BLUE BLOOD

BLUE BLOOD

CRAIG
UNGER

WILLIAM MORROW
AND COMPANY, INC.
NEW YORK

Library of Congress Cataloging-in-Publication Data

Unger, Craig.
    Blue blood / Craig Unger.
        p.   cm.
    ISBN 0-688-05081-6
    1. Harkness, Rebekah West, d. 1982.   2. United States—Biography.
3. Philanthropists—United States—Biography.   I. Title.
CT275.H3834U64 1988
973.92′092′4—dc19   87-34761
[B]   CIP

Printed in the United States of America

First Edition

1 2 3 4 5 6 7 8 9 10

BOOK DESIGN BY RICHARD ORIOLO

CONTENTS

Happy families are all alike;
every unhappy family is unhappy
in its own way.

–LEO TOLSTOY, *Anna Karenina*

Money!
You got lots o' friends,
Crowdin' 'round the door,
When you're gone
And spendin' ends
They don't come no more

Rich relations give,
Crust of bread and such,
You can't help yourself,
But don't take too much

Mama may have
Papa may have
But God bless the child that's got his own
That's got his own

–ARTHUR HERZOG, JR., BILLIE HOLIDAY,
"God Bless the Child"

GENEALOGICAL CHART

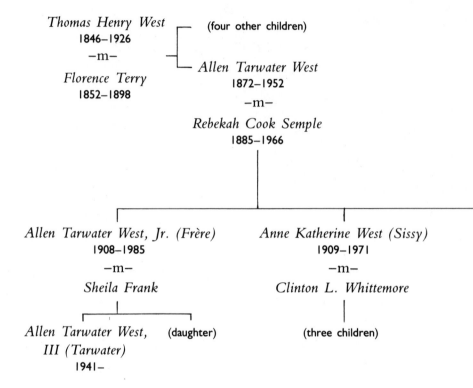

Thomas Henry West
1846–1926
–m–
Florence Terry
1852–1898

(four other children)

Allen Tarwater West
1872–1952
–m–
Rebekah Cook Semple
1885–1966

Allen Tarwater West, Jr. (Frère)
1908–1985
–m–
Sheila Frank

Anne Katherine West (Sissy)
1909–1971
–m–
Clinton L. Whittemore

Allen Tarwater West,
III (Tarwater)
1941–

(daughter)

(three children)

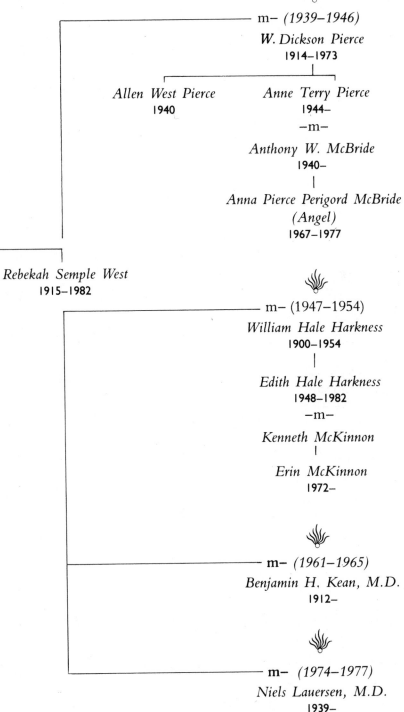

m— *(1939–1946)*

W. Dickson Pierce
1914–1973

Allen West Pierce
1940

Anne Terry Pierce
1944–
—m—
Anthony W. McBride
1940–

Anna Pierce Perigord McBride
(Angel)
1967–1977

Rebekah Semple West
1915–1982

m— (1947–1954)

William Hale Harkness
1900–1954

Edith Hale Harkness
1948–1982
—m—
Kenneth McKinnon

Erin McKinnon
1972–

m— *(1961–1965)*

Benjamin H. Kean, M.D.
1912–

m— *(1974–1977)*

Niels Lauersen, M.D.
1939–

BLUE BLOOD

PROLOGUE
A MOTHER'S
LEGACY

N

EW YORK CITY,
June 17, 1982
Edith Hale Harkness sat in the living room of her mother's large suite in the Carlyle Hotel apartments on the Upper East Side. Rebekah Harkness, sixty-seven, had not been fully conscious for days. Edith, her thirty-three-year-old daughter, waited patiently for her to die, as she had for the last month. After a lifetime of bitterness, she had finally come to terms with

her mother, and now she was about to lose her. Everyone—Rebekah included—had given up her fight against cancer. There was not even a remote chance of successful surgery, and because the growth blocked her intestines, Rebekah had not eaten for days.

At about 7:30 P.M., Willard Wallace, Rebekah's black Bahamian butler, went to the master bedroom. He was a huge St. Bernard of a man who had ably cared for Rebekah's estate in Nassau for almost twenty years. He was one of the few who had survived years in Rebekah's employ without losing her trust. During her long downfall—well before her terminal illness—he had often found his employer in a drugged and drunken stupor, picked her up, and put her to bed. Even Rebekah, so fickle and capricious she had fired dozens of housekeepers, lawyers, and administrators on a whim, had never found fault with Willard.

"He would never let anything happen to me," she had told friends. "I'll never go anywhere without him again."

Daunted by the prospect of her death, Willard had left the changing of Rebekah's linen to his wife, Augusta. Even after Augusta had come down with a cold, Willard had been reluctant to go into the room. But Augusta had been sick for more than a day, and finally Willard relented. He entered the room. Rebekah's grand piano, on which she had struggled for years to become a composer, sat silent in one corner. Rebekah herself lay lifeless in her gilded Louis XIV bed, a nurse watching over her.

Rebekah had always taken extraordinary measures to stem the onslaught of age—her rigorous dance regimen, plastic surgery, special injections, and countless drugs. But now it had caught up with her with a vengeance. Her skin had lost its tone and color and become slack on her emaciated frame. She was so ravaged that it was hard to believe she had once been a vital physical presence. A few weeks earlier, when the chemotherapy caused her hair to fall out, she had bought a wig from Kenneth's. But now she was far past worrying about cosmetic details.

For most of her life, no such frivolity was beyond Rebekah. But she had given up trying to fool anyone. She knew she was dying and wanted it to be over with.

As Willard entered to clean up, Rebekah's respirations came farther and farther apart. Then she took a final gasp and stopped breathing. Willard looked at the nurse.

"She told me we would be together at the end," he said.

Edith went to take one last look at her mother. Altogether, there were eight or nine people scattered through the sprawling apartment. Rebekah's friends, relatives, employees, and hangers-on had been coming and going for days like retainers in a royal court, waiting for the queen to die. All of them seemed to have someone to comfort them.

But Edith was alone. She didn't even know some of these people, and she wished they would leave. Only the servants and nurses really had any business being there. Rebekah had given them everything they had. She had been so generous with her vast wealth. She had built their careers. They had devoured Rebekah while she was alive, Edith thought. They had waited out her last days only by consoling themselves with fantasies of how much money she would leave them. As she lay dying, they had brought in groceries and invited their friends over to cook for them. Rebekah was dead now, but they were still drinking, telling jokes, and laughing. Later, Edith expressed her distress to a friend. "Now they're having dinner while my mother is lying here," she said. "And these are supposed to be her friends. Don't they care? Don't they care?"

The obituary in *The New York Times* told the official story: REBEKAH WEST HARKNESS, 67, PATRON OF DANCE AND MEDICINE, read the headline, running across three columns that detailed Rebekah's philanthropic gifts to dance and medicine. It discussed her comfortable upbringing in St. Louis and mentioned three of her four husbands, including Standard Oil heir William Hale Harkness. The text gave a nod to her wry sense of humor, and some of the extravagances and controversies for which she was known. Rebekah had transformed an elegant East Side town house, with its marble staircase and crystal chandelier, into Harkness House, a dance center that rivaled the splendor of the great royal ballet schools of Europe. Her dance company, the Harkness Ballet, had won acclaim for its spectacular dancers but constant criticism for its uneven choreography; even in her obituary, *The Times* could not resist taking one last potshot at it, describing it as an "unlikely" blend of classical ballet and modern dance "flavored by the 'neo-Freudian' churnings of the 30's and early 40's." Scant mention was given to her career as a composer, which meant so much to her.

For the most part, the real story of Rebekah Harkness remained untold. *The Times* only hinted at how, with her enormous wealth and eccentricity, she simultaneously captivated and infuriated the dance world and café society in the sixties and seventies. Determined, disciplined, with a powerful will and the extravagance of a latter-day Catherine de Medici, she created a dance company that always seemed to be on the verge of greatness. But time and again, she herself sabotaged it. Ultimately her dance empire fell apart.

The irony, of course, was that all Rebekah's dreams had come true. She had shown everyone—including her father, who had laughed at her dreams of glory; who believed if you broke the rules, if you refused to abide by stuffy midwestern sensibilities, you could not possibly make a go of it. The reckless debutante; the demure society matron; the world-famous arts patroness; the eccentric, capricious, decadent heiress—in whatever guise she had worn, she had gotten exactly what she wanted. Betty West, as she was known when she was a dazzling deb, had come East to conquer New York, and had done precisely that with her marriage to William Hale Harkness.

And after his death, Rebekah had flirted with heads of state and billionaires and aristocrats. She toyed with Aristotle Onassis on board the *Christina*. She was propositioned by President Lyndon Johnson at the White House. She took what she wanted of New York society and said to hell with the rest of it, just as she had done back in her debutante days. She had defied them all. This was the woman who dyed a cat green, who baked cakes with money in them, who cleaned her swimming pool with Dom Pérignon.

Even at the height of her powers, though, Rebekah loved to repeat her father's prophecy, as if daring it to come true. "Shirtsleeves to shirtsleeves in three generations," he had often said. She fulfilled his prediction in a far more spectacular way than he could possibly have imagined. By the end, her money—or most of it—was gone. The vast fortune Harkness had left behind—the equivalent of $250 million in 1987 dollars—had been dissipated in a haze of alcohol and drugs. Like an aging prizefighter, punch-drunk, flailing about desperately in search of old reflexes and responses that no longer were there, Rebekah ultimately paid the price for the blind pursuit of her fantasies.

"Rebekah's problem," says one of her lovers, "was that she really was the American dream. Rebekah was the pursuit of happiness. But only the pursuit is fun. After the dream comes true, it becomes a nightmare."

The press humiliated her. No one took her music seriously. Her dance companies folded. Once, she had been known the world over as dance's greatest patroness. Now, if she was remembered at all, it was with knowing smirks, as irrational and capricious, driven by her own childhood fantasies rather than a real artistic vision, incapable of discerning between real genius and the parade of sycophants who demanded her attention.

She died surrounded by the detritus of those dreams, and it became painfully obvious that Rebekah's greatest failure in life was as a mother. For the real victims were her children, to whom she left a legacy of abandonment and neglect that scarred them for life. As a result, a dynasty had come undone. One of her children had tried suicide several times; one had even been convicted of murder.

At about ten-thirty that night Dr. Morton Coleman came to pronounce Rebekah dead. Edith helped provide the requisite information on the death certificate. In the box for her mother's occupation, they filled in "Artist." After midnight, the body was taken away.

There was still much to be done. Edith and her half sister, Terry McBride, had to plan the funeral, organize the memorial service, and make plans for the future of Harkness House. This was no simple matter. Edith and her mother's entourage were natural enemies. Over the years they had battled each other bitterly for Rebekah's affections.

In many ways, Edith was more the outsider than they were. She had come to her mother's side only as the disease reached the final stages. As usual, she played the part of the heiress reluctantly, wearing blue jeans and a tank top, while surrounded by her mother's finery—apricot chiffon Austrian draperies, five grand pianos, inlaid ivory furniture, and elaborate murals. In the living room hung a portrait Salvador Dali had painted of Edith when she was just a child. Back then, the image he chose to capture her spirit was that of a young girl trapped in a gilded bird cage.

Edith stood out in such sharp contrast to Rebekah that many people found it hard to believe they were mother and daughter. Unlike Rebekah's two other children, Edith was a Harkness, the only child Rebekah had borne during her seven happy years of marriage to Harkness. But it was not just that Edith took after her father. Rebekah was given to lavish displays of wealth. Edith was modest, unpretentious, painfully embarrassed by the family riches. Rebekah was impulsive, highly susceptible to sycophantic praise. Edith was deliberate, thoughtful, impervious to flattery. Both women had rapier wits, but even there they differed: Rebekah delighted in playing havoc with the boundaries of propriety; Edith's wry humor was that of someone who knew only too well where those limits begin and end.

Bobby Scevers had been Rebekah's lover on and off for eighteen years, sharing her suite at the Carlyle with her during her last days. "I dislike Rebekah's children," he says, "because I saw all the unhappiness and irritation they caused her. I don't see that those kids have any right to complain. Me and my friends were Rebekah's real family."

From Edith's point of view, that, of course, was precisely the problem. Just as Rebekah had embraced young dancers like Bobby, so had she neglected her own children. To one close friend, Edith confided that it was because of Rebekah that she had had eighteen years of psychoanalysis.

"Eighteen years!" the friend said. "Edith, that's ridiculous. At most you needed two years."

"I know," Edith replied. "But which two?"

In Bobby, one could hardly have found a more conspicuously unlikely mate for a woman who had married into one of America's great dynasties. It was not just that Bobby, forty-one, was twenty-five years younger than Rebekah. The son of an oil worker from Aransas Pass, Texas, he was at the opposite end of the social ladder as well. And, most shocking of all to those from her staid midwestern background, he was homosexual.

Those familiar with Bobby's limited talents as a dancer and choreographer suspected that his motives were mercenary or political or both. He had never made much of an impression on the New York dance world, yet under Rebekah's auspices he had risen to a powerful position in one of the major ballet companies in the country.

Edith gave Bobby more credit than that. She saw how Bobby attended to Rebekah loyally day and night in the hospital, often spending the evening sprawling out on a makeshift mattress on the floor near her bed. Whatever one thought of him, it was clear to Edith that Rebekah took genuine pleasure in his visits.

The others were a different story, and their presence was part of Edith's problem. As Rebekah was dying, Edith's battle for her affections had reached the endgame stage. This was the conflict that had indelibly marked Edith's life. In Rebekah's last days, Edith tried to make the most of what time was left. "They were trying to make sense of a whole lifetime in just a few moments," says one friend. After years of relegating Edith to a backseat behind her entourage, Rebekah finally apologized. For the first time ever, the two had become close. And Edith had responded to her mother's warmth with a constant bedside vigil that lasted weeks.

For the funeral, Terry and Edith arranged a small, intimate service for close friends and family. They chose St. James Episcopal Church on Seventy-first Street and Madison Avenue. Rebekah was in a coffin, and the organist played Pachelbel's *Canon*. The music was stately, solemn, and somber—all qualities Rebekah had detested.

Bobby was dismayed. "I didn't want to have anything to do with it," he says. "Rebekah didn't want a religious ceremony. She didn't want to be in a coffin. She hated organ music. The piece of music she hated most was Pachelbel's *Canon*. Edith and Terry gave Rebekah everything she didn't want. They had to, for their social image. The whole thing was done with so little love and care."

On Thursday, June 24, a week after her death, a memorial service was held at Harkness House. This time, however, things were different. Bobby and his friend Nikita Talin, the executive director of the Harkness Ballet Foundation, were in charge along with other foundation officials.

At 5:30 P.M., about a hundred people from the dance world gathered in Studio B, after marching up the winding staircase to the sounds of Rebekah's orchestration of Rachmaninoff's *Sonata for Cello and Piano in C Minor*.

It was a curious assemblage. Although some of those whose work was most closely identified with Rebekah couldn't make it and wired their regrets, there was an impressive cross-section of people Rebekah had known in her twenty-five years in the arts. These were the people whom Rebekah had pampered as though they were her own children, in whose accomplishments she had taken such pride. These were people whose careers she had fostered and those she had fired on a whim. This was not just a memorial service, it was a reunion as well. Some hadn't seen each other in more than fifteen years.

A portrait of Rebekah, painted when she was fifty-nine and still trim and fit, dressed in blue leotards, her back to the barre, overlooked the mourners. The family was seated in the first row. Terry, in a pink cotton-candy dress, inspired comments on her astonishing resemblance to her mother; she was heavier, but had the same inflections in her voice, the same laugh, the same toss of her head.

Edith, wearing culottes and a navy-blue polo shirt, was composed. She barely knew anyone there, but she played her part dutifully nonetheless. That had been her role in life—to be polite, diligent, bright, presentable—and she was not about to stop now. She greeted an old friend of the family she barely knew and hadn't seen in nearly two decades. "I was surprised she recognized me," he says. "She was so warm and full of life, even though it must have been a difficult time."

"She looked adorable," says a friend who attended the service. "But can you imagine what she felt? All those people Rebekah loved, all those people she was so good to! I could see back through the years and watch the dancers running in and out of Rebekah's house, slamming the doors, complete strangers taking over, hangers-on winning her mother's affection, while Edith just stood by watching.

"What could Edith think? 'If this woman is so great, if she loved all these people and didn't love me, then I must be terrible.' It was just dreadful."

The next day before noon, Terry went over to Frank E. Campbell's funeral home on Madison Avenue. Rebekah had been cremated. There was nothing in which to carry the ashes, so Terry was given a brown paper bag from Gristede's, a nearby supermarket. In the meantime, at Harkness House, Dali's Chalice of Life, a $250,000 jeweled urn that Rebekah had bought nearly twenty years earlier, had been taken out of its display case and cleaned. Of all the pieces by Dali that Rebekah had bought, the chalice was the most important to her. Out of a base of gold and malachite grows a tree in sculptured relief that winds around a seventeen-inch-high golden urn. Some of the leaves give the appearance of being half devoured by caterpillars. Others open mechanically into jeweled butterflies studded with diamonds, emeralds, sapphires, and rubies, and then close again. Rebekah had stipulated that her ashes rest inside the urn.

When Terry returned to Harkness House, Bobby, Nikita, Edith, and another member of the entourage waited in the main reception room. There was no ceremony.

"Terry just stood there with a stupid, vacant look," says Bobby. "A couple of people were horrified that she had brought back her mother in this grocery bag."

Finally, a security guard, with some difficulty, opened the lock to the case holding the chalice. Terry gave him the paper bag and he poured the ashes in. But the chalice was too small. "What was she talking about, having her ashes in there!" says a friend. "Just a leg is in there, or maybe half of her head, and an arm."

When Terry peered into the cabinet a few hours later, somehow the top of the urn had been displaced.

"Oh, my God," she heard someone say. "She's escaped."

Next to the display case was an inscription written by Dali; on this occasion, it seemed especially appropriate: "Man exists amidst putrefaction," it read. "Like a worm he crawls through terrestrial existence, but by virtue of divine metamorphosis, as in the metamorphosis of the butterfly, he transforms himself into spiritual life."

Later that week, Edith was finally alone in her mother's apartment. She rummaged through Rebekah's drawers and medicine cabinets. There were over forty vials of drugs. Some were there, of course, to dull the pain she had suffered in her last days. But there were many others as well—antidepressants, barbiturates, and tranquilizers—a virtual history of drug dependency.

Edith picked out the ones she wanted and packed them in her suitcase. She handed the empty vials to her mother's maid, saying that she had flushed the drugs down the toilet.

Others had ransacked Rebekah's apartment for far more valuable things. After the funeral, everyone had returned to the Carlyle for drinks. "It was unbelievable," says a friend who was there. "People were grabbing things right and left, saying Rebekah had promised it to them." Within minutes a lapis lazuli clock that had been on the mantelpiece was gone. Two matching sconces were missing as well.

A friend was appalled and told Edith what was going on. "You're a little bit late," she said. "I would love to have half of what was hauled off."

As it was, the press was already trumpeting Rebekah's gift of her jewels to the Smithsonian. HER WILL IS A DAZZLER, read the headline in the *New York Daily News*. Unfortunately, there was not much left in her estate apart from her various residences. Relative to the once vast Harkness fortune, it was hardly worth fighting over. Yet everyone was up in arms. Terry and her fiancé had already talked with a lawyer about contesting the will.

In addition, there was Harkness House, crumbling like Tara after the Civil War. In its current state of decay, it was an ironic reflection of Rebekah's shattered dreams. It reeked of overripe opulence. Its marble floors smelled from spilled hors d'oeuvres left to spoil. One visitor likened it to an aging, once beautiful woman whose wrinkles were painted over with too much makeup. Edith had begun to feel a responsibility toward restoring it; but to bring it back to its former glory, she knew, would take a small fortune and, no doubt, an ugly battle with Bobby and Nikita.

Already relationships between Bobby and Rebekah's children were at the breaking point. "I have no sympathy for any of the kids," he says. "None of them. Here their mother was doing so much for the world—all the money she just gave away. And those kids were doing nothing. They had gotten so much money from Bill Harkness. They were the most worthless, selfish, useless creatures I've ever seen."

Most people were more generous than Bobby, but no matter how one looked at it, the fate of Rebekah's children was tragic. Allen Pierce, Rebekah's son by her first husband, had not even attended the funeral—much as he wanted to. Years earlier, he had been ripped off for millions of dollars by unscrupulous businessmen. Desperately angry, with his explosive, violent temper, he had subsequently shot and killed a young man and been convicted of murder. During Rebekah's last rites, he languished in a Florida jail.

Allen's sister, Terry, more closely resembled Rebekah than had any of the three children, and had gotten along well with her mother for most of her life. But then had come Terry's only child, born with multiple defects. That tragedy had scarred Terry's relationship with Rebekah forever.

That left Edith. She was the special one. The brightest, most beautiful, the most sympathetic. Rebekah cared most for her, but was so deeply conflicted she still neglected her. Many thought Edith was the only one in the family who was really sane. But she was so out of place, so alone that she had tried suicide several times and had been put away in mental hospitals for much of her youth. "She knew exactly what was going on," says a cousin. "That's why she spent so much time in mental hospitals. It was other people's intention that she be insane, that she be under control."

After the funeral, Edith returned to her estate in Potomac, Maryland. A friend watched, horrified, as Edith unpacked. Bright orange, yellow, and green capsules, and lavender tablets spilled out. There were barbiturates like Seconal and Nembutal, tranquilizers like Valium, Haldol, and Librium, painkillers, and much, much more. Ironically, the drugs were about the only possessions of her mother's Edith could take with her. The portrait of her by Dali was virtually the only thing that had been left to her in her mother's will, but it couldn't be distributed until the estate was settled. No one knew how long that would be.

The entourage that had stood between Edith and her mother for Edith's entire life was now battling greedily over each and every scrap she had left behind. Edith had spent most of her life trying to escape her mother and the pain she had caused her family. By now Edith knew, of course, that one never could do that. But that didn't make it any easier to come to terms with the truth: that her mother had presided over the disintegration of the entire family. What was remarkable was that Edith had not only survived all that pain, but that Rebekah and she had finally reconciled during those last days. And now Rebekah was gone for good.

"Just when I thought I found my mother again," Edith told a friend, "I lost her."

Edith's friend demanded an explanation of the drugs. She replied with the self-conscious irony of someone who was weary of searching for the reasons for her family's tragedies.

"This," Edith said, "is my mother's legacy."

BETTY AND THE BITCH PACK

They lived in an imposing three-story house at 48 Westmoreland Place, one of the most fashionable addresses in St. Louis, Missouri. Developed at the turn of the century by Rebekah's grandfather, Thomas Henry West, and several other St. Louis businessmen, Westmoreland Place provided St. Louis society with a private residential enclave. It consisted of several dozen mansions on both sides of an elongated tree-lined oval and was sealed off from the rest of the city by wrought-iron gates. One could enter only through a small side street. At night, private guards patrolled the area, walking back and forth from the guardhouse.

Westmoreland Place's fifty-four Tudor, Georgian, and neo-classical mansions, some with as many as forty-five rooms each, came to be regarded as a high point in American residential architecture. Portland Place, adjacent to it, was equally striking. When Count Apponyi of Hungary visited the World's Fair in St. Louis in 1904, he said the city had more beautiful residences than all of Europe combined.

The people who lived there were the families who had brought the World's Fair to the city, who had backed Charles Lindbergh's transatlantic flight, whose sons prepped at Groton, Choate, and Middlesex before going on to Princeton and Yale, and whose daughters went to the toniest finishing schools. These were the people who ran St. Louis, who were on the boards of the banks and the major corporations in town. Of the three hundred or so families who were members of the exclusive St. Louis Country Club, as many as 90 percent lived there and on equally prestigious Portland Place and Vandeventer Place. One could not simply be wealthy and expect automatically to gain admittance to either the country club or the more exclusive "places." The so-called lager Germans, for example, including the Busches with their brewery empire, were not particularly welcome, nor were the wealthy Jewish merchants.

The Wests, however, had been prominent for two generations—enough, by St. Louis standards at least, to qualify as an "old" society family. It was Rebekah's grandfather, Thomas Henry West, who had catapulted the family into its exalted position in the city's social hierarchy.

At the age of sixteen, Thomas West fought with General Nathan Bedford Forrest in the cavalry of the Confederate Army. After the Civil War, he left his home in Tennessee for Louisville, Kentucky, and then moved to Mobile, Alabama, where he started a cotton brokerage. The firm, Allen, West, & Company, prospered, but a yellow fever epidemic in Mobile forced it to relocate to St. Louis in 1880. Within a few years of his arrival, West became a major figure in the bustling city.

At the time, American business, unhampered by income tax, estate taxes, and the like, was expanding westward at an unprecedented pace. For St. Louis, this was a period of extraordinary growth. The population of the Lion of the Valley, as the city was called, was 350,000 in 1880. By 1900 it had become the fourth largest city in the nation, with 575,000 people, second only to Chicago as a railroad crossroads. With Anheuser-Busch and many other breweries, the city was one of the leading centers of beer production in the country as well as a diversified manufacturing center. One of the city's slogans was "First in booze, first in shoes, and last in the American League."

For all that growth, there was still no trust company west of Cleveland. In 1889, West, then forty-three, and three other wealthy St. Louisans created such a company. It thrived and later merged with a rival to become the St. Louis Union Trust Company, with West as its president. His financial acumen was so highly valued that he was given a quarter share in the company without putting up any equity.

He became so financially powerful in the era of Progressive reform at their turn of the century that fiery articles in small magazines like *The Iconoclast* began attacking him. Along with lawyers, merchants, and manufacturers known locally as the Big Cinch, West was named as part of a "nobility" that owned "everything worth owning," buying aldermen "like cattle," holding the city "at their mercy." His wealth and that of his friends, the Progressives argued, was based not on earned income, but on a monopoly of the city's resources.

Such barbs came with the territory, however, and were little more than confirmation of how far he had come. In addition to being president of the trust, he was a director of the local electric and gas companies as well as of the St. Louis–San Francisco Railroad Company. The Wests had arrived.

In 1906, thirty-four-year-old Allen Tarwater West, one of Thomas's four sons, was vacationing in Winter Harbor, Maine, when he met a young woman named Rebekah Semple. The two soon spent nearly every day together. By late summer, Allen wrote to her mother announcing their forthcoming engagement: "It seems a quick thing to you no doubt but being in the same house here we have had a chance to know each other in a way that in a city would have taken two years."

In November, the two wed in Minneapolis. Semple was the daughter of one of the wealthiest families in the city. Her father was a prosperous merchant and her mother was part of the richest family in Indiana, the Culbertsons. The family lived in the most opulent private residence in Minneapolis, an extraordinary seventeen-room, 25,000-square-foot Italian provincial mansion, with vaulted ceilings ornamented with frescoes, stained-glass windows, and brass doorknobs in wrought relief. The entire third floor was designed for ballroom dancing.

According to the local press, "The handsome and lavish appointments of the wedding were in keeping with the social prominence of the event, which was witnessed by one of the most fashionable assemblages in Minneapolis society."

West and his bride settled in Westmoreland Place in St. Louis, less than two blocks from his parents' house. Their home was equally stately, with more than twenty elegantly furnished rooms.

Allen, Junior, the oldest of the Wests' three children, was born in 1908. He prepped at Choate in Connecticut. When he was home, it was clear he would never be satisfied with spending his life in the stuffy confines of St. Louis.

The Wests' older daughter, Anne Katherine—"Sissy"—was a year younger than Allen, lovely, demure, self-possessed, and pure St. Louis. "She was just peachy," says one friend of the family, "as comfy as an old shoe. Terribly attractive with coal-black hair. But she didn't have any of this wildness in her."

Rebekah did. She was born April 14, 1915, when Sissy was six. A pudgy adolescent, with a round face and brown hair, she was irrepressible and mischievous, and looked as if she would do just about anything to get into trouble. Everyone called her by her nickname, Betty.

★   ★   ★

St. Louis was staunchly midwestern, but many of its most prominent citizens were originally from the South and had brought with them southern gentility and southern attitudes toward race. It was not unusual among Betty's crowd, for example, to have separate dining facilities for black and white servants. The city was hit hard by the Great Depression, but the Wests and their friends were so well off that they had worried more about the onset of Prohibition.

Young women in Betty's group went to finishing school after they graduated from one of the St. Louis's elite private schools. The idea of a woman going to college was frowned upon, and a career was out of the question. Even the men were not really supposed to work; for many young men there was sinecure waiting for them in family-owned businesses. Betty's father had tried that for a year, working at the St. Louis Union Trust Company. He didn't like it, however, and instead went off to help found the stockbrokerage firm of G. H. Walker. But he was more interested in golf, at which he was quite accomplished, even winning the Trans-Mississippi Tournament one year. There was little reason to worry about money. He had his wife's considerable wealth, and when his father died in 1926, a sizable portion of his $3 million fortune was passed on to him.

"This was a country club bunch," a friend says. "There was no incentive to work. We had just about anything you could want, so everyone was really living it up." St. Louis was a hard-drinking city, and liquor flowed in homes and private clubs even when it was illegal. This group dined, danced, and went horseback riding at the St. Louis Country Club and other exclusive spots such as the Log Cabin Club and the Claytonshire Coaching Club. Duck hunting was a popular weekend sport, and they attended the annual Retriever Trials, where labradors and golden retrievers were shown in competition. On weekends they chartered steamship packet boats like the *Golden Eagle* and steamed up and down the Mississippi with a Dixieland band on board. Betty's father founded the Deer Creek Club for hunting and trapshooting. The family's best friends, the Johnsons, had a fifteen-hundred-acre ranch called Trail's End Stables where they raised show horses and held big parties.

When it came to the children's upbringing, no expense was spared. There were lessons of every sort for Betty and her siblings. The family traveled frequently to New York City and Miami Beach. Gus, the chauffeur, was always available to take Betty and her friends wherever they wanted to go.

But for all the material wealth, there were few signs of real affection in the family. "We weren't a very close family," says Betty's brother. "Our nanny, Rose Sackberger, practically raised us. My parents wanted someone with a firm hand, and Rose had worked in an insane asylum. I guess they thought we were insane. We were scared of her, but we loved her and respected her. Betty loved Rose better than her mother or father."

The real problem was Betty's father, who ruled the family like a tyrant. If the rolls were too hard at dinner, he threw them at his wife. His gruff demeanor and sardonic humor terrified Betty. She would do anything for his approval, but she never could seem to live up to his expectations. Her friends stayed away even when he wasn't there, claiming that the house was haunted by him. Mrs. West could be quite sweet, but her husband completely dominated the household. His usual greeting for Betty and her friends was a blustery, "Harumph." Sometimes he ignored them entirely.

By the time she was sixteen, Betty was tall and athletic. She was not a classic beauty, but she was pretty and she knew there was more to one's appearance than pleasant features. She knew how to toy with men and how to project an energetic, physical charm that made her girlfriends pale by comparison.

"One day she was a roly-poly little fat girl," recalls a friend, "and the next thing you knew, she discovered boys and became very glamorous, slim, and sexy." Betty had taken up dancing to lose weight and subsequently decided to pursue it more seriously. She never could learn to keep time, but that didn't stop her. She took up figure skating as well. Again, she wasn't exactly a natural, but she kept going to the old Winter Garden skating rink until she was good. She was compulsive, highly disciplined, and spent several hours every day practicing both. It was a way out of the stuffy debutante parties she was expected to attend, and it was possible her skills might someday provide her with a one-way ticket out of St. Louis.

In 1929, Betty went off for three years to Fermata, a finishing school in Aiken, South Carolina, where the daughters of the wealthy were prepared for marriage in antebellum splendor. A town where polo was the number-one priority, Aiken prided itself on providing a milieu for society girls to go on hunts and steeplechase rides.

Education took a backseat. "Fermata was a school of rather low academic standing," says a classmate of Betty's. "If a girl even thought about going to college in those days, she was called a queer."

Fermata counted among its pupils Roosevelts, Auchinclosses, Biddles, and tobacco heiress Doris Duke. That these were families with far higher social standing than anyone in St. Louis didn't faze Betty or discourage her from being the mischievous prankster she had always been. At parties, she was the first to turn off all the lights and "do everything bad," as she wrote in her scrapbook. She raided the school kitchen and convinced schoolmate Alice Aldrich that her lovely eyelashes would grow even longer if she cut them off first. At the end of the year, Betty was voted the funniest girl in her class.

She graduated in 1932. Several years later Fermata burned to the ground. The cause of the blaze was arson, but the culprits were never caught. "Her school was completely destroyed, its doors closed for good," says one friend "and Betty thought it was an absolute scream." Many years later she and a friend bragged that they had set the fire themselves. The story was untrue, of course, but it does suggest her bravado. If Allen West wanted a daughter who was a quiet, unassuming society girl, he would have to settle for Sissy. Betty could never be like that. If she had to be restricted to the stuffy confines of the St. Louis debutante world, she was going to do it on her own terms.

She took refuge in a group of friends who called themselves the Bitch Pack. Quick, sharp-witted, and attractive, its members were extraordinarily sophisticated and daring for their time. The name was bestowed upon the group, with some affection, by Jodie Drew, a thwarted suitor who kept asking out Betty's best friend, Jane Johnson, only to find that she, Betty, and the rest of them would rather be off pouring mineral oil into the punch at a debutante ball or putting Coke bottles under the tires of the cars in the parking lot.

In the eyes of many, the most sought-after woman in the Bitch Pack was not Betty at all—who was certainly the most mischievous—but Jane Johnson, the granddaughter of Jackson Johnson, president of the International Shoe Company, the largest shoe company in the world. Jane had been Betty's classmate first at private school in St. Louis and later at Fermata.

In 1933, Jane and Betty vied for honors as Queen of Love and Beauty for St. Louis's Veiled Prophet Ball, a Mardi Gras–like society event. The debutante parties in St. Louis were taken with utmost seriousness by the powers that be, and the local papers afforded them pages of coverage in the rotogravure section. Now the society pages played up the battle in their outlandish purple prose, touting Betty's chances: "Rebekah, or Betty, as she is familiarly called by those blue blooded enough to be on informal terms with her is, verily, a favorite of the fairy godmothers. She has everything to make a reigning belle—pulchritude, personality, and pelf—the magical trio of attributes that can't help but win out. Early as it is, the quidnuncs are hinting that the Veiled Prophet's crown will grace her fair brow."

But they were wrong. Betty narrowly lost to Jane, a striking beauty with reddish brown hair and green eyes. She was so stylish and glamorous that just by casually pinning flowers above her breast or putting on an old scarf, she somehow ended up the picture of elegance. "She had the smartest clothes," says one friend. "She could put on any old rag and look terrific." Betty, by contrast, had to work at it.

In St. Louis, this was an era of elaborate Junior League parties and costume balls with big swing bands. Both Betty and Jane had mixed feelings about the deb parties at which they and their friends were feted. They were not unaware that the country was in the middle of the Great Depression. By 1933, unemployment in St. Louis was over 30 percent. On the levee of the Mississippi River were Hoovervilles and Happy Valleys where the homeless sought shelter in large wooden shipping cartons and galvanized metal shacks. Yet nearly six hundred society people attended Jane Johnson's coming-out party.

Still, the girls were conflicted by all the attention. "Jane always had high ideals," says Jack Shinkle, a cousin. "She had a social conscience and she didn't quite know how to handle it. She expected a little more from a man than a routine club life and being a figure in the business community."

For Betty, these stuffy society functions represented everything she hated about her father. He was a reasonably successful stockbroker, but his success was largely the result of his father's fortune and accomplishments. Born into society, he clung to its values and ideals. He took a dim view of anyone—his progeny above all—who questioned the ethos of this world. When Betty's suitors came to pick her up, he made sure they were from good society families.

Betty and Jane, the two most popular women in St. Louis, thus ended up in the curious position of scoffing at the social world they ruled. They used the Bitch Pack to make their feelings known. They could make or break almost any party. If they decided to go elsewhere, all the attractive men would go with them. And if they deigned to appear, they could radically alter the character of the evening.

Betty did the kinds of things that everyone else just talked about. She arrived at one party by climbing the roof and going down via the chimney. At another, she did a suggestive semi-striptease on the dining table. At one especially formal event she wore sneakers under her evening gown. At another party, she and Jane waited stealthily until the chauffeur took a break so they could take a joyride through every driveway in the neighborhood. Called on to provide corned beef hash for a weekend brunch, Betty served canned dog food instead. Once, she brought dozens of stickers reading, "Repent, Your Time Is At Hand," and discreetly stuck them on the backside of unsuspecting party-goers.

Costume parties in those days were serious affairs—so serious that one young man named Vincent Price ended up making a career out of his when he came dressed as Count Dracula. Betty, on the other hand, might come with blackened-out front teeth, a toilet seat around her neck, or dressed up as a maid. And on Wednesday afternoons, she and Jane would go to the "local loony bin for tea and dance with the inmates." For a time, she was known as Mademoiselle Annetsky Pesky Fresky, "the girl who made the century of progress that much more progressive."

Jane, who was seen as the leader of the Bitch Pack, usually went along with Betty. But Jane always knew where the lines of propriety were drawn. It was Betty who was the ultimate prankster.

Not all their friends delighted in their antics. "You had to compete in that aggressively sophisticated atmosphere," says one. "There was enormous pressure to fit in with these terribly sophisticated, attractive girls from the best families with their quick, sharp, cutting remarks. I felt inferior, not quite able to compete. Betty dressed beautifully in these slinky evening gowns. You had to have these gorgeous, expensive, wonderful-looking dresses and tweeds for the daytime. And then they would go out at night, drinking for eight or ten hours and come home at six A.M. and sleep all the next day. It didn't occur to us that we were all spoiled brats being introduced to the worst possible values."

For all their rebelliousness, Betty and Jane continued to dominate the society pages. Betty appeared in the paper as a model for Kline's, a local department store. When she went to Miami Beach, the press featured her as a favorite of the Bath Club debutante set, who dated the heirs to various fortunes. She studied both piano and dance, taking ballet lessons from Victoria Cassau, herself a student of Anna Pavlova's. At nineteen she performed in the dance school's ballet recitals. Dressed in black tie, top hat, and tails, she did a tap dance at a Junior League program the same year, and performed in a rumba recital as well.

That same year, Betty auditioned for a role in the chorus of a production of *Aida* to be staged by the Chicago Opera Company in St. Louis. She won a small role in the triumphal scene. This was not just another opera debut. This was the inauguration—at the nadir of the Depression—of St. Louis's magnificent new Municipal Auditorium. At the opening, Mr. and Mrs. West took their seats in the second row. Anticipating their disapproval, Betty had not even told her parents about her role. Distracted by her father's presence, she forgot all her steps.

Mr. West was outraged. He told her she wasn't wearing enough clothes and that the whole display was disgusting. "He raised hell," says her brother, Allen. "That's when the walls came tumbling down. He didn't believe in the things Betty did. It just wasn't done."

None of which stopped her. In September she went to Chicago to spend several months at the Ned Wayburn Institute of Dancing. A well-known figure on Broadway, Wayburn had been Florenz Ziegfield's executive producer for ten years. In addition to directing *The Ziegfield Follies,* he had such Broadway hits as *Showboat* to his credit. The Wayburn Institute had trained Fred and Adele Astaire, Al Jolson, Fannie Brice, Mae West, and the Marx Brothers, among many other stars. Betty practiced rigorously and soon caught Wayburn's eye. When he told her he wanted her for his next production, she was ecstatic, but she advised him that it would be difficult to get her father's consent.

In November, Wayburn wrote Betty's father:

My dear Mr. West:
Last evening I had a talk with Betty after she heard me explain my forthcoming musical play, "The Year Round." . . .

. . . I would like very much to have her as a member of the group . . . And, I sincerely hope that you will realize that her environment, if you will consider allowing me to have her in this new attraction, will be all that can be desired.

. . . I am a father and I fully realize what I am asking, but I have been watching Betty for sometime and from reports that her work has been 100% I feel very sure she will make good if given the opportunity. . . ."

Yours very sincerely,
Ned Wayburn

Mr. West was not impressed by the letter. "He figured Wayburn was just playing on his ego, trying to get money out of him to help finance a production," says Betty's brother. "He was against the whole idea of her going to New York."

Still, Betty knew there was more to the world than what she saw in St. Louis. In 1937 she and Allen took a cruise around the world on the *Empress of Britain*. The 760-foot Canadian Pacific ship was one of the most luxurious of its era, with two swimming pools, a full-size tennis court, and twenty-eight-foot-long staterooms. Society from both sides of the Atlantic was sure to be on board. "It was quite a group," says one passenger, "young, very attractive people representing the greatest fortunes from all over the world." A daughter of the Duke of Wellington was there, her thirty-carat blue-white diamonds glittering in the moonlight. The Wertheimers, perhaps the wealthiest merchants in all of Germany, found the cruise an elegant means of fleeing Nazi Germany. There was also Robert David Lion Gardiner, heir to the oldest fortune in the United States, dating back to 1639 when King Charles I allowed his forebears to become the first English family to settle in what is now New York.

Midway through the voyage, a short, pudgy man with a conspiratorial grin on his face approached Gardiner. The man, a putative Brazilian banana king, had had more than he could take of Betty. Her behavior, he said, was entirely unsuitable for a cruise. It was just a question of time, the man insisted, before the captain put her ashore.

"She was game for any prank," says Gardiner. "But there wasn't a mean bone in her body. I had to come to her defense. This man was being ridiculous. So I bet that awful Brazilian one hundred dollars that Betty wouldn't be thrown off."

Betty had already startled passengers by breaking into impromptu pirouettes and performing an occasional adagio. At night she went skinny-dipping in the foredeck pool. She wrote obscene poems about the cruise director and posted them on the ship's bulletin board.

On March 19, the *Empress*, more than halfway through its four-month voyage, docked in Manila harbor. As a gesture of goodwill, the Philippine government saluted the vessel that afternoon with a band playing the "Star-Spangled Banner" and the Canadian national anthem.

"It went on and on and on," says Gardiner. "*Oom pah pah, oom pah pah*—too much of a good thing really."

Betty couldn't stand it. "Can't someone get them to shut up?" she yelled.

There was no response. The band continued to play. She rounded up some silverware and china, leaned over the deck, and looked down at the orchestra. When she had the conductor in range, she let a plate fly.

"She happened to be quite a good pitcher," says Gardiner. The plate landed at the conductor's feet and shattered into dozens of pieces. The orchestra stopped. There was complete silence.

"The captain wanted to put Betty ashore right there," says Gardiner. "She had created an international incident. But to throw her off in Manila would have put her in serious danger."

Instead, the captain cabled back to Canada about appropriate disciplinary action. After the *Empress* pulled out of Manila, word spread about his decision. Meanwhile, the Brazilian, predictably pleased by the events, smugly sidled up to Gardiner.

"You owe me a hundred dollars," he said. Betty, accompanied by her brother, was put ashore at Shanghai, and the two were given passage on another vessel back to the United States.

GOING

EAST

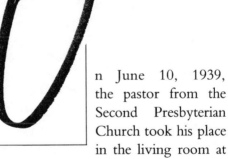

n June 10, 1939, the pastor from the Second Presbyterian Church took his place in the living room at the West house on Westmoreland Place. An elaborate flower arrangement of white Easter lilies was set against a mass of dark greenery. Betty's mother had taken the ivory-colored Duchess satin from her own wedding gown and remade it into one for her younger daughter. Betty, twenty-four, was marrying a twenty-five-year-old Yale graduate named Charles Dickson Walsh Pierce.

Mr. West had examined the social credentials of the young man, and Dickson had passed the test admirably. The son of a prominent St. Louis attorney, Pierce lived on Vandeventer Place and was a member of both the exclusive St. Louis Country Club and the Racquet Club, as well as the Claytonshire Coaching Club. He had returned home from Yale a few years earlier to work for a local advertising firm in the then-new field of color photography.

Many, however, were surprised by Betty's choice. Dickson was a handsome, dashing figure on the debutante circuit. And his interest in photography, in a world where everyone was going to be a stockbroker or lawyer, gave him an exotic appeal. But to some, he was a Walter Mitty of sorts, full of impractical dreams and harebrained schemes. He needed a simple, loyal St. Louis society hausfrau. How could someone as lost in the clouds as he possibly handle the wild, stubborn, and uncontrollable Betty West?

"I told Dickson it was the stupidest thing I ever heard," says one friend. "He had to be out of his mind. It was an impossible match."

Betty was not one to let such minor details interfere with her plans. She had been swept off her feet before, and she was not sure that was really what she wanted. A few years earlier, she had been seeing Potter Stewart, a handsome Yalie who invited her up to New Haven. "She was in love with him," says a mutual friend. "But he was already thinking of becoming President or getting on the Supreme Court. He told me he had to marry a girl who would help his career."

Stewart did indeed make it to the Supreme Court, when he was appointed by President Eisenhower in 1958. But back then he wrote letters to "Mademoiselle Snakehips West," and he sent her nude photos of himself from a skinny-dipping session in Maine. When Betty visited "Potsy" during Harvard-Yale weekend, she stole the key from the New Haven inn she stayed at, and kept it for the rest of her life. Their relationship continued for more than two years, but when it came to marriage, Betty was much too wild and unpredictable for someone as ambitious as he.

Dickson wasn't clever like Potsy, but that only made it that much easier for Betty to stay in control. More to the point, she wanted to leave St. Louis, and Dickson was as likely to provide a ticket out as anyone. Besides, as World War II approached, everyone else was tying the knot—among them, three or four more of Betty's close friends that spring alone. Jane Johnson had married John Hylan Heminway, a handsome New York investment banker and Princeton graduate from a well-known New York family, and had already moved to New York. Betty, one of the last single people in her crowd, was determined not to be left an old maid in St. Louis.

Her wedding was not as big as Jane's, but because of the social prominence of the couple, it received a great deal of attention in the local press. The small, private ceremony was attended by only a few friends of both families. Sissy was Betty's matron of honor. Jane and her husband came from New York.

As the ceremony was about to begin, Betty made last-minute preparations. Over her forehead, a pearl halo was secured. A veil of lace was attached to it and draped over her shoulders. She marched to the landing at the top of the stairs, the railing of which was entwined with white flowers. At twelve-thirty Betty's father took her arm and they descended into the living room. By then, it was too late to back out.

"As soon as I walked down the aisle," she said later, "I knew that I had made a terrible, terrible mistake."

The newlyweds lived briefly in her parents' house before finding a place of their own on Clara Avenue, less than a mile away. The Bitch Pack days were over. Dickson went off to his job each day. Betty got pregnant and on July 1, 1940, gave birth to a blond blue-eyed son, Allen West Pierce, whom she named after her father.

In 1941, Dickson joined the army. Betty worked as a nurse's aide in Barnes Hospital in St. Louis. Over the next three years the family was constantly on the move as Dickson was transferred from base to base—Denver, Salt Lake City, Miami Beach, Washington, D.C., and Dayton, Ohio. Betty hated the moving around. She passed the time during the cold Ohio winter by working on her figure skating. On January 5, 1944, she gave birth to her first daughter, Anne Terry Pierce.

When she returned to St. Louis later that year, Betty found being a mother confining. "We went for walks pushing our children in their prams," says a friend. "But as soon as cocktail hour rolled around—bingo, she would find a nanny to take care of them. She would have been much better off without children."

When Dickson got out of the army in 1945, he and Betty moved to New York, where Dickson launched a commercial photography studio called the House of Color. But the studio failed, and friends who had invested in it lost their money. "Dickson was always going to beat the world," says one friend. "To listen to him talk, he could do anything."

In comparison with Jane Johnson, Betty was not faring terribly well. Jane's in-laws had bought the Biddles' oceanfront villa in Palm Beach and lived in the Waldorf-Astoria Towers in New York. Dickson's family was unknown in East Coast society. It was not just that Dickson had failed to measure up to Betty's notion of worldly success. "Of all the people she could have picked," says one confidante, "he was absolutely the worst. They had nothing in common except they were from St. Louis and had some of the same friends. They just weren't fit for each other." Dickson had already served his purpose: Betty had her foothold in New York society.

By July 1945, Dickson had left their Park Avenue apartment and moved into the Yale Club. A few months later, Betty filed for divorce. She claimed Dickson objected to the presence of her girlfriends. She added that she had accepted the "hardship and inconvenience" of being transferred from town to town while he was in the service, but that he was "thoughtless and selfish."

Betty never wanted to see him again. She was granted custody of Allen and Terry, and was awarded a property settlement. Dickson went back to St. Louis. Because of the war, his children had seen little of him during their early childhood, and now he was gone for good.

Betty was thirty years old, a bright, attractive, engaging divorcée who could finally enjoy the high life of New York. She was briefly employed as a receptionist at the advertising firm of Batten, Barton, Durstine, and Osborne. Then she got a job at the showroom of Mainbocher, the fashion designer, working mainly as a "bouncer" of sorts—making sure that the "wrong" people didn't come into the shop. The job didn't pay particularly well, but that was not the point. In those days, Mainbocher was one of the most fashionable—and most expensive—designers in town; dresses went for more than a thousand dollars even then. For Betty it was less a career than a way of meeting the right people. She boasted that she sold only one dress during her tenure there.

And so, Betty managed a life on the fringes of café society. She tried her hand composing music, a hobby about which her friends teased her. They knew her as a party girl who stayed out until three or four in the morning at the Casino in Central Park, or at La Rue on East Fifty-eighth Street, or at El Morocco, with its blue-and-white zebra-striped banquettes and white palm trees. On summer weekends, she went to Southampton, just eighty miles from the city, where New York society partied in Georgian and Colonial oceanfront mansions. "Things were booming socially," says one friend. "We were the 'Drink today, because tomorrow we die' generation."

A year after her divorce, at a party at the River Club, Betty met John Archbold, an heir to Standard Oil. He was one of several men who clustered about her, each of whom had been favored at one time or another. Betty was not the type of girl who could be easily won. She was unable to endure being dominated and was so self-assured that she could easily overpower most of her suitors.

Still, Archbold was not easily dissuaded. "She was so vivacious and intelligent, but untrained—just out for a good time," he says. "She was a very physical person, full of vim and vigor. She loved dancing and staying up all night. She'd go to Atlantic City and do cartwheels up and down the boardwalk."

Betty enjoyed his company. With him as her escort, she could at least move comfortably in the same circles as Jack and Jane Heminway. As the summer of 1946 approached, Archbold went off to his family's vacation place in Bar Harbor, Maine, while Betty went to her parents' summer place in Watch Hill, Rhode Island.

Watch Hill was the beach resort where the Wests and many of their St. Louis friends summered. It was the one constant in Betty's life. Her family's position in St. Louis society carried no weight in New York, but in Watch Hill the Wests were a presence. They passed the summer in their cottage, called Stoneleigh, along with Allen and Sissy and their families.

Instead of the baronial pomp of Newport or the Gatsby-like splendor of Southampton, Watch Hill had the quiet charm of a small New England town. Whereas Newport was the summer playground for the families of East Coast industrialists, Watch Hill catered to mostly midwestern money from St. Louis and Cincinnati, as well as Pittsburgh and Philadelphia. There were the Lamberts of the Warner-Lambert pharmaceutical fortune, Richard Mellon of the Pittsburgh banking family, Douglas Fairbanks, Sr., the Brecks of the shampoo empire, the Engelhards of the South African gold fortune, and various heirs to the Anheuser-Busch brewery fortune.

Watch Hill never became as well known as its neighbor forty miles up the Rhode Island coast, but regulars resented the suggestion that it was "a poor man's Newport." They looked down upon the better-known resort towns as too showy and pompous.

Watch Hill was a community with a "higher moral tone," they insisted; it was more subdued and conservative by design, not because it wasn't as fashionable. "Watch Hill isn't as vulgar as Southampton," says one matron. "We wanted it to be simpler, not as society-minded." Tudor and Georgian homes lined streets with Indian names. There were also huge clapboard and shingle houses surrounded by pine and fir trees, their gables peeking out over the coastline.

Still, in the postwar era, Watch Hill, for all its simplicity, was not informal. Dinner parties, even on weekdays, were always black-tie affairs. Golfers wore coats and ties on the links. Virtually all the good families had their own chauffeurs take them to the beach or the yacht club, many in their Rolls-Royces. While the parents were off drinking at the club or playing golf, they would send George Hoxsie, Watch Hill's only cabdriver, to pick up the children and their nannies and take them to the beach. Each year, the town's own version of the social register, the *Book of Names,* was published. The comings and goings of houseguests was reported by the weekly *Seaside Topics,* the local "shiny sheet." (Every resort of note, society writers have pointed out, has a paper printed with a glossy sheen so as not to stain the white gloves of its readers, and Watch Hill was no exception.)

The community's social order was rigorously maintained by the powers that be at the Misquamicut Club. Jews generally were not admitted, though there were occasional exceptions. It was a very in-bred, closely knit group, requiring just the "right" society credentials to get in. Those who were accepted ended up being the people who ran Watch Hill. If a person could not obtain membership in the Misquamicut, he might as well not move to the resort.

Betty had the same problems with Watch Hill that she did with St. Louis. "[She] thought the Old Guard should be put on a shelf somewhere and stuffed," says one friend. "They were handsome enough. But who wants to hang around with these people who hate Jews and think of nothing but money?" It was everything she had wanted to leave behind in St. Louis.

That summer, however, a newcomer arrived who not only aroused Betty's interest, but whose credentials also happened to be impeccable. He was tall, handsome, and forty-six years old. On his mother's side he could trace his family back to the *Mayflower*. Through his father, he was an heir to one of America's great industrial dynasties. He had already inherited a fortune estimated at well over $50 million. Newly divorced, he was suddenly one of the most eligible bachelors on the East Coast. With his eighty-one-foot yacht, the *Ardea*, anchored nearby, he could hardly have escaped notice. The social hierarchy in this staid resort was turned upside down. Everybody was desperately eager to meet Watch Hill's newest summer resident.

"There is an aura that goes with people like the Vanderbilts and the Rockefellers," says one of his friends. "And William Hale Harkness had it."

John Archbold continued his ardent pursuit of Betty throughout the summer. Despite the distance between Maine and Watch Hill, the two saw each other almost every week. Occasionally, Betty went up to Bar Harbor to stay at his family's summer place, but more often Archbold came down to Watch Hill. He looked forward to their weekends. When he wasn't there, however, Betty had a full social calendar.

Bill Harkness's yacht, was the official boat of the Harvard-Yale Regatta in New London, Connecticut. Before the race on June 12, Harkness went to the marina near Holdredge's Garage on Bay Street in Watch Hill. It was a convenient anchorage for commuting by boat to New York or neighboring coastal towns. As usual, he made a point of having a friendly chat with the Holdredges; then the *Ardea* pulled out for New London. Late that evening, when he returned to Watch Hill, the Holdredges noticed he was not alone. By his side was Betty West.

By this time Archbold had thoughts of marrying Betty. She invited him down to Watch Hill for the weekend, but she discreetly decided not to inform him about her outing on the *Ardea*. Normally, Archbold stayed at the Wests' house; he had become quite friendly with Betty's father. "I assumed I would stay at her parents' house as usual," he says. "But when I got there, she said, 'No, I've got a room for you at the Misquamicut Club.'"

Archbold was perplexed as to why Betty would change the regular arrangements. "Finally my information department clued me in," he explains. "She had met up with this Bill Harkness. They were seeing each other. He'd moved in very rapidly. I said to hell with it. It was a complete shock to me."

It was sheer coincidence both Harkness and Archbold came from families that had played crucial roles in the birth of Standard Oil. The two men did not even know each other. Archbold's heritage was not inconsiderable: His grandfather had been one of the great early pioneers in the oil business.★

The Harkness family, however, had wealth of a different magnitude. They, after all, were partners with John D. Rockefeller in starting Standard Oil, the world's greatest oil company. It was a formidable legacy. It began a hundred years earlier with Bill's great-uncle, Stephen Vanderburgh Harkness, a successful businessman in a small town in Ohio, who staked John D. Rockefeller in the founding of the company.

Originally a harness-maker from the Finger Lakes region of New York, Stephen Harkness had moved to the Bellevue, Ohio, area, just sixty-five miles from Cleveland, in 1839. He worked first at harness-making, then at livestock-trading. By 1848, he had saved enough money to open a combination inn-grocery

---

★"Great" sometimes was a synonym for "ruthless," at least in the early days of the oil business. Archbold's grandfather, after whom he was named, had grown up in Titusville, Pennsylvania, where the first oil well was drilled by Edwin Drake in 1859, and initially headed the opposition of independent oil producers to John D. Rockefeller's young but enormous powerful new company, Standard Oil. By 1872, however, Archbold had been converted to Rockefeller's side and later became his right-hand man, president of the company, and one of the most ruthless men in the business. According to *The Rockefellers: An American Dynasty,* by Peter Collier and David Horowitz, Archbold bribed his way into rival companies and besieged them with stockholder fights until they sold out to Standard. Nor was he above buying off politicians in the name of the company, sending one U.S. senator fifteen thousand dollars in return for lobbying against some potentially damaging legislation.

store-lunchroom-ten-pin alley. Lodging and breakfast cost 19 cents. Patrons could buy anything from a pint of sugar brandy for 28 cents to five pounds of coffee for 50 cents.

In addition to running a store, Harkness began to deal in such diversified fields as livestock, whiskey, and the buying and selling of agricultural commodities from farmers as their goods awaited distribution. He even had his own bank. As he accumulated capital, he cultivated friendships with a number of high-ranking politicians, including John Sherman, U.S. senator from Ohio and the brother of General William Tecumseh Sherman. During the Civil War, Sherman tipped him off that Congress was about to pass a tax of two dollars on each gallon of spirits.

Harkness saw the opportunity to make a killing. He took every available dollar from his bank to stockpile whiskey before the tax took effect. Before long, the bank's funds were virtually depleted. One day a farmer tried to withdraw seventy-nine dollars for a load of corn. Harkness himself stalled the farmer with a discussion about the weather while a cashier snuck out and borrowed money from the druggist next door.

Harkness survived the crisis, but just barely. Scores of farmers were so angry he had tied up their funds to build his own fortune that he had to hire a man to stand on street corners telling people that "old Steve Harkness" was all right. Before it was over, he wired a commission firm in Cleveland that owed him money. "Why in hell don't you remit for the last car of corn I shipped you?" the telegram said. "Unless I get it soon, I will go bust."

Harkness was lucky he had not gone completely bankrupt. But he emerged from his whiskey gamble one of the wealthiest men in Ohio, with a profit of more than $300,000. Even more important, a twenty-year-old commission agent from the firm that owed him money would make up for his egregious error many, many times over. His name was John Davison Rockefeller.

By 1866, Harkness was no longer just the biggest businessman in a small town. He had moved to Cleveland and had quickly become one of the most powerful men in the city. He was an owner of the Union Elevator Company and a director of the

Euclid Avenue National Bank, oversaw various mining and railroad interests, and was buying up large amounts of real estate in the city. His income that year was $120,000—this in an era when a shot of gin at his country store went for four cents.

By 1867, Henry M. Flagler,★ a relative of the Harknesses by marriage, had become a partner of Rockefeller's. Their firm needed a huge sum of capital—variously reported as $60,000 to $90,000—in order to expand their refineries, and Flagler went to Stephen Harkness for the money. Harkness put up the money and became a silent partner in the venture. Dr. Lamon Harkness, Stephen's uncle, also invested. Less than three years later, the firm was recapitalized with $1 million and incorporated under a new name, the Standard Oil Company. By the time of its incorporation, Standard Oil was not just the biggest oil company in Cleveland; it already handled 10 percent of the petroleum business in the country. Of the original 10,000 shares issued, John D. Rockefeller owned 2,667, Stephen Harkness 1,334, and Henry Flagler, 1,333.

The company grew rapidly as new uses were discovered for oil, but at its inception none of the men had any idea what they had created. By 1882, six members of the family had invested heavily in the company. One of them, Daniel M. Harkness, Stephen's half brother, became a trustee.

The company expanded so fast that at the time of Stephen Harkness's death in 1888, his holdings alone were valued at more

---

★Strictly speaking Flagler was not a blood relation, but he was very much a part of the Harkness clan by both birth and marriage. Flagler's mother, Elizabeth Morrison Harkness Flagler, had been widowed twice before marrying Henry's father. During her marriage to her second husband, David Harkness, she gave birth to Daniel M. Harkness. Eight years later, after she married Isaac Flagler, Henry Flagler was born. As recounted in *Florida's Flagler,* by Sidney Walter Martin, the two half brothers became quite close friends, despite the age difference, and Henry followed Dan to Bellevue, Ohio, where they worked for L. G. Harkness and Company, which was owned by Dan's uncle Lamon Harkness. Both young men became fond of Lamon's daughters. Dan married Isabelle, a first cousin, and Flagler married her sister, Mary. Thus, Flagler, in addition to being a close friend of Dan's, was both his half brother *and* his brother-in-law.

That left Stephen Vandenburgh Harkness. Dan's father, David Harkness, had already had a son, Stephen, by his first wife prior to his marriage to Dan's mother. Dan and Stephen Harkness had the same father, so they were half brothers. Dan and Henry Flagler had the same mother, so they were half brothers. Henry and Stephen were not related at all—at least until Henry married Stephen's cousin.

than $30 million. It is difficult to convert the value of such a sum a century ago into current dollars, but his share would certainly be the equivalent of several hundred million dollars today, perhaps billions. Still, the Harkness fortune had not come close to its peak. The most important single use for oil had yet to reach the American public: the automobile.

Bill Harkness came by his fortune as the grandson of Daniel M. Harkness, Stephen's half brother and also one of the original investors in Standard Oil. Daniel's son, William Lamon Harkness, was an active yachtsman who devoted his time to managing his enormous inheritance. He married the former Edith Hale, who bore him two children, Louise and Bill. Bill was deeply devoted to his mother.

Bill prepped at St. Paul's before going to Yale. In 1919, while he was still at college, his father died. In 1922, the year he graduated, Bill made his own contribution to the family fortune, albeit somewhat reluctantly, when two friends from the Yale *Daily News* approached him for financial backing to launch a weekly newsmagazine. Bill was wary of people who came to him because of his great wealth. But he heard out Briton Hadden and Henry Luce's proposal and was sufficiently impressed to put up $5,000 and suggest they see his mother. Mrs. Harkness was quite deaf by then. She heard little of what they said, but she read the prospectus and liked their looks. "That will do, boys," she said. "I'll put in twenty thousand dollars." Other relatives put up another $10,000. The new magazine was launched with 40 percent of its $85,000 capitalization coming from the Harkness family.

The first issue of the new publication sold 9,000 copies. By 1924, its circulation was up to 70,000 and *Time, The Weekly Newsmagazine,* as it was called, was beginning to attract advertisers. The investment, of course, was eventually worth millions.

After graduating from Harvard Law School in 1925, Bill set out on a voyage around the world with a Yale classmate. When he returned, he began working as an attorney for the New York firm of Murray, Aldrich, and Roberts (now merged into Milbank, Tweed), occasionally commuting from Glen Cove,

Long Island, by one of the family yachts. In 1930 he gave up his position at the firm. In addition to managing his vast fortune, he served as a vice president and trustee of the Columbia Presbyterian Hospital and as a director of Time, Inc., and was an officer of the National Geographic Society, the American Museum of Natural History, the New York Trust Company, and the Boys Club.

In 1932, he married Elizabeth "Buffy" Grant. Their daughter and only child, Anne, was born in 1935.

By World War II, the Harknesses were so wealthy that their name was virtually synonymous with philanthropy. At the time of his death in 1940, Bill's cousin, Edward Stephen Harkness, had given away so much money that he was in the same league with Andrew Carnegie and John D. Rockefeller as a philanthropist. The most notable of his gifts to more than thirteen hundred charities included a donation of more than $11 million to Harvard University, $25 million to Yale, and $30 million to Columbia University, part of which went to the Columbia Presbyterian Medical Center. In addition, he and his mother were instrumental in founding Harkness Pavilion at the Medical Center. Those gifts alone created the undergraduate residential house system at Harvard, the equivalent residential college system at Yale, and one of the most prestigious hospitals in New York. In all, Harkness gave away over $129 million—billions in today's dollars.

During the war Bill served in army intelligence with the Eighth Fighter Command in England and Belgium and oversaw the making of aerial reconnaissance photos of the Normandy coastline in preparation for the D-Day invasion. He was decorated with the Bronze Star and the Croix de Guerre, as well as various African, Middle East, and European campaign ribbons.

When he returned from the war, he was shocked to find that Buffy was divorcing him. In 1950, she would marry the film star Robert Montgomery. It was a shocking and unexpected blow. After all, one just did not leave a Harkness.

3

PRIM
AND
PROPER

They were an unlikely couple. Betty was uninhibited, spontaneous, unpredictable, reckless. Bill was restrained, repressed, aloof.

"I don't think you could make him colorful," says Malcolm Aldrich, one of his best friends. "He wasn't that type."

Harkness, however, was seduced by Betty's effervescence. And Betty sensed the romance she had always been looking for.

She toned down her behavior considerably. Now, when she went out, she ordered nothing more than an occasional Dubonnet. Only when the waiter was safely out of Bill's earshot did she go over and whisper, "Put some gin in it."

Within a few months, Bill asked her to marry him. A small private wedding was held at his Park Avenue apartment. Among those attending were Betty's parents, her two children, Allen and Terry, and Bill's daughter, Anne.

Mr. and Mrs. West were understandably ecstatic over Harkness's money and social position. Moreover, here was a man who might exercise some control over their daughter. When the ceremony was over, Mr. West turned to a friend of Betty's and smiled. "Well," he said. "I finally got a built-in policeman to take care of Betty."

But just because he had been one of the most sought-after bachelors on the East Coast didn't mean Bill Harkness was an ideal match for Betty West. The Harknesses were not just an ordinary family. They were an institution. It would have been difficult for any man to carve out his own identity in this context. But Bill, far from wanting to rebel, as Betty did against a far more modest legacy, was determined to live up to his family's name.

Harkness's first book, *Totem and Topees,* is a case in point. A privately printed collection of letters to his mother written during his trip around the world, the book is a travelog full of lengthy descriptions of churches leavened with patrician bromides. Each time a personal voice threatens to reach the surface of the narrative, the author buries it in self-effacing homilies. He lovingly dedicated the book to his mother, and described it as a "conglomeration of uninteresting misinformation."

In 1939, Harkness privately published another book, *Ho hum, the Fisherman,* detailing the adventures of a fishing trip aboard the *Ardea,* in Cat Cay off Bimini. It describes at length the group's fishing expedition and tennis matches and also contains some of Harkness's occasional efforts at light verse. He prefaces it with the warning that "this book will be of no value . . . its existence cannot have the excuse even of literary merit. It does not claim to have any."

Excruciatingly shy, self-conscious, and diffident, Bill distrusted the affection of all but his closest friends. He was painfully aware that people sought him out because of his family's wealth. When he lost at backgammon—even fifty cents—he almost always forgot to pay. But if he won, he played the poor boy, hounding the losers incessantly. At restaurants, even in small towns where no one knew him, he told friends to ask for the check—reimbursing them later, of course. "If they think I'm paying the bill," he explained, "they'll charge twice as much."

He attended parties only out of his sense of duty to his great family. When a friend attempted to make light conversation with him at a charity ball, he said, "Don't even try. You can't make me have a good time." Cocktail chitchat—at which Betty excelled—was not his forte; he was too stiff and formal for that. With his keenly developed sense of noblesse oblige, he chatted more easily with the servants than with friends. The day he became engaged to his first wife, he threw his hat out the window. That, however, is about the only spontaneous act of his that friends can recall. Even the most daring investment with which he is credited, the backing of *Time,* is disputed. Betty's brother, Allen, insists that when approached by Henry Luce to help launch the magazine, Bill, predictably, was so cautious that he referred Luce to his mother. "Bill wouldn't go for it," says his brother-in-law. "The story is always told that Bill put up the money. But the only reason the investment was made at all was because of his mother."

But Bill was quite likable, and if circumstances were right, he could loosen up. He had a winning way with children. He was not entirely without a sense of humor; one had to have one if one spent any time at all with Betty.

Still, he was forty-six, fifteen years older than Betty, and the age difference seemed even greater. Betty had long railed about the stuffiness of society. Who embodied that more than Bill Harkness? Could she possibly be happy with someone best known for his resolute colorlessness? She might give up her late-night carousing for the time being, but how long would she settle for sipping Dubonnet?

"We were worried," says one friend. "She was a really a wild dish and he was so set in his ways."

There was one factor that set Harkness apart from all the other men in Betty's life. Unlike them, he was forceful, commanding, and strong. Shunning publicity with patrician assurance, he radiated glamour and a brightness so irresistible that virtually everyone in Watch Hill bowed in his wake. "I've seen them come and go," says one old-time resident, "but there was no comparison. When he got off the *Ardea* with his ascot and sport jacket, he was the most elegant and charming man I have ever seen."

Betty was not immune, even though she had always avoided relationships she could not dominate. But this time she let herself go. It was not just the money. She loved Bill, and by all accounts he was crazy about her. "I don't think money was her primary cause," says a friend. "He was a terribly nice man and she realized it."

Nevertheless, Betty's status was profoundly altered. Prior to her marriage, her entire social identity was still that of a West from St. Louis. But now things were different. Here, for the first time, was a man who could take care of her, a man who would turn the heads of her friends in New York, let alone St. Louis and Watch Hill. Bill could even impress the one man who had never been impressed by anything Betty had ever done—her father. The tables were turned: Now her parents were the hangers-on; they had to ride her coattails.

No longer would she take a backseat to Jane Johnson. The Veiled Prophet Ball, Jack Heminway—none of the glamorous things Jane had done were worth anything compared to William Hale Harkness. The Harknesses *were* the social order. One's level of social acceptance was simply a measure of how many invitations one got to the fabulous parties they gave. Betty had come from the stuffy, provincial world of Midwest debutante balls to a world of infinite possibilities.

"She adored money and needed it," says one friend. "Here she was from the Midwest, rich but basically a simple product of pork chop Americana. She didn't know how to buck the New York social game. Those sophisticated bitches will spit in your eye and cut you to shreds. But with that name, Harkness, she was safe."

The year after they married, Bill bought the single most imposing structure in Watch Hill, Holiday House. Situated on the bluff after which the town was named, the white clapboard house dominates the area. It is so large and rambling—with more than forty rooms, four chimneys, and half a dozen terraced sundecks—that it is hard to believe it is a single-family summer dwelling. Near the top deck is a room with windows on three sides from which one can see for miles up and down the Rhode Island coast.

Betty's parents kept Stoneleigh, but it was so modest in comparison that they spent most of their time at Holiday House. Her father was around so often that her myna bird began repeating the question he asked each time he entered: "How's the market doing?" it chirped. "How's the market doing?"

To everyone's surprise, the marriage seemed to work. Betty's spontaneity helped draw out Bill. But it was she who changed the most. Now that she was so rich that she could get away with anything, suddenly she was the picture of respectability. "We thought Bill Harkness was just great," says her brother, Allen. "He wouldn't let her get by with the things she did before. He wouldn't stand for it. Everything had to be accounted for."

"Bill looked on Betty as a naughty child and set about to reform her," said one friend of the couple. "He tried to teach her about banking and investments and that sort of thing. He was so much older, and she had always had this father complex." When he learned that she had invested in a Broadway production, he was appalled. But the play, *Kiss Me, Kate,* was a smash hit and Betty made a substantial profit. She was delighted that in her own modest way she had actually succeeded on his terms.

"She was scared of him," says another friend. "But she loved him being the dominant figure. She'd never had that before, except possibly with her father, and she always thought he was a clown."

The couple commuted between Watch Hill and their rambling duplex at 778 Park Avenue in New York City. They went to New York each Monday on the *Ardea* and returned to Watch Hill on Thursday; even though Betty hated boats, she never missed a trip. Yachting was a Harkness tradition; Bill's mother had owned a 270-foot vessel, the *Cythera*. Every day at Watch Hill, as the Block Island ferry crossed in front of their house, Bill and Betty went for a swim. Promptly at seven o'clock, Bill arrived at the dinner table wearing his satin house slippers and a satin smoking jacket. Their formal dinner parties were equally sedate. Guests were to arrive at seven o'clock on the button. One drink was served, then dinner began at seven-fifteen. After dinner Bill occasionally indulged in a rousing game of backgammon with Jack Heminway.

Jane Johnson Heminway and Betty had drifted apart somewhat because Jane thought Betty should have outgrown her Bitch Pack antics. Now, if anything, the opposite was true: Betty acted like the queen summoning commoners for a brief stay at the castle. "This wasn't the Betty we used to know," adds one friend. "She had been a real rip-roarer, and suddenly she was so prim and proper. She was simply not the same person."

But that was the price of Betty's charmed life: Her impulsiveness was curbed. There was no running around or kicking up her heels, Bill told her, and she complied. She confided to one friend that she was terrified he would find out she dyed her hair.

There were also constraints on her behavior that had nothing to do with her wildness. Before she met Bill, Betty had taken music lessons and composed songs about which she had been teased mercilessly. But she stood her ground. With Bill, she was still passionate about the arts—music, sculpting, and painting—but pursued them on the sly, as if she were afraid he might not approve.

Bill was something of a would-be lyricist himself, and with Betty writing the music, they began composing songs together. Even here, she took a deep bow to his tastes. Their most renowned effort, a western song, had the unlikely title "Giggling with My Feet." On the rare occasion that Betty tried to take the lead in aesthetic matters, she had little success. One summer she dragged him to a ballet performance in nearby Stonington, Connecticut. "Get me out of here," Bill said. "I've had enough faggots for the rest of my life."

But such contretemps were rare. Betty was finally cultivating a real family. She was actually spending time with the children, if only because Bill loved them and expected the same of her. Terry was a miniature of her mother, with beautiful dark chestnut hair and the same eyes and mouth. "For the first time, we had someone who spent time with us," she remembers, "someone who gave us a clearly defined world."

The children adored Harkness. Uncle Bill, as they called him, soon became closer than their natural father. There were plenty of nannies around, but he took them under his wing as if they were his own.

On October 24, 1948, Betty gave birth to her first child by Bill, a daughter named after his mother, Edith Hale Harkness. The myna bird soon picked up another phrase. "I love Edith," it squawked. "I love Edith."

But it was not entirely clear whether Betty West, the reckless society girl, was really gone for good or just buried under a controlled exterior. No longer did she have to outrage to win attention; that now came as a matter of course. No longer did she have to worry about propriety; she and Bill defined it. Her determination, her stubbornness, her compulsiveness to be the finest figure skater, dancer, musician, or whatever was still there. It was just focused in another direction, which was equally demanding and exacting, and required the same kind of discipline. She had decided she was going to be the best possible Mrs. William Hale Harkness in the world.

The only dark spot was Bill's health. In the fall of 1953, he had a heart attack while playing squash at the New York Racquet Club. Betty's father had died the previous year. Then, in the spring of 1954, Bill, only fifty-three, had his second heart attack.

He was told to give up playing squash, but, to Betty's dismay, he continued. He was also told to give up alcohol, but refused to forsake his cherished old-fashioneds. His father had earned the appellation "Whiskey Bill" for reasons that had nothing to do with the family's history as liquor barons.

Despite his health problems, the Harknesses went to Watch Hill as usual that summer. A special elevator was installed at the house so Bill wouldn't have to climb the stairs, but he refused to use it. Terry, only ten, was exasperated. "I tried to make him use it," she recalls. "It was almost like he wanted to do himself in."

On the first weekend in August, Watch Hill was alive with social activity. The last month of summer was peak season for the tiny resort. Many families had guests. As usual, an invitation to Holiday House was the most sought after of all.

Betty asked Bill to sit for her so she could work on a bust of him. While she molded the clay, Harkness was stricken with sharp chest pains, and could barely breathe. Bill was moved to Westerly Hospital, just a few miles away. His cardiologist was called up from New York. At first no visitors were allowed beyond the immediate family, but finally Betty said they could visit. They were greeted by an uncharacteristically unshaven Bill. The white streaks on his black bristles made him look roguish, almost piratelike, as if he had finally thrown off the constraints of being a Harkness and decided to have some fun. But his appearance belied his medical condition; his heart had sustained irreparable damage. His condition quickly deteriorated, and on Thursday, August 12, he died.

Two days later, a large service was held at Holiday House. It was a magnificent day. "It was like an MGM special, a huge marvelous Watch Hill cocktail party," says one friend of Betty's. "No one would have missed it for the world."

As the sea gulls circled overhead, a service was conducted on the front terrace at the top of the cliff overlooking the ocean. That afternoon, a small party of family and close friends accompanied the body by train to New York, where Bill was buried in Woodlawn Cemetery, in the Harkness family plot. The Reverend

Arthur Lee Kinsolving of St. James Episcopal Church conducted the service.

During her marriage to Bill, Betty's friendship with Jane Heminway, among others, had receded. Jane wanted to attend the burial, but she was no longer certain she belonged at such an intimate gathering. That amused Betty. Already they were lining up. No one could pass up a chance to pay final respects to the king.

"Jane's just looking for a little excitement," she said.

Meanwhile, her friends offered their condolences and did what little they could—fielding phone calls, making various arrangements.

Grief-stricken as she must have been, Betty did not share her feelings with anybody. To the extent she discussed Bill's death, she concerned herself with logistical questions. Without him, she had no one in whom to confide. The two most powerful figures in her life, her father and her husband, had died within two years. It was only through her marriage to Bill—an accomplishment she clung to tenaciously—that she had finally won the approval she so desperately sought from her father. She had eagerly become the proper Mrs. Harkness, the sedate society matron. She had suppressed her wildness, stopped drinking, even repressed her love of the arts—yet she had still lost Bill. She would have to find something to fill the void he left. The money, the boat, the house, even the family—all of them had been his. As far as Betty was concerned, she could do without them. But Bill had transformed her world, and now that he was gone it was likely to undergo an equally radical change. She had his great fortune at her disposal. And without her father or Bill, there was no one to hold her back.

On the morning of August 30, Hurricane Carol, with winds hitting a peak of 125 miles an hour, smashed into Rhode Island. At 11:30 A.M., forty-foot-high waves struck the Misquamicut shores, tearing houses from their foundations. Less than an hour later, a state of emergency was declared. A one-year-old baby was swept out to sea in nearby Stonington. The entire Watch Hill Beach Club was destroyed, with more than thirty cabanas washed away. The public bathhouses down by the carousel were ruined. Stores on Bay Street in the business section of town were destroyed; Atlantic Avenue was buried under eight feet of sand. More than three hundred homes were damaged beyond repair. In all of New England, there were forty-nine dead, and property damages were estimated at up to $500 million.

Many boats at the yacht club were totally destroyed. The *Ardea* went out to sea to wait out the storm and survived, but Betty decided to sell it immediately. Yachting had been a Harkness family tradition, one of Bill's greatest indulgences; he had instructed accountants never to tell him how much it cost to maintain the yacht. Betty, however, had always hated it. She had boarded it only to please him.

Holiday House escaped with only broken windows and minor damage. But Betty sent in the contractors full force anyway. Bill was gone and now Betty remade the house in her image. She ordered workmen to demolish the grand stairway, which Bill had climbed just before his final heart attack, and the enormous kitchen, both of which had been focal points of the house. She had several new kitchens installed, for a total of eight. Each child had one, as did servants and guests. New bathrooms were added, making twenty-one in all. There would no longer be any need to have the family dinners over which Bill had presided. The mansion was now effectively transformed into eight separate units, each entirely self-sufficient. It was as if Betty were making fundamental changes in the family structure itself. Even though her mother retained her cottage, Stoneleigh, Betty made sure one of the "apartments" in Holiday House was for her. The top unit was Betty's. When the door was closed, it was understood that under no circumstances was she to be disturbed.

As Bill Harkness lay in an oxygen tent, Edith, only five, had been horrified by the exotic paraphernalia surrounding him. She resembled him more than she did her mother; she had his dark coloring, enormous oval eyes, and brown hair. She had adored bouncing on her father's knee. Then, suddenly, he had disappeared. There was no one to explain things to her. Desperate for comfort from her mother, she entered the music room one day as Betty was practicing the piano. Betty didn't seem to notice the young girl and continued playing. Tentatively, Edith drew closer. Still, Betty continued playing, either not noticing her daughter or intentionally ignoring her.

Finally, Edith was so close that it was impossible not to take note of her. Bill would have known how to deal with such a tragedy; Betty had been able to tell the children only that Daddy had gone to the angels, and let the nannies take care of the rest. Sitting on the piano bench, her back arched, almost imperious in its erect posture, Betty looked at Edith with a scowl.

"What do *you* want?" she said.

AN
EMBARRASSMENT
OF RICHES

n Thursday, May 26, 1955, Betty arrived at Carnegie Hall full of anxiety as the eight-thirty performance was about to get under way. She took her seat next to her mother in their first-tier box. She had good reason to be nervous: She had composed—with some assistance, of course—the work that was being debuted.

Since Bill's death, Betty had thrown off the constraints he had imposed on her. She had decided not to be just another rich society matron, but to use his fortune to pursue the dreams her parents had denied her. "Since I took up the study of music seriously five years ago I've developed one ambition," Betty told a reporter. "I want to write something that will last, something that will be remembered."

It was such a complete transformation that she even changed her name. "Betty" was too simple, too St. Louis, too inelegant for a serious composer. Henceforth, she would be known as Rebekah.

The Carnegie Hall concert featured *Safari,* her twenty-minute tone poem, to be performed by sixty members of the New York Philharmonic. Leading the orchestra was Alfonso D'Artega, a Spanish composer-conductor who had had one pop hit, "In the Blue of Evening." He had shown particular interest in Rebekah's compositions; a Cavalcade Records album by D'Artega containing some of Rebekah's work was on sale in the lobby. Rebekah's father would not have believed it and even her mother, who was present, was highly skeptical. They had sneered at her dance performance in St. Louis when she was a teenager. Now she was playing Carnegie Hall.

Safari had grown out of a 1952 trip Rebekah and Bill had taken to Africa, and she dedicated it to him. They had traveled to the plains of Kenya during the great Mau Mau uprisings against the colonialist British. After Rebekah listened to the rebels chanting outside her tent at night, she put down her impressions in music. The work was structured in six movements. In one of them, "Dance of the Spears," the program notes said "brass, percussion, cymbals, and jungle drums . . . pyramid in volume and intensity until the Spear Dance [becomes] a mad, delirious nightmare as the revenge-maddened tribesmen leap into the air like Whirling Dervishes."

Safari was the last piece before intermission. The work was received politely. Fred Werle, Rebekah's piano teacher, a bookish, professorial sort who had put in hours working on the piece, fought through the crowd to congratulate his student. He approached Mrs. West, who was standing next to her daughter.

"Well, how did you like Rebekah's piece?" he asked her.

"What do you mean, what did I think of it,". Mrs. West said. "*You* wrote it!"

Rebekah looked away sheepishly. Her mother was right, of course. Only by the wildest stretch of the imagination was Rebekah Harkness a serious composer.

The cultural education of Rebekah Harkness had begun immediately after Bill's death. Rebekah invited artists, writers, painters, many of them world-renowned, to visit her in Watch Hill. She traveled constantly, usually with the children in tow, to France, Switzerland, and Haiti, often seeking out the best-known teachers in each country. She even enlisted the assistance of France's Nadia Boulanger, the world's preeminent teacher of composition and harmony.

The society pages lapped it up. "One of the world's richest women, Mrs. Harkness, could sleep until noon or later every day and party all evening," said the New York *World-Telegram*. Instead, the paper reported, Rebekah was probably the first woman to have an album devoted to her "semi-classical compositions." At least three labels issued recordings of her works. And the New York *Daily Mirror* predicted that Rebekah's pop song, "My Heart," would place its composer in "the top brackets of the musical nabobs whose earnings are computed by ASCAP."

Rebekah eventually devoted all her time to the arts. Holiday House was turned into her salon. She secured introductions to composers Samuel Barber and Gian Carlo Menotti, and invited them as guests. She became the patron of a French sculptress named Guitou Knoop and made considerable progress as a sculptress herself. She bought the old volunteer firehouse in Watch Hill and with a friend transformed it into the Holiday House Art Center, with films, art exhibits, lectures, crafts, and ballet.

She made arrangements—later aborted—with CBS records to release an anthology of historic works of American composers. She even got her children into the act with piano, dance, and painting lessons. She saw particular promise in the songwriting of Terry, now eleven, whose oeuvre consisted chiefly of a piece called "The Bunny Parade."

Rebekah's "My Heart" was released as a single on the Cavalcade label and debuted in a Carnegie Pops Orchestra program starring Eddie Fisher. "When Love Is New," on Mercury, had its premiere at a performance at Town Hall in New York. "Music with a Heart Beat," her first album, was issued on the Design label. In 1957, the Buffalo Philharmonic premiered a work she composed called *Mediterranean Suite.*"

Rebekah's earnestness notwithstanding, it was clear to the few people who knew her real abilities that she was not a great talent. She frequently conjured up bits of melodies on the piano. But that was about it. Without a teacher telling her what to do note by note, she foundered.

Working on a composition about nature, she pointed to the sheet music and looked at her teacher. "Do you think we could have a few more birds here?" she asked.

"It was so naive of her, it was almost touching," the teacher recalls.

When it came to orchestration, Rebekah was totally lost. "She really couldn't tell the difference in range between a piccolo and a tuba," a teacher says. Some of the "composing" was done through the tutelage of her regular piano teacher in New York, others with the help of a Russian composer-arranger, Nicholas Stein. "She'd fool around on the piano a little bit," recalls Arnold Arnstein, her music copyist at the time. "Then Nicholas Stein would listen carefully, and play with it. He'd write it down and we'd orchestrate it."

Even with all that help, the completed product was sometimes embarrassing. Most of the rave reviews Rebekah got were from society columnists. On the rare occasion real music critics discussed her work, they dismissed it. The only reason her works were ever played in public was because she subsidized the performances. And in truth, she was not under contract to all those record companies at all: Her records were vanity pressings, paid for by her.

"She played piano very badly, year after year," says a teacher who worked with her between 1952 and 1960. "Nothing jelled. Some days she would look far, far away, and it was like she wasn't there. Absolutely nothing would register."

Even the legendary Nadia Boulanger, who taught Aaron Copland and Virgil Thomson, couldn't do much with her. "I wrote Boulanger that Rebekah was very well-to-do," recalls one of her teachers. "And I said if one were very diplomatic with her, one might be able to get her to contribute a few scholarships to Boulanger's school."

After spending a few private sessions with Rebekah, Boulanger wrote back: "The meeting may need more diplomacy than I naturally have—but you have really well prepared me." Then she gave her assessment of Rebekah's progress. "I am sorry to answer so badly," she wrote, "but—these weeks *are hopeless*."

Boulanger was so hard-nosed, Rebekah said, "She gave me such an inferiority complex, I felt like I wanted to shoot myself." But she persisted. She was at the keyboard by 6:00 A.M. and spent six hours a day composing. "There are, of course, interruptions from the children, but those are the only distractions I allow," Rebekah told a reporter. "The social calendar bows to my work."

The extent of her self-deception was not immediately apparent to others. Few people knew how her composing was actually accomplished. They accepted her uncritically, and were swept away with the glamour of her wealth.

Now that Bill was gone, she also treated herself to luxuries he would never have allowed. Her florist bill got as high as $2,600 a month. She sold their seventeen-room Park Avenue residence and moved into a penthouse in Madison Avenue's elegant Westbury Hotel. She even began to dabble in mysticism and took on a yogi named B.K.S. Iyengar.

Rebekah bought a third home, Le Pavilion, a chalet owned by violinist Yehudi Menuhin in the Swiss ski resort of Gstaad. Gstaad was not quite as aggressively chic as neighboring St. Moritz, but it did count among its regulars David Niven, Elizabeth Taylor, Richard Burton, and Princess Grace of Monaco.

When the posh boarding schools like nearby Le Rosey let out, the pâtisseries and cafés filled up with pint-size Beautiful People.

In 1956, her distaste for boating notwithstanding, Rebekah chartered the *Virginia,* a 210-foot yacht, so family and friends could enjoy a Caribbean cruise while she attended the wedding of Prince Rainier and Grace Kelly. They anchored near the *Christina,* Aristotle Onassis's 325-foot yacht, and when they boarded it, Onassis began flirting with her.

Suddenly, Rebekah realized just how rich she really was, and she could not believe it. Once, when she wired for a large sum of money, she expressed her delight. "Isn't it amazing!" she said. "It was so easy." She was now one of the richest women in the world, in charge, more or less, of a fortune totaling some $54 million; Bill had left roughly half to their children, and Rebekah squirreled much of the other half away in foundations and trusts.★

The only problem was that Rebekah was so wealthy that she was now capable of fulfilling the wildest dreams of just about everyone who came in contact with her. She presented a most tempting target to hustlers on the fringes of café society.

In 1956, she met a portly, reddish-haired woman in her late fifties named Jane Gray. A woman of extraordinary presence who espoused her own peculiar brand of eclectic spiritualism combining astrology, reincarnation, and various mystical theories, Gray was a leader of the Great Work, a California-based sect that vaguely followed the teachings of British black-magic occultist Alastair Crowley. "We did special rituals," says one former disciple. "We were taught that the number 666 was the number of 'the Beast,' which represented evil. The idea was to make us special beings with special knowledge. And there were these trances."

★Harkness left $54,387,830.98 at his death. By the time of his estate's final accounting, it had grown to about $63 million, which would be more than $250 million in 1987 dollars. Over $52 million of that was in stocks and bonds, the largest single component of which was 185,000 shares of Standard Oil, worth about $16 million at the market price at the time. Of that, $25,972,300.07 was transferred to Rebekah. An additional $25,955,801.56 was left in various trusts to be split four ways between Anne Harkness, Bill's daughter by his first wife, Buffy; Allen and Terry Pierce, Rebekah's two children by Dickson Pierce; and Edith Hale Harkness, the only child of Bill and Rebekah's. That meant that each of the four children would get about $4 million, most of which was held in trust until they turned thirty. The remainder of the money, less than $4 million, went to estate taxes.

Rebekah hired Gray as her "executive secretary." What that entailed was unclear, but Rebekah leaned on her for advice, and they went to Spain together. When they returned to the United States, Rebekah gave Jane a mink coat. Then, suddenly, Jane was gone, never to be heard from again. "Only later did we decide Jane's trances consisted of having a few drinks and getting blotto," says an apostate. "I'd always thought she was in it because she believed in it. But when she met Rebekah, for the first time it seemed that what she really wanted was money and fame. Jane Gray smelled money."

Rebekah seemed oblivious to what had happened. "But she was riding for a fall," says a good friend. "When people were after her, she didn't even know it. Bill had kept the fast track away from her. But now that she was out there by herself, there was absolutely no one to protect her at all."

5

THE
GOLDEN
CAGE

ne evening in early
1958, Salvador Dali
arrived at Rebekah's
New York apartment
with his wife, Gala,
to meet Rebekah and three or four other potential patrons. After
dinner, the party made its way to the living room, where the
huge bird cage that held Rebekah's myna bird was kept.

With the help of jeweler Carlos Alemany, the fifty-three-year-
old Dali was making giant surrealist jeweled pieces, including a

working version of his "melting clock"; an extravagant dia-
mond-ruby-emerald "Star of the Sea," its five jeweled fingers
extending from a gigantic pearl; and the Chalice of Life. Some of
these works cost as much as $250,000.

Rebekah was interested in the jewels, but she also commissioned Dali to paint a portrait of Edith, then nine years old.
"Edith was just a little girl," says Joe Wade, a beau of Rebekah's
who was present that evening, "but she was really beautiful and
had long dark hair down her back."

When the finished portrait was unveiled a few months later,
Rebekah's friends were horrified. The painting showed Edith
trapped in the gilded bird cage. "I can't imagine why Rebekah
ever allowed it to be done," says one friend. But Rebekah
proudly displayed the portrait, completely oblivious to its meaning.

"You knew instantly that this girl wanted to be free and wild
and was trapped," says one observer. "It was so touching it was
overwhelming."

One could see the difference between Edith and her siblings at
a very early age. Physically, she looked so unlike Terry and Allen
that she could have been from another family.

But it was more than physical. "At a birthday party you might
see Edith, only six years old, in a corner reading an enormous
book—*Gone With the Wind, A Tale of Two Cities* or something
even more erudite—that would be more appropriate for a child
ten years older," recalls a friend of the family. "She would be
sitting alone, in a starched, scratchy organdy dress that she hated,
having totally blocked out everyone there. She was very bright,
precocious, but it was almost as though it was an affectation on
her part, like a little freak who was kept apart, not allowed to
live a childhood that was real, that she was not allowed to make
mud pies.

"The difference was striking. Here was this young girl in her
little glass bubble reading Tolstoy or something while Terry was
playing the dumb blonde, and Allen, stranger than strange, just
one big clumsy goofball, was shooting off his mouth, usually
saying exactly the wrong thing."

"Edith was my mother's conscience," says Terry. "She looked like Uncle Bill and my mother could not look at her without seeing him. My mother knew that she had abandoned us, but Edith was something she could not escape. Edith was a love child, but she still didn't treat her any better."

Rebekah had great expectations for Edith. When the child returned from a shopping mission wearing a new camel's hair coat, Rebekah complained, "It's too big for you."

"The tailor wanted to leave me room to grow in," said Edith.

"I don't want you to have any room to grow in," Rebekah barked. "I want it to be perfect now!"

The young child was expected to be a grown-up. When she was invited over to a friend's house to play, she often had to return home to have "cocktails"—sometimes a brandy Alexander—with the family. Rebekah charted the child's life by proxy, through nannies and governesses. "One nanny, a Scotswoman, manipulated Edith in the most sadistic and ruthless ways," says one relative. "She told Edith, 'Nanny's going to leave. Mama's going away, and when Nanny goes, Edith won't have anybody. Edith will be all alone.'"

When Edith was ten, Rebekah required that two very stern nannies accompany her when she went to the Misquamicut Club for tennis lessons. "I could tell her to pick up the ball, and Edith would pick up the ball," recalls Spencer Gray, the tennis pro. "I could tell her to stand on her head, and she'd stand on her head. She was very nice, very polite. She was beautiful, and she could do anything she wanted athletically.

"But there was still something about Edith that made it very difficult to give her a lesson. She was never allowed to do whatever the hell she wanted, to go around with friends or tell jokes, or whatever kids do. I could tell she was bothered by these nurses, so I asked if they would be good enough not to come down. Then I asked Edith if she wanted to sit down and talk. I knew she didn't want to hit the ball. She was just going through the motions. So we sat on the bench and talked. She wasn't able to show any emotion. At that age, they should feel great when they win or horrible when they lose—within limits, of course.

Sometimes we would be there for half an hour, just talking. She always seemed very unhappy. You could see she was beaten down, that she was sick and tired of doing things her mother had mapped out for her."

"Even as a child she was not naive," says a friend, Sophronia Camp. "She saw through the pretensions of Terry's friends better than Terry did, and Terry was four years older. You could not pull the wool over Edith's eyes." When Allen, eight years older, affectionately nicknamed her "Little Bug," Edith responded by mocking his imperious affect, calling him "His Lordship."

"She was not exactly mercurial, but there was an intense quality to her personality, especially for someone so young," says Camp. "She was very verbal, high-spirited, a riveting conversationalist. Her attitudes and observations were much more sophisticated than the other kids her age; she had a sense of irony and wit. She knew how to put on people even when she was a young kid."

One morning Edith was making faces at the breakfast table when Rebekah's music teacher, Lee Hoiby, cautioned her to stop. "When I did that as a child," he said to her, "my mother told me if I didn't stop, my face would freeze in one of those horrible silly faces."

Edith thought it over for a second. "Well," she said, "your mother was absolutely right."

Terry eagerly took piano lessons, learned guitar, and tried out painting, but Edith, even at that early age, rejected her mother's demands. "Edith reminded me of Eloise," says one of her best friends from childhood, referring to the holy terror of children's literature who turned the Plaza Hotel upside down. She taunted Mademoiselle, as they called the French governess, chanting, "Mademoiselle from Calamaziers, Where did you get such enormous ears?" Once, she spat and stomped on the ingredients of a cookie mix before baking the most revolting cookies imaginable. Then she approached her unsuspecting nanny. "Here," she said proudly, as if mocking the expectation that she was the most perfect little girl in the world. "Try some of my cookies."

Frequently, Edith sought to escape and become part of another family. "This Mademoiselle was a real witch," recalls Courtland Loomis, whose father, Bob Loomis, headed the staff at Holiday House. "She used to treat Edith terribly." When no one was looking, Edith used to sneak away and come down to eat lunch with the Loomises because she was so lonely. "Then that damn French governess would go down to our place and chase after her."

Edith loved going fishing for flounder with her friend Sophronia and her father. Friends who were awed by the extravagance of Holiday House were perplexed. "I never could understand why she liked our pot roast family dinners so much," says one.

"Edith played with my daughter," says another friend of the family, "and I allowed my child a good deal of freedom. Whenever they were together Edith kept whispering, 'Let's get away, let's get away.' My child didn't quite see the point."

At Holiday House, with each of its many kitchens perpetually busy with servants preparing for huge parties, a kid could easily get lost in the endless corridors. Thus, the children were under strict orders not to be out of shouting distance of their nannies. But Edith would spend hours in a room called the Cockpit. A pink, glassed-in, polygon, the Cockpit jutted out from the house with a dramatic 180-degree view of the Rhode Island coast. It was not meant to be Edith's room alone, but she spent so much time there that it became hers by fiat. "Keeping her occupied was difficult," says one of the house staff. "Her mother was rarely home. She never talked about her father. She was not close with her sister or brother or anyone. She was pitiful, quite bright, very alert mentally, but so alone."

On winter nights in Watch Hill, Edith sometimes snuck outside. As a friend looked on, Edith, thinking no one was watching, wearing only a nightgown in the subfreezing weather, danced alone in the moonlight on the sea wall overlooking the ocean.

One afternoon in the summer of 1958, when Rebekah and the family were in Watch Hill, Edith's cousin, Allen Tarwater West III, known in the family as Tarwater, strolled about the great house. Passing Edith's suite, he called out for her. There was no response. He peaked into her quarters and saw steam issuing from the bathroom.

"Edith!" he called again. There was still no answer. He opened the bathroom door and saw the nine-year-old child slumped unconscious in the steaming bathtub. He picked her up and shook her, but she failed to awaken. He yelled for Rebekah, then called for help. A doctor arrived within minutes. He administered smelling salts, then gave two sharp slaps to the child's face. She returned to consciousness and was then rushed to nearby Westerly Hospital, a few miles away, where her stomach was pumped and emptied of enormous quantities of aspirin.

"Children do that all the time," says one of the doctors who treated her, "but we never consider them suicidal, especially at that early age. To them, it's just like eating candy. Anyone that young just can't understand what death is about."

Others close to the family, however, saw Edith's overdose differently. "I always thought Edith was a little disturbed," says one member of the house staff. "I would ask if there was anything I could do for her, but she always said no, that she could do it herself. She was very, very sad. There was only one time that she asked me to do something. She gave me a bottle with a note in it and asked me to throw it in the ocean."

Instead, the housekeeper waited until Edith had left, and read the note.

"When somebody finds this bottle," it said, "I'll be dead."

When she entered Brearley, a posh private school on New York's Upper East Side, Edith was one of the more popular girls in her class. "Everybody liked Edith," recalls Heyden White, Edith's best friend. "They found her interesting and very likable, but a little mysterious."

The daughter of historian Theodore H. White, Heyden was overwhelmed by the Harkness wealth. Edith did her best to ease the disparity, buying her some records and sending her a whole carton of potato sticks when her friend went away to summer camp.

"When you went over to the Westbury, it wasn't like a home,

it was like a Hollywood set," says Heyden. "Seeing Edith at the Westbury, you were preoccupied with the strangeness more than the wealth. This was not a place where a family would grow up."

Heyden was welcomed to the family as a regular guest in Watch Hill and was invited to join them in Gstaad and Nassau when they were on vacation, but Rebekah always greeted her as if she hoped the friendship would give Edith something that she herself was unable to provide.

"I felt like I was supposed to be Edith's lifeline for a while," says Heyden.

From a distance, even Heyden's mother looked on at Rebekah's family in dismay. "She knew Rebekah was completely disciplined and dedicated in so many ways," says Heyden—"in her music, in her exercise—and yet she couldn't spare the time to take care of her own daughter. My mother almost wanted to adopt Edith. Not seriously, of course, but she knew Rebekah was not giving Edith enough care."

That was the least of Rebekah's concerns, for she had become newly obsessed with dance. Her composition, *Journey to Love*, had its premiere as a ballet with the Marquis de Cuevas's company at the Brussels World Fair in 1958—to seven curtain calls and shouts of "author" calling her to the footlights—and the experience was so heady that she determined to become a dance patron. By 1959, she had launched the Rebekah Harkness Foundation for precisely that purpose, backing Jerome Robbins, a major figure both on Broadway (*West Side Story*) and in ballet (*Fancy Free, The Cage*), and his troupe, Ballets: U.S.A.

On February 3 and 4, 1961, New York was hit by the biggest blizzard it had seen in nearby fifteen years. Manhattan was covered with seventeen inches of snow, and more than two feet had fallen in nearly Rockland and Westchester counties. At Newark, LaGuardia, and Idlewild airports, twenty-seven hundred flights were canceled, stranding a hundred thousand passengers. Garbage collection was suspended. An army of fifteen thousand men went out to clear the snow. Mayor Robert Wagner toured the city by helicopter and issued emergency decrees closing all schools and banning all private vehicles from the city for all "nonessential driving."

By Tuesday afternoon, February 7, the temperature rose briefly to forty-one degrees, which helped ease the burden of snow removal. But there was considerable fear that the city might get hit again by either of two storms that were approaching the area.

Even though New York had come to a standstill, Rebekah's life went on as usual. On Wednesday, Edith, now twelve, was at home with her nanny and Rebekah. Just before five o'clock, Rebekah and Edith's nanny went upstairs to the child's bedroom on the fifteenth floor of the Westbury. It was time for Edith's dance lesson.

Edith, who had no interest in dance, refused to budge. "Nothing you can do can make me take that lesson," she said. But neither woman would listen to her. They told her to get on with it. Then Rebekah, fed up, left the room.

"That nanny was so nasty to Edith," says a friend in whom she later confided. "Edith utterly despised her." But when Edith had tried to have the nanny fired, Rebekah refused. Edith felt completely abandoned. She had fulfilled her mother's every demand, having learned very early, and in the most painful ways, exactly what she was allowed to do and to feel, what was acceptable and what was not.

The nanny continued to goad Edith.

"If you don't stop," Edith said, "I'll jump out the window."

The nanny went over to the window and opened it. "Go ahead," she said. "Jump! Do it." Then she, too, left the room, leaving Edith alone.

There was nothing to make Edith believe she would ever be loved for what she was, that anything would ever change. She ran to the window. She leapt free and fell toward the icy pavement fifteen stories below.

At the last second, her body veered in a slightly different direction. As a result, she didn't fall directly to the pavement, but instead plummeted to the roof of a three-story wing of the hotel.

Even so, her body had accelerated to a speed of about sixty miles an hour. The fall would certainly have been fatal were it not for the storm of the preceding week: Instead of crashing into the roof, Edith landed in an extraordinary snowbank several feet deep.

She was rushed by private ambulance to New York Hospital nearby. Her left elbow and several ribs were fractured, but exploratory surgery showed no major organic injuries.

When she recovered consciousness, she saw Ben Kean, a doctor who had been dating her mother, hovering over her.

"I'm so sorry I caused all this trouble," she said.

"You're a very lucky girl," another doctor said. "You should be dead."

"I still wish I was."

Betty West, as she was called in her youth, when she made her debut as a nineteen-year-old in the winter of 1934. The local press said they thought she would be chosen Queen of the Veiled Prophet Ball. They were wrong.

The Wests' home
at 48 Westmoreland Place
in St. Louis

Betty as
a baby at the
West home

As a young girl, Betty was
sometimes called "Chunky"
because of a weight problem she
had until she took up dancing as a teenager.

With his gruff demeanor, Betty's
father, Allen T. West, often terrified
his daughter and her friends.

Rebekah Semple West, Betty's
mother, was warm, but it was Betty's
father who ruled the family.

Siblings: Anne Katherine "Sissy" West, who grew into a demure society matron,
and Allen Junior—later, Frère—Betty's alter ego, who knew he
had to leave St. Louis

Finishing school: Betty *(right)* with friend Kate Shinkle during their schooldays at Fermata

Debutante days: The "vivacious" Betty West, the local press noted, "is a member of the Bath Club debutante set."

Repent
YOUR TIME IS AT HAND

Society asses: At one party, Betty discreetly placed these stickers on the backsides of stuffy St. Louis socialites.

Stage fright: When *Aida* came to St. Louis in 1934, Betty won her first dance role, but she was devastated when her disapproving father unexpectedly showed up in the audience.

Naked justice: Potter Stewart, long before his appointment to the Supreme Court, wrote to "Mademoiselle Snakehips West" and signed his letters, "Love Always, Potsy." He enclosed photos of a skinny-dipping session.

Model daughter: During her brief career as a model, Betty appeared in newspaper ads for local department stores.

Poolside hijinks aboard the *Empress of Britain*, during Betty's 1937 round-the-world cruise, in which she and her brother were put ashore because of her pranks

Betty has a drink during a stopover.

A quiet moment offshore during the same cruise

During the *Empress*'s stopover in Ceylon, Betty and a friend went elephant riding.

At twenty-two, Betty was self-assured and sophisticated beyond her years.

Betty, standing, second from left, and her brother, Allen, sitting, fourth from left, enjoy dinner aboard the *Empress*.

Alter egos: Betty and her brother, Allen, at the Claytonshire Coaching Club in St. Louis

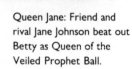

Queen Jane: Friend and rival Jane Johnson beat out Betty as Queen of the Veiled Prophet Ball.

Betty and the Bitch Pack: Betty, with best friend Jane Johnson next to her, and three other members of the Pack, make a toast at a party.

The center of attention: At Bitch Pack gatherings, Betty was
always the most outrageous.

Rejected suitor: Betty's brother, Allen (right), courting Jane Johnson, but Jane later
turned down his marriage proposal.

An impossible match: Betty and her first husband, Dickson Pierce. Friends predicted that Pierce was a dreamer who would never be able to rein in anyone as wild and uncontrollable as Betty. They were right.

6

THE BLACK SHEEP

*I*n September 1961, Rebekah, then forty-six, brought Ben Kean to her chalet in Gstaad. She had first met the forty-eight-year-old Kean when she returned from travels abroad and he treated her for a parasitic infection. They had begun dating not long afterward. Recently divorced from his wife, Kean, with his ruddy good looks, was capable of consider-able charm.

They decided to get married. With just two days' notice, Rebekah had a Tyrolean peasant dress made to wear as a wedding gown. Kean wore an embroidered shirt. On a warm Friday, they took off with a few friends in a Land Rover filled with champagne. In the car ahead of them was an accordionist with the unlikely name of Johann Sebastian Bach who provided the music during the trip. The entire village showered them with flowers as they drove by. Then a quiet civil wedding was performed.

"The ceremony was in French, so we're not too sure what it said," Rebekah wrote her family, "except I know that I didn't have to promise to 'obey' like they do in those barbarian countries like New York . . . Anyway, after 15 minutes we signed a book and the operation was over . . . I'm sure no Queen or anyone ever had a gayer, more amusing or happier wedding. By the time we got back to Le Pavilion the farmers were yodeling three octaves higher & my bridesmaids were doing a weird ballet through out strange Italian garden & the next thing I knew I was swept off my feet by a pair of massive arms."

Kean nicknamed Rebekah "Karma," in reference to the Buddhist doctrine that present actions can determine one's destiny in future lives. Rebekah, a devout believer in reincarnation, delighted in the name.

Rebekah's son, Allen, now twenty-one, regarded Kean with suspicion, believing he had married Rebekah only for her money. Oddly enough, Allen had given the couple a dark blue Rolls-Royce as a wedding present—which was later painted the color that Rebekah adopted as the family trademark, "Harkness blue." But that gift reflected Allen's erratic, often extravagant behavior more than any positive feelings about Kean.

About nine months after the wedding, on a cool June night in 1962, Allen's true sentiments toward his new stepfather surfaced. Terry, eighteen, was having her debutante ball, and Rebekah had pulled out all the stops, renting a Circle Line boat and decking it out in a tropical motif for the occasion.

Allen arrived at the pier in his own Rolls-Royce with his twenty-year-old cousin Tarwater. "You know, a Rolls is such a good investment," Allen said. "Everyone should have one."

Tarwater had heard it all before. For years he had worn Allen's hand-me-downs from the best tailors all over the world. "Allen was always displaying his wealth," he recalls. "His new skis, his stepfather's yacht, his speedboat. It was as if he was nothing more than these extraordinary objects that surrounded him." Allen's East Side apartment was a case in point. In it were a Dali, some old Italian tempera paintings, and a Degas over the fireplace. His youth notwithstanding, Allen already found such luxuries commonplace. As he put it, there was "nothing overly priced. It was just normal."

The two got out of the car and boarded the Circle Line ship, which was adorned with palm trees and grass huts. Terry, dressed in a seven-thousand-dollar off-white gown, looked resplendent. The guests wore leis. Some 350 socialites, A&P heir Huntington Hartford among them, had arrived from as far away as Central America. Lester Lanin's orchestra was playing, with Lanin wearing a grass skirt instead of his usual attire. Dali scribbled on napkins and signed them, giving them away as party favors. As the boat pulled out from its berth, guests scrambled for the limited supply of tables and chairs.

Tarwater quickly downed a few drinks and began chatting with an attractive girlfriend of Terry's. She was not responsive. When Tar persisted, abusively, she was distressed to the point of tears, and ran to Allen for help. "This is my sister's coming-out party," Allen told his cousin. "Do you mind cooling it?"

Tar was smashed. Moreover, he was enraged by Allen's attitude that he was defending the family honor against some upstart trash.

"Allen," he said, "you're full of shit."

Allen hauled off and slugged him three or four times. Ben Kean came over to investigate the commotion. This time Allen, completely out of control, slugged Kean. "Most of us have some self-restraint," says Tarwater. "That never entered Allen's head. It didn't exist."

Rebekah sent over security guards to control her son. Allen couldn't understand why. He had stood up for the family against his cousin. He had fought off his new stepfather, who, he thought, had married her only for her money. And after all that, Rebekah sent over the "goon squad" to hold him down.

"My own mother almost had me arrested!" he says. He was the black sheep in the family, and he knew it.

Blond, with blue eyes, Allen most closely resembled his father, Dickson Pierce, whom Rebekah had divorced shortly after World War II. Dickson's visits to Allen and Terry were rare and perfunctory. "You'd be talking to him and suddenly he'd fall asleep," says Allen. "Might as well talk to the wall."

Then Bill Harkness had come into the picture. "I'll never forget when Uncle Bill first showed up," Allen says. "You knew the minute he walked in the door that he called the shots."

When Rebekah and Harkness got married in 1947, seven-year-old Allen, dressed in his coat and tie and short pants, beamed proudly at their side. Harkness was not the most indulgent parent in the world, but he was so attentive that the children respected him even when he disciplined them. A year later, when Allen stole a small knife from a store, Uncle Bill made him return it immediately, go to his room, and write one thousand times, "I shall not steal." He never stole again.

Allen was delighted by the way Uncle Bill dominated Rebekah. "She had met her match," says Allen. "She could push around Dickson Pierce, but Uncle Bill knew how to rule the roost. I'd never had a family. Suddenly I had one. There was somebody I could look up to and respect."

More than anything, Allen looked forward to returning from boarding school to Watch Hill each summer to be with Uncle Bill. But all that came to an end in the summer of 1954, when Allen was fourteen. He was taking a golf lesson at the Misquamicut Club. "I'll never forget it," he says. "The flag was at half-mast. Everybody else in town knew. I was just about to take a swing, and Aunt Sissy came up and said, 'Your Uncle Bill died last night.' That was really the saddest day of my life. Bar none."

After the funeral, Rebekah asked Allen if he would like to change his name from Pierce to Harkness. "It wouldn't be fair to Uncle Bill," Allen said. "I'm not good enough."

Despite his grief, Allen stoically hid his feelings. "Allen didn't act appropriately shocked," says Tarwater, who saw him immediately after Harkness's death. "He didn't reveal emotions directly."

Allen had a tough time facing life without Harkness. With his stepfather's death, he was expected to behave not only as an adult, but as a Harkness. When he started looking under the hood of the family car one day, the chauffeur chastised him, "What are you doing? You will shut that hood immediately!"

"Allen loves to get dirty," explains one friend. "He's a hard worker. He loves that. But he was brought up like Little Lord Fauntleroy, not allowed to touch anything. All he wanted was to tinker with the motor or something. But his upbringing was so upper-class."

Soon even the neighborhood cop was on his back. "When I was around sixteen, I went into one of the slum bars where all the whores were in Westerly, near Watch Hill," he says. "I was out whoring around. Well, one of the cops recognized me. He steps right in front of me, puts his hands on his gun, turns around, and says, "What are *you* doing here? This isn't your element. Get out."

But no one could really control him. He terrified locals in Watch Hill with his high-speed driving. And he frequently went off on his own little jaunts away from the family. "I used to pick him up at the train station in New London," says one member of the house staff at Holiday House. "Goodness knows where he went."

For her part, Rebekah indulged Allen as Harkness never had. While she was in France studying with Boulanger, she let Allen, fifteen at the time, pick out and drive a Mercedes 220S. When he promised to refrain from smoking and drinking, Rebekah gave him an eight-thousand-dollar teak-paneled Century Coronado "Safari" speedboat, in which he zoomed recklessly toward the Watch Hill Yacht Club at fifty miles an hour.

"He was left alone so much and so ignored that he had all this time to fantasize," says one family friend. "There was no one to be his friend, and he wondered why we had to be in bed at a reasonable hour. They were essentially kids without parents. You could be there for six hours in that huge house without any adult knowing where you were. They had no rules. Rebekah abandoned them. She would go for days without knowing where they were.

"He could be warm, open and loving. One day he might give you five or six records because he knew you liked music. Then he'd think you had tricked him into it. He was totally infantile, but with an enormously big heart. He didn't know how to bring anything into perspective. He might say, 'Let's go for a hot dog,' and we'd assume he'd take us to the nearest hot dog place. But before you knew it he would be driving us off to some greasy spoon miles away in New Haven."

When one of Terry's friends spent the weekend at Holiday House, Allen burst into her room at six-thirty one morning and ripped off her nightgown. "It wasn't rape," she says. "Allen knew me very well. Terry was in the room. He really did think it was amusing. But I was so shaken that I returned home early. Very few men would do that. Only someone who was very unstable."

It did not help that Allen had been shuttled from one boarding school to another since he was six. There was the Malcolm Gordon School, the Harvey School, St. Paul's, and finally Collège Aiglon in Switzerland, from which he was expelled when he beat up the headmaster.

Alarmed at his frequent outbursts, Rebekah sent Allen to a therapist. "The psychiatrist started telling me about everybody's weirdo sex habits," Allen says. "I didn't want to listen to all this crap. If he thinks I was gonna listen to it all day, guess again."

When Allen was twenty, he took off for Munich, where he studied languages and worked in the Bavarian Union Bank. He loved it. No burdensome expectations were thrust on him as a result of the family fortune; few people knew the name Harkness, and family tensions were thousands of miles away. But Rebekah pleaded with him to come back after a year. When he returned, he enrolled at Columbia University, but dropped out less than a year later. "I just didn't blend in," he says. "Anything I wanted to learn I always learned myself."

To make matters worse, Allen hated the fact that Rebekah had decided to become a dance patroness. "Allen was naturally jealous," says Tarwater. "He was hypersensitive that his mother cared more for her art than for motherhood."

Getting her attention had been difficult enough. Now, as Allen saw her start to surround herself with "parasites, dancers, fortune-tellers and conniving shyster lawyers," it was next to impossible. They all wanted something. At one party Rebekah gave, Salvador Dali became angry that a full dinner was not being served and later told his colleague Carlos Alemany he would get back at Rebekah for her dinnerless evening. When he sold her his "Star of the Sea" brooch for $45,000, he confided to Alemany that he had jacked up the price.

Dali, of course, was not the only one. And it was not just that they were after her money. "I objected to all the perverts running around," Allen says. "It blew my mind. There's no way I was going to put up with all the fairies flying off the floor, the blackmailing lawyers, the weirdos, the people in the trances. They thought *I* needed help!"

All this would never have happened if Bill Harkness were still around. Rebekah was well-meaning, Allen thought, but so naive. In his own way, however, he was as trusting, highly impressionable, easily manipulated, and vulnerable as his mother. "You can see the hurt in his eyes," says a friend. "He has a lot of hate in him, and I don't think it was born in him. It was put there by people. Even as a little boy, Allen could see that something was wrong."

"When children don't feel love they are crippled forever," says another friend. "That's what's wrong with Allen. He is bright, he is intelligent. But he is so screwed up emotionally. He is so full of holes."

Angry, armed with a substantial trust fund left him by Bill Harkness, Allen decided to strike out on his own at the age of twenty-two. A male dancer asked him if he was going to Watch Hill for the summer.

"Not if I can help it," Allen said. Then he boarded a plane to Chicago and left the family for good.

DREAMS
OF
GLORY

ebekah first met cho-
reographer Robert
Joffrey in 1961, and
arranged to observe
his dance company
from the dark recesses of the Phoenix, a dusty, run-down, off-
Broadway theater on Second Avenue and Twelfth Street in New
York City. As she waited, Joffrey explained to the dancers in his
ballet company why they were going out onstage. "We're going
to give a very special performance," he told them. "This is for

just a couple of people. I can't tell you who they are. But if it's successful, our futures are assured."

For about an hour, the young troupe performed various excerpts from favorite pieces in their repertory. "It was very strange," recalls Lawrence Rhodes, a Joffrey dancer at the time. "We were all in our practice clothes. It was so dark that we could hardly see the audience. It was rumored that there was a woman there named Rebekah Harkness."

Joffrey had struggled since 1956 to keep his small ballet troupe afloat. For his company to make its mark on an international scale, however, he needed money to hire choreographers, build scenery, make costumes, and, most importantly, have the luxury of rehearsing new works. Rebekah had already had some significant successes with the Marquis de Cuevas and Jerome Robbins's Ballets: U.S.A. Robbins, however, had gone off to other projects, and Joffrey was the ideal choice to fill the void left in Rebekah's life.

And so, after they privately auditioned for her, Rebekah decided to take on the sponsorship of the Joffrey Ballet. She invited him and his entire dance company to spend the summer of 1962 in Watch Hill, preparing for an international tour that fall. In addition, she invited up six choreographers and commissioned them to create new works. She also hosted the production and administrative staffs, managers, lawyers, members of her extended family, dance teachers, and so composition teachers, not to mention artists and musicians she admired.

Rebekah transformed the volunteer firehouse in Watch Hill, which she had previously turned into an arts center, into a dance studio. "Money was no object, so she did things others wouldn't dream of," says Lee Hoiby, her composition teacher at the time. "The ceiling was too low at the firehouse for the dancers, so she literally raised the roof."

Rebekah basked in her newly found glory as a dance impresario and indulged her entourage as if they were her own children. During the summer, the dancers were put up in a rooming house on Bay Street at the other end of town. Key staff members and honored guests like Samuel Barber were given their own suites in Holiday House, complete with a kitchen, whose refrigerator was freshly stocked each day. There were at least half a dozen grand pianos in the main house, so that each composer and music teacher had one for his own private use. She sent all the men dancers to Saks Fifth Avenue for formal wear, the women to Bergdorf's for evening gowns. If a dancer required a nose job or orthodontics, she paid the bill. Traveling accommodations for the troupe were always first-class. She showered them with gifts of perfume or scarfs or expensive leather purses.

"We were the favorites," says one dancer. "We were the loved ones."

Rebekah stopped at nothing to win the affection of her new surrogate family. "She'd invited us over for dinner at Holiday House," recalls one of her music teachers, "and before desert she announced loudly, 'I can't cook very well, but I can make a wonderful cake.'"

When the guests cut into their portions, they found that she had wrapped ten-dollar bills in aluminum foil and dropped them into the batter. She waited until everyone had discovered her joke. "Well," she said, "now who wants seconds?"

Once on tour, the company quickly made its mark. Original works by Joffrey himself and the young black choreographer Alvin Ailey fared especially well. In India, the Bombay *Free Press Bulletin* hailed Joffrey as a "miracle worker." The Teheran *Journal* said his dancers had "unbelievable grace."

When the tour was over, the Robert Joffrey Ballet had stamped its name indelibly on the international dance world, and Rebekah was acclaimed one of the great patronesses of dance. "It was an utterly magnificent gesture," said *Holiday* magazine, "and utterly successful." The international press compared the new partnership between Joffrey and Harkness to the golden era of Diaghilev and the Ballets Russes in Paris.

Only thirty-one, Bob Joffrey was already a veteran of the New York dance scene. He demanded complete independence as a choreographer and artistic director, and he had earned it. He had made his mark early as a dancer and was offered a contract with the Ballet Russe de Monte Carlo when he was fourteen. But it was as a teacher at his own dance school, the American Ballet Center, where he combined modern dance with rigorous classical training, that he gained the respect and loyalty of his colleagues. His taste was considered impeccable, his judgment flawless. "Even though he was only two or three years older than some of the dancers, he was like a father to us," says one member of the troupe. "We would have jumped out of the window for him."

Not that working under him was easy. "Bob had many good features, the greatest of which was he cared," says his former production manager, Jack Harpman. "But sometimes that meant he was a professional procrastinator, delaying decisions until the last minute. That made getting my work done very difficult. I needed decisions so I could get the scenery constructed, to get a tour planned and plotted, and he would always put things off. He was so intensely focused on whatever he was doing that the house could be burning down and he wouldn't notice."

The five foot-four Joffrey was such an exacting taskmaster that some dancers in the troupe called him "the dictator," others "Napoleon." The nicknames were meant—and taken—in the best of spirits; Joffrey himself even collected Napoleana as a hobby. But there was an element of hard truth in the names. "He was such a perfectionist," says one dancer, "that he never allowed us to feel we were good enough."

Joffrey and Rebekah were both dreamers, but their visions had little in common. That became apparent by the opening number of the troupe's European premiere on their 1962 tour. Specifically, the dilemma arose over a ballet score entitled *Dreams of Glory,* which Rebekah had written. She made certain that no expense was spared in producing it; twelve ornate Spanish chairs had to be hauled all over Europe, costing a small fortune in cargo. But more troublesome was the scenario, the story of a teenage boy and girl who visit a museum, fall asleep, and dream they become President and First Lady. "*Dreams of Glory* was a disaster," says Françoise Martinet, a dancer. "The music wasn't that bad because Lee Hoiby must have helped Rebekah a lot. But the story was inane." Says Larry Rhodes, who danced the male lead, "I was on stage the whole time, so it was really embarrassing for me."

It was a vanity production for Rebekah, and everyone, including Joffrey, knew it. But Joffrey had to humor her. "His only hope was that the piece would self-destruct," says one dancer, "that everything would go wrong in rehearsal so that he could tell Rebekah it wasn't ready." At the dress rehearsal in Lisbon, half the costumes weren't ready. One dancer's Greek tunic wouldn't stay on; another's buttons popped off. One dancer, wearing a Statue of Liberty outfit, kept getting her spiked crown stuck on the other dancers' costumes. Another's zipper broke.

"Bob doesn't like to make waves," says one member of the troupe. "It's important to him to give the illusion that things are running smoothly. So when he began drumming his fingers, that was a serious warning sign."

The programs had already been printed saying *Dreams of Glory* would open the show. But his dancers were collapsing around him in hysterics. "Once he decided to cancel it, he was devilishly happy," says Martinet. Joffrey told one dancer that if anyone asked, they should explain that the sets weren't ready. *Dance* magazine was told there were too many problems with the costumes. The work wasn't performed on tour until Rebekah caught up with the company in Teheran, where it was staged in a special performance for her and the Shah of Iran. Then it was withdrawn from the repertory for good.

That episode did not resolve the problem, however. If Joffrey failed to shower praise on his own dancers, whom he genuinely admired, he was even cooler to Rebekah, who demanded constant attention and affirmation. Rebekah behaved as if the age of nobility had returned. "She was the queen," says one dancer, "and we were her subjects."

Many dancers adored her because of her generosity. "It was extraordinary," says one. "It's unheard of for a dance company to be able to take the entire summer off to rehearse and build its repertoire. We were given every weekend off and could eat a magnificent buffet at the house and swim in the ocean. It was

ideal." But with the largess came problems. "There was no logical way to deal with her," says Jorge Mester, a musical director
of the Joffrey. "She was either composing or taking lessons or
meditating or just erratic, and there was such a whirlwind of
people seeking her favor."

Worst of all, no one knew what to do about her delusions
about her talent as a composer. In the beginning, she was totally
inept, and so completely ignorant of musical styles that she could
not even distinguish the counterpoint of Bach from the fervid
romanticism of Wagner.

"I felt very sorry for her," says Hoiby. "We would tell her
exactly what to do, and then she would do it, and she ultimately
would think she had really done it all by herself. She really
thought she was pretty good.

"She did everything as a pupil to be as good as she could possibly be. But even her best was not good enough," he says.
"There were enthusiasms of hers that turned my stomach—castanets, Chinese bell trees, glitzy cheap Mantovani orchestrations.
It was so hard for her. There was a basic lack of understanding of
the nature of music, of composing, a lack of intuition. Why her
incompetence in music should be coupled with such an impas-
sioned desire to do just that is something I could never understand."

Previously when Rebekah tried to have her music accepted by
major figures in the dance world, she had met with no success.
She wanted to get George Balanchine, the legendary choreographer and co-founder of the New York City Ballet, to choreograph some of her music. "She offered him a lot of money,"
recalls his wife at the time, Tanaquil LeClerq. "And it was at a
point when we really could have used it." Initially, Balanchine
expressed interest in the project. But after he heard Rebekah's
composition, he said, "Nobody needs money this bad."

Rebekah was herself totally oblivious to her lack of talent.
Some of her teachers didn't have the heart to tell her the truth.
Since they were dependent on her generosity, she was the last
person a struggling musician would want to alienate. Others
shamelessly exploited her naïveté. One composer kept sending

her flowers, telling her again and again he would make her the greatest woman composer in history. "He knew where the money was," says a colleague.

Occasionally Rebekah was aware that a new acquaintance had ulterior motives. Every once in a while she threw her hands up in dismay when another hanger-on approached. "Well, how much money am I supposed to have?" she said.

But more often than not, she believed the flattery. The Teheran *Journal* had compared her to Barbara Hutton, Doris Duke, and Elizabeth Taylor before gushing with relief that she was just a down-to-earth, regular girl, doing her best to be a serious composer. The Delhi *Statesman* called her an "eminent composer." Insecure and eager to prove herself, she lapped up the slightest bit of encouragement.

On October 1, 1963, the Joffrey Ballet performed at the White House at the invitation of President Kennedy, during a state visit by Ethiopian Emperor Haile Selassie. With the help of Lee Hoiby, Rebekah had put together a medley of vaudeville tunes, called "The Palace." Choreographer Gerald Arpino reworked about a dozen vaudeville acts for ballet. *Dreams of Glory* had been extravagant, but it was nothing compared to *The Palace,* as this piece was called. There was a Charleston number, men dancing in black tie and top hats, tap dancing, and a number with dancers wearing 1912 Gibson girl bathing suits. All the costumes were designed and created especially for this one-act production at an unbelievable cost of over $135,000—more than the entire annual budget for the company before Rebekah had hooked up with them. Still, many in the White House audience were less than impressed. One State Department aide mused, "Well, we just lost Ethiopia."

When Joffrey took the ballet on tour to Russia the next month, the audiences, unfamiliar with the idiom of vaudeville, were initially baffled by *The Palace.* But they were soon won over. The Charleston number was encored at every performance. The head of the Kirov Ballet called it "one of the most thrilling performances" he had ever seen. "We had so many curtain calls I couldn't count them," said one dancer. Even *The New York Times* reported that *The Palace* had been a hit in Russia.

Its limited success notwithstanding, all Rebekah had really done was to string together and orchestrate a few old vaudeville tunes—and for that she needed the help of a real composer. The response was mainly due to the excellent choreography by Arpino and the lavishness of the production. But Rebekah wanted to believe her good reviews. And it was easy to. In New York, her parties were the hottest ticket in town. In September 1962, when the Bolshoi Ballet arrived to play New York's Metropolitan Opera, Rebekah's party for them was the event of the season. She had bought a fifteen-room penthouse apartment, which, *Time* magazine reported, "covers the entire top of the Westbury like a two-acre astrakhan hat." The Russians had never seen anything like it.

"If they're going to be exposed to capitalism," Rebekah told a reporter, "it might as well be in one fell swoop." Hollywood stars attended. Russian-speaking waiters passed champagne and served beef Stroganoff on sterling silver platters as the Russian dancers tried to figure out how to do the Twist.

When Rudolf Nureyev and Dame Margot Fonteyn made their first visit to America in 1963, Rebekah and Ben Kean feted them with a lavish party. Such dance-world luminaries as Jerome Robbins, Agnes de Mille, Alvin Ailey, and Martha Graham were present. The guest lists at her parties included New York Mayor Robert Wagner, Adlai Stevenson, and Salvador Dali, his wife Gala, and their pet ocelot.

After the company returned from Russia, it began a ten-week cross-country tour that took it to Seattle, Denver, Buffalo, and Chicago, among other cities. Rebekah did not join the troupe, preferring to spend some time with Dr. Kean at Capricorn, her winter retreat in the Bahamas. In fact, Rebekah had begun to lose patience with Joffrey. She had put the entire company up at Watch Hill for two summers, as well as furnishing it with a new repertory and the costumes and scenery that went with it. She had spent millions, providing the dancers with a masseur, swimming facilities, and medical attention. It was because of her support that the company had been asked to perform for President Kennedy, Prime Minister Nehru, the Shah of Iran, and King Hussein. Yet the more time and attention she gave to it, the colder Joffrey himself grew. He disappeared for long periods. He refused to answer her calls and questions. In the summer, Rebekah, always an early riser, was so furious with him for sleeping late that she and her husband would wake him up and tell him to get to work. He occasionally waited so long to decide what program the company would dance that it would be too late to have an orchestra rehearsal or costume fittings. Worst of all, the company had performed only two ballets to the music she had written, forcing her to seek out other companies to perform her compositions. It was her money; why should Joffrey get all the credit? Shouldn't she be able to do what she wanted with the company?

When Joffrey defended his position in the name of artistic integrity, Rebekah was incensed. He was just an "inadequate beatnik," she said. Did he really think he could do exactly as he pleased while she paid for it, allowing her the honor of participating in his great creative project?

In February 1964, as the troupe toured the United States, Rebekah arranged for the company's general manager, Jeannot Cerrone, to meet with the dancers in Joffrey's absence. She had decided to form a new company with Joffrey dancers; she would call it the Harkness Ballet. She later offered Joffrey the post of artistic director, but she refused to assure him he would have final authority over the company's artistic direction.

Joffrey was outraged: Rebekah wasn't starting her own company, she was stealing his. When she asked him if he would take the job, he did not respond. She had gained control of everything: Costumes, sets, musical scores, many of the best dancers, the entire repertory—even the works choreographed by Joffrey himself—were owned by her foundation. If he refused her offer, he would lose everything. Yet if he gave in to her demands, he would be legitimizing her piracy. The company would be hers, both in name and artistic control. He had been betrayed.

In March, Rebekah flew to New York for a special meeting at

which she expected Joffrey's reply. He did not show up. He had decided not to work with Rebekah again. On March 17, Joffrey told *The New York Times* the whole story. "Although my decision may temporarily cripple the Joffrey company," he said, "I must take this risk." After eight years of building one of the most promising dance companies in the world, he was going to have to start from scratch again.

"It's not often you meet the goose that lays the golden egg," says one colleague. "Well, all of a sudden the goose went away. It hurt him a great deal. She wanted it to become her ballet company. It wasn't. It was Bob Joffrey's."

If the dancers had had a real choice to make between Rebekah and Joffrey, most would have picked Joffrey, difficult though he could be. "He was the first truly analytical teacher I had," says one of the dancers. "He made things so clear technically, so utterly logical, simple and pure. We went from tour to tour, and each one got better. There was a great deal of love and warmth, a minimum of politicking. Somehow, he managed to get rid of the manipulators. He was a real perfectionist, with an incredible sense of taste."

But Joffrey was left with no money, no jobs to offer, no scenery, no repertory. "He told us, 'Do what you want,'" says one staffer. "It just killed him."

The dance world rallied to Joffrey's side. George Balanchine offered him use of his ballets at no cost so he wouldn't be entirely without a repertory. The press castigated Rebekah. "If Mrs. Kean wants a company that reflects her attitudes about ballet, no one should complain if she is able to find the money to go out and buy one," said Allen Hughes in *The Times*. ". . . But if the new company must be built on the ruin of an old one, no right-minded person can rejoice in that. The Rebekah Harkness Foundation has paralyzed the Joffrey Ballet for the present and imperiled the company's future. . . . A moral issue is involved here."

The Times and other papers all over the world reported the episode as a coup by a capricious millionairess against one of most brilliant young artistic directors in America. The Russians, once so impressed with Rebekah, now attacked her. *The Palace* was nothing more than "a potpourri of popular melodies of the twenties," charged *Sovetskaya Muzika*. "Even a composer's laurels were not enough for Mme. Harkness. Now, she desired to become a second Diaghilev."

Suddenly, Rebekah was a pariah in the world to which she had so long sought admission. How could *The Times* possibly believe Joffrey, she wondered incredulously. He needed a psychiatrist. She was enraged that he had spoken to the press directly rather than to her. "If nothing else," she wrote in a letter to the paper, not for publication:

> Where were his manners? Didn't his mama ever tell him to shake hands and say "good-bye" when leaving a party—even if he didn't have a nice time? . . . I know that some of this must sound light and airy, but I have worked too hard to be so foolish as to become emotional over the hysterical complaints of a "Tom Thumb" masquerading as Napoleon.
>
> There seems to be a fallacy that if you have money, you can't possibly have artistic ability, taste or judgment.

But Rebekah truly believed she was an artist. She rose at 6:00 A.M. and took dance class daily. Of the fifteen ballets in the Joffrey repertory, two were done to music she wrote, and one of them was a hit in Russia. "For these and other reasons," her letter said, "I feel qualified to know when I should participate; however, I guess what I really need is a beard and some horn-rimmed glasses."

Finally, her letter took the issue directly to Hughes, who had so vigorously defended Joffrey.

"Now, my dear Mr. Hughes, I am not going to challenge you to a duel, but maybe we could have a ballet class together. Just a few quiet pliés while you contemplate your contributions to the future of the dance. Don't worry, no adagio! I could never expect you to have the strength to lift me up or to let me down."

STRANGE
BEDFELLOWS

o the Old Guard in Watch Hill, Rebekah's marriage to Ben Kean only underscored the extent to which she had become estranged from them. She now scorned them, although she could not ignore them completely. The same old families were always there, hovering in the background, a scolding, disapproving presence, tittering when Rebekah defied conventions by bringing a dance troupe to the sleepy society resort, gossiping about her marriage to an outsider like Benjamin Kean.

Kean was not born into society, yet he was comfortable in the sophisticated, international world in which Rebekah traveled. He had made a name for himself specializing in tropical medicine at New York Hospital. In the course of his career his work brought him into contact with such luminaries as the Shah of Iran, Joan Fontaine, Henry Kissinger, and David Rockefeller.*

One might have thought Rebekah's old friends would have been delighted that she finally settled down, seven years after Harkness's death. But they were not. Never partial to outsiders to begin with, they now saw Kean as a potential threat to one of their own, and they closed ranks. "I had reservations about him from the start," says one of Rebekah's longtime friends there. "He was totally disconnected. You had to think, here's this girl with a lot of money and somebody has laid a trap for her."

"When the girl has the money, nine times out of ten the guy is not an all right guy," says Joe Wade, a former beau of Rebekah's. "Maybe it happens sometimes, but nine times out of ten it's the dough re mi." Kean's dilemma was inescapable: Any man without the resources of a Harkness or Rockefeller would have been subject to the same suspicions. Any man who married Rebekah was destined to be seen as little more than a fortune hunter.

---

*Many years later, Kean became a figure of controversy when he played a key role in the Iranian hostage crisis that toppled the Jimmy Carter presidency.

It began in 1979 when the Shah of Iran, Mohammed Reza Pahlavi, was forced to flee the country he had ruled for thirty-eight years. Seriously ill, the shah finally asked for asylum in the United States. President Carter had refused the request, fearing danger to Americans in an Iran where the Ayatollah Khomeini was gaining power, and the shah went to Mexico. Meanwhile, David Rockefeller and Henry Kissinger flew down to meet privately with him and lobbied with the Carter administration for a change in its policy. Despite the shah's illness, it was still possible he might try to regain power in Iran, and in that case Rockefeller's Chase Manhattan Bank, which had handled billions in transactions with Iran, would be in an enviable position.

In late September, an assistant to Rockefeller asked Kean to examine the shah in Cuernavaca, Mexico. He recommended that the shah, suffering from cancer, advanced jaundice, and fever, undergo extensive tests at New York Hospital-Cornell Medical Center or one of several other hospitals in the United States. Dr. Eben Dustin, a State Department medical officer, consulted with Kean on the phone. President Carter later said, "I was told that the shah was desperately ill, at the point of death. I was told that New York was the only medical facility capable of possibly saving his life." Kean contends that Carter was misinformed about the urgency of the shah's condition. Nevertheless, under the impression the shah's life was in danger, Carter finally admitted him to the United States. The Iranians seized sixty-three American hostages in retaliation.

Such enmity aside, Kean went everywhere with Rebekah. He was admitted to the Misquamicut Club, since it was perfunctory to elect spouses of members. But he was sufficiently out of place that Rebekah built him his own three-hole golf course at Holiday House. On occasion, he could be seen lining up a putt on his course overlooking the Atlantic.

Whatever one thought of Kean, he was not a weak man. "Of all the men she was involved with after Harkness," says one relative, "Kean was the smoothest, most independent, most believable. He could live without her money. He was a relatively agreeable, self-made doctor with his own life to lead, and he had gotten in the middle of this intrigue. I guess it was very enjoyable for him to be the center of it and to make hay while the sun shined. But he was not as desperately attached to it as other people were."

Kean began to play an active role in Rebekah's life. He traveled with her and the dance troupe. He served on the board of the ballet company. He accompanied her to the White House and co-hosted their various soirees. He advised her on her investments. He oversaw her expenditures. "He had gotten married to this wonderful rich lady," says the company's music director, "and now he was going to do some grand artistic thing."

It was not just her marriage to Kean that disturbed her old friends. The more savvy among them, Jane Johnson Heminway in particular, were alarmed by her headstrong determination to become a great dance patroness. It was as if she had something to prove but didn't know what it was. How different she was from Jane, who seemed to have style and grace in the most natural, effortless way. The transition from St. Louis to international café society had been much easier for Jane than Rebekah, and to Rebekah that was precisely the problem. St. Louis seemed even more provincial than ever before, and it became increasingly important to prove that she was far more sophisticated than the people she grew up with, that she was really an artist in her own right, that the wealth that had been left to her was completely justified. The two did not openly fight, but there were long periods when they lost contact. Jane frequently mused aloud about "crazy Betty's" latest stunt. But it was impossible for anyone to give advice to someone so complicated, intense, and unpredictable as Rebekah. And, Jane wondered, what was becoming of Rebekah's children? Already Edith had tried suicide, and Allen was a time bomb ready to explode.

When Jane contracted cancer in 1964, Rebekah kept her distance. Only when her old friend was on her deathbed did Rebekah finally visit, and then Jane reproached her on her absence. "I had to die to get you to come," she chided.

For all the pleasure Rebekah got out of her new dance company, having so many people vying for her attention had made the summer of 1964 terribly draining. Rather than be bothered by the minutiae of everybody's daily needs, Rebekah simply erred on the side of excess and left it at that. Standing orders were given to prepare fifteen or so meals every night, just in case any one of the ever-changing assortment of musicians, dancers, choreographers, or staff joined her and Dr. Kean for dinner; she even allowed for people like Tarwater, who downed as many as five lobsters in one sitting. But often only a handful of people showed up, meaning that a dozen or more steaks or lobsters had to be thrown out.

At long last, it was early September, the best time of all in Watch Hill. The Old Guard had trooped back to their midwestern homes. Most of the dance company had returned to New York. Even Kean was away from Holiday House for the day. The weather was still warm. Rebekah was elated; it was as if, for this moment at least, she had the entire village to herself.

Only a few select members of Rebekah's retinue had stayed behind so she could continue her dance and music lessons. Among them, Rebekah had become particularly fond of twenty-four-year-old Bobby Scevers, a six feet four-inch dancer she had hired several months earlier to partner her in pas de deux work each day. To be sure, his great height and fine Nordic features were part of her attraction to him, and she delighted in his youth and refreshing lack of sophistication. But his age also made her self-conscious about her own advancing years; she was nearly

fifty now. So far, at least, her war against time had been spec-
tacularly successful. Firm and fit and lean, she could hold her
own in ballet class without unduly embarrassing herself. She had
shed the pudginess of youth and her face had acquired a lean
angularity. Although at times she seemed hard and tense, more
often she was serene and beautiful. It was hard to believe she was
more than twice as old as Scevers. Still, she was so deeply concerned about aging that she secretly returned to the city in the
middle of the summer to have a face-lift. Scevers, naive about
the wonders of cosmetic surgery, could not get over how she
had suddenly become so youthful again.

A native of Aransas Pass, Texas, a town of five thousand, near
the Gulf port of Corpus Christi, Bobby Scevers was the son of a
foreman at the nearby Atlantic Richfield storage facility. The
Sceverses were deeply religious southern Baptists who attended
church regularly and forbade alcohol in their home. Bobby's father deplored dancing, even his son's attendance at school
dances. They had no formal education, but they worked hard,
and doted on their only child.

"We had a hamburger stand and a jukebox, and all the kids
from school would drive out there and scream and yell," says
Scevers. "All there was to do in town was drive from one end of
town to the other and turn around." The major outside cultural
influences were Elvis Presley and the Everly Brothers. Occasionally, Bobby and his friends would go to the Rialto, the only
movie theater in town, and when they were old enough to drive,
they took off for Corpus Christi twenty miles away. With its
population nearing 170,000, Corpus was the big city. "I didn't
know I was miserable, because I just didn't know any better."

In 1958, Scevers went off to Texas Western College, now
known as the University of Texas at El Paso. He played the tuba
in the college band and majored in theater. For the first time in
his life he became aware of dance as a classical discipline. "I had
no idea what dance was," he says, "but I thought I could do it
instantly." His key influence was Nikita Talin, a Dallas dance
teacher who was to become one of the most important figures in

his life. Bobby soon transferred to Texas Christian University in Fort Worth and then to Southern Methodist University in Dallas, so he could live with Nikita and major in dance. "Dallas was so big, I was scared to cross the street," he says. "But it was exciting. I am very single-minded, and once I started dancing, all I wanted to do was dance."

In June 1963, after three years in Dallas, Scevers, then twenty-two, took off for New York alone with just five hundred dollars to his name. He took classes at the School of American Ballet. He gave dance recitals with friends. At the end of the summer, however, he was denied a scholarship at the School of American Ballet. He was simply not good enough to make it as a soloist in a major company. And he was far too tall for the corps de ballet.

Bobby was broke. He sometimes walked to class because he didn't have money for a bus or subway. When the soles in his shoes wore out, he put plastic in the bottoms to keep the snow from sloshing through. For food, he bought lamb patties at eleven cents each, and mopped up the grease with bread. He got a job as a busboy at the Automat, but lasted only a day. In desperation, he landed a job as a temporary typist, earning fifty dollars a week. His career was going nowhere.

Finally, through his various recitals and lessons, he met Leon Fokine, the nephew of the great Russian dancer and choreographer Mikhail Fokine, Diaghilev's chief choreographer in the early days of the Ballets Russes. Leon had never quite attained the stature of his fabled ancestor, but he was widely respected as a teacher when Rebekah hired him to teach class for her new company. And in the dance world he had become legendary as a hard-drinking, gambling, womanizing figure. "He was unique— charming, Russian, romantic, and sexual," says one dancer. "He was a man who lived by his cock."

Fokine established an unusual avuncular relationship with Scevers. Bobby was his protégé, but his interest in him extended beyond his potential as a dancer. Fokine was fed up with Ben Kean constantly interfering with the company. And if Bobby's greatest talent was not at the barre, but in the bedroom, perhaps, Fokine thought, he had found a way around his patron's meddling husband. When Rebekah needed a dance partner—a tall one, to complement her five-feet-nine-inch frame, Fokine recommended Scevers.

"I know this poor kid from Texas," Fokine told Rebekah. "He's not very good. But he's strong. He can pick you up. He can pick me up. He can pick up the piano."

That was good enough for Rebekah. She offered Bobby fifty dollars a week to help her in daily lessons of two hours each.

Scevers was staggered by her generosity. He had never been paid so much to dance before. This was as much as he was making from his full-time job as a typist, and it would allow him to continue dancing. Not having followed the Joffrey saga, he had never even heard of Rebekah. He wondered who could afford to be so magnanimous.

"She's a crazy old woman," explained Fokine, adding that Rebekah Harkness just happened to be "richer than God."

Bobby approached his new patroness with trepidation. He was eager to join her new company, but didn't stand a chance since all the other dancers were far more accomplished than he. And there were other reasons. "In Aransas Pass, the richest person I knew owned a towboat company," he says. "I thought that was rich. So I was scared to death."

Rebekah's friendliness and informality quickly put him at ease, however. They met each afternoon in Rebekah's private studio at Carnegie Hall. She told him he was very talented and a terrific partner. He was not accepted into the company, but she invited him up to Holiday House for the summer to help with her lessons.

"I'll never forget the first time I saw that enormous white structure," Bobby says. "I nearly fainted. I'd never seen anything so big in my entire life." In many ways, he was treated better even than the soloists in the company. The troupe boarded in town, as they had in previous years, but Bobby stayed at Holiday House, sharing Fokine's quarters. Moreover, he had close contact with Rebekah every day. Even the highest-ranking staff members who vied for her attention were not able to see her so frequently.

But there was a certain amount of distance between them. After all, Rebekah was still reeling from the Joffrey debacle and occasionally flew off to Nassau for a few days' rest and recuperation. "It was all nice and friendly, but she was Mrs. Harkness and I was who I was," says Bobby.

Rebekah's relationships with men worked only so long as she called the shots. Bill Harkness, of course, was the great exception to that rule. After his death, Rebekah grew even more insistent on dominating her relationships. In the late fifties, she secretly took an extra apartment on Manhattan's Upper East Side, just a few blocks away from her residence at the Westbury, under the name of Mrs. Foster. No one was certain why she resorted to such subterfuge, but acquaintances suggested that it was a meeting place for various and numerous romantic relationships.

"She had never been allowed to express herself," recalls a close friend. "And now that she could for the first time, she became a nymphomaniac. There was no way that we could hold her back."

During that same period, Rebekah became involved with Nicholas Stein, a Russian composer-arranger she hired to help with her composing. He left his wife and kids behind in Paris, and Rebekah put him up in an apartment on the Upper East Side for a few years. "He thought he had it all," says a friend of Stein's, Arnold Arnstein. "He was getting about thirty-five thousand dollars a year from her. You could buy a lot of hamburger for that in those days." But one day Rebekah and he had a fight, and he was sent packing. "He and his wife had become quite accustomed to the money. But all of a sudden, just after that fight, he was cut off completely."

Then came Ben Kean. At Rebekah's behest, he launched an abortive attempt to start a symphony orchestra to compete with the New York Philharmonic. He tried to interest Rebekah in buying Twentieth-Century Fox. When those ventures failed to get off the ground, however, he was left in the uncomfortable position of playing second banana around the Harkness Ballet, of which Rebekah was clearly in charge. Ultimately, Kean was disturbed by the various factions battling for her attention.

Rebekah could be as willful and unyielding as even the most obdurate Hollywood star, but she was also impressionable and insecure, and capable of developing strong dependent ties to people. One of these was with her attorney, Aaron Frosch. A partner in the firm of Frosch and Weissberger, Frosch was the preeminent entertainment lawyer in the nation, counting among his clients Judy Garland, Marilyn Monroe, Elizabeth Taylor, and Richard Burton. With his urbane, powerful presence, he had taken on a role in Rebekah's life far greater than that of an ordinary attorney, spending so much time at Holiday House and the Westbury that the kids called him Papa Aaron. He made certain that Rebekah's Rolls-Royce met her at the airport and that she could breeze through customs wherever she traveled. Whatever crisis might arise with his other clients—the death of Marilyn Monroe, the Burton-Taylor divorce—Frosch was always there for Rebekah. As a result, she consulted him for everything, from major policy decisions concerning the dance troupe to the most banal day-to-day questions. "She let Frosch pick her dresses for her," says her daughter Terry. "He was always there for dinner. Mother could always let someone rule her emotional life like that."

Kean didn't trust Frosch, and it wasn't long before he began to lock horns with him. "Ben looked into all the paperwork and thought he found various discrepancies," says Terry. "He told mother to fire Frosch. Ben said it's either him or me." Three years after their wedding, it was an open secret that Rebekah's marriage to Kean was in trouble. "Every time Dr. Kean comes into the room," her masseur would say, "her muscles get so tense I can't even massage her."

A number of people in the dance company were delighted by Rebekah's marital problems. "Everybody hated Dr. Kean and his meddling," says Bobby Scevers. "It was always why are you spending this or that, why don't you do such and such? We couldn't wait to get rid of him."

Kean's interests often competed with the ballet for Rebekah's time and money. In July 1963, New York Hospital announced that Rebekah had made a donation of $2 million for the construction of the William Hale Harkness Medical Research Building. Being married to such a munificent donor could not have hurt Kean's standing at the hospital. Various members of the dance company couldn't stand having Kean around.

Toward the end of the summer of 1964, Leon Fokine took Bobby aside to discuss the problem. If Fokine's plan worked, his protégé could be a most powerful ally, someone who would always have Rebekah's ear.

"What the boss really needs is a new boyfriend," Fokine told Bobby in his thick Russian accent. "You know, boy, she really likes you. I'm sure if you wanted to, you could get to be a real good friend of hers. . . . But I know you don't like that."

"If I wanted to, I could," protested Bobby. "It's not that I don't want to. It just never occurred to me."

"Then why you don't get to be good friends with her? You do everybody a big favor. Anything to get rid of Dr. Kean."

On a blustery September night in Watch Hill, Rebekah and Bobby took their usual after-dinner walk along the jetty. The moon was out. At a small inlet, where the tide was washing in with increasing intensity, Bobby suddenly kissed her.

"We were both surprised," says Bobby. "She said we couldn't stand there because she didn't want Dr. Kean or any of the neighbors to see us. So we went back to the main house and sat in the living room. She fixed me a brandy. And as the wind was blowing and howling we started necking, and I got more and more nervous because I didn't know what I was doing. I was so nervous I must have had six brandies."

The two retreated to a room in the back where the linens and mattresses were stored. They unrolled the mattress and made the bed.

"You know what alcohol will do to you, but I didn't know that then. I was absolutely loaded. I couldn't do anything. I just couldn't get it up. I mean zero."

Rebekah was patient. "I know you're nervous," she said. "We'd better stop here."

Embarrassed, Scevers returned to his quarters. Early the next morning, Fokine, who was anxious to find out how his protégé had fared, told Bobby that Rebekah was looking for him.

"You do good job last night?" he asked Scevers.

"Well, uh, I did my best," Bobby stammered.

It was hard to know what was worse—that he had actually dared to bed down with his employer, or that having done so, he had failed as a lover. "I thought, 'Oh, buddy, you blew it. You'll get your walking papers,'" says Bobby. "I was so scared."

When Rebekah was halfway down the staircase, she ran down the stairs and kissed him. "I just wanted to give you something," she said. She took him back through the house to another room, where she had set aside a portable stereo for him.

"I nearly fell over dead," Bobby says. "I thought I was going to get sacked for not performing, and she ended up giving me a stereo."

9

SEXUAL

POLITICS

nitially, Rebekah kept her relationship with Bobby secret. When the Kirov Ballet came to New York later that month, she and Ben celebrated the occasion with a spectacular party at their Westbury apartment, with the Duke Ellington Orchestra entertaining. In October, the Harkness Ballet performed at the White House before President Lyndon Johnson and Filipino President Diosdado Macapagal. Later be-

hind the scenes, Rebekah met with Bobby. The first few times, however, Bobby repeated his performance at Watch Hill. "I saw her four or five times before I got anything going. I would try and try and try. But eventually the miracle happened."

Rebekah was ecstatic. "We've got to go to Nassau," she said.

Rebekah told Kean that she couldn't go to the Bahamas without taking her music and dance teachers with her. She packed up, bringing with her her house staff, two piano teachers, Fokine to teach her dance, and another pianist to play piano for her lessons. Bobby fit in inconspicuously enough in that group, ostensibly coming along to partner Rebekah in her daily dance lessons.

Kean was warm and friendly to Bobby. As they planned the company's European tour that winter, Kean even insisted that Scevers accompany them. "You can't go without Bobby," he told Rebekah. When they got to Nassau, he invited Bobby to join him out on the golf course. If Kean suspected anything, he didn't show it.

Capricorn, Rebekah's six-acre beachfront estate in Nassau, had been constructed by Sir Francis Peak, a wealthy British lawyer, in the 1950s at a reported cost of $300,000. It consisted of a white stone main house with ten rooms, a two-bedroom guest cottage, a Japanese-style artist's studio, and separate servants' quarters. In back was a sunken swimming pool. A grove of palms shielded Rebekah's house from the main road, and she had her own private beach. Willard Wallace and his wife oversaw the house staff.

Even in the tropics, Rebekah was as disciplined as ever. Hers was a punishing regimen. She woke up by six each morning and began playing scales on the piano. Lee Hoiby taught her composition, orchestration, and counterpoint. Her second hour was spent with Stanley Hollingsworth, a friend of Hoiby's and a composer who, like Hoiby, was also a Menotti student. Together they tackled rhythmic problems, technical assignments, and orchestration. Next came a dance class with Bobby and Fokine. She delighted in showing off her long legs at the barre, particularly in the développés and grands battements. Then she swam and did her exercises. "Even professional dancers tell me when they have a cramp," says one of her teachers. "But when Rebekah had one, she just stayed there, holding a very painful position. She had this ability to drive herself mercilessly." When her energies flagged, she fortified herself with drugs, including amphetamines.

Rebekah's houseguests served the dual function of entertaining her and acting as a smoke screen for her affair with Bobby. She had brought down a sculptor to do a bronze of her and Bobby dancing, and a pianist friend of Bobby's, Raymond Wilson, who was the most flamboyant member of the group, who sometimes did mudpacks with Rebekah.

The group assembled daily: Bobby Scevers, Raymond Wilson, Leon Fokine, Lee Hoiby, Stanley Hollingsworth, Benjamin Kean, and of course, Rebekah. Rebekah often confided in Raymond.

Bobby's only task was to dance with Rebekah for two hours a day. He shared a guesthouse with Fokine, not far from Capricorn's main residence. "I had my own bedroom and bathroom, and we went snorkeling all the time, and you pushed buttons and the servants would do everything," Bobby says.

After lunch, Fokine often got Kean to go fishing out on the reef, taking off in a rickety little skiff called the *Queen Rebekah*. "As soon as they left, Rebekah would come tippy-toeing through the bushes and we would have our little fling in the afternoon until finally we heard Dr. Kean in the boat," Bobby recalls.

These afternoon trysts were conducted with utmost discretion. "You could tell she loved having this big blond giant throwing her around in her dance class each day," says one guest at the time. "But I wouldn't have guessed they were having an affair." Only Fokine knew of it, and he was delighted with the progress his charge had made. Initially, even Raymond was kept in the dark. At times, Scevers had to climb Rebekah's balcony to avoid being seen by other guests. "It was terribly romantic," he says. "I felt just like Romeo."

After making love, they would get to know each other. "I told Rebekah all about my Aunt Ella and all my hillbilly relatives," says Bobby. "I didn't think it was anything but amusing. It wasn't something you'd shy away from, unless you were a social climber. Rebekah told me she admired me for being so open and honest."

When they returned to New York, Bobby was more firmly ensconced in Rebekah's life than ever. But the disparity in their backgrounds was now painfully evident. In the Bahamas, everyone had dressed casually and lived on the same estate. But in New York, Bobby had no appropriate clothes for Rebekah's lifestyle, and would return from their rendezvous in her chauffeured Rolls-Royce to his shabby apartment on the Lower East Side.

So Rebekah bought him a complete wardrobe and found him an apartment on East Seventy-fourth Street, in the same building as her psychic, Eva Brach, who served as the cover for her frequent visits. Before he moved in, Rebekah took him on a shopping spree to Bloomingdale's. "She furnished the whole apartment," he says. "It was, 'Take this, take that, we'll get one of these.' Everything—knives, forks, rugs, furniture." As they shopped, however, Rebekah noticed a well-known dancer from another company. Fearing he would spot her with Bobby, she ran to another part of the store and hid.

In January, Rebekah divorced Kean. As his settlement, he received the earnings from a $1 million trust, the principal of which was to revert to the Harkness Foundation upon his death.*

The Harkness Ballet spent the first few months of 1965 getting ready for its debut. Rebekah had inherited the vast majority of the Joffrey's excellent corps of young dancers and some of its administrative staff. But this was not going to be just a carbon copy of

---

*In her autobiography, No Bed of Roses, actress Joan Fontaine writes about her seven-year relationship with a man she calls Dr. Noh, a New York physician who specialized in tropical diseases—who, sources say, was in fact a thinly disguised Benjamin Kean. In the book, the doctor called Fontaine at her New York apartment at about the time of Kean's divorce from Rebekah and told her he was coming over. "With brief 'hellos' to my guests, [he] led me into the dining room and without a word put his arms around me and kissed me," she writes. "The psychologist in him knew exactly how to handle me, gave me no time to demur, to think twice. I was putty when faced with a strong man and I knew it." In another passage, Fontaine describes their courtship: "[He] unloaded the luggage, brought out two roast grouse he'd had his hotel prepare, a bottle of Château Haut-Brion. He lit the fire, served the midnight supper, poured the wine, lowered the lights. If this was a honeymoon, it was the best I'd ever had. At least I felt attractive, desirable. I felt like a movie star."

the Joffrey. Rebekah set about making a new, bigger company in her own image. She had hired forty-four-year-old George Skibine, the former director of the Paris Opera Ballet, as artistic director. With him came his wife, Marjorie Tallchief, the sister of Maria Tallchief and a highly regarded ballerina in her own right. Alvin Ailey was brought in as a choreographer. As guest artist, they hired Erik Bruhn, the former star of the Royal Danish Ballet. Rebekah plowed $2 million into the company's coffers.

Seventeen works had been in preparation since the beginning of the summer, including two with music by Rebekah. She had composed a new piece, and the company was going to perform a version of *The Palace,* now renamed *Vaudeville—1920* with new choreography by Donald Saddler. The troupe was heady with excitement. "We all believed that we were going to write the history of ballet," says a musician who was with the company. Even the press, so hostile to Rebekah just a few months earlier, saw the occasion as an historic event. "The first major cultural event of the new year is the launching of an American ballet company on a scale unprecedented in dance history," said the New York *Morning Telegraph.* ". . . Not since brass heiress Lucia Chase started her American Ballet Theatre in 1940 has a company been formed with such expectations of success."

If there were one person after whom Rebekah was modeling herself, it was probably the Marquis de Cuevas, whose company had premiered her composition *Journey to Love* as a ballet at the Brussels World Fair in 1958. Skibine had been a principal dancer and choreographer with de Cuevas's company, and Marjorie Tallchief its star. Even Rebekah's association with Salvador Dali could be traced to the marquis, for whom the Spanish surrealist had once designed stage sets.

It was not that the marquis was such a terrific impresario. In fact, his erratic tastes were widely criticized as capricious and overly reliant on big-name dancers. Like Rebekah, his biggest qualification for running a company was his bankroll. He was a relic of a different era, given to wearing blue velvet cloaks lined with red satin, a crown of diamonds on his lapel, even going so far as to fight in duels to defend his honor.★ Such quaint customs were at the heart of his appeal to Rebekah. And, coincidentally, his wealth, like Rebekah's, came from marriage to an heir to the Standard Oil fortune, Margaret Strong Rockefeller, the grand-daughter of John D. Rockefeller.

In February 1965 the Harkness Ballet flew to Nice to begin rehearsals for its February 19 debut in Cannes and the beginning of its European tour. There was enough ill will left over from the Joffrey fiasco that the company could not possibly open in New York. On the plus side, Rebekah was now known throughout Europe, the Middle East, and the United States as the most gen-erous philanthropist in the dance world.

From its very first performance, critic Clive Barnes hailed the company's "remarkably gifted young dancers," mentioning Lawrence Rhodes, the Danish ballerina Lone Isaksen, and the young Icelandic dancer Helgi Tomasson, among others. He sin-gled out works by choreographers Alvin Ailey and Stuart Hodes for praise. "Naturally, the company is still on trial," he wrote in *The New York Times*. "The indications are that it will come out of this trial with distinction."

In the rest of Europe, the company fared even better. Its Rome opening was lauded by the critics. *Unità* called their perfor-mances "triumphal." In Bucharest, a sellout crowd of three thousand in the Palace of the Republic Hall cheered the troupe and showered the stage with flowers.

"We were put up in the best hotels and given very handsome rooms," recalls Barnes, who came representing both *The Times*

★ A few months before the Brussels World Fair, the marquis made headlines with a highly publicized duel with choreographer Serge Lifar, then the fifty-two-year-old ballet master of the Paris Opera. As recounted in the May 1958 *Dance* magazine, the marquis had angered Lifar by staging his ballet *Noir et Blanc* without the choreographer's consent. At intermission, Lifar threw his handkerchief at the marquis, who in turn slapped him. A few days later, the two met by accident and Lifar challenged the seventy-three-year-old marquis to a duel. "I'll make you dance a minuet to my épée," said Lifar. Replied de Cuevas: "Your handkerchief was so starched it could almost have drawn blood."

Over the next ten days, the two opponents decided they were willing to forget the whole thing, but an eager press made that impossible. On March 29, 1958, they met "in secret" outside of Paris with about fifty reporters and photographers in attendance. In the course of the duel, the marquis's blade nicked Lifar's arm.

"Blood! blood!" cried Lifar. "Honor is saved." His arm was bandaged, he embraced the marquis, and the two declared their mutual respect.

of London and *The New York Times*. "There was champagne and baskets of fruit waiting in our rooms and all that kind of stuff laid on at a very, very high level." The opening at the Casino Municipale was attended by everyone from Princess Grace and Paulette Goddard to former Paris Opera ballet master Serge Lifar.

Yet for all the cheering, the world tours, the lavish receptions, White House performances, for all the extraordinary talent in the company, something was drastically wrong. It was evident even in the very beginning. "The first performance was fairly disastrous," Barnes says. "One wouldn't want to be too damning on a first venture, but the best I could do was to make encouraging noises. Nothing more." At a party after the Cannes debut, Barnes sat next to Rebekah, who launched into a long anecdote about being stranded with the Joffrey in Russia. Rebekah's story finally reached its end as she explained how she was able, despite the Soviet bureaucracy, to charter a plane. When she finished, she turned to Barnes triumphantly.

"You see," she said. "Money can buy anything."

He turned to her. "You wanna bet!" he said.

The one thing money could not buy, at least in Rebekah's case, was an artistic vision. It simply was not clear, at least in aesthetic terms, why Rebekah was throwing all her time, money and energy into starting a dance company—unless she was trying to prove something. Indeed, when her troupe toured Europe, the stars of the company were not the dancers, even with the likes of Erik Bruhn, Marjorie Tallchief, and Larry Rhodes. The star was Rebekah. *Paris-Match* hailed her as a "patron on point," with full-page photos of her dancing with Bobby. Even *Time* magazine featured her doing lifts with Bobby, rather than the principal dancers. "If her mind had really been on the company," says one of the ballet's publicists, "she would have said, 'Why don't we photograph the best dancers in the company?'"

Throughout the tour Bobby and Raymond stayed with Rebekah, as members of her inner circle, rather than with the dance troupe. In Cannes she took a villa with Bobby, Raymond, and Fokine, giving Bobby a Mercedes in which to run about. In

Paris, they all dined at Lasserre, Maxim's, and Tour d'Argent. But her relationship with Bobby was still sub rosa; she was the toast of Europe, but he was not even a member of the company, and no one knew his name. "I hated it," he says. "I've never been so out of place. It was always Mrs. Harkness, Mrs. Harkness. But I had no identity myself. I just stayed in the background. The sophisticated people knew what was really going on."

Meanwhile, Rebekah convinced Skibine to give Bobby a chance with the company. Bobby rehearsed his role in *Vaudeville—1920* diligently, and took pride in the "gorgeous tuxedo" he wore as a costume, with a bib in front with the collar and tie, all fastened at the waist.

On March 15 the piece premiered in Paris. Finally, the Charleston sequence began, with Bobby on the stage of the Opéra-Comique, performing in a major professional dance company for the first time in his life. Midway through the number his bib became unfastened at the neck.

"It just fell out dangling, connected by the bottom button at the belt," he says. "It was swinging loose, hanging, and the whole audience started booing."

Mortified, Bobby retreated to his room at the Ritz and didn't come out for three days. Rebekah salved his wounds, saying the booing was not for him, but that the French were appalled to see vaudeville in their opera house. "She would blame the ballet or the costume," says one observer. "Anything but Bobby. That was her kind of loyalty."

When they returned to the States, Rebekah insisted that Skibine admit Bobby to the company. At Watch Hill that summer, she and Bobby no longer snuck around. Bobby stayed in Holiday House, but he did not have to share Fokine's quarters; this time he was upstairs, on the same floor with Rebekah. "By now," he says, "everyone knew exactly who and what Mr. Scevers was."

That didn't mean they liked him. Initially, his relationship with Rebekah was not a major issue in the company. For one thing, at first few believed that the two were actually lovers, if only because Bobby was so open about his homosexuality. Besides, there was so much going on that few dancers had time to pay any attention to him. "Everyone was busting their ass eighteen hours a day," says one musician with the company. "And we were loving it. We thought, God, we have the whole world in our hands. There is nothing we can't do. We were dancing at the White House, touring world capitals. She was putting together this big fancy mansion for us on the East Side."

Even though Bobby was now a member of the troupe, he kept his distance from the other dancers in the troupe, and vice versa. "I didn't have any real friends in the company," he says. "I was just never a part of it. I had my own life. They never said anything to me. But they resented me because of my relationship with Rebekah."

As time wore on, things just got worse. Bobby was cold, suspicious, always on guard. He seemed to take pride in his insensitivity. Not much of a diplomat, he traded in caustic insults and cutting barbs. No one was immune. After one performance, he told Skibine that he was rather "unmusical" as a dancer, and Rhodes that he "had no stage presence." Finally, he approached the thirty-seven-year-old Marjorie Tallchief. "What a wonderful dancer you must have been once upon a time!" he said. With Rebekah at his side, he was invulnerable.

"He went around insulting people all the time," says one rival dancer. "If he wasn't Mrs. Harkness's escort, he wouldn't have been in the company. He was an arrogant houseboy."

Bobby's personality was not the only issue. There was also the question of whether he belonged on the same stage with world-class dancers. Few dancers are over five feet ten; at six four Bobby was much too tall. Moreover, he had not begun to study dance until he was nineteen; most dancers start much earlier, and his lack of training was apparent. "Those were terrific handicaps," says one friend of his. "That is very, very late to begin a career. And his height only accentuated the awkwardness. But Bobby had incredible drive. He was extremely focused. He is extremely headstrong. Once he gets something into his head, he never reflects for a moment, never gives it another thought. Everything else be damned."

Well aware of his limitations, Scevers had resolved to turn his great height to his advantage. "I realized I was too tall and too old," he says. "But I was going to do it, and that was that. Besides, being tall helps if you are partnering a tall ballerina. So I became a wonderful partner."

Good enough, anyway, to partner Rebekah. But taking private class with a fifty-one-year-old woman was a long way from sharing the stage with world-class dancers. Skibine knew Bobby could never progress to being a soloist.

But increasingly, his power over her became evident. As early as the Cannes debut, after he loudly criticized one piece, Rebekah promptly yanked it from the company's repertoire. Privately, he touted various dancers to her, and they suddenly became her favorites. She even chose his choreography for the White House.

All the while, Bobby insisted that his motives were not political. "I really like Rebekah," he told a friend. "I really do." Yet if he was going to be involved with a woman, he could hardly have done better. "The fact that those two could find each other at that particular time!" says one of his friends. "He was highly, highly ambitious. He is a driven person. This was his way to achieve. Without her, he would have found some other vehicle. But he would have been a player no matter what. Still, I think that Robert genuinely, genuinely cared for her. He really did. That she had all the accoutrements to go along with it—well, she was just a gift from God!"

Now that she had invested millions of dollars to live out her dreams, Rebekah's critical judgment further deteriorated. Martha Graham, like all the other great choreographers who passed through Rebekah's doors, ended up leaving in consternation.

"That woman has a lot of money," Graham told a colleague. "But she will never have what she wants. All she wants is to be a swan."

Instead of going to Graham, Balanchine, Jerome Robbins, Robert Joffrey, or Alvin Ailey for artistic advice, Rebekah relied on Bobby Scevers. Some thought the reason for her devotion to him was quite simple. "Rebekah had a thing for tall men," says one musician in the company. "You can joke about it, and people did—about what hidden assets a taller man would have to offer her. But she filled the whole company with these big, tall, muscular, good-looking young men. She had several male dancers over six feet three inches. And in Bobby she had this very tall, extremely attractive, very striking man. He was so much like a Nordic god, people even called him the Viking. Who knows what seventeen-year-old fantasy she was living out."

Still, there was more to it than sex. Bobby also listened to her ideas in a way that no other man had. He believed in what she was trying to do. Everyone gave her advice, but Bobby reminded her that she was paying the bills and she ought to be able to run the show as she pleased.

In Watch Hill, Rebekah's mother, now an elderly dowager, smiled politely when she saw her daughter with Scevers. She was aware of their relationship but did not comment on it; the closest she came was when Bobby escorted her at the White House. He took her arm and tried to help the stately matron down the stairs. Instead, he tripped and fell on the White House floor. As he pulled himself to his feet, Mrs. West looked at him and laughed. "Some help you are!" she said.

10

THE GO-GO YEARS

early two years into its existence, the Harkness Ballet had performed in the United States only twice—at the White House and for a benefit—and neither of those appearances had been open to the public. From a public relations point of view, it was crucial that they perform at home. Bob Joffrey had won grants from the Ford Foundation and other since moved to New York as dance critic for *The Times,* could not resist comparing Rebekah's troupe to the efforts of the man she ditched. "The better of the two, by a fair distance, is the new Robert Joffrey Ballet," he wrote, "and it might be instructive to consider why."

Barnes argued that the reason for whatever success there was in either company had been Joffrey's keen eye for talent. Indeed, all the principal dancers in the Harkness—Larry Rhodes, Lone Isaksen, Brunilda Ruiz, Elisabeth Carroll, Helgi Tomasson, and Finis Jhung—and most of the soloists originally had been discovered and developed by Joffrey. "Where the Joffrey company scores most clearly over the Harkness is in its repertory," he added. "There are too many uninteresting classical divertissements [in the Harkness], with flavorless and tired choreography . . . The troupe is young but rich. Yet being born with a silver spoon sticking elegantly out of your mouth can be an initial disadvantage, even though the security of the Harkness Ballet should eventually ensure its success." Outraged, Rebekah bought a huge African carved wooden spoon and had it painted silver before sending it off to Barnes. "A spoon this big can feed a lot of dancers," Rebekah wrote in an accompanying note.

Bobby often urged Rebekah to become artistic director herself, but ultimately she did not have the confidence. Meanwhile, George Skibine was working on creating a new repertory that was veering toward modern dance rather than traditional ballet. Rebekah kept complaining she wanted something more classical, though she hated *Swan Lake.* Beyond such vague, often contradictory, statements, she was capricious and easily swayed. Any criticism of her company made her furious.

On September 29, 1965, the Harkness Ballet went to Washington to inaugurate a portable stage designed by Jo Mielziner that Rebekah had donated to the White House the previous summer. The occasion consisted of remarks by Lady Bird Johnson, followed by three ballets, including the premiere of a piece by Scevers, *Classical Symphony,* to music of Prokofiev.★

Immediately after the White House performance, the company took off for a six-week tour of thirty American cities. At the same time, Rebekah returned to the Westbury with her staff to oversee the opening of Harkness House, the East Seventy-fifth Street townhouse she had bought for $625,000 as the permanent home for her dance company. It was not just an office, school, and dance studio; it was a home for Rebekah's extended family of thirty-five dancers, fifty trainees, and ten staff members, in the tradition of the Imperial Ballet School in nineteenth-century St. Petersburg.

Rebekah had bought the mansion, once owned by IBM founder Thomas J. Watson, after abandoning plans to build her own high rise devoted to the arts. "I want to give splendor back to ballet," she told a reporter. "I think today our artists deserve such elegance, for they are our true aristocrats. As an artist myself, I know that I am affected by my environment."

Each of Harkness House's four dance studios was painted a different color—gray, blue, red, and peach—and outfitted with special "springy" floors and eight-foot-high mirrors. There was also a music classroom, a costume room, locker rooms, masseur's room, bathing facilities, a laundry, record-listening rooms, canteen, and administrative offices. A room with a magnificent beamed ceiling became the library, decorated with thick red rugs, velvet wall coverings, an elegant chandelier, leather furniture, a portrait of William Hale Harkness, and sculptures Rebekah herself had done. On the fourth floor, in the back of the building, was Rebekah's private office-apartment, furnished elegantly with two grand pianos. The elevator cage was decorated to resemble a butterfly-encrusted jewel box. Murals were painted on the walls of the elevator depicting famous ballet scenes from

---

★Afterward, President Johnson approached Rebekah privately and told her he would like to see her again. She said she would be delighted to return with the company. That, however, was not what he had in mind.

"No," he said. "You come back without them." Rebekah never took him up on the offer, but she delighted in telling the story to friends.

Firebird, Daphnis and Chloe, and *Spectre de la Rose.* On the ground floor, the mansion's former coach room was transformed into an art gallery, initially displaying work by Picasso, Braque, Derain, and Matisse. Finally, there was the reception hall, with a magnificent black-and-white-checkered marble floor and an extraordinary Louis XVI crystal chandelier.

On November 18, 1965, Rebekah hosted the grand opening of Harkness House. More than 1,000 notables in dance, theater, music, and the arts attended, among them Governor and Mrs. Nelson Rockefeller, Lynda Bird Johnson, Rosalind Russell, and Salvador Dali. At one end of the hall was Dali's golden Chalice of Life. Rebekah wore her Star of the Sea broach. Later that month, Rebekah gave a reception for the Royal Danish Ballet. "Big new love affair: Dali's ocelot is stuck on Rebekah Harkness," one gossip columnist gushed. "It all happened at a reception for the Royal Danish Ballet at Harkness House. Rebekah made a gorgeous descent on the great marble staircase with the ocelot draped around her neck, eyes flashing fire and all that. But it can't last. Those things never do."

As Rebekah's empire grew, it became increasingly unclear who was running things. In the normal scheme of things, Skibine, the artistic director, should have been calling the shots. But he was always being second-guessed: Scevers was at the center of Rebekah's growing and ever-changing Inner Circle, and Leon Fokine was delighted he now had a direct pipeline to Rebekah through Bobby, which he wasted no time in putting it to good use.

Increasingly, Skibine was becoming irrelevant. By the fall of 1966, Rebekah was completely fed up with him. She wanted the company to be more classical, but he balked. "He just looks at me with those bleary blue eyes and he doesn't know what I'm talking about," she told Bobby. "He just doesn't know what to do."

Meanwhile, Aaron Frosch told Rebekah that she was spending far too much on the dance troupe. She had blown more than $1 million on it the previous year alone. Even with her gains in the stock market during these go-go years, she couldn't continue forever. To discuss the fate of the company, Frosch scheduled a meeting in Rebekah's office at Harkness House. If he was persuasive enough, her dream would be over.

Less than an hour before the meeting was to take place, Skibine was walking down Madison Avenue just a couple of blocks from Harkness House, when at autumnal downpour forced him to take shelter under a nearby awning. Standing next to him was a man he hadn't seen in ten years, Bertrand Castelli.

A writer-producer of Corsican ancestry, Castelli had made a name for himself in Paris in the fifties during the heyday of St. Germain des Prés, when French youth culture was discovering bebop, blue jeans, Camus, and Sartre. *Les Algues,* a 1953 ballet Castelli wrote with Janine Charrat about the inmates of an insane asylum, mixed despair and mystery in exactly the right combination to become a success with the existentialists. He moved easily in the smartest cultural circles, mingling with Picasso, Raoul Dufy, Jean Cocteau, and Colette. A play he wrote called *The Umbrella* had been produced off-Broadway. These days, Castelli was collaborating with Dorothy Parker on an adaptation of her short story, "Big Blonde," for public television.

"Bertrand was that mysterious, crazy showman you saw in the sixties, the guy with the business suit and the beads," says his colleague Michael Butler, with whom Castelli later produced the musical *Hair.* "He had a remarkable manic energy. He could work tremendously hard, chain-smoking so much we had to have someone follow him around with an ashtray. He was a charming, attractive guy. It was hard not to like Bertrand."

Skibine grabbed Castelli by the lapel and dragged him two blocks to Harkness House. On the way, he explained: Rebekah had decided to hire Brian Macdonald, the Canadian choreographer whose *Time Out of Mind* had been a success, as the new artistic director, but he wouldn't be available for six months. Skibine wanted to leave as soon as possible. In the intervening months, with no artistic director to protect the company, it was altogether possible that Rebekah's lawyers, who saw what a mess she was making of the company, would succeed in closing it.

"Bertrand!" he said. "It's a miracle running into you like this. You are the only man who can save us."

Castelli had just shared three bottles of wine with Dorothy Parker. "I was a little bit drunk," he says. "But I could see it was a crisis for them. They were frantic. All the dancers wanted to quit. The lawyers were coming at eight o'clock. No one knew what to do. We met in her exquisite office—very elegant with a fireplace, a bar, piano. She asked Skibine to leave. She closed the door."

After nearly fifteen years in this country, Castelli's French accent had, if anything, become more pronounced, thickening into a gravelly soup of Gallic charm spiced with the argot of the sixties. Tall, with dark good looks reminiscent of Yves Montand, Castelli was certain to get a fair hearing from Rebekah.

"I realized she was trying to create in America what the Marquis de Cuevas had done in Europe twenty years earlier," he says. "And I had to tell her she was finished. There is no fortune big enough to support ballet the way it used to be done. Those days are over. I knew the lawyers must be right. I broke the image, the mirror of Rebekah Harkness, by telling her what no one else would tell her, what she was thinking inside. It was a very important moment.

"Then she cried. She cried a long time. Her lawyers were waiting, beeping impatiently. But she paid no attention. She was a shy woman, but she was not shy with me. She and I looked at each other and I knew she was a little girl. She began this long monologue, for two or three hours talking about all the people who were taking advantage of her. She was totally paranoid about those people, the pimps and gigolos that surrounded her. Her frustrations were enormous, but she had never spoken to anyone honestly. We were like two children who are happy to be together because maybe, together, we can get out of the mess of our lives. It was as if we were two camels in the desert who suddenly know that the only way to make an oasis is to really talk sense. She wanted to expose herself. It was a tremendous relief for her."

Rebekah walked across the room and sat on Castelli's knee.

"She put her arms around me," he says. "Then she said, 'How glad I am to be alone with you. Kiss me. The others, they just know how to bite.'"

Outside, Frosch, Skibine, and the others continued to buzz her office impatiently, waiting for the board meeting to begin. "They must have thought I was Rasputin," says Castelli. Rebekah and he ignored them. As the buzzing continued, they made love in her office. "She was a racehorse," says Castelli. "She had a superb body, a natural elegance, marvelous hair, exquisite skin. She was giggling like a little seventeen-year-old girl going to her first ball."

When they emerged, Bertrand Castelli had become the new artistic director of the Harkness Ballet.

With Skibine gone, one would have thought that Rebekah would insist the company return to its classical roots. Instead, she let it go in precisely the opposite direction. "I considered dance not art, but show business," says Castelli. "I had no respect for big names and traditions. I was bored with the very precious, static, obsolete world of ballet. It was a world totally corrupted by the dilettante and café society. When I was nineteen I started my own company in Paris. I was doing my own trip. I was making money. It really blew their minds." With just a few months to try to remake the dance company, Castelli tried to do the same thing with the Harkness, bringing in people like Andy Warhol and Tom O'Horgan, who was later the director of *Hair* and who had absolutely nothing to do with classical ballet.

"I didn't understand what was happening," says Bobby. "I thought Rebekah hated all that sixties modern crap. So Castelli came along, and suddenly she wanted to try it and said I was too closed-minded."

There was more than just artistic confusion. "It was total pandemonium," says Jane Remer, an administrator who joined the staff without a clearly defined job. "It was disorganized and bizarre. I was made assistant director—to do what, nobody knew. I sat at a desk worth more than my apartment! On any given morning when she and I had something to talk about, Rebekah would come down in her pink and blue leotards and literally stand on her head, and we would have the conversation with her standing on her head. It would be all very Proustian and never made too much sense. It was fascinating, but we never got anything accomplished."

"Few of the staff had specific duties," says Stuart Hodes, who choreographed *Abyss,* one of the most successful pieces in the Harkness repertory. "Nobody reported to anybody, and no one knew what the others were doing. Yet everyone had an impressive title. There was a director of Harkness House, director of administration, director of the library, director of the canteen, and director of special projects." Hodes himself became "project coordinator" and was asked to reject various grant requests, saying they did not fall within "foundation guidelines"; in fact, even he could not discern what the guidelines were.

Rebekah's lawyers still tried to curb her lavish expenditures. But the outside perception was that there were no limits to her resources. At a dinner at her place in Nassau it was said that she had more than $400 million. The figure was a gross exaggeration, but it was widely repeated, even published in national magazines, fueling the grandiose dreams of her hangers-on. An Italian accordionist wrote asking for money, with an application that appeared to be a thinly disguised offer of his body to Rebekah. A dancer with a Russian-Bronx-Cockney accent whom Rebekah thought was a mad genius ended up masterminding a rash of thefts at Harkness House. An angry overweight woman came in claiming to be the inventor of jazz dancing and demanding to be so honored. A swami asked Rebekah for a Fifth Avenue mansion.

In some measure it was amusing. Members of the inner circle vied for her attention, and the lucky ones were rewarded with free trips to the compound in Nassau. They admired her quick wit, and she played to them with a camp sense of humor, much as she had to the Bitch Pack in her debutante days. At parties, she dressed up as a maid passing out drinks, eavesdropping on conversations and winking at those in the know. She didn't like the color of chocolate mousse, so she had it dyed blue when it was served for dinner. And in Nassau, dressed in evening clothes and wearing hundreds of thousands of dollars' worth of jewelry, she left a restaurant by walking through its fountain and emerged soaking wet. Thinking her goldfish were not perky enough, she tried to pep them up by filling the fish tank with Scotch whiskey—killing them in the process. She flaunted her belief in reincarnation, insisting that in a previous life she had been the Egyptian queen Nefertiti. "We've been here before, honey," she said. "And you know what? We'll be back again."

When she showed guests around one of her spectacular weekend retreats, she said, "Well, it's not home." Then, with a pause for effect, she added, "But it is much."

And, referring to whatever problems she was having with the company: "If it's perfection you're looking for, dear," she would say again and again, "you're on the wr-ro-n-ng planet."

Everything was not fun and games, though. At Harkness House, people moved in and out of favor so fast that the high turnover became a standing joke. Even at the top administrative levels, Rebekah hired people before firing their replacements, allowing them to fight it out on the job.

"Rebekah really had a talent for bringing together people who hated each other," says Bobby. "I used to tell her she collected people. But she was very perceptive. She knew exactly what everyone was after. No one took her for a ride unless she wanted to be taken. Rebekah liked to have people around to do things her way, so whatever she needed she would have the person who was able to do that come into her little group, whether it was to teach her music, ballet, or Spanish dance. And then they wouldn't like each other and there would be all this intrigue, but she rather enjoyed all that."

The more unconventional these people were, the more likely they were to be taken seriously by Rebekah. At least one person was usually able to secure a semipermanent place in Rebekah's entourage serving as her "spiritual consultant," a task that over the years had fallen successively to Iyengar, Jane Gray, and finally, to a woman named Eva Brach. The daughter of a well-known German author, Brach had gained Rebekah's attention for her unorthodox amalgam of psychoanalysis and mysticism, and "automatic writing," in which she claimed her hand, taken over by "spirits," just started writing. Eva put forth the teachings of a spirit known as the Guide, in hopes of letting "all of life's energies stream through body and soul."

For years Rebekah put her up in an apartment on Third Avenue and flew her down to Nassau, and in the summer of 1965 she invited her to Holiday House so she could write a book. By the end of the summer, however, Rebekah got tired of seeing Eva out by the pool, accompanied by her obese white cat, Mickey. When she heard that Eva had been ordering specially prepared filet mignon for the animal's dinner, Rebekah had had enough. Furious, she bathed the cat in food coloring until it was a horrid green. Eva was appalled. "What vicious and stupid person could have done this horrible cruel thing!" she asked Rebekah, not knowing who the culprit was. "Vicious and stupid, vicious and stupid!"

Eva's place was taken by Yukiko Irwin, the Japanese-American physical therapist who had already achieved a certain popularity with the company by virtue of her acupressure massages. Yuki, or Yuki-san as she was sometimes called, also introduced the dancers to Zen Buddhism and the Buddhist mantra *"Nam myo horenge kyo."* Suddenly, a new issue split the company: There were the chanters and the nonchanters. Three of the male soloists began chanting and proselytizing the unconverted, claiming Buddhism made them jump higher and dance better. Even Bobby and Rebekah began chanting for a brief time. "If you wanted to get anywhere in the company," says one musician who was with the company, "you had to find out whether the chanters were running things or not."

Castelli, many thought, was only the latest in a long line of charlatans. The dancers were so dumbfounded at the sudden and radical change in the direction of the company that they called him "Skibine's Revenge."

"The company was very paranoid about me," Castelli says. "I came from nowhere and I didn't want to tell them where I was going. I was totally detached and yet very concerned, because I felt it was an opportunity to do something good and serve well. But there was a lot of paranoia among [Rebekah's] advisers. It blew their minds. If I had said to Rebekah, 'Let's get married,' it could threaten their jobs; it was 'Good-bye, Charlie.'"

As a surprise to Castelli, Rebekah had his new office completely redone, knocking down walls and buying two magnificent antique English desks. He was mystified; part of his mandate was to drastically cut costs. Regulars at Harkness House were astonished at the change in her. For the first time in years, she appeared euphoric, as if she were truly in love. Intellectually insecure, she could still be dazzled by the sophistication of someone like Castelli. Bobby couldn't compete with that. Fokine warned him, "Boy, she's going to throw you out any minute now."

Meanwhile, Castelli asked each member of the corps de ballet to audition. "I knew right away Bobby couldn't dance," Castelli says. "But Rebekah hadn't told me that she had had an affair with him. I took him to my office. I just talked to him as a father. I thought it was pathetic wasting a life like that. I told him not to dream. And I said I think you should really look for a job. There is not much future for you in dance. You are a really good man, but the space you need is different than dancing. Bobby was a very beautiful man, very handsome. In a way I was sorry. He was dancing very well with her."

Bobby was livid. "Castelli got me out of there fast," he says. "I knew what was going on. I hated him with all my heart. Rebekah was a real sucker for that greasy European gigolo type, who had that wonderful smooth polish where he would ooze and gush and slobber at the mouth and pull out her chair for her and click his heels. Castelli gave such a sales pitch, and suddenly we were estranged. My security blanket was out the window. I had no way of making a living. I was living in an apartment that wasn't mine. I was scared to death."

Not long after he talked to Bobby, Castelli began receiving threatening notes. Once, Stuart Hodes returned to his office at Harkness House and began fiddling with his typewriter. He had picked up the rather peculiar habit of looking at the ribbon on his

IBM Selectric whenever he sat down to write. "If I looked at the ribbon I could see, written backwards, of course, the last few words of the last thing I had written," he says . . . "This time, the last word on it was one I hadn't written. DAED . . . Dead . . . I got curious and began unrolling the ribbon and it was a hate note . . . As I recall, it said, 'You think you are all powerful but you are a nothing and we will be here long after you are dead. . . .'"

The notes continued. "Many times when I came back to the office," says Castelli. "I found saying notes that I was going to be killed, so I gave them to Frosch. I couldn't figure out who it was."

As she traveled about the world with Castelli, Rebekah seemed to feel like a young girl again, playing pranks as she hadn't done since her Bitch Pack days. On a lark, she switched three or four hundred thousand dollars from one bank account to another just to confuse Frosch and her accountants. When Castelli told her he hoped to adapt the short stories of J. D. Salinger for dance, she accompanied him to the New Hampshire home of the reclusive writer. She rang his doorbell dressed up as a cleaning lady, in an unsuccessful attempt to get a job as his maid.

"In Switzerland, we went to a beautiful place with wine and a fondue in a poor village," Castelli says. "She didn't want to leave and she had suddenly discovered that life could be simple and marvelous and wonderful.

"She knew with the dance company she was reenacting her childhood," he says, "but she couldn't explain it to the others. She knew the $400 million did not exist. She was very self-aware—yes, very, of everything all the time, never a fool. That was her privilege—to appear a fool. She shouldn't have done what she did. All those investments were for me totally grotesque. Show me those Dalis—I wouldn't give him ten cents. When we had dinner with Dali, and when he saw me, Dali knew that. It's a world that has disappeared. And in a way it is good she exposed it. The ballet is full of parasites. They steal youth. They want the glory, the intrigue. You are giving them Pandora's box. Then you have the sharks waiting for ten percent, making the deal. Those things were totally absurd. But she had been abused and misled by all kinds of people who wanted to take advantage, so she had never spoken to a man since Harkness, or since her father.

"I think she was courageous. She was willing to accept destruction. She was widely portrayed as a fool, but she was not. When she got into a room, she knew immediately what was going on. If she paid more, it was because she wanted to pay more. Rebekah was a man, a buddy-buddy of anyone—the maid, the doctor, the bullshit artist, the gigolos. Rebekah had a lot of man in her. Even her attitude to her own children—she was more a father than a mother. She was like a man, like a truck driver. Even physically, she was tall, a man in drag. When she wanted to be coquettish, she was like a man in drag.

"And yet she was a mirror. I could see so many people in front of her, playing the game of the moment, and she liked being in that position. She was very shy about it. She was embarrassed. She had a way of washing her hands. When they left, she used to clean her hands. I caught her many times washing her hands. I used to call her Pontius Pilate. She died laughing. She used to wet her pants. She had a sense of humor about it. The thing with money was a trip. She knew how to make believe that she had so much money. She used to enrage Frosch and those people. She was like the gardener in Kosinski's *Being There,* the mirror into which we could look and see what we wanted, an idiot who says profound things."

Meanwhile, Bobby, devastated over Rebekah's desertion, was desperate. "I was very close to suicide," he says. "Aaron Frosch was like the marriage broker, listening to me cry on the phone."

At the same time, it was clear there were limits to Castelli's relationship with both Rebekah and the company. He had told Rebekah in the beginning that he was married, and his wife was now expecting his child. "Rebekah understood that I would disappear. She knew that I wouldn't marry her. We were friends, but in the deepest sense. We met in the desert, we did the oasis and we went our own ways." But by the spring of 1967, his six-month tenure with the company was coming to a close.

"Frosch still wanted to close the company," says Castelli. "He begged me, 'Please tell her to stop.' I tried to make her understand. But she was like an alcoholic. You can save them for a while, but after they take one more glass, they go back."

For Rebekah to follow Castelli was to give up the dream her dance company represented. That was something she could not do, no matter how much she was aware of its flaws. At the same time, Frosch regularly kept Rebekah abreast of Bobby's state of mind. After a particularly upsetting conversation with Scevers, Frosch called her in Gstaad. Later she sent a telegram to Bobby: "Coming home soon," it read. "Don't do anything. I'll see you when I get back."

When she returned, the two of them flew off to Nassau.

The second time around: Betty, thirty-one, and William Hale Harkness, forty-six, at their wedding—the second for both of them—in their Park Avenue apartment in 1947.

Six-year-old Bill Harkness and his
sister, Louise, in Palm Beach, Florida,
in 1906

Bill, flanked by his sister, Louise, and
his mother, Edith Hale Harkness,
about to hop into their horse-drawn
carriage. About 1905

Bill aboard one of the family's many
yachts

The Harkness family gathers on their estate in Glen Cove,
Long Island, about 1907.

Young Bill and his sister, probably in St. Augustine, Florida, one of the resorts built
by their great-uncle, Henry Flagler

Intrepid explorer:
Bill Harkness, twenty-six, in Cairo,
during his 1926 trip
around the world

Patrician assurance:
Harkness not long after
his marriage to
Betty in 1947

How to marry a millionaire:
After her 1946 divorce from Dickson Pierce,
Betty was a bright, young, attractive divorcée
who had no intention of going
back to St. Louis.   RAWLINGS

A new role:
After she married Bill, Betty,
here with him and Terry, was
finally forced to become
a real mother.

The house on the hill: With over forty rooms, twenty-one bathrooms, and, at one point, eight kitchens, Holiday House was the most imposing residence in Watch Hill, dominating both the beach and the town.

A home at last: When their mother married Harkness, Allen, five, and Terry, two and a half, finally had a real family. Here they attend their mother's wedding.

Her father's daughter: Even as a baby, Edith, the only child Rebekah had by Harkness, had her father's eyes and coloring.

DOROTHY WILDING

Friends who knew her as a rip-roaring party girl were shocked to see Betty
transformed into a sedate society wife. "This wasn't the Betty *I* knew," said one.

Betty and Bill in 1952, two years before his death. One's social standing in Watch Hill was measured by how often one was invited to Holiday House.

Nothing Betty did ever won her father's approval—until she married Harkness. Here is her father, Allen West, Sr., who was often compared to W. C. Fields, with an unidentified woman.

Shortly after her father's death, Edith
went to her mother for solace. "What do
you want?" Rebekah asked.

When Harkness died, Rebekah asked
Allen Pierce, who was devastated by the
tragedy, if he wanted to take on his
stepfather's last name. "No," Allen said.
"I'm not good enough."

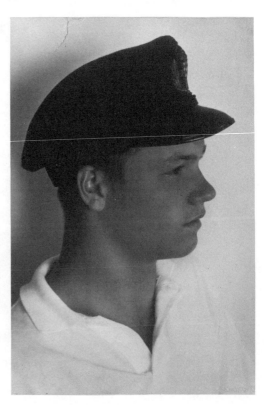

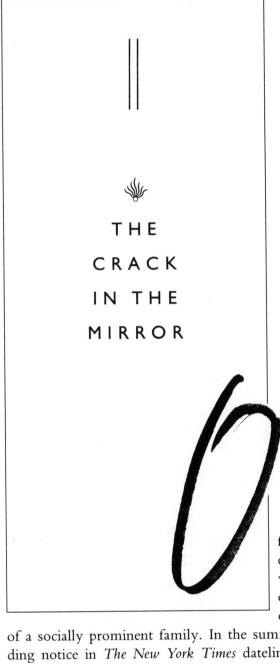

THE
CRACK
IN THE
MIRROR

Of Rebekah's three children, only Terry was even remotely on an acceptable path of life for a member of a socially prominent family. In the summer of 1966, a wedding notice in *The New York Times* datelined Watch Hill read, "Announcement has been made here by Mrs. Rebekah Harkness of Holiday House and New York of the marriage of her daughter, Miss Anne Terry Pierce, on May 2 in St. Thomas, the Virgin

Islands, to Anthony Wallace McBride, of New York and St. Thomas. The ceremony was performed aboard a ship by the ship's captain."

In fact, no such wedding had taken place. Terry's best friend, M'liss Crotty, fabricated the announcement at the request of the family. Terry was pregnant. An abortion had been considered but rejected, and Terry and McBride decided to get married instead. They moved into Holiday House to prepare for the formal ceremony September 3. The entire entourage, including the dance company, was in Watch Hill for the summer season as preparations for the wedding got under way.

Bobby Scevers and his friends, who had had the run of Holiday House, now had to make way for the nuptials. "I thought the whole thing was so stupid," Bobby says. "I hated Terry and Tony. When Terry came to Watch Hill, she and her friends would put spaghetti in the Waring blender without a top on and let it splatter all over the ceiling, just to see how big a mess they could make. It was their home. We were just guests. But we felt that they were intruding on our territory. Everyone was working to create something in the arts, and here were young Terry and her yacht club friends just making a mess."

Bobby was particularly irritated that the wedding party had commandeered Rebekah's 1919 American LaFrance fire engine. Each summer he and Rebekah used to race through the streets of Watch Hill in it wearing fire hats. "We had more fun in that fire engine," he says. "Rebekah turned up the siren every time she passed one of her snooty neighbors. Raymond Wilson was dressed up in his makeup and a lavender antebellum gown."

For the wedding, the fire engine was covered with flowers, and Bobby reluctantly chauffeured the bride and groom through the town. "I was so disgruntled at having to drive them around—the two people I hated most in the world," he says.

The ceremony took place with all the pomp and circumstance of a state occasion. The topiary trees were specially trimmed. Peter Duchin and his orchestra played at the reception. Harkness House staff photographer Michael Avedon, a second cousin of Richard Avedon, took the photos. The ceremony itself took place in the library before just a few members of the family and close friends, but hundreds of guests were present for the reception. After Tony and Terry took their vows, Rebekah, anxious to have the whole affair over with, clapped her hands. "Well," she said. "That's that."

Terry had beautiful dark chestnut hair and her mother's eyes and mouth. Like Rebekah, she had been a bit heavy as a child; back then she was called Little Chunky. She was sent to private schools all over the world including Brearley, Hewitt, and Burleigh in New York, and to schools in Arizona and Switzerland, before going to Rollins College in Florida. Despite all the moving around, she managed to make friends easily wherever she went. She did reasonably well in school and was enthusiastic when it came to the arts.

Terry had dutifully been introduced to society at her coming-out party. She attended social functions for her mother and the ballet company and was conspicuously featured on the society pages with Dali and his ocelot. She delighted her mother with her guitar-playing and her painting—she was taught by Dali—and Rebekah found it easier to be with Terry than her other children.

"When you consider the trauma she was exposed to, she was very calm, very serene, remarkably stable," says one former classmate. "Terry may look back now, and wonder why she was alone for weeks on end. But at the time, she certainly didn't complain. She was terribly proud of Rebekah. She adored her."

The previous summer, Terry, twenty-two, had met Tony McBride, the twenty-five-year-old stepson of CBS newsman Mike Wallace, at the Southampton Beach Club to which she belonged. McBride had the blond, athletic, all-American good looks of the archetypal California beach boy. Indeed, to Bobby, that was the only redeeming feature of the wedding. "Tony was gorgeous," he says. "Just like a Greek vase—beautiful, but absolutely nothing inside."

The son of Lorraine and Paul Orlopp, Tony had taken his maternal grandmother's maiden name, McBride, after his parents' early divorce. He spent his childhood first in Los Angeles, and then with his mother in Puerto Rico, Haiti, and the Virgin Islands. In 1955, his mother, a painter, met Wallace, then about to begin his show *Night Beat,* which established his reputation as a relentless interviewer well before his long tenure with *Sixty Minutes;* she became his third wife, and the family moved to the suburbs of New York.

Tony finished high school in nearby Nyack and later attended Bowdoin College in Maine. Then he returned to Los Angeles, where he discovered the surfing scene through his stepbrother, Mickey Dora, known as the "King of Malibu," "Da Cat," or, quite simply "the best surfer in the world."

In the fifties, surfers were the true bohemians of the West Coast. But by the early sixties, the surfer subculture had exploded, with gremmies, hodads, woodies, surfer girls, and the Beach Boys making their way into the middle-American market place. Dora was in no fewer than six beach films, including three Gidget movies and the 1964 hit *Ride the Wild Surf.* He was hounded for interviews, and asked to endorse products. All of which he did, albeit reluctantly, aghast at the commercialization and trivialization of all he held dear.

Tony followed suit. Capitalizing on his good looks, he signed a contract with Columbia Pictures, where he landed television roles in Alfred Hitchcock episodes, a TV pilot, and a 1963 film called *The Victors,* with an unlikely cast including George Hamilton, Albert Finney, George Peppard, Vince Edwards, Melina Mercouri, and Jeanne Moreau. But he soon became disenchanted with the phony Malibu surfing crowd and Hollywood, and returned to New York to run a limousine service called Classic Coaches. At night he hung out at chic watering holes like Le Club, with a crowd that included Prince Juan Carlos of Spain. Then he began a whirlwind romance with Terry that ranged from New York and Los Angeles to the Caribbean and Hawaii.

About three months into their courtship, Tony went out to the north shore of Oahu, where hundreds of spectators line the cliffs to watch surfers take on waves as big as twenty and thirty feet.

Terry joined him for a couple of months, then the two went back to the Caribbean, where Tony skippered charter boats.

But their idyllic romance had its problems. "I had visited Tony in California before the wedding," says Pauline Dora, his half sister. "This was before abortions were legal in this country, and there was pressure from Rebekah to have the kid and get married. Otherwise, I don't think they would have gotten married. They had nothing in common."

Terry, however, couldn't seem to get enough of Tony's family. As wedding presents, she gave Pauline, also a bride-to-be, an extravagant canopy bed and expensive clothes. "I refused things from her because I was embarrassed," says Pauline. "Someone giving you that amount of things—it's strange. I had to stop her. It's as if she wanted to get close to me, because that meant getting close to Tony."

Luci Baines Johnson and her groom, Patrick Nugent, had honeymooned at Capricorn in August, and immediately after their wedding Terry and Tony followed suit. About three days into their stay, Terry called her friend M'liss Crotty. "Marriage isn't exactly what it's cracked up to be," she said. Terry returned immediately to her East Side apartment in New York.

"Terry was pretty sure the marriage wasn't going to work out," says M'liss. "But it was damn late to have an abortion, and Japan was the only place that would consider it. Terry got the plane tickets and got as far as the airport. But Rebekah must have had the phones tapped and paid off the doormen for surveillance, because she got wind of what was happening and sent guards to the airport to keep Terry from getting on the plane." After a few weeks, she and Tony reunited in Hawaii. Rebekah and the Wallaces had convinced them to give the marriage another try.

On March 7, 1967, Terry gave birth to a daughter, Anna Pierce Perigord McBride. Terry called her Leilani, a Hawaiian name, but others later called her Angel, and the name stuck. Several weeks later, Terry and Tony returned to New York with their baby. She and Tony had not been getting along well. "There was very little warmth or affection," says Pauline. "You could tell they were drifting apart. The marriage was under strain. Terry was not happy. There was this tension between them over Terry's weight. Tony was fasting a lot, and was very strange."

Adding to the tensions were medical problems with their baby. "In the first two months her eyes should have focused, and when they didn't I thought I should have her checked out," Terry says. "So when I came back to New York, I took her to a doctor. After two weeks we began to find out what was really wrong. That was the beginning."

Rebekah had Angel admitted to New York Hospital, where several top specialists were called in. Among them was Dr. Maria New, a rising young star in the hospital's pediatric department, best known for her work in endocrinology.

"Angel was extremely beautiful." says Dr. New. "At first, except for the roaming of the eyes, it did not appear that the child was very damaged."

But as the weeks went by, Angel failed to develop normally. "At three months, a baby should be able to prop herself up on her elbows and hold her head up," says Dr. New. "Angel couldn't do that. She had a very floppy head. A newborn with a floppy head is okay, but a three-month-old is not."

Angel's prognosis changed from day to day and from doctor to doctor. But as the child grew, the signs of severe neurological damage became inescapable. Mike and Lorraine Wallace thought Angel should be put in a home because the chances of her living very long were minimal. "They didn't think that Tony and Terry should be burdened with the kid," says Pauline.

Finally, the newlyweds approached Dr. New. "Terry and Tony asked me about placing the child in an institution," she says. "I said that if the baby was not capable of being cared for in a normal environment, then we would help with that."

Rebekah, however, objected. "One day [she] went in—she went in every day—and picked her up and held a bottle to her mouth, and the child began to slightly suck," says one of the child's nannies. "That's where you get the sentiment. Granny felt she had done something wonderful. She knew she could give the baby something."

After that, Rebekah insisted the child stay with the family. "She was adamant that Terry and Tony should take care of the kid," says Pauline. "When they said no, she took over. She was determined. If they were not going to do it, she was."

Rebekah set up a nursery in the Westbury, hired nurses, and began meeting regularly with the baby's doctors. "Mother was very good about it," says Terry. In June, the baby and her nurses joined Rebekah's entourage at Holiday House. When necessary, Rebekah sent a chauffeur-driven car to New York Hospital to pick up Dr. New and take her to Watch Hill. It was still too early to give a complete diagnosis of the child's condition, but there was reason to believe she would never live a normal life. Nevertheless, Rebekah showed her more love and devotion than she had given any of her own offspring.

"Angel's birth was the glaring crack in the perfect glass," says Rebekah's nephew Tarwater, "the perfect, terrifying manifestation of everything that could have gone wrong with the woman who, of course, had everything."

In time it was learned that Angel was afflicted with septooptic dysplasia syndrome, a brain malformation characterized by atrophy of the optic nerve, and by an absence of corpus callosum, the central part of the brain that connects its two hemispheres. As a result, Angel was almost completely blind and there was probably no communication between the two halves of her brain. Angel also suffered from epilepsy and was subject to recurrent seizures. In addition, she had a severe condition known as right spastic hemiplegia, which meant the entire right side of her brain was spastic, leaving all functions on the left half of her body almost useless. Finally, Dr. New determined that Angel suffered from diabetes insipidus, a pituitary dysfunction that often results in chronic dehydration.

Taken individually, each of the infant's problems posed great difficulties. But cumulatively, they made each day a life-and-death struggle. Most life-threatening of all was the fact that her condition was complicated by diabetes insipidus. Most normal patients can stave off the threat of dehydration through regular feeding. But Angel could not. Even the most primitive, infantile urge of all—feeding—did not come easily to her. Because she was spastic, she could not even put her lips together, much less bite anything. She could barely suck. Yet the slightest irregularity in feeding put her life in jeopardy.

Terry was devastated.

Rebekah's relationship with her, once the least complicated in the family, was now colored with guilt and bitterness. Devoted as Rebekah was to the infant, ultimately she blamed Terry and Tony. "Every mother with a child like Angel has a guilt complex," says the child's nanny. "But Rebekah never stopped telling Terry it was her fault."

Too make matters worse, Rebekah told friends that Angel's birth defects came from Tony's alleged use of LSD. In fact, it was impossible to establish a cause, and such allegations were mere speculation on Rebekah's part. (Later scientific studies showed that LSD does not damage chromosomes in humans.)

Tony dismissed the idea that drug use was responsible for his daughter's birth defects. "Terry never did any [drugs] herself," he says. "I might have experimented here and there, but I never got into the drug culture."

But Rebekah voiced her disapproval strongly enough that he felt he had to return to Hawaii. "He said he was leaving because nobody liked him," says Terry. That left Terry caught in the middle. Sometimes, she avoided her mother by leaving town, giving her number to Dr. New with clear instructions not to inform Rebekah of her whereabouts.

Most of the doctors who examined the infant thought she would live only a year or two. Dr. New, however, was slightly more optimistic. Not all of the disorders were untreatable. A drug called Dilantin was effective for controlling her epilepsy, though how long she could survive and how much progress she would make was a question that no one—not even Dr. New—dared to predict. Even so, Terry expected more from the medicine. "I heard Dr. New had this fabulous new medicine," she said. "We were given hope for a real recovery." When the medicine proved to be not a cure, but a treatment to prolong the life of her severely damaged child, Terry's agony was exacerbated.

"The baby was dying when I was called in," says Dr. New, "and as a result of my treatment the baby turned the corner and did very well. Terry turned against me, partly because I supported the grandmother's role in this baby's life. I did so because in the beginning at least the grandmother was the constant force in the baby's life, the one who provided the stimulation, the desire for the baby to do better. The mother was an occasional guest. The primary person was Mrs. Harkness."

Terry was increasingly suspicious of Dr. New, who now accompanied Rebekah occasionally to Watch Hill and Nassau as Angel's physician. If psychics, dancers, and musicians could take Rebekah for a ride, Terry thought, it was not out of the question for a doctor to exploit her tragedy to get close to her mother. Terry returned to Tony in Hawaii, leaving Angel in the care of Rebekah and Dr. New, but she was uneasy. "As soon as we went back to Hawaii," she says, "Maria New came swooping in like a Valkyrie."

12

DON'T
DRESS HER
IN
ORGANDY

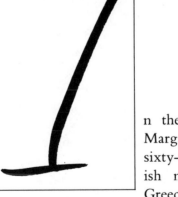

n the fall of 1967, Margaret Weeks, a sixty-year-old British nanny, was in Greece caring for the child of a wealthy family when she received a telegram from Rebekah asking her to come to New York. A letter followed in which Rebekah said Broadway producer David Merrick, a former employer of Miss Weeks, had given her his highest recommendation. Miss Weeks had been entertaining thoughts of retiring to a two-bedroom flat in London's West End after her tenure in Greece, but such notions vanished when she read Merrick's name—he had treated her handsomely, once sending her twelve dozen daffodils on her birthday—and Rebekah's description of her "delicate little grandchild."

Rebekah, however, did not reveal the whole truth about how handicapped the child was, so Miss Weeks was somewhat baffled by the apparent urgency of the situation. "Mrs. Harkness said she wanted me that very day," she recalls. "I told her I would like twenty-four hours, but she said, 'I really can't wait.' She had such persuasive powers! So I came that afternoon."

On November 13, Weeks met Rebekah, Dr. New, and Angel. The baby was vomiting. Dr. New explained that nobody expected the child to live very long, nor did they know what kind of life she was capable of living if she did survive. Then the three of them consulted with Dr. Samuel Levine, then chairman of the department of pediatrics at New York Hospital. Levine told Miss Weeks, exactly what she was getting into. Whatever happened, he said, the child would probably require total infant care for her entire life. "If you take this baby," he told her, "you must not leave her. She has got to have a rock to cling to. If you leave her, she will die."

Miss Weeks did not give it a second thought. "If I am given an order professionally," she says, "I obey. I knew I had a lot to give that child. I was that rock. I wanted that baby."

The stout, white-haired Miss Weeks had a religious devotion to her charges. She was the epitome of a dying breed—the starchy, old-fashioned British nanny. In *The Rise and Fall of the British Nanny,* author Jonathan Gathorne-Hardy describes the nanny as a surrogate mother who is unmarried, lonely, often wise, at her best anticipating Freud and Spock as she adopts her charges as "her" children. She is devoted, reliable, beaming a steady benevolence, possessed of an innate ability to enter and understand the world of a child. At the core of this sensibility is a finely tuned class-consciousness. The nanny often idealizes the mother as a beautiful, untouchable goddess who is distant but can do no wrong. Within that context, the author says, the nanny sits, all-

12

DON'T
DRESS HER
IN
ORGANDY

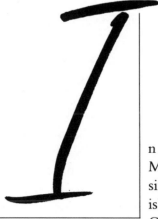

n the fall of 1967, Margaret Weeks, a sixty-year-old British nanny, was in Greece caring for the child of a wealthy family when she received a telegram from Rebekah asking her to come to New York. A letter followed in which Rebekah said Broadway producer David Merrick, a former employer of Miss Weeks, had given her his highest recommendation. Miss Weeks had been entertaining thoughts of retiring to a two-bedroom flat in London's West End after her tenure in Greece, but such notions vanished when she read Merrick's name—he had treated her handsomely, once sending her twelve dozen daffodils on her birthday—and Rebekah's description of her "delicate little grandchild."

Rebekah, however, did not reveal the whole truth about how handicapped the child was, so Miss Weeks was somewhat baffled by the apparent urgency of the situation. "Mrs. Harkness said she wanted me that very day," she recalls. "I told her I would like twenty-four hours, but she said, 'I really can't wait.' She had such persuasive powers! So I came that afternoon."

On November 13, Weeks met Rebekah, Dr. New, and Angel. The baby was vomiting. Dr. New explained that nobody expected the child to live very long, nor did they know what kind of life she was capable of living if she did survive. Then the three of them consulted with Dr. Samuel Levine, then chairman of the department of pediatrics at New York Hospital. Levine told Miss Weeks, exactly what she was getting into. Whatever happened, he said, the child would probably require total infant care for her entire life. "If you take this baby," he told her, "you must not leave her. She has got to have a rock to cling to. If you leave her, she will die."

Miss Weeks did not give it a second thought. "If I am given an order professionally," she says, "I obey. I knew I had a lot to give that child. I was that rock. I wanted that baby."

The stout, white-haired Miss Weeks had a religious devotion to her charges. She was the epitome of a dying breed—the starchy, old-fashioned British nanny. In *The Rise and Fall of the British Nanny,* author Jonathan Gathorne-Hardy describes the nanny as a surrogate mother who is unmarried, lonely, often wise, at her best anticipating Freud and Spock as she adopts her charges as "her" children. She is devoted, reliable, beaming a steady benevolence, possessed of an innate ability to enter and understand the world of a child. At the core of this sensibility is a finely tuned class-consciousness. The nanny often idealizes the mother as a beautiful, untouchable goddess who is distant but can do no wrong. Within that context, the author says, the nanny sits, all-powerful and beneficent, comforting, watchful, chiding, ruling her kingdom consisting of various nurses and nursery maids, medicine, toys, and chamber pots.

Margaret Weeks had always known this would be her calling. "All my life I wanted to be a nanny," she says. "I played with dolls as a child and dressed them for charity. I always got the first prize for doll dressing. I was taught to sew a fine seam."

As a young woman, she was engaged to be married, but her fiancé was killed in World War II, and she took refuge in her work. "During the war, dealing with the underprivileged, the broken, the maladjusted, the hurt, it was wonderful to see them mend," she says. "And some of the little rich children are far worse off than those in Council care. You can't have a private life and bring up other people's children. You are proud of your family. You give up your life for them."

In the postwar era, a ravaged Britain could ill afford its vast domestic class, so the most highly trained servants soon found themselves in the employ of Greek shipping magnates and Park Avenue industrialists. By the mid-sixties, Tom Wolfe, in *The Kandy-Kolored Tangerine-Flake Streamline Baby,* asserted that New York's chic East Side was really run by "the Nanny Mafia." English nannies were the smartest status symbols of all. It was a different milieu from that in England, but the same rules applied. In New York, Miss Weeks met with the other members of the Nanny Mafia. There was the Uzielli nanny, the Ford nanny, and the former Kennedy nanny, who had had Caroline Kennedy as her charge but was now with another family—all pushing their prams in Central Park.

"You could tell who was who," says Miss Weeks. "But I was never one who stood in the corner with five prams gossiping."

By the time she began working for Rebekah, she had already been employed by families in locales ranging from St. James Palace to David Merrick's New York home. She specialized in what she called "the damaged ones"; she even had to care for one infant whose mother was on heroin at the time she gave birth—hardly proper behavior in the highly placed precincts in which she worked. It was partly because of her special talents in such sensitive areas that she was recommended so highly. Her associates wrote a poem about her. Its last lines read:

It's hard to find an area where Nannie doesn't shine
She may be only human, but I find her quite divine.

Her newest assignment was to be the most challenging of her life. No one had even known what to call the child until she came along. "They called her Anna or Angela, all sorts of things," says Weeks. "But once I had her twenty-four hours, I called her Angel. That's what we call them in England. If they are not whole, they are God's angels. 'Angel' stuck to her, and she answered to it."

Their day began as early as five-thirty. "She had a musical thing tied 'round her cot," says Miss Weeks, "with these little bluebirds, and you pull them and play Brahms's Lullaby. She could twist herself 'round from top to bottom of the cot as soon as she woke. If she was well, she would pull the bluebird, and I would relax and know that she was perfectly well. But if six o'clock came and there was no sound, I would sneak in and look. Her signaling was a sign of intelligence. She was telling me, 'I am awake and I feel well.' If you took the bluebird away, she would be feeling for it. She had a tremendous sensitivity to sound. I only had to call out a high-pitched 'Cuckoo' and she would go crazy. She would shriek out."

As soon as Angel was awake, she needed her medicine. "Then I would go to the icebox and bring up nasal medication, five drops into each nostril. This instantly gave her strength to move. Without it she would be very limp. This was repeated five times a day.

"Then I put her into a clean bed. Her bed needed a lot of changing, so I used to put her on the floor on a blanket and change the whole cot while still in my nightie, go down and make my own tea, and give her a feed, which was made the night before. She had cold food always—couldn't touch anything warm."

Feeding was no simple matter. Miss Weeks spent half of each morning preparing food for the child. Most frequently, a mixture of fruit—usually baby food—and milk was put in a blender. Crushed phenobarbitol and thyroxine was added before the resulting mixture was put in baby bottles with big slits in the nipples. "Everything had to be very smooth or she would choke. She ate no meat or vegetables except corn. Toward the end we managed to get a bit of biscuit on a string called a bickey peg— you give them to teething babies." Sometimes she prepared other dishes such as strained plums or egg custard, always specially blended to a thickness to go through the rubber nipple.

Occasionally she ate when held by others, including Rebekah, but Miss Weeks was the only person with whom she could feed consistently. She was incapable of closing her mouth entirely, and could only be fed from one side of her mouth, so the liquid food always spilled onto whoever was feeding her. All the while the music of Burl Ives, *Peter and the Wolf,* or the *Nutcracker Suite* played, as Angel fed more easily when she heard the same songs over and over again.

This painstaking ritual was repeated five times daily. Somehow the baby managed to drink two quarts of milk a day. The slightest irregularity in feeding was life-threatening. When she was unable to take food by mouth, she would have to be subjected to nasal or intravenous feeding.

"That was my life," says Miss Weeks. "I could do it sound asleep."

Rebekah gave Angel attention she had never shown any of her own children. Each morning, she looked in on her and Miss Weeks, and then again at around four o'clock she joined them for tea or an afternoon drink. She took the baby everywhere she traveled—to Watch Hill, the Westbury, Nassau.

Angel responded in kind to Rebekah. "She adored her," says Miss Weeks. "She could hear Granny [Rebekah] walking along the side of the pool in her bare feet, coming toward the nursery in Nassau, and her left leg would kick the floor. That was Angel's way of saying, 'Granny is coming.' That's how I knew she was coming into the nursery for her evening visit and a drink of Bacardi." Every night Miss Weeks brought a photograph of Rebekah over to Angel and said, "Kiss Gran good night." The child would not go to sleep until the ritual had been completed.

Rebekah took pride in her granddaughter, delighting in showing her off to visitors. Whenever anyone visited Angel, we dressed her up," says Miss Weeks. "Normally, she lived in long trousers and T-shirts that required no ironing. We had to make work light. But in the beginning Granny came to me once in a while and said, 'I have someone coming I want to show the baby to. Has she got anything decent to wear?' So I went to Saks for her, and we had her looking rather beautiful."

Tony never saw Angel after he and Terry moved to Hawaii, though his mother visited occasionally. Terry visited her a few times, but even friends were struck by her seemingly offhand attitude toward her child.

"Was she a good mother?" asks Dr. New. "No. It would have been very easy to love this baby. There are many twenty-four-year-old mothers who would cherish a beautiful baby like that, very blond and externally perfectly formed. There were no outward deformities. She had beautiful facial features. But Terry never was the real mother. I learned from her that the child was left with some Hawaiian person in infancy. Most young parents love their babies and nurture them. There is a very mundane process to raising a baby, and Terry and Tony were not involved in it. They were very immature. There was a certain degree of narcissism. They were very interested in how they looked. They constantly traveled from one resort to another. He was teaching diving and snorkeling. I didn't keep track of them. She would leave me telephone numbers from time to time, and I had to keep them in my pocket because Terry never wanted her mother to know where she was. I would know how to reach her, but my main contact with the child was through Rebekah."

Others saw it differently, however. "Underneath it all, Terry had a lot more real feeling for the babe than anybody gives her credit for," says Miss Weeks. "She got no sympathy. She was told to leave the baby, that it couldn't live. Once or twice at Nassau there were a few tender moments. She brushed Angel's hair, and then she put the brush down and ran away and burst into tears. Terry would love Angel for a few moments and then break down, and I would say let's go out to the garden. She would be sobbing her heart out. Every time ended with a sobbing. She had to give Angel back to me. She couldn't have coped with it."

To Terry, Miss Weeks was part of the problem: She couldn't tolerate the nanny's relentlessly cheery mien in the face of her tragedy. Miss Weeks had raised self-denial to a fine art, and it drove Terry crazy to hear her chattering on as if everything was just fine, investing so much love and affection in a child that would never walk, talk, or speak, a child who no one expected to survive more than a few years. When she put Angel to bed, saying, "It's time for your nappie-nappie," Terry couldn't stand it.

Rebekah cut a striking figure, coming up to the hospital with her granddaughter for the child's physical therapy in her Harkness-blue Rolls-Royce, still wearing a tutu from her dance class. "It was a fairy tale," says one doctor who treated Angel. "I didn't believe it. It was like magic. She wore a ballet dress, and I thought she was young enough to be the mother. But no, she was the grandmother, dressed as a ballet dancer. I had never seen this magic world in all my life."

But as early as the summer of 1968, it was becoming evident that Rebekah's patience as a grandmother to Angel, just a little over a year old, was beginning to wear a bit thin. "Granny came in every morning to visit at nine o'clock as I was having my breakfast," says Miss Weeks. "[She] was particularly beautifully done up one day with a large gray bow in her hair—she was going on a TV program. She picked up Angel and said she was such a beautiful little thing. You must remember Angel could perceive light somewhat, though practically speaking, she was blind. But somehow Angel must have seen the gray bow in Granny's hair, and she reached and pulled the bow out of Granny's hair." Miss Weeks was thrilled at the progress it suggested; Angel had never been able to see much of anything before and she had never done anything with her hand.

Rebekah's reaction was different. "Granny hated it," Miss

Weeks recalls. "She flung Angel at me. She said, 'Now I'll have to have it done all over again.' I'd never seen Granny so cross."

Rebekah apologized a few minutes later but it was clear the novelty was beginning to wear off for her.

Edith observed the scene surrounding Angel with a critical eye. One day she picked up the child in her arms and held her. "You won't let anything hurt her, will you?" she asked Miss Weeks. Miss Weeks promised always to watch out for Angel. Once, after they had just brought Angel a shawl and white dress from Saks Fifth Avenue, Edith recalled her own childhood, when her mother had dressed her up for cocktails to show her off to company in a horrid, starchy, scratchy dress.

"Whatever you do," Edith said to Miss Weeks, "don't dress her in organdy."

13

A CHIC
WAY
TO GO

For Terry's wedding, Edith had been released for the day and allowed to attend the ceremony accompanied by orderlies. She was then seventeen and had been confined to Payne Whitney Psychiatric Clinic since her attempt at suicide by jumping out the window. She looked beautiful. "But she was in the shadows the whole time," says one member of the wedding. "There was an incredible sadness about Edith."

And with good reason. Bobby and his friends were vying with Terry and the wedding party for command at Holiday House. Rebekah was furious because her first husband, Dickson Pierce, had arrived without notice. Allen had not shown up at all. There was so much tension and confusion that the photographer couldn't even get a shot of Rebekah together with Terry. All the while, Rebekah insisted that Edith be accompanied by attendants wherever she went.

"Nobody could be sane with the life Edith had," says Tarwater. "She always had someone with her, a caretaker, someone who was watching her. She knew exactly what was going on. Edith was angry, very, very angry. And finally she expressed it verbally, and there was this flurry of four-letter words." As members of the ballet company and Rebekah's entourage danced to the music of Peter Duchin and his orchestra, Rebekah discreetly had a guardian take Edith away.

Now that all three of her children were nearly grown, it was painfully obvious to everyone that as a mother, Rebekah was a failure. It was not that she didn't care. At times, she cried because she didn't know if she was being responsible enough toward her children. But whenever the blame shifted to her, she became petulant and defensive. She had given those kids everything; how could anyone possibly say she neglected them? "Maybe I was not there every minute," she said, "but I never left them alone. There was always someone there. I took them all over the world, and they had a beautiful place to live and the best education you can get. I did the best I could with my shaped brain."

It was Edith with whom Rebekah had the most volatile relationship. No one, least of all Rebekah, had ever known what to make of Edith's suicide attempt. It went without saying that she was deeply disturbed by her daughter's "accident," as she called it. She dispatched a Harkness House employee to investigate whether there had been any intermarriages within the Harkness family in previous generations, as if incest might account for her daughter's problems. She lashed out at the servants. "She blamed it all on that sadistic nurse," says Rebekah's brother, Allen. But it never occurred to her that the episode might have had something to do with her own relationship with Edith.

Still, it ate away at Rebekah. "Edith's suicide attempt stayed in her gut," says one dancer with the company. "She never got over it." She attended weekly sessions at Payne Whitney with Edith and her psychiatrist, and always left more frustrated and bewildered than ever. "Nothing they do is helping," she told Bobby. "They just sit around with their drugs and their neuroses and they don't do anything." Once she idly scrawled "Edith" on one piece of notepaper, the word "Sane" on another, then stuck them in her scrapbook. Dali had painted Edith in a cage. Now she was living in one.

Part of Rebekah's problem was that she could not understand why her children did not share her passion for dance. It was ironic, of course: Rebekah was painfully aware of what it meant not to fulfill her own parents' expectations.

At a loss of what to do with Edith, Rebekah tried to launch her into a modeling career while she was still in and out of Payne Whitney. The two of them posed in *McCall's* magazine for an article on "admittedly privileged" mother-daughter duos, including Lynda and Lady Bird Johnson and Dina Merrill and Marjorie Merriweather Post. Then Rebekah arranged a sitting for Edith with Harkness Ballet photographer Michael Avedon. Rebekah had posed for him earlier herself, fresh from another face-lift, with the skin of her face tightened so she could barely talk. She made certain that he was properly briefed about Edith.

"This wonderful old nurse told me they were going to take Edith out of the hospital for the day for a fashion shooting," Avedon says. "They told me she was very unbalanced, that it was a delicate situation, that they were hoping she would start relating with someone outside. I was ready for a lunatic, but instead, Edith talked totally openly about her mother. She was very beautiful. She talked so honestly, looked so frail, so fragile, almost poetic. I thought I was touching base with her. I was shocked because I didn't understand how they thought she could be unbalanced. She made much more sense than her mother."

Edith, like Terry and Allen, felt deserted by Rebekah ever since

Bill Harkness's death. When she was just six or seven, she would hide behind a piece of furniture and pretend she was not there when her mother entered the room. The only person in the family she had ever been able to really talk to after her father died was Ben Kean, but he was long gone from Rebekah's life. As an adolescent, she posted signs on her door at the Westbury saying STAY OUT, THIS MEANS YOU and OFF LIMITS TO EVERYBODY. Rebekah seemed to take the signs at face value. "Her mother was a complete stranger to her," says one of Rebekah's personal secretaries. "That's why I left. I heard someone telling Mrs. Harkness that I, little old me, was more of a mother to Edith than she was. I thought, it's time I got the hell out." During one of Tarwater's stays at Watch Hill, he indirectly tried to tell Rebekah about Edith's problems in a film script he wrote called *Bird in a Golden Cage,* a thinly disguised roman à clef about Rebekah's family in which the Edith character ends up dead, facedown in a swimming pool.

"I didn't see it this way, but there were people who thought Rebekah was trying to kill her off," says Edith's friend Heyden White. "In fact, it was clear she loved Edith more than her other kids. But many people felt that Rebekah didn't take care of Edith enough."

Edith was often identified during this period with a Peter Sellers film called *The World of Henry Orient,* a comedy about a concert pianist and a pair of teenage girls. The parallels were striking. Edith, already tall and beautiful, bore a striking resemblance to Valerie Boyd, the movie's heroine. Their lives were almost identical: their neighborhoods, their schools, their mothers' Rolls-Royces, their society parties. Intellectually sophisticated, with a sharp, sardonic sense of humor, Edith, like Valerie, was an incredibly mature social animal. And no one could deny that, like Valerie in the movie, she was woefully neglected by her mother.

Even though Edith was a patient at Payne Whitney, she attended school, first at Brearley, then the Masters School at Dobbs Ferry, New York. Many who knew her thought she was far more sophisticated and better adjusted than most teenagers. "She was so attractive—extraordinarily nice, poised, sensitive—

and I was not exactly the Don Juan of my class," says Tony Movshon, who dated Edith in 1966 and 1967, when he was a sixteen-year-old junior at Browning High School on Manhattan's Upper East Side. "I don't know why she decided to go out with me. Maybe I wasn't threatening in some way. But the whole relationship was very natural, given the sensibilities of sixteen-year-olds, because she treated it that way. Her psychiatric problems simply didn't show. The only way our relationship was affected by her treatment was that I took her home to Payne Whitney, where it was architecturally difficult to find a place to kiss her good night.

"Edith had a peculiar, independent quality about the way she dealt with her family. Her father continued to be important to her through his absence. He was the guy who would have made everything all right. She talked only a little about her mother, and then as a person who just happened to be there. Her mother had no important involvement in her life, and that was her mother's choice. The dance stuff was in full swing. But Edith was not a fan of the ballet."

Most striking was the equanimity with which both mother and daughter appeared to accept their tormented relationship. It was as if it were essential to both of them to maintain the fiction that everything really was just fine. Edith helped fuel the notion that things were not so bad. She seemed so assured and self-possessed, how could she possibly want to kill herself? "She wouldn't have jumped if her nanny hadn't egged her on," says a close friend. "Edith wasn't nearly as suicidal or troubled as you might assume."

When she talked about it herself, Edith dismissed her "Peter Pan episode," as she called it, as merely a childish impulse. And because she appeared to be so levelheaded, it was easy to believe her. "It obviously tickled her fancy, her sense of irony to talk about it," says Movshon. "She showed me the window out of which she jumped, pointing out the Dali portrait of her in a bird cage, as if it were this spookily perceptive painting, a prophecy that became true. She talked about it as if it were a very spur-of-the-moment thing, as if she were saying, 'Isn't it bizarre that a person like me would do this crazy thing?' She described suicide as something she just decided to do one day, as a call for help. She mentioned that she had considered suicide from the age of five. I knew that she was capable of it, but I was still startled by it. It was as though she talked about another person when she talked about the girl in the portrait. 'I jumped out of this window and, guess what, I lived'—that was her attitude. Being as normal as she was was the extraordinary thing about her, that she was able to separate that time in her life."

It was often said of Edith that even as a young child, there was never anything naive or childlike about her, perhaps because of the burdens and expectations Rebekah imposed upon her; since the possibility of receiving unconditional love from her mother had ceased to exist, Edith could not really be a child. Even the reference to Peter Pan, which she made repeatedly, was suggestive—after all, this childhood fantasy figure was someone who had run away from home to the Neverland, a place for lost children who had "fallen from their perambulators when the nurse was looking the other way"; Peter Pan "had not the slightest desire to have [a mother]. He thought them very overrated persons."

Yet no matter how deep Edith's pain, there was not much point in expressing it. No one could hear her. Even her most desperate pleas were ignored. Rebekah saw Edith's jump from the Westbury penthouse as nothing more than an unfortunate accident, and tried to make everyone else see it the same way. Typically, one newspaper article, headlined FALLS 12 STORIES INTO SNOWBANK—SOCIETY CHILD SURVIVES, focused on Edith's miraculous survival and added that her mother, "said to be one of the richest women in the world, is noted as a composer of light and semi-classical music." Even those close to the family had difficulty finding out exactly what had happened. Edith was instructed to explain the episode as a horrible accident.

"Edith didn't really want to die," says a friend. "She was trying to get her mother's attention." For her efforts, she was confined to a mental hospital. Meanwhile, she conducted herself with an aplomb that her siblings never had, acquiring an astonishing amount of poise as she matured, as if it were essential to her survival that she play-act the role of the perfect daughter her mother wanted. The difference between her and her siblings became even more pronounced with time. At the grand opening of Harkness House, Lee Hoiby, Rebekah's composition teacher, saw an "incredibly beautiful young woman, very intelligent and sophisticated and warm" who approached him looking "like she stepped out of the pages of *Vogue*." It was the first time many of Rebekah's friends had seen her since her fall nearly five years earlier.

"You don't know me," she asked Hoiby, "do you?"

"Edith?" he said. "It can't be."

"She started talking about herself in a very open way, and we got to talking about the jump," Hoiby recalls. "I told her they said that she was reaching for an icicle and fell."

"I know they said that," Edith replied. "But I want people to know that I jumped."

Yet only occasionally did the real rage Edith felt for her mother break through. Then she would scream at Rebekah, "I wish you were dead! I wish you were dead!"

When that happened, Rebekah didn't have the vaguest notion of how to deal with it. "There are parents who are incapable of giving the milk," says one friend of Rebekah's. "There *is* no milk. You can try and try and try. Edith was trying to show that she was a bad mother, but Rebekah didn't want to play that game. She didn't feel the pain of Edith's drama. She felt Edith was very intelligent, much more intelligent than she. But Rebekah had nothing more to give than what she gave."

When a maid called Rebekah in Nassau not long after Terry's wedding and said Edith once again threatened to take her own life, Rebekah was enraged. "Rebekah thought it was in bad taste," continues Rebekah's friend. "The child is not there to remind you that you didn't have milk. You don't jump out the window. She thought it was a lack of basic behavior."

Now, in vowing to kill herself, Edith was making the ultimate demand on her mother. "I'm going to tell her to do it and do it well," said Rebekah. "I've got to call her and tell her how she should do it. How should she do it? Is there a chic way to go? 'This time, don't fuck it up.'"

A
PERFECT
MARK

hen Allen Pierce left the family in 1962, his first stop had been Chicago. He obtained a commer-cial pilot's license, bought a plane, and hired a pilot to fly him and a friend all over the world. He learned to speak Spanish, Russian, French, and German. At five feet eleven inches and close to two hundred pounds, he was overweight but powerfully built, with blond hair and steely blue eyes, and he seemed made for the outdoors. He went on expeditions to South America and Africa. And he counted among his hobbies raising horses, hunting, gun collecting, tropical fish, and photography. When he wasn't traveling, he raised Lipizzaners and show horses in Lake Forest, Illinois, forty miles from Chicago.

Leaving home, however, had not solved his problems. "It was difficult for him to establish genuine friendships," says one friend from Illinois. "As soon as anyone learned how much money Allen had, they became more interested in that than in anything else."

It was not that he was stupid. "He had a very high IQ," says one friend. "But he was emotionally immature." Stripped of the love his Uncle Bill had given him, he now sought to buy affection with the great wealth and material possessions Harkness left behind. He was not particularly good at handling his finances. He would go into a tropical fish store and buy $450 worth of rare fish without thinking. He also went for such high-ticket items as cameras, motorcycles, and cars. "In two years he went through at least half a dozen very expensive luxury cars," says one friend. When he tired of a car after a few months, he got rid of it, often at a considerable loss. Sometimes he just gave them away, even to people he didn't know well.

"I saw my mother giving cars away so I figured that was the way to be," he says.

But he was so improvident, and so boastful about his profligacy, that if was hard to know when to believe him. When a friend allegedly forged a check on Allen's account, Allen was furious—at first. "I was gonna blow his ass away," he says. On second thought, however, he decided not to pursue the matter. "It wasn't for very much," Allen says. "Only six hundred thousand dollars. Big deal."

Allen soon moved to the Max McGraw Wildlife Foundation, in Dundee, Illinois. Forty miles west of Chicago, the 1,350-acre preserve has dozens of artificial lakes and ponds, game farms, rich woodlands and hilltops sloping down to the Fox River. It is populated with deer, raccoons, trout, wild ducks, and 250 species of birds. Allen's close friend was the general manager at the foundation, a former colonel in the OSS named Jack Young Cannon, a man in his mid-forties. "Allen was looking for an older figure he could style himself after," says Cannon's son Kurt.

The Colonel, as Cannon was known, fit the bill perfectly. A powerfully built, extremely physical man, well traveled, multi-lingual, he spent endless hours regaling Allen with stories of his undercover days. "Cannon was a guy who never got over his World War Two experience in the Pacific," says one colleague at the wildlife refuge. Among other exploits, the Colonel boasted that he worked as a hit man breaking up drug traffic in the Far East. "If you had a problem with him, you died," says Allen. "It was that simple. You got shot in the head or chest. Take your pick."

"Most everybody was scared to death of the Colonel," says one employee. "He carried at least two guns on him all of the time—a .45 automatic and a .357 magnum. He was quite a shot. I watched him shoot dogs while all the kids were around. Finally, I said, 'If you hit one of those boys, well, Colonel, if it comes to court, I'm going to tell it the way I see it.' He pulled that gun out, and said, 'You'll tell it the way I tell you to.'" At night he would sometimes go out on his motorcycle with a .243 Winchester to shoot rabbits.

"He really turned Allen down the wrong path," says another employee. "When Allen first came here, he liked kids. But later he said, 'Hell no, I don't want to get married and have no snotty-nosed brats.' That was the Colonel talking. Allen was polite, thoughtful, friendly, and dressed well and kept himself looking good. He didn't have any guns when he came out here. But by the time he left, he had so many he had to catalog them." There were shotguns and rifles, even automatic weapons such as the AR-15.

Allen and the Colonel were so inseparable that they were referred to as Batman and Robin. A number of people suspected the Colonel's motives. "Allen was like a lost sheep around him," says one friend at the refuge. "The Colonel was going to help him spend all his money." When they played cards and back-gammon, the Colonel sometimes cheated. "But when Allen tried the same thing, the Colonel put his guns on the table and said, 'You keep doing that and I'll blow your brains out.'"

"You had to watch your back with the Colonel," Allen says. "He had his good points, but he could be a scumbag."

Ultimately, Allen was hypnotized by the Colonel's thirst for adventure. They went on an expedition to Africa together. "Cannon used to read *Argosy* magazine and believed everything he read about buried treasure," says one acquaintance. "He was going to find it. And Allen was a devoted disciple."

In 1966, at the Colonel's suggestion, Allen bought a Unimog, a four-wheel-drive vehicle made by Mercedes, in preparation for a trip to South America to search for gold. They attached a heavy-duty trailer to the Unimog in hopes that it could be lowered into gullies to get gold out in the backcountry where nobody else could get it. They loaded the trailer with motorcycles and hunting paraphernalia, sent it by ship to Panama, and took off. The other employees at the wildlife refuge were skeptical about the trip, but they were not sorry to see the Colonel go.

"They were leaving," says one colleague, "and that was all I cared about."

Early one morning in Los Esmeraldos, Ecuador, the Colonel woke Allen up with the news that an American had been killed the previous night. The Colonel was scared.

Allen was startled: The Colonel had always talked tough, but now that they were down in Ecuador, he was afraid. "If you're such a big rough-tough guy," Allen said, "you want to be in badlands, don't you? What're you gonna complain about if you're the big rough-tough guerilla, right?" Disgusted and disappointed, Allen bought the Colonel a ticket back to the States and said good-bye. "He was just putting on a big show for me," he explains.

Alone once again, Allen moved to Panama, settling in an upper-middle-class section of Panama City called El Cangrejo, where he launched various business ventures, including an electronics firm, La Companía Panameña de Electrónica; a large-format photo company called Panafilm; and a third company called New World Trading.

But there was not much of a market for large-format photography, and Allen blamed the problems of the other companies on poor management by his business associates—not that he himself had made much progress in handling money since his days in Illinois. "He was always buying camera equipment and funny vehicles—tractors and things like that," says Camilo Quelquejeu, a friend. "But it never really worked. He was more of a collector."

"Every few days he would come in and buy a Hasselblad for two or three thousand dollars," says a local merchant. "He would play with it for a while and then give it away. He had all types of camera and laboratory equipment, but I can't tell you what he did with it."

"You had to wonder why the hell someone with all those resources would go to Panama,' says Edward F. Hutton IV, a stockbroker and descendant of the brokerage house family of E. F. Hutton who met Allen in Panama. "And he didn't have a phone. It didn't add up. He marched to a different drummer. He was like a kid who was always finding something new to devote his attention to: If that's no longer fun, let's try this. He had that adolescent tendency to be interested in one thing at a time, not for terribly long, and whether it was cameras or guns, always to get the best."

"That was his favorite word—'the best,'" says a friend. "When he would get tired of them, he would find new toys. He was like a grown-up kid."

One of his passions was the search for buried treasure. "Whenever he heard about buried treasure, he tried to get together an expedition," says Quelquejeu. But he was surrounded by freeloaders. "People sensed he had money and crowded around him trying to milk him," says Michael Bettsak, who sold him photo equipment.

Allen kept his gun collection at the National Guard headquarters, and frequently went down to the armory and signed out weapons for the day. In addition, he designed and built specially crafted hunting weapons, which he gave as gifts to friends in the Guard. "Weapons were his weakness," says Quelquejeu. "They made him feel powerful. He was close to the military because they would give him his permits for his weapons. They saw him as someone who would buy anything under the sun, so they got along fine. The military and he were having a ball showing off their new toys."

"But they were not toys to him," says Quelquejeu's wife, Charitas. "They were a means to power. There were closets full of guns. They weren't toys. He wasn't playing with them. They were a way of living, a way of life."

In 1968, Allen made elaborate plans for an expedition with his Unimog to traverse the 250 roadless miles of rain forest that separates Panama and Colombia. "Indians have walked through the jungle, but with four wheels no one has ever done it," says Charitas Quelquejeu. "The rivers are terrible, and it is a dangerous proposition."

In the meantime, however, Allen's close friend, Brigadier General Bolivar "Lilo" Vallarino, had been ousted as commander of the National Guard. "Everybody started double-crossing each other, and when Lilo stepped down, then the whole country got mixed up," says Allen. "I figured, what am I going to get involved in this for? I was an innocent bystander. The place got too hot with all the political unrest. The country was falling apart."

He had already been bitterly disappointed by the Colonel. His businesses were failing. Now his friends in the National Guard were in the midst of a major political upheaval. After nearly three years in Central America, Allen had had enough.

"Suddenly, he abandoned his project," says Charitas Quelquejeu. "He abandoned his car, his furniture, his apartment, his maid, his friends. He left everything thrown every which way." It was 1968 and it was time to return to the United States. His first stop was Miami. He had already lost hundreds of thousands of dollars on his expeditions and failed businesses to so-called friends who had mercilessly exploited his trusting disposition.

Highly impressionable, in equal measures bighearted and angry, full of bravado and vulnerability, he made an irresistible target for any con man on the make.

"He was so easy to set up, just like a little kid," says one friend, Raleigh Jordan. "He would have been better off growing up like a junkyard dog, doing all the things you have to do to survive. But he never had those street smarts. Once these con men started, they were all over him like a bag of maggots. It was a feeding frenzy, like throwing five hundred pounds of bloody beef in a shark tank. First they sent the Alpha team after his mother, with their tutus and dancing shoes. Then they sent the Bravo team after Allen."

Allen was not the first person in his family to settle in Florida. Three generations earlier, Standard Oil co-founder Henry M. Flagler had made his presence known in a way that shaped the state for a century to come. In the late 1880s Flagler was fabulously wealthy and had left Standard Oil for other worlds to conquer. He started by transforming the tiny hamlet of St. Augustine, Florida, into a major resort. Then he almost single-handedly turned Palm Beach, a shard of sparsely populated scrubland, into the most elegant society resort in the country, creating a winter home for Astors, Vanderbilts, Goulds, and Harknesses—including William Hale Harkness, who vacationed there when he was a young child. And it was only after Flagler's Florida East Coast Railroad chugged to the southern tip of the state that Miami became a real city. He built and ran the entire town. Even today the name Flagler there conjures up spectacular wealth and power.

Allen's relationship to Flagler was convoluted at best. William Hale Harkness, Allen's stepfather, was Flagler's great-nephew. But Allen's fortune could be traced directly to Flagler's role in the founding of Standard Oil.

Allen's Miami, however, was a far cry from the elegance of Flagler's. It was modern, often garish, on its way to becoming the so-called Casablanca of the Eighties, but not yet mythologized as an international capital for drug smuggling. Allen arrived there with no friends, relatives, or business contacts. He signed a lease on a plush one-bedroom apartment in the Four Ambassadors, a luxury high-rise complex downtown with an ocean view. Like his mother, he awoke each morning at five or six. Much of his day was spent taking photos or shopping for photography equipment and guns. He often went to the local shooting range and on weekends would go hunting for wild boar.

For female companionship, Allen relied on prostitutes. Among his regular haunts were huge, flashy, Miami Beach-style hotels and restaurants. "I was out whoring at night," he says. "These were not cheap pickup places. You wore a coat and tie. You went to make a connection. It was very cozy. You always met a girl, although, shall we say, in a professional category, and you'd make your little arrangement and go. No one ever thought anything of it. I enjoyed it. I'd always meet somebody and have a good time."

In early 1969, he hired the Triple B Security Company to investigate the possibility of importing fish from South America. Nothing came of his queries, but he had another interest with which Triple B might be of more help. "To Allen, being important meant being the guy who stood outside in a uniform with a gun to help and protect," says one friend, "not being an executive or having all that money."

"I wanted a security company to protect myself from evil," Allen says. This need for protection involved fantasies that went back to childhood. He had always thought his family's homes resembled police stations. He wanted to be a cop. Short of that, he would settle for anything in the line of security work.

Triple B Security appeared to be the answer. It was run by Philip Mansfield, then in his late fifties. Born in Russia with the name Manischewitz, Mansfield was given to polyester leisure suits and wore a gold chain with *"l'Chaim"* on it. Of medium height and slight build, he projected an authority and kinetic energy that belied his size. "He didn't weigh more than one hundred thirty," says one retired Miami police officer, "but he talked like three hundred pounds." Largely uneducated, Mansfield took pride in being streetwise, and therein lay the source of his success. "He was arm's-length honest," says one cop. "If you could buy it retail, he could get it wholesale. You had to be pretty good to outmanipulate Phil."

"He reminded me of Sergeant Bilko," says another, referring to the Phil Silvers television character of the fifties. "He was always pulling some scam, figuring out how to get money out of this or that. Always something going on."

From their first encounter, Allen was transfixed. Mansfield knew police talk. Many of his friends and employees were present or retired cops. He claimed to be a retired officer from Chicago and carried a lieutenant's badge as proof, all of which gave him great authority in Allen's eyes. One day he took Allen aside. "There's something I have to tell you about your mother," he said. "I don't know how you're going to take it . . . well, your mother is oversexed."

Allen was stunned. Mansfield seemed to know everything there was to know about him—his adventures in Panama, the Colonel, Rebekah and her dance company, Uncle Bill's drinking habits. Only one other person could have had such connections. By now, Allen had endowed his stepfather with superhuman powers; anyone who remotely filled that void instantly became the object of his complete trust and devotion.

"He was very much like a god," says Allen of Mansfield. "Someone to look up to. When someone knows that much about you, your family, you wonder what's going on. Evidently Mansfield was plugged somehow into the Federal agencies. Or he had good connections in the underworld. He knew that my mother wanted me to change my name to Harkness when Uncle Bill died. If somebody knows *that,* what else do they know? He had damn good information, and I don't know how he knew it. Either our house was wired or he had information from a spy in the sky. I knew then I was going to listen to him and find out what makes him tick."

Not long afterward, Mansfield put Allen in a Triple B uniform and sent him down as a security guard to Little Havana's Trojan Lounge, a raucous, rough bar on Miami's Cuban strip that was a hangout to some of the less desirable elements of what then appeared to be a decaying Cuban community. There were frequent shootings. Guns were confiscated on a regular basis. "Only an idiot would work there," says one former cop who worked at Triple B.

Allen loved it. He was elated at being able to put on a uniform and carry a gun, and saw it as the kind of training you had to have before going on to the police department. He was impressed by the cops hanging around Triple B, by the badges, guns, uniforms, and police paraphernalia.

He drank and spoke Russian with Mansfield. "My husband had studied to be a rabbi," says Mansfield's wife, Mary, "but he was not a particularly religious Jew. Allen hated the Jews. He thought the Jews ran the world. I didn't understand how could he be so anti-Semitic and love Phil so much. He didn't even think of Phil as being Jewish.

"I used to ask Phil, 'Why do you keep him around?' You had to keep Allen busy and tell him what to do almost like he was a child. Phil would put him everywhere to keep him busy. Nobody wanted to work with him."

Anything Allen did, he did to excess. If he went bowling, he would bowl seventeen games. When asked to buy a magazine for Mary Mansfield, he returned with dozens. Occasionally, he would go on and on about having spent time as a child with Onassis on his yacht; he claimed Onassis had covered the yacht's barstools with the skin from a whale's penis. For the most part, no one at Triple B really believed him.

But Mansfield remained attentive and loyal to Allen. "They had a special relationship, and it was a mystery to me," says Berlin Barry "Bert" Bindschadler, who worked with Mansfield for several years and for whom Triple B was named. "Mansfield was very streetwise. He played the emotions. He played the mind. You could make Allen do anything in the world by giving him a pat on the head and saying 'You are the greatest.' He was starved for affection."

Meanwhile, Mansfield had plans. Since leaving Chicago several years earlier, he had been in a number of businesses, the latest of which, Triple B Security, was in and out of financial trouble. He had dreams for others—motels, hotels all the way down to Key West, boats, airplanes, even banks—an empire worth hundreds of millions of dollars.

There was just one thing holding him back—money. But Allen had plenty of that, and would do anything to please his mentor. "Allen thought Phil was perfect," says Mary Mansfield. "He just adored him. He worshiped him in this strange way. He always called him Mr. Mansfield. He took his word as an order. If Phil told him to do something, Allen would do it."

Before long, Mansfield asked Allen to invest in real estate. He said the investments should be made in cash, in small bills no larger than a hundred dollars. Allen, who would come into control of the principal of his trust on his thirtieth birthday, complied without a second thought. "To me, I was just transferring money from one trust to another," he says. "I had never paid much attention to financial matters because I had never had to. Suddenly, I was doing all this for myself."

In the ensuing months, Allen made frequent trips to the Pan American Bank in Miami and the First National Bank of Hialeah. Occasionally Mansfield accompanied him, but usually he went alone. "He would tell me what he needed, and I would go get it for him," Allen says. "Usually, it was fifty to a hundred thousand dollars." The money was put in a bag, stamped, and wrapped in little wrappers. Sometimes Allen went to the drive-in window to pick it up and brought it right back to Mansfield. "We used to stack 'em up. Stacked it up all over the place."

When more of Allen's money came in, Mansfield purchased a the Hurricane Motor Lodge in Marathon in the Florida Keys. At first Allen received a few income checks from Mansfield for his investment, but they soon stopped. "He'd say, 'We need it for this, that, and the other thing,' Allen recalls. "I said fine. I never argue."

On one occasion, Allen balked at the amount Mansfield requested, saying he had put in enough already. Mansfield looked surprised. "Why, that's no money at all," he said. For every dollar Allen invested, he said, there were ten more behind him. He told Allen repeatedly that by the time he was forty-five, he would be worth over $500 million.

"If that's the way it is, I'm not gonna ask any questions," Allen says. After all, he figured, Mansfield was twice as old as he was and must have known what he was doing.

Even after dozens of injections of cash into Mansfield's businesses, Allen never got a lawyer to represent him. Mansfield had given him his word. "I know people whose word's good for any amount of money," says Allen. "Ordinarily you wouldn't need a contract from somebody like that." And Allen's own sense of honor was so great that he would have turned over his entire fortune without giving it a second thought.

By the same token, anyone who soiled that honor did so at his own peril. "Rage came to Allen very easily," says a friend from Panama. "He couldn't control it. There was a volcano behind him."

Allen had been warned about Mansfield. "I was told the people surrounding him were nothing but crooks. Another friend said, 'They don't have any money. They're just looking for a money man.' But when I saw these other people come into his office, from the police, the FBI, I figured this guy's got to be all right because I see police lieutenants keep coming in the door. If there's anything wrong, surely they would know. There was even a photo of him shaking hands with President Roosevelt. I just trusted him."

So for the time being, he cast aside his suspicions. After more than forty trips to the bank, he had given Mansfield more than $2.6 million, and he had absolutely nothing to show for it—not a contract, not a receipt, not even a canceled check. If he found out his trust was being betrayed, however, what happened next was anybody's guess.

"You get me mad," Allen says, "somebody's gonna get hurt. I don't care who it is. I'm automatically on my guard. I automatically figure somebody is going to fuck my ass over. I'm ready. If I have to go get a machine gun, I will get a machine gun. I will take everyone out if I have to. Somebody's gonna go down."

15

THE
DREAM
IS
OVER

hile Allen's need for attention was reaching a dangerous stage, Rebekah's battle with the Old Guard at Watch Hill, where the Wests had held sway for more than forty years, had finally broken into the open. In the summer of 1966, Rebekah took the area at Holiday House that had once been Ben Kean's golf course and built an outdoor stage with an inflatable roof known as "the Bubble." Even before its construction, however, the Bubble had earned the ire of Rebekah's neighbors, who banded together to file suit against it as a zoning violation.

"It was an eyesore," says one neighbor. "They used to start at eight-thirty every day including Sundays, with all this music and coaching, and it was not what you come up here for."

This was no mere zoning squabble. With her dance troupe, Rebekah had effectively made Watch Hill her private kingdom, and many summer residents resented it. Her neighbors were going to pay her back by taking it all the way to the Rhode Island Supreme Court. She responded to her adversaries with contempt. "Isn't it interesting that all those peasants hate me," she told one friend.

The irony was that even the dancers hated the contraption. Its ceiling was so low that a grand jeté was likely to take their heads off. Besides, as the company began to tour year-round, it appeared there would be no more summer workshops and no further need for the Bubble.

Rebekah found an alternative "summer cottage," in Sneden's Landing, where Mike and Lorraine Wallace had a place. A bucolic hamlet just half an hour from New York, Sneden's Landing has been the home of such actors, artists, and writers as Helen Hayes and Charles MacArthur, Ben Hecht, Kurt Weill and Lotte Lenya, Burgess Meredith, Carson McCullers, and *New Yorker* magazine writers Roger Angell and Calvin Tompkins. "The houses are old and beautiful," says Pauline Dora, "but there's not that kind of lavish money and glitzy crowd that Rebekah wanted. It's just a quiet little community."

For $275,000 Rebekah bought actress Katharine Cornell's house overlooking the Hudson. It was hard to imagine that the mansion, with its parquet floor and great stone mantel, had ever been a farm. Its forty-five-foot-long drawing room, once a barn, had a thirty-foot ceiling and pale yellow walls covered with yellow and gray silks and velvets woven to order by Scalamandre in Europe. Two crossbeams supported enormous chandeliers. Cornell and her husband, Guthrie McClintic, the theatrical producer and director, had added an entrance hall, library, kitchen, and two terraces, plus a three-room upstairs suite and a lower suite.

Rebekah made the place even more lavish, importing a painted wooden ceiling from Iran. She installed a fireplace from William Randolph Hearst's estate. She added seventeen adjoining acres to the estate, put in a magnificent swimming pool, enlarged the garage so it could house her blue Rolls-Royce, her lemon yellow Mercedes, and other cars, and then built a forty- by fifty-foot ballet studio.

"She spent millions building it up," says Pauline Dora. "It was totally out of place, absolutely outrageous."

Rebekah left Watch Hill, vowing never to return. To get even with the Old Guard who had chased her out, she spread rumors that she was going to sell Holiday House to any one of a number of inappropriate parties including Martin Luther King, Frank Sinatra, and Alcoholics Anonymous.

Rebekah's whirlwind romance with Bertrand Castelli had ended with his departure from the company in 1967 to launch the musical *Hair*. She now insulated herself with a coterie of younger male admirers, with Bobby Scevers once again at the center. Her increasingly bizarre entourage inevitably included psychics, gurus, and spiritualists, each putting her and her friends through a new set of occult rituals. To add to the intrigue, several of her personal servants traveled with her, and although some of them were relatively selfless and dedicated, many of them fought among themselves for access to their mistress.

Occasionally, Rebekah was still the charming debutante who had come East twenty years earlier. "When she was relaxed and not surrounded by the gang, she was completely different," says her nephew Tarwater. "As soon as the sycophants split, she was great fun. Nothing was better than sitting around sipping gin and tonics."

But more often than not, she was campy, eccentric, capricious. Her age was beginning to show. Her temperament grew increasingly brittle. Her attention span became shorter and shorter. "You never knew which of her you were meeting," says one friend. "All you knew was whichever one it was, she would change." One New York journalist saw her for the first time walking serenely on the beach at Watch Hill and remarked that she was one of the most beautiful women he had ever seen. But when he saw her at a dinner party later that summer, her features were hard and cold. "My God," he said, "don't tell me that's the same woman."

When Castelli left, Rebekah hired Brian Macdonald as the company's third artistic director in as many years. Macdonald soon realized a crucial part of his job was keeping Rebekah happy.

"We could have had an extraordinary American company, but it was impossible to get any continuity of purpose," he says. "One day she would be sweet and caring, and the next day she would talk to you only through her lawyers. We would make decisions together and then the next morning I'd get a memo reversing all the decisions we had just made."

In order to survive in his job, Macdonald had to allow Rebekah to play an active role in the company. That meant chaos. As critic Clive Barnes put it, she had a "whim of iron." Every passing fancy of hers became the order of the day. She backed fashion designers, swamis, musicians, jazz choreographers, all ranging in caliber from serious artists to out-and-out frauds. "The money was there to be taken," says one aide.

With each shift in direction, new people were suddenly in and out of favor. Rebekah hired Joanna Kneeland, a dance teacher with "revolutionary" methods of kinesiology, to head the Harkness House dance school—without firing her more traditionally trained predecessor, Patricia Wilde. That meant two diametrically opposed approaches were pitted against each other, dividing the dance school into two warring camps. She commissioned ballet music from major composers, seemingly oblivious of the fact that it is the choreographer who normally picks the composer for a ballet. Often, at great expense and embarrassment, the composition was paid for, then abandoned when no choreographer showed interest in it.

People came and went so quickly that it became a standing

joke. "I once told her she used people like Kleenex," says a former press aide. "She used them once and threw them away. She had the capacity to make a mess of everything. I remember the stiffness and the rigidity of her back, the fear in her eyes. She was not at ease. The turnover was very high. Every time things started to settle down, she would find new butterflies to chase."

"At heart, she sure as hell meant well," says one administrator at Harkness House. "But she could easily be swayed, especially if you could convince her that people were not acting in her best interests or were making a fool of her. No one wants to be made a fool. No one wants to be taken for granted. Since she was a rather uncertain person, it all came across as sort of an 'off with their heads' attitude."

There was so much intrigue that Harkness House itself was bugged so that Rebekah could listen in on her minions. "After the Castelli period they came in with all the bugging equipment," says one musician. "So we would say things like, 'Mrs. Harkness is such a nice person and does so many lovely things. Isn't it great to have such a wonderful patron? I just pray for her.'"

At the same time, Rebekah held fast to her own artistic ambitions—often to the chagrin of the company. To the embarrassment of several dancers, she had them do a ballet to music she wrote called *Macumba,* in which she actually performed onstage with Alvin Ailey in Barcelona. "It was this tacky, gussied-up, pseudo-Brazilian number that was really terrible," says Larry Rhodes. "Then at some point she got nutty about Spanish and flamenco dancing. It was pretentious to think we should do that. We weren't trained to do flamenco. It didn't make sense." Rebekah took her castanets everywhere, annoying fellow passengers on a transatlantic flight by clacking them ceaselessly, driving her chauffeur crazy to the point where he told her that if she didn't stop, he would. When enough people complained, she broke down and had mink mufflers made for the castanets so she could clack away in quiet.

Rebekah's most ambitious—and problematic—project was a thinly disguised autobiographical ballet called *Cindy*. The Cinderella story of a shop girl who marries a millionaire, the dance kept faltering as she vainly tried to push it into production. There were hints of her experience as a shop girl at Mainbocher and of Bill Harkness, though the male lead role, that of a Texan, was to be played by Bobby. The music was a pastiche of two compositions by Rebekah, *Journey to Love* and *Musical Chairs,* as well as some new music she had written for it. It was all very important to her, but she was too insecure and self-conscious about it to put all her energies into making certain it got a serious production. She proposed it to the company again and again—always halfheartedly. "It was the story of her finding Harkness," says Raymond Wilson. "She used very obvious cowboy music that was so erratic you couldn't tell what was happening. We went stark raving mad trying to put it together. It was a disaster, just pitiful."

The discrepancy between the caliber of the dancers in the company and its choreography widened. All of the principals and many of the soloists were acclaimed as world-class dancers. Yet few disagreed with *Times* critic Clive Barnes when he wrote, "The company seemed to have an unerring instinct for the choreographic bomb, and threw them almost indiscriminately." Barnes gave Brian Macdonald some credit for weeding out many of the real duds, but he felt the Harkness still had a long way to go. Rebekah seethed with anger in the face of such criticism. "She would telephone me and harangue me about my notices and ask me what I had against her," says Barnes. "She thought there was some kind of conspiracy against her, in part organized by Joffrey and in part prompted by the fact that she was rich. She felt very strongly that people resented her riches."

By now, Larry Rhodes, the company's leading principal dancer and a mainstay since its inception, had become the unquestioned leader of the troupe. Since the Harkness rarely surfaced in New York, Rhodes was not nearly so famous as Nureyev or Erik Bruhn, yet Barnes called him "one of the greatest male classical dancers I've ever seen," but he added, "for all his genius, Rhodes did not have a great career."

Rhodes was versatile enough to make his mark playing both

classical and contemporary dramatic roles. "As a young dancer, watching Larry Rhodes was awe-inspiring for me," says Sal Aiello, a Harkness soloist. "He was fabulous, breathtaking, a joy to watch. He had a wonderful, serene quality and an incredible technical facility. He was perfection." In a company with such an unsettled aesthetic identity as the Harkness, Rhodes was a constant, associated in particular with the most contemporary dramatic pieces that managed to survive in such an erratic repertory.

By the time the company neared the end of its European tour in Spoleto, Italy, in the summer of 1968, most of the dancers were fed up with the absence of leadership in the troupe. Macdonald, having taken on the choreography of a Broadway musical, was no longer even traveling with the company; ultimately, he had ceded to Rebekah much of the authority that an artistic director normally would have. "Other directors had fought against [Rebekah's work], but it appeared that Brian was content doing his own work and allowing her to do the rest," says Rhodes. "So she became the director." For the next season, she was enthusiastic about an evening-length three-act ballet about the great Russian dancer Olga Spessivtseva. Many of the dancers thought it sounded awful.

Indeed, the company's best dancers—including the Danish ballerina Lone Isakson, who was later to marry Rhodes, Rhodes himself, and Helgi Tomasson, later of the New York City Ballet—were so upset about the plans for the upcoming season that they were on the verge of accepting offers from other companies. In all, twenty-four dancers—more than half the company—considered a walkout. "Finally, we decided that if twenty-four of us were leaving, maybe we should try to reverse it," says Rhodes. At a meeting in Spoleto they voted to replace Macdonald with Rhodes. If Rebekah refused to accept their decision, they vowed to walk out.

Rhodes's first duty was to inform Rebekah. "I told her the plans she and Brian had made were terrible," he remembers. "They were the reason everyone wanted to leave the company. That was hard for her to swallow." In effect, the dancers had staged a coup directed against her more than against Macdonald.

She had always asserted she would never sit on the sidelines and write the checks. But with so many dancers threatening to quit, she had no choice. On August 5, 1968, it was official: Larry Rhodes, twenty-eight years old, became the new artistic director of the Harkness Ballet. It was an unusual appointment because Rhodes was not a choreographer, and it was rare for a principal dancer to become artistic director of a company. But most importantly, Rhodes had been selected by the dancers themselves, not by Rebekah.

The dancers were elated with the new leadership. So were the critics. The first reviews under Rhodes's directorship came early in the 1969 season, only its second ever in New York, just five months after he had taken over. Clive Barnes began his review with a one-word sentence: "Gorgeous." He went on: "There may be a better word to describe the Harkness Ballet dancing Benjamin Harkarvy's 'Grand Pas Espagnol' at the Music Box last night, but if there is, it does not readily come to mind. Until it does, will you believe—Gorgeous." For the first time, he even ended on a upbeat note about the company's choreography.

But serving as both a principal dancer and artistic director soon proved to be too difficult a task even for Rhodes, and he persuaded Rebekah to hire choreographer Harkarvy, then thirty-eight, as co-director. By the end of the year, Barnes wrote that the Harkness Ballet had survived its difficult rite of passage and was truly on the road to greatness as a dance company. In an article headlined HARKNESS BALLET REACHES DANCE PEAK BECAUSE OF DETERMINED DIRECTOR, he credited Rhodes with the company's success. Of its past, in which Rebekah played such a large role, he wrote, "It had dancers—but then so does Roseland." Now, he said, Rhodes had weeded out the worst of the company's overstuffed repertory and strengthened it with the work of Harkarvy. "Its dancers are superb, rehearsed to within an inch of their glory. They are crisply motivated, and yet it is the tiny marginal freedom of their discipline that truly counts. This has become a company superbly disciplined, yet never regimented." Nor was Barnes the only critic to tout the Harkness's new direction. From *The Wall Street Journal* to the *Village Voice,* dance critics applauded Rhodes and Harkarvy.

There was just one problem with the troupe's newly won success: Rebekah didn't like it. Even though Rhodes was commissioning classical works, she still identified him with the contemporary dramatic pieces she detested. Yet she couldn't bring herself to confront him directly. Chastened by the coup in Spoleto, she had less direct contact with the dance company than ever before. When they were on the road, she kept in touch through a liaison. Even when they were in New York, she attended rehearsals with less and less frequency. She did not like to think her absence was responsible for the troupe's good fortunes, but now that she was just a hands-off patroness, the company was succeeding beyond her wildest dreams.

Meanwhile, the Harkness School of Ballet at Harkness House was producing dozens of fine dancers, and there wasn't nearly enough room for them in the main company. Having lost control of the Harkness Ballet, Rebekah had formed a second company, the Harkness Youth Dancers, in the summer of 1968, under the direction of choreographer Ben Stevenson. It was an ideal outlet for the young dancers trained at the school. Moreover, she and Bobby could participate in it in a way that seemed impossible with the main company so long as Rhodes and Harkarvy were in charge.

None of the artistic directors had ever wanted Bobby in the company, and Larry Rhodes was no exception. "I had no relationship at all with Bobby," says Rhodes. "We knew he was unhappy, but he was not really of the quality to be in there except in a limited way. I didn't want to be in a position where I said, 'No Bobby, you can't choreograph. You can't dance in the company.' So I avoided him entirely."

Nevertheless, since Castelli's departure, Bobby's star had begun to rise, if not in the company, at least in Rebekah's eyes and at Harkness House. "After Castelli, Bobby was given more control than ever before," says one of Rebekah's assistants. "Everybody got a memo saying that all purchases—linen, office supplies, everything—had to be approved by him."

Meanwhile, Bobby did everything he could to undermine Rhodes. "Larry was such a sneaky little thing," Bobby says. "I didn't like him, but he was a wonderful dancer. I couldn't understand why he wanted to be a pseudo-intellectual, suffering, modern-type dancer. I was always telling Rebekah it was her ballet and she should run it however she wanted. She should treat the artistic director like a maid. They should do exactly what she said or be fired."

By now, most of the company viewed Bobby with suspicion. "I worked in a congressional office, and it's exactly the same," says one of Bobby's friends. "There is always someone who is closest to the power, and that was Robert. It would be hard to get near Mrs. Harkness with him there. Robert couldn't touch Larry as far as real talent goes. How would you feel if you knew you could dance rings around this guy and yet had to take orders from him?"

"He was a maneuverer," says Eivind Harum, a rival dancer. "I didn't feel that way until he started gaining power. He was really close to Rebekah, and he started giving her bad advice just to get control of the company. He was the bad apple."

"Everybody dealt with it differently," says Dennis Wayne, a soloist in the company. "Most of the troupe ignored him, but a lot paid homage to him because of his position with Rebekah." Bobby's friends, however, were shunned by the dancers. "I desperately wanted to be with those people," says Raymond Wilson. "But they would ask me, 'Are you a spy?' Are you a spy?' They were always asking me that."

Bobby became one of the stars of the Harkness Youth Dancers, playing lead roles in performances, choreographing, and taking an active part in the junior company's direction. Just months after it was launched, Rebekah sent it to the White House to perform for President Johnson. By 1970 she was so involved with it that she didn't even bother to attend the main company's New York season premiere.

Many attributed her attitude to Scevers. "It was Bobby's influence," says Christopher Aponte, a dancer who was close to him. "He brainwashed Rebekah to think that the Youth company was a much better one. I would see Larry Rhodes and think he was the greatest dancer in the world. Then Bobby would tell me how terrible Larry was, going all over the world spending all her money on ballets she didn't like."

By this time Rebekah often seemed to be either drugged or to have been drinking heavily. She made sure doctors were always there for the company, with special "vitamin" shots that she herself indulged in. She claimed she didn't know what was really in the injections, but took them regularly. Moreover, her fondness for rum become increasingly apparent. Her favorite was "the Pink Drink," a Bacardi cocktail made with rum and grenadine.

All of this made it more and more difficult to deal with her. Increasingly, Rhodes ran into interference from her and Bobby. Much of the time, Rhodes was conciliatory. But when the issue was a work-in-progress called *L'Absence,* he and Harkarvy held their ground. "She said it was too expensive, she hated it, and we should get rid of it," Rhodes recalls. "But Ben and I decided to go ahead, over her objections. We said we believe in this work. In the end, people didn't like it. It was too long, too diffuse. So there was some justification for her saying, 'I told you so.'"

Worse, Rhodes and Harkarvy made public the degree of independence they had from Rebekah. In late 1969, an article in *Dance* magazine said, "Gossip has swirled about her considering the company as little more than a personal toy." The two artistic directors dismissed such rumors, but Harkarvy said *L'Absence* was important partly because Mrs. Harkness "has made it clear that she is less than enthusiastic about it."

Rebekah went through the roof. "She decided right then she didn't want to keep Larry Rhodes because he was such a strong-willed little bastard," says Bobby. "He was hell-bent on defying Rebekah."

Between the two companies and the dance school, Rebekah was losing a fortune. She could not afford all three. Her advisers told her with renewed urgency that she had to stop spending so much money. Meanwhile, she had become increasingly angry. After spending $7 million on the company, she had less control than ever before. She felt she had treated the dancers as if they were her own children, and now they were betraying her. Rhodes and Harkarvy almost automatically turned down any idea she had. They laughed at her behind her back; they sneered at her favorite choreographers. This was not the company she had envisioned.

The dancers, of course, saw it completely differently. The Harkness Ballet had finally achieved unquestioned acceptance as a major company. They had begun their 1970 European tour and were playing Monte Carlo with spectacular success. The hard work, long hours, the enforced intimacy of traveling together, the intense, insular world in which they lived, and the fine reviews made the tour an arduous but heady experience. A powerful sense of camaraderie had developed. The company finally had a stable aesthetic identity. "We were a family," says one soloist. "Morale was high. We were a real unit. For the first time, we were proud of the repertory."

During a rehearsal not long into their Monte Carlo run, soloist Sal Aiello went offstage for a drink of water and saw Renzo Raiss, former ballet master of the Bremen Opera Ballet, hiding behind a column, secretly watching rehearsal. Raiss had studied in Munich, and as director of the American Festival Ballet had choreographed a composition by Rebekah called *Letters from Japan*. In that capacity he had won Rebekah's loyalty.

"What are you doing here?" Aiello asked.

"I'm just passing through town," said Raiss.

Aiello was not sure whether to believe him or not. Most of the dancers were oblivious to Rebekah's dissatisfaction, but Aiello knew it would be just like her to send someone four thousand miles to spy on her own company. He asked Renzo if he wasn't there under secret instructions from Rebekah.

"No, no, no, no, Sal," Raiss said. "Not at all."

Aiello did not pursue the matter any further. But he was not convinced.

A day or so later, on March 26, Jeannot Cerrone, the company's general manager, received a telegram from Milton Kayle, an attorney representing Rebekah. Citing financial pressures, Rebekah, in the midst of the company's greatest success ever, was canceling most of the remaining engagements and ordering the company home. The tour was not nearly over. Performances were scheduled for Paris, London, Switzerland, and Italy.

"It was a total shock," says Rhodes. "I was bitter and upset. She had no real knowledge about how good we were. I knew it wouldn't make any difference what I said to her. So I said, 'Jeannot, you have to do something about this. This is impossible.'"

Cerrone called the entire troupe together after rehearsal and read them the telegram. Everyone was devastated. "The company died with that announcement," says one dancer. "It was like the death of a close friend. It changed the lives of everybody in the company. Nobody had any warning."

Renzo was there to tell the dancers that some of them would be invited to join the Harkness Youth Dancers to form a newly merged company. But that only made things worse. They called him "Renzo the Rat" and chanted "Renzo Raiss, and his advice."

The dancers asked if they could borrow the costumes and continue the tour without salaries. Rebekah said no. A press aide blamed the action on the recent decline in the stock market. "When you have five hundred million dollars," he said, "it bombs hell out of your holdings. It wasn't possible for Mrs. Harkness to support two companies."

When they returned to New York, selected dancers were invited to Rebekah's suite in Harkness House and were asked to join the new company. But they were shell-shocked: Rhodes had been fired. "I had liked her very much," says Aiello. "She was always very nice to me. I think she had an honest concern for us. She cared for us. That's what hurt so much when we were fired. We were basically lined up against the wall and shot."

Dennis Wayne was one of the first dancers to meet with her. When he told her he had sublet his apartment and lent his car to someone in the expectation that the tour would continue, she said she would get him a new apartment and a new car. Then she asked him to join the new company.

"She had fired the best director we ever had," he says. "I didn't want to be a part of it. I said she could shove it up her ass."

In all, Rebekah asked sixteen members of the old company to be members of the new one. All but one refused. Helgi Tomasson joined the New York City Ballet, Rhodes and Lone Isaksen went to the National Ballet of Holland; the rest scattered. A spokesman for the American Guild of Musical Artists said, "It's the most tragic situation that's ever happened in the dance world. The company was built to a success and then dashed on the rocks. Every other company that's failed has failed for lack of money."

The telegram had said that the "structure of the company will be reevaluated upon its return but the company will continue—repeat will continue—as a major group in the ballet world." That, however, was just bravado. The main company was dead. What was now called the Harkness Ballet was really just the Harkness Youth Dancers under a new name. Many members were not yet even real professionals; they were trainees, some of them just sixteen and seventeen years old. Within a few months, Clive Barnes wrote in *The Times* that the Harkness Ballet has "descended beyond the necessity of serious consideration." Rebekah's dream was over. Everybody knew it but her.

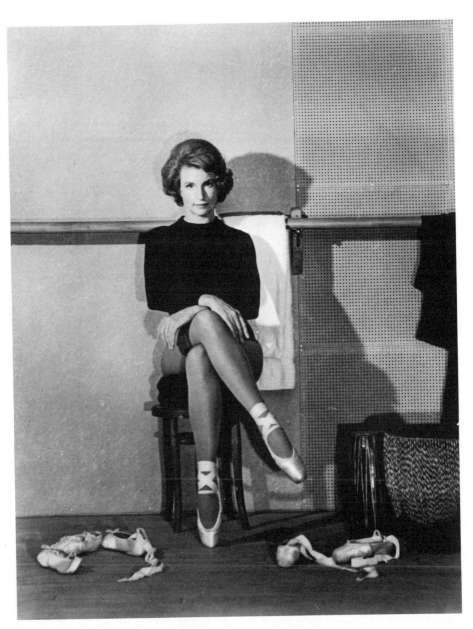

Born again: "Betty" was too simple, too inelegant a name for someone with such
lofty dreams. After Harkness's death, she asked to be called Rebekah.

The new guru: In 1955, Rebekah invited B.K.S. Iyengar to Holiday House for six weeks to teach the family yoga. From left: Edith, Terry, Rebekah, Allen, and Iyengar

Mediterranean cruise: When Grace Kelly wed Prince Rainier, Rebekah took the family with her while she attended the wedding. From left: Mrs. West, Rebekah, Edith, nanny, Allen, and Terry

Far East: In 1959, Rebekah took the family on a tour of Asia. Here she and Allen board the plane to Hua-Hin, Thailand.

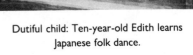

Dutiful child: Ten-year-old Edith learns Japanese folk dance.

Cultural crash course: In each country, Rebekah sought out the best-known music and dance teachers.

Guilt complex: "My mother could not look at Edith without seeing Uncle Bill," says Terry. "But that doesn't mean she treated her any better."

Different from the others: "Edith was the only one to have stature," says a cousin. "She had so much it was heartbreaking. It was in her bones. It was of the blood. She was a Harkness and they were not."

Ben Kean and Rebekah—or Karma, as
he called her—during their 1961
Swiss wedding.

A 1963 painting by
Terry of her mother.
Golf flags suggest the
golf course Rebekah
built for Kean at Watch
Hill, and, at right, is
Kean's ubiquitous cigar.

The Harkness Ballet rehearses on Rebekah's patio overlooking the
ocean at Watch Hill.

Rebekah's Pekingese, Miss Ting, a favorite
of Bobby's, sometimes joined select
members of Rebekah's entourage for
drinks on the Holiday
House terrace.

Now that both Harkness and her father
were dead, the irrepressible Rebekah of
Bitch Pack days returned.

Artistic Director George Skibine, left, had to contend with dance teacher Leon
Fokine, second from left, whose protégé, Bobby Scevers, near right,
had become Rebekah's lover.

In June 1964, Bobby Scevers, twenty-four,
had just been hired to partner Rebekah.
Three months later, they were lovers.

Bobby and Rebekah practicing one of
their favorite routines.

Rudolf Nureyev and Rebekah at a party at her apartment in
the Westbury, 1963. Above them is Salvador Dali's
portrait of Edith.

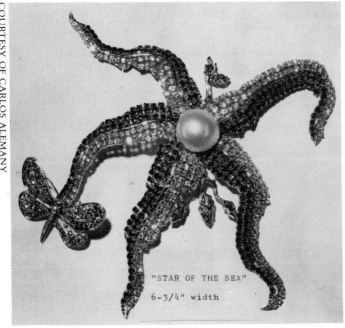

"STAR OF THE SEA"

6-3/4" width

Sometimes referred to
as the "Octopus," the
diamond, ruby, and
emerald "Star of the
Sea" was one of
Rebekah's favorite
pieces in her collection
of jewels designed by
Dali.

Salvador Dali, with his waxed moustache and cane, holding forth with Rebekah and other members of the dance company at the Ritz Hotel in Barcelona in 1966. At far left is Assistant Artistic Director Donald Saddler. Also standing is Artistic Director George Skibine. Seated, at Rebekah's near right, is Brian MacDonald, who later became artistic director.

Rebekah and Ben Kean, center, with Lyndon Johnson at the White House. During one of her visits with the dance company, Johnson invited Rebekah back—alone.

JACK MITCHELL

Now that she had her own company, Rebekah could finally live out the dream her
father had denied her. Here, at the age of fifty-one, she is partnered by
Alvin Ailey in a 1966 performance in Barcelona.

16

SMACK
AND JAB

Bobby had been so vocal in urging Rebekah to regain control of the company that everyone thought he had orchestrated the coup in Monte Carlo. In fact, he hadn't, and he resented being blamed for it. "It's like the days of the kings and the queens," he told a friend. "If you're too close to the throne, they're always going be gunning for you."

To be sure, Rebekah had listened to Bobby more than anyone

else over the past five years. But now she was about to appoint Raiss, the tall, dark choreographer with whom she was infatuated, as the company's new artistic director, and Bobby despised him. "Renzo was just like the other greasy gigolos Rebekah fell for," he says. "They were marvelous salesmen, selling this lovely swampland. And she would buy it. She was gullible for that. She would think, 'At last someone who understands me.' And off they would go and ruin me."

As they were taking a sauna together at Sneden's Landing, Rebekah finally told Bobby she was promoting Renzo.

"Goddamn it," he said, "You are not going to do that to me." With Renzo in charge, Bobby was no more likely to get a spot in the company than before. Rebekah swatted him with a wet bathing suit. Bobby threw her against the wall of the sauna, then put her over his knee and started spanking her. Rebekah bit his leg. When Bobby stormed out and jumped in the pool, Rebekah yelled, "I hope you drown, you son of a bitch!" Then she laughed; she loved these cat fights, she thought he was so attractive when he was mad.

Until recently, Rebekah had been reasonably satisfied with her unusual arrangement with Bobby. Given his sexual preference, it was a source of great satisfaction to her that he had come to care for her. Moreover, she valued his honesty, even if his brand was marked by insensitive, sardonic comments spewed forth at the slightest pretext. "He used to say things to her I couldn't believe," says one friend of his. "He told her off all the time. That's what she liked about him. She knew he was telling the truth, that he was never just another ass-kisser."

For example, Bobby would rail about Rebekah's devotion to Angel. "I had no sympathy," he said. "I thought the whole thing was so absurd. Maybe she thought she had made a mistake earlier with her kids and was trying to repay it through Angel. When they started talking about putting the nursery over my room at Sneden's Landing, I just hit the ceiling. I don't want this screaming baby over my room! The whole thing was a colossal waste of money. Let the little creature die!"

Rebekah had a salty tongue herself, of course, and given the nature of their relationship, such pointed give-and-take came with the turf. She also appreciated Bobby's disregard for the stuffiness of society, but sometimes she cringed when he embarrassed her in company. "She loved Bobby to take her out, because he was very, very tall," says Cappy Pantori, who began working for Rebekah as a hairdresser and companion around 1970. "But she always felt bad because he could be very nasty. She was trying to train Bobby. When he would speak his mind or insult houseguests or say whatever he felt at a dinner party, she would be a little ashamed. She used to always say, 'I'll straighten him out. He's got to learn to talk the right way.'"

When it came to important public receptions, Rebekah often left Bobby home, relying on more sophisticated escorts who were closer to her age. Bobby didn't particularly mind, since he hated going to these kinds of affairs, where no one could remember his name. Instead, he maintained his own circle of friends. He shared his apartment with a teenage dancer, Christopher Aponte, a dancer who was one of his protégés. His friends, including Nikita Talin, were often flown to New York or Nassau. Raymond Wilson came and went as well.

All of which was fine with Rebekah. The only problem was that Bobby had fallen for Aponte. "On Sunday night when Bobby came back from Sneden's Landing he would tell me that he missed me and how happy he was to see me," says Aponte. "He hated having to go away. He would call it having 'to go with the Dog.'"

"Rebekah and I still had an active sexual relationship," says Scevers. "But I could be difficult to deal with when I was madly in love with someone. I really wanted to be with Chris. But I knew that anything in my personal life had to be secondary to Rebekah. And I would grumble about having to sleep with her, 'Oh, I can't come over tonight; I'm working.'"

Even if such acid comments escaped Rebekah's ears, she was not immune to Bobby's neglect. In Nassau, she complained that her own sexual appetites had inexplicably waned, and, deciding there must have been foul play behind it, she sent a batch of her favorite drink to a lab for chemical analysis. "When the results came back, she said it was spiked with saltpeter," says a guest who was there. It could only have been Bobby, she thought.

At the same time, Rebekah saw Bobby spending more and more time with Joy O'Neill, a dancer-choreographer who was working at Harkness House. Rebekah had composed music for a ballet based on the life of Helen Keller, and Joy did the choreography for it. But it was Joy's purported psychic powers and reading of tarot cards that had won her entrée to the inner circle of friends Rebekah brought to Sneden's Landing and Nassau.

As Renzo began organizing the latest version of the Harkness Ballet, Bobby went off to Europe, with plans for Rebekah to join him there later. "Renzo was clever enough to get Rebekah's close friends out of the way," says Bobby. "So he proceeded to plant all these lies—that Joy was a woman of the night and that she and I were having an affair."

Any suggestion that Bobby was seeing another woman made Rebekah furious, but it was pointless to have a showdown— Bobby would deny everything. Instead, before going to Europe, Rebekah, accompanied by her chauffeur and security chief, Joe Pantori, secretly broke into Bobby's apartment in Manhattan. "She told Joe to pack Bobby's clothes, and change the locks, and do this and do that," says a housekeeper. "Bobby had about twelve very, very expensive bathrobes that cost hundreds of dollars, shirts, pants, every kind of charge card you could imagine. She took everything."

Rebekah arrived in Europe icy and remote, and did not tell Bobby what she had done. "We had always stayed together," says Bobby. "But this time she had gotten an apartment and made me pay my own hotel bill, and she was never available."

When they finally had it out, Bobby denied everything. "None of it was true," he says. "Joy and I were together all the time—talk, talk, talk, talk, but that's all. We were just sisters under the skin. We gabbed and shrieked and read cards. That was it."

But he could not convince Rebekah. For more than nine months, he stayed with friends, and Rebekah refused to speak to him.

Rebekah's grudges may have been impetuous and irrational, but she did not hold them forever. In 1970, before Christmas, she not only gave him back his apartment, she also gave him a Mercedes. Yet she was still suspicious. When Bobby returned from an out-of-town dance tour a few weeks later, Rebekah had heard that some dark-haired woman was staying in his apartment. "She assumed it was Joy and we had started up again," he says. "But I had just let a woman friend stay in my apartment to water the plants."

Again, Rebekah didn't believe him. She had heard rumors that he had been taking her fine silver. "I had found a way to open the silver cabinet, and I put some of Rebekah's silver in my room," says Bobby, who was sometimes enamored with Rebekah's frills. "But I told everybody about it. One day I came home and [Rebekah's maid] said don't worry, that the workmen had left brown dust all over. But they had really hired some people to fingerprint my room and the silver cabinet. They were trying to put it on me. I didn't want to sell it. Things got so bad I was told I had to leave."

This time it was over for good. Rebekah dismissed him from his job teaching at Harkness House. She had her lawyer demand back not just $100,000 she had loaned him, but everything his investments had earned. She even evicted his friend Joy, who had been living in her own apartment—which Rebekah also subsidized.

"I was so naive," says Bobby. "Her lawyer tricked me into signing the apartment back to her. Lots of times Rebekah hurt me, and any relationship must be full of that," he says. "But this was devastating to me. It was like one of those Italian courts or Louis XIV. Everybody was sneaking around. It was embarrassing, scary. Here I am strung out like that with no backup, no reserves in both my emotional and professional lives."

Rebekah gave the apartment to Angel and Miss Weeks. It would serve Bobby right, she reasoned, to see that she considered this paralyzed, hopelessly damaged child a better bet than he. That, she knew, was something he could never understand. "It was such a beautiful apartment," he recalls. "It had pressed velvet on the walls. It was like Versailles, a baby Versailles. Oh, it was beautiful." As he arranged to go to Chicago to work in a small dance company, his life in tatters, he surveyed the damage to the magnificent world he had created for himself. They had taken over his apartment and torn down the velvet. They made it look exactly like "the inside of a pressure cooker. "That way," he says, "Angel, being nothing more than a vegetable, could be right at home."

Those who saw Bobby as insensitive, self-serving, and ambitious were delighted that he was out of the picture. But whatever one thought of him, he had served as Rebekah's lover and aide-de-camp for six years. He had acted as a pivotal figure in her life and in determining who had standing with her. It was a role that Renzo Raiss had no intention of filling. Without Bobby, there was a vacuum at the center of Rebekah's world, at a time when Rebekah was particularly vulnerable. By now, her inflated fantasies, held together by her fortune, had metastasized to the point where they were beyond her control. Anyone with even a modicum of talent or integrity saw that the egregious errors she consistently made were destroying her dance empire.

Increasingly, she relied instead on people who could be enslaved by her money. Her dismissal of Bobby was typical, not an aberration. "She constantly used people," says one housekeeper. "She'd wine and dine them and spoil them so much that they got used to it. Everyone was looking for a little nest egg, one way or the other. They were always looking to feather their nest. She had them on call—demand, demand, demand. And after she was through with them and she got tired of their stories, she found a new toy—another person. They were out, and the next one was in. That's the way she operated."

"The power she had from her wealth frightened her," says a dance teacher at Harkness House. "She would be totally contradictory. One minute she would be contemptuous of that power. Then she would say, 'Everybody has got their price, and if you can pay that price you get what you want. That's when money is useful.'"

As each person came and went, Rebekah became increasingly

erratic. "She became the image that would satisfy the most profound dreams of those around her," says one relative. "There was a crazy, kinky, spur-of-the-moment sense that at any time, she was going to drop a Rolls-Royce on you or send your kid through college or whatever. And because of the unpredictability of her nature, things happened very quickly and everyone was very tense and on edge. The experience of her was obliterated by the steamroller effect of whatever was going to happen next."

By 1971 Rebekah was imprisoned by the realm she supposedly ruled, a dominion as extensive and Byzantine as any royal court. She maintained lavish residences in New York, the Bahamas, Sneden's Landing, and Gstaad, any one of which might employ up to a dozen people, including caretakers, gardeners, handymen, house cleaners, security guards, and cooks. The number of people she had to deal with both professionally and socially had grown exponentially. The war for her affections was out of control. No longer was it possible for her to pursue her own dream; she had become the object for everyone else to pursue, and she hated it.

One reason she was less in command was her use of drugs and alcohol. In the late sixties, hoping to keep the dance company in good spirits, she brought in John Bishop, a physician to many show business personalities and an advocate of vitamin shots. This was a period during which several doctors, including the much-publicized Max Jacobson, administered "special" injections to countless society patients and celebrities. Jacobson's unusual medical practice was exposed in 1972 in *The New York Times* when one of his patients died of acute amphetamine poisoning. But in the sixties his most celebrated patients included President Kennedy, who received injections during the 1961 summit meeting in Vienna with Nikita Khrushchev, and the First Lady. Among the other luminaries who frequented his office were Truman Capote, Tennessee Williams, Cecil B. DeMille, Eddie Fisher, Otto Preminger, Anthony Quinn, Alan Jay Lerner, and more than a hundred major figures in government, finance, society, and show business.

Bishop was considered the most avant-garde of this group of

doctors. Others treated jet-setters and socialites, but his clientele consisted of underground filmmakers, the cast of *Hair,* and Timothy Leary. His office was decorated with huge abstract paintings and included a sauna for the use of patients. In the waiting room live music was often provided by a live guitarist, and many patients said they often met there, smoked marijuana, and discussed pop philosophy.

In an interview in *The New York Times,* Bishop acknowledged that he had become linked with the other doctors in the minds of many people, some who saw both him and Jacobson for injections in the same day. But he denied that he ever gave amphetamines "the way Jacobson did." He added, "It's possible to give people good feelings with vitamins—niacin, for example, without using amphetamines."

In any case Bishop was available to the entire dance company at Rebekah's expense. "He used to have parties at his home," says dancer Dennis Wayne. "And we had champagne and injections, and it was fantastic." At times, a nurse would be brought around to give shots before the dancers went onstage. On tour many of them used the shots for recreational purposes after a performance. "It was the greatest thing invented by medicine," says Wayne. "Mrs. Harkness used to send us on the road with it. I used to play doctor and smack and jab, smack and jab."

Not everyone reacted so benignly to the injections. Raymond Wilson couldn't sleep for days after receiving one. At least four or five dancers had severe anxiety reactions. "I was told we were taking Vitamin B-12 shots," says dancer Sal Aiello. "I mean, I didn't even know what speed was. I used to think that I could jump and jump and never come down. It was incredible. After a lot of performances, I remember just crying. I never knew why. I thought it was just because we were so tired."

One patient of Bishop's told *The New York Times* he experienced severe withdrawal symptoms when he was unable to get the injections. "The crashing process is pretty bad—nausea, chills, sweating, headache, anxiety, a feeling of total despair. It's a matter of physical exhaustion. Sometimes you've stayed up three or four or five days."

Whatever was actually in the shots, some of Rebekah's dancers did suspect they contained amphetamines. "Bishop experimented on big guys like myself," says Eivind Harum. "He would give us twenty cc's consisting of speed with vitamins." Others were told the injection "consisted of serums from pregnant cows and vitamins and minerals."

Rebekah herself didn't really know what was in the shots either, but she adored them. Composer Stanley Hollingsworth, one of her teachers, got an injection and spent the whole day furiously cleaning windows, then tried to convince Rebekah the shots contained speed. But she refused to listen. "She couldn't recommend them highly enough," says her nephew Tarwater.

"She was always searching for perpetual youth," says one member of the entourage. "She was constantly jabbing herself in the ass with whatever drug she could find." She was fascinated by medicine, and usually made sure that a doctor was part of her entourage. Sometimes she carried a black bag full of drugs herself, including esoteric ones not approved in this country. To strengthen herself as a dancer, during this period, she began injections of testosterone, a male hormone. Her voice dropped an octave, to a husky tenor. Her musculature began to change. "She told me never to try it," says Cappy Pantori, "because it made her voice raspy and gave her a masculine build. She took so much stuff, I wouldn't even remember half of them. She took a lot of other things the FDA didn't pass here. She tried the stomach of a goat to keep you younger, and so much garbage. No matter what they told her, she tried it."

By the early seventies, when Rebekah was afflicted with arthritis and hip problems, she began taking regular injections of Talwin, a powerful painkiller sometimes compared to morphine and used as preoperative medication and as a supplement to surgical anesthesia. Capable of inducing euphoria, dizziness, and drowsiness, Talwin can lead to physical and psychological dependence in some patients. "She was using it very, very heavily when I first went there," says Cappy. "I never saw anything like it—I'd see blood on the sheets and blood on the bathroom rug. There were splatters of blood all over the bathroom floor.

233

"She was always drugged. She knew what she was doing. She took pills to wake up, Seconal to go to sleep—like Judy Garland and everybody else. At first she could handle it, but then, when she was depressed, she would take it like it was going out of style, and it did her no good, and she kept giving herself more and more. And every time the tension got greater, she'd take more shots."

Rebekah shot up Talwin so much that her muscles calcified at the injection sites in her upper thighs, necessitating painful surgery. When she was taking drugs and drinking, she frequently passed out and often slept past noon the following day. But attempts by the household staff to help curb her drug use met with little success. "I used to get nervous that she wouldn't wake up in the morning, so I used to hide her medicine," says Cappy. "She'd ask me to help her that way. But the next day she'd have second thoughts. She was her own person—you couldn't tell her what to do. And she'd go to the doctor and would get a Percodan or something. And she'd just hoard it. She was a hoarder of medicine. I don't know who prescribed it initially, but she got it from the drugstores. Half the time they didn't even need a prescription at the drugstore, because they were glad to have her business. When you have that kind of money and you want something from the drugstore, you get it."

Initially, Rebekah tried to hide her habit, but over the years she became increasingly lax. "She left needles in her bathroom, all over," says Cappy. "You'd go in to pick up something, you'd get stuck with needles. If she was in the lady's room at a restaurant, she was so scared of getting caught that the minute she finished injecting herself she would put the needles back down into the bag. And when you cleaned out her evening bag, never thinking an open needle was there, you'd get stuck. This happened constantly. Pascale was stuck so many times. We never knew about AIDS then. But if we had, we would have run."

If she didn't get her requisite dose, she took it out on those around her. "It was the end of the world, if we were to forget her earplugs or her eyeshield," says Cappy. "Life would stop.

And it was like you were going to your execution, because she'd get so nasty."

Rebekah, once so disciplined and rigidly bound to her schedule, began to sleep late in a drug-induced stupor. The events in Monte Carlo had changed everything. "Bringing them back from Monte Carlo was the worst decision she ever made—that was the turning point," says Tarwater. "From there it was all downhill." Occasionally she deluded herself into believing in the new dance company, but she often retreated into drugs instead. "She was on drug weather, cellophane-wrapped into her own cellophane world," he adds.

Bobby's most recent dismissal meant that the entourage he once dominated was now in flux. A new team took over. Among them were Terry's friend M'liss Crotty, who was hired as Rebekah's social secretary, and Maria New, Angel's pediatric endocrinologist. Miss Weeks and Angel, now ensconced in what had been Bobby's apartment, often traveled with Rebekah to Sneden's Landing and Nassau.

Rebekah had come to depend on her servants far more than ever before. She used to talk to her chauffeur, Joe Pantori, Cappy's husband, for as long as two hours every night. "She had nothing better to do than to talk to Joe," says Cappy. "It was as though she didn't have any family at all, any friends."

What friends and relatives she had saw Rebekah as increasingly insulated by her servants, and they resented it. And it was not just that the two groups were at war with each other. Among themselves, the servants vied for control. "I was the closest of them all," says Pascale Olave-Uriarte, who had become Rebekah's personal maid after being hired away from the Ritz Hotel. "Of all the little workers, I alone talked to Madame. It was only me she wanted to see. She would have been bored talking to all the personnel, so she told me to hire those you need to keep the house in order. Madame fled everyone all the time. She would go in her dance studio, her sauna, so that no one could see her or bother her, so we left her alone."

Access to Rebekah could only be attained by catering to the

various powers in the new coterie that surrounded her. "Mrs. Harkness would promise things without knowing what she was really doing," explains Cappy. "The next day she would be flying with a drink or two—and if she wanted to renege, she'd say, 'Well, talk to Joe.' She put Joe in the middle, and it made me sick. Joe was hated completely all the time, because he used to have to be the heavy and say no."

The servants fought among themselves, hoping to get closer to Rebekah. Joe and Cappy Pantori were pitted against their own brother-in-law, Carmine Pontillo, who was Rebekah's chauffeur until he was succeeded by Joe after a bitter battle. Pascale was also at war with the Pantoris. "They were bad," she says. "Jealous of everybody. You cannot fight those kind of people. They were saying things against me. They wanted to be masters of everything."

"The name of the game was divide and conquer," says Tarwater. "It was almost impossible to communicate with [Rebekah] without going through this coterie. Anyone who got close would hold on as long as they could. The intrigue you could cut with a knife. It was not the kind where certain people had an absolute position of authority based on defined objectives. Instead, people came and went. Heads rolled. It was never clear who was in command, and those close to power were always terrified."

Rebekah played them all off against each other, writing each of them in and out of her will, making promises she often withdrew. "Whatever she said caused earthquakes or delusions of Nirvana," says Tarwater. "It caused frantic scurrying of the minions who wished to control and dominate her." Various servants were accused of theft. Thousands of dollars' worth of luxurious Porthault linen were mysteriously billed to her; one of her servants apparently shipped them to a relative who had a linen store in Europe.

It was difficult to know what was true and what wasn't—not that it seemed to matter anymore. "For twenty-five thousand dollars a year, a fortune in those days for a personal chef, she hired a very elegant French chef," says Tarwater. "It was a real coup to get him. But each time he brought out a magnificent meal, she was so drugged that she ate none of it. Instead, she asked very politely if he could bring some soup, and she gave him instructions on how to heat up a can of Campbell's."

On his own time, the chef was allowed to cook whatever he wanted. But his magnificent meals were just for the servants. Rebekah wanted none of it—just Campbell's soup and an occasional tubful of Kentucky Fried Chicken. Exasperated, the chef resolved to get back at her. According to Tarwater, when she asked for a can of soup, the chef would sometimes urinate in it before heating it up. Rebekah didn't seem to notice until she finally caught him in the act. Even then, she didn't fire him. "She just hired a Pinkerton and told him to shoot if the chef pissed in the soup again," says Tarwater. "Those were the stories you heard. Even if they are not entirely true, that is the way things were."

For all the drugs she took, Rebekah did not give up on her dream. When Renzo Raiss left the dance company in 1972, she took over the reins herself. The troupe toured Europe and got good reviews, though it shied away from New York. At the same time, financial cutbacks began in earnest at Harkness House.

In November 1973, Rebekah agreed to perform a Spanish dance at a benefit for the Alvin Ailey Dance Theater. She had studied Spanish dancing for five years and was scheduled to perform a flamenco dance with Roberto Lorca, but at age fifty-eight, after years of heavy alcohol and drug abuse, she was terrified of appearing in public, especially before an audience of celebrities. In the wings waiting to go on that night, she stood anxiously in front a spotlight. The heat from the light bore down on her. "Cappy," she said, "my ass is on fire."

Rebekah was closer to the onstage microphone than she realized, and her words went out to the entire audience. Dustin Hoffman, one of the masters of ceremonies, introduced her. "Mrs. Harkness is here," he began, "and she says her ass is on fire."

"When she came out, she was frozen," says a friend who was

there. "She was petrified, like petrified wood, and the stare—it was like she didn't know what to do. Finally somebody in the audience screamed out, '*Olé!*'"

The dance began. "Seeing her dance was one of the saddest experiences I've ever had," says one member of the audience . . . "to see this pale, haunted, stiff figure who couldn't move, who was too controlled."

Some compared Rebekah to Florence Foster Jenkins, a wealthy socialite who promenaded across on the New York concert stage in the 1940s and unwittingly became a hilarious camp spectacle. Jenkins's soprano was so ludicrous that audiences doubled over in laughter, and cruelly called her back for encores so they could hoot through the final rendition. As a composer, Rebekah had always been able to fool herself about her talents, but it was a secret that only her music teachers really knew. But now the distance between reality and her dreams of artistic glory was exacting a psychic cost that thousands of people could see.

"She was a tragic figure, stiff and pained," says a spectator. "I knew what the effort must be costing her. She held herself so tightly, she had no access to expression. Your heart went out to her. It was painful. I was crying."

17

DOCTOR
LOVE

*I*t had been almost a decade since Terry had been introduced to society on the Circle Line cruise in 1962. In the intervening years, her marriage to Tony McBride had ended in divorce. Now Rebekah wanted to help her start over. She called on her friend Maria New.

"I'm going to give her a blast," Rebekah told Maria. "I want young people there. Can you get any young doctors there?"

Maria asked the chief resident at New York Hospital to invite several young single male doctors to the party. Among them was a thirty-three-year-old Danish gynecologist named Niels Lauersen. Handsome, curly-haired, and tall, Lauersen cut a striking figure. He would later become a minor celebrity by writing popular books on gynecology, appearing on television talk shows, showing up in gossip columns linking him to actress Liv Ullmann.

When Lauersen arrived at the Westbury for the party, Rebekah was instantly impressed. Just five years older than Terry, the young doctor seemed a likely enough prospect. But it was not Terry who was entranced with Lauersen. It was Rebekah.

From the beginning, Lauersen's courtship of Rebekah caused a stir. Rebekah, fifty-seven, had once again picked a man who was much younger than she. She was now drinking so heavily and was so deeply involved with drugs that she didn't know where to turn. Desperately lonely, wide open to flattery, she had become the perfect victim: the highly impressionable, vulnerable millionairess.

"She used to hate to have dinner alone," says Cappy Pantori. "The cocktail hour was her very bad time of the day. She had to have someone to talk to. If I wanted to go home at six or seven o'clock, it was very hard for me to leave her. She would keep you talking until the company would come. She couldn't stand to be alone."

Often when Rebekah was depressed—several times a day—she phoned Frank Andrews, a man in his thirties who reportedly read palms and tarot cards for Yoko Ono, Christina Ford, and Princess Grace. Frequently, she was desolate. "Lie to me," she told him. "Tell me somebody loves me."

"Rebekah would call me at two or three in the morning crying, and I had to go over there and pick her up in her own vomit," Andrews says. "I used to find big hypodermic needles. She would call me four or five times a day. She desperately needed someone to hang on to."

But she had no idea who that should be. In a reading with

Andrews, she reflected on her dilemma. "I don't know who I can trust, I don't know who I can trust," she said.

"It's almost impossible to escape people taking from you," said Andrews.

"I know it. I know it."

"It's like your plague. You'll just have to accept it to some degree."

"I do sometimes. It depends on what they take. Sometimes I think I'm overly suspicious, paranoid. But then sometimes I'm right."

More often than not, however, Rebekah was wrong. "She was a bad judge of character," says Andrews. "She picked the worst. She had a hard time saying no. I realized I wasn't helping her. If I am talking to her every day, then I'm like a psychiatrist, and that is not my goal in life. She became so dependent on me, everybody in the entourage hated me. They thought I was a Rasputin. But I didn't need her—I had Princess Grace as a client."

Despite the disapproval of family and friends, Rebekah determinedly pursued Lauersen. In the beginning, she was the aggressor. If Terry minded her mother's sexual competitiveness, she didn't articulate her grievances. "Terry was not particularly angry," says a friend. "But she was amused and a little horrified at the idea of her mother and Niels."

Even Maria New, who inadvertently had introduced the two, did not think highly of the match. "I had never met Lauersen," she says. "How did I know he would turn out to be the kind of person he is?"

Meanwhile, Rebekah began her most ambitious dance project to date. In early 1972, she paid $1,500,000 for the old Colonial Theater on Broadway near Sixty-second Street with the intention of making it into the most elegant dance theater in the country. Just across from Lincoln Center, the Harkness Theater, as it was renamed, would enable her to go head-to-head against the dance establishment.

Inspired by the Kirov Theater in Leningrad, Rebekah pumped $5 million into the renovation. Black *negro marquina* marble was shipped in from Granada, Spain, to line the foyer. The front doors were of specially made ironwork and, like the plaster moldings, were decorated with extensive gold leaf. Sixteen crystal chandeliers hung from the ceiling. The stage had absorption units beneath the floor to give it special resiliency, making it one of the best dance floors in the world. Finally, Rebekah had 1,277 hand-carved Louis XIV chairs made in Valencia, Spain, and upholstered in velvet in her own color, Harkness blue. Much as she had once disdained the pretensions of society, having her own color—even though some said it was never the same shade of blue—had become a trademark of hers as much as a royal coat of arms.

One of her key advisers throughout the planning stage was Lauersen. "She was willing to listen to anything he said with great attentiveness," says one of her attorneys. On Lauersen's advice, Rebekah engaged a Spanish artist named Enrique Senis-Oliver, at a cost of $200,000, to paint a 120-square-yard mural, *Homage to Terpsichore,* on the stage's proscenium arch. Despite the fact that he had touted Senis, as opening day for the theater approached it became painfully apparent to insiders that the artist was having trouble executing the masterwork.

"I got a call from a staff member asking me sort of apologetically if I could take nude photographs of some of the dancers," says Michael Avedon. As Senis sat in the studio drinking beer, a male and female dancer posed naked on a glass platform so Avedon could photograph them from below. He made fifteen hundred prints of his work. "Senis used my photos either through tracing or projection to finish the mural. It was like painting by numbers," says Avedon. On the mural, a hand-lettered sign in the corner modestly noted that the completion time for painting was three thousand hours—many of which were spent by Senis on his back.

There were other problems as well. The theater was perfect for a medium-size dance company, but it was barely big enough to be able to pay off its high overhead even if it sold out. When costs increased, it became virtually impossible for it to be financially viable. But Rebekah rejected all advice that she abandon it.

"She was very determined, opinionated, and strong-willed," says an attorney who advised her on the undertaking. "She was so headstrong. Regardless of what was told her, she was going to do it."

Indeed, Rebekah was more completely committed to the theater than to anything since the launching of the dance company nearly ten years earlier. She spared no expense. She looked over every detail. One night, she and Maria New donned wigs and went down to the theater to check the progress without being recognized. The theater would be her ultimate monument to herself, her retort to the dance establishment and critics who had spurned her.

Since the grand opening would be her first great public event with Lauersen, Rebekah had still another face-lift. Cappy stayed by her bedside in the hospital. "She needed more drugs than they were willing to give her to put her out," says Cappy. "She would not take any pain. She said, 'Why should I have any pain when there's drugs? Just put me to sleep, and let me sleep for three or four days.'" She was released from the hospital more deeply addicted to Talwin than ever before.

Then she prepared for the April 9, 1974, opening of the theater, an evening two years in the making. Rebekah was to be accompanied by guests of honor Betty and Susan Ford, but she was upset because Lady Bird Johnson and her daughters could not come. Tickets were $150 each. The most important figures in dance were to attend—George Balanchine and Lincoln Kirstein of the New York City Ballet, Lucia Chase and Oliver Smith of the American Ballet Theatre, Alvin Ailey, Bob Joffrey, and Rudolf Nureyev. Rebekah also invited the same segment of society she had always sneered at—Angier Biddle Duke, various Vanderbilts, Prince Egon von und zu Furstenberg, and other assorted nobility. Rebekah wore a white gown with white mink trim and a tiara designed by Dali with a string of diamonds dripping down her forehead. The sedate society matron who was once married to William Hale Harkness was now making a spectacularly garish display of her riches.

Rebekah's nephew Tarwater appeared at her apartment a few

hours before the opening. He was battling his own drinking problem and had sworn he would abstain that evening. Nevertheless, Tarwater arrived "with only three and a half quarts of beer in me," he says. "I probably had some coke, some tranquilizers, and two doubles on the way over—nothing very heavy, you understand, just enough to even things out. Finally, like the trembling of the gods of Valhalla, she came sweeping down the stairs.

"There was a whole hierarchy of who got into the limo with Rebekah. Carnations were worn to identify us as family. We drove over in separate cars and met at the theater. It was *the night*. Geoffrey Holder looked spectacular. Alvin Ailey was there. Andy Warhol arrived wearing blue jeans, tennis shoes, and a tuxedo top, and they wouldn't let him in.

"At the theater, the gigolos and the entourage were all dressed up by the same tailor, wearing eight-hundred-dollar tuxes, double-breasted, midnight blue, cut by the same hand, and I had an After Six job and felt really third-rate. And they had that ghastly painting. You could tell all [the artist] had done was project slides onto a canvas and copy them. There were so many limos downstairs, and a vapor of alcohol pervaded the whole thing. On [Rebekah's] right was Betty Ford, Rudolf Nureyev, Monique van Vooren, and me.

"Rebekah was drinking this pink Bacardi garbage. Bacardi had run out of it, and someone at the factory told her we can't give you just one bottle, we have to make a run of at least twenty thousand or two thousand bottles or whatever. So Bacardi gave it one day's run, and she had thousands of bottles. Since then, this pink Bacardi cocktail was her favorite, and people were looked on rather favorably if they chose this peculiar garbage drink. It was awful, but I liked it. It was a quick route, reddish violet, the most expensive sneaky Pete wine there is. So I was the pink Bacardi gofer, carrying the flask for Rebekah. I took it to the chauffeur, who filled it up, but by the time I got to them, I had drunk so much of it myself that I had to go back for a refill."

At intermission, at one of the first performances, Rebekah snuck off to the bathroom. "She was straight at the beginning of the night," says Cappy. "but she must have given herself one or two shots when I wasn't with her. She had this long gown and she must have hit a vein in her leg, and the blood came streaming down all over the back of her shoe, and it stained the satin shoe, and the dress. She had blood running down her leg. I had to walk her back covering her with my shawl, and put her in the bathroom and lock the door. Meanwhile, they had had the bright idea that somebody might steal the gold-plated faucets in the theater, so opening night they took all the faucets off, and you couldn't run the water. It was so sick. I had to tell the maid not to let anyone in, and everybody was knocking, and here I was with toilet paper, trying to clean her shoe. I was so embarrassed for her."

After the opening-night performance Rebekah went backstage to congratulate the dancers. "She came back to my dressing room," says one of the soloists, "and she said how proud she was of me. Then she fell. It was really embarrassing. She just fell. And she got up and started walking up the steps. And she fell several times. I excused it. I thought, well, she's celebrating."

But there was not much to celebrate. In *The New York Times*, Rebekah's nemesis, Clive Barnes, could not fail to note that what was happening offstage was far more interesting than what was taking place onstage. He savaged the troupe's choreography in several separate reviews during it's two-week stand, and said the theater was too hot, had poor sight lines, mediocre acoustics, and a claustrophobically tiny lobby. "Getting to know a new theater is rather like getting to know a ship on its maiden voyage," he wrote. "The first night out might tell you something—especially about the quality of the champagne and the garishness of the fittings, but it is only when you are well out to sea that you learn about the menu, the heat of the cabins and, occasionally, that the name on the lifebelt is the *S.S. Titanic*."

The dancers themselves were given excellent reviews, but the repertory, Barnes said, was "extraordinarily weak." He added, "I am reminded of a colleague, years ago in London, who, during a sad performance, startled the woman in front of him by tapping her on the shoulder and saying in a penetrating whisper:

'Excuse me, madam, would you mind replacing your hat? I can see.'"

In retaliation, Rebekah got Senis to dash off a caricature of a nude, overweight Barnes in toe shoes on the sinking *Titanic,* which she immediately hung in the theater's lobby. But Barnes's review was by no means the most vicious. *Time* magazine compared Rebekah's shrine to the Wagnerian theater that Mad King Ludwig paid for, adding that "One can only sorrow that so much love, money and care was expended to such little result." *New York* magazine compared the "garish bordello of a dance theater" to a "Staten Island beauty parlor." *Dance* magazine said the theater looked like "a lavish ladies' powder room."

And everywhere, Senis's painting came in for the most brutal criticism of all. *Newsweek* called it "the ugliest mural ever painted." Noting that one should not ridicule any theater designed for dance, *Dance* nonetheless asserted that Senis's work

> gives the word vulgarity a whole new meaning. Done in the Daliesque vein, it is redolent with that sort of come-hither nudity that porno magazines have thrived on for years. Flying, leaping, standing or sitting male and female figures (some, portraits of Harkness dancers), glisten in tautly suggestive poses. Amidst them all, stands the *soi-disant* visionary figure of Mrs. Harkness, her head held high, but unfortunately painted in such a way that she seems to be looking straight at the buttocks of her more fleshy male dancers. I was especially amused at one section of the mural, showing a group of grimly caped and hooded figures, whom I assumed to be those Harkness dancers banished from the company some years ago.

The Toronto *Globe and Mail* critic John Fraser said it was

> . . . perhaps the most tasteless, ludicrous and eminently vulgar mural of any theatre in the world. There is more genitalia per square inch floating around in this horrid mural than any hardcore rag could dream up. This all reaches its apogee with the top-most figure directly over centre-stage so that the audience's perspective of him is through turned-out feet, buttocks and testicles.

Senis's painting of Clive Barnes on the *Titanic* added "the perfect final touch," Fraser wrote, "to an evening with the Harkness—the theatre and the company that dares to be known by bad taste alone."

Rebekah had survived the attacks on her after the Joffrey debacle and the coup in Monte Carlo, but they were never this savage. Moreover, since she was now the company's artistic director, there was no one left for her to blame. What did they want from her? She could have been just another society dame; instead, after all her previous setbacks, she had made a greater commitment than ever before. The reviews were so cruel that for the first time, some reporters actually began to feel sorry for the woman who had everything. After thoroughly eviscerating both the theater and the company's choreography, one New York critic wrote:

> None of this, however, seems to me grounds for the gossipy, often vindictive-sounding way much of the Eastern press has puffed and hammered a sad situation into a national issue . . . Harkness says she wanted to leave the world something besides a hangover. She already has, even though she may not be doing it the way you or I would want it done. . . . In return, we could let her keep a little self-respect.

When it's two-week run ended at the new theater, the Harkness Ballet went on tour in Europe and the Middle East, mercifully out of reach of the New York critics. Meanwhile, Rebekah sought, without much luck, to rent the theater out to other dance companies, Broadway shows, or whomever might want it. By the fall of 1974, the company itself was in danger of folding, not from the internal strife that had marked Rebekah's past efforts, but because of financial problems. The theater had already cost her millions; and dark as it usually was, it was a continuing drain on her resources. In addition, the bear market of the seventies had left her finances in a shambles. She would not be able to carry the projected $1,500,000 deficit the company would run up each year.

Rebekah agreed to put up $500,000 for the company that year, but unless they were able to raise the additional $1 million over the next few months, the troupe would fold the following spring. "This is not a gimmick," said her accountant. "The stock market has been severe—people have been losing thirty to forty percent of their capital, and this, combined with inflation, is definitely the reason" the company needs outside money. The dancers literally took to the streets, passing out pamphlets to raise funds. "Save our Company," read one, "The Harkness Ballet must raise $1 million by March 31, 1975, to survive." It noted that a donation of $100 would buy one costume, $25 one hour of class time, $10 a pair of toe shoes, and $5 a pair of tights. The company that had everything, Rebekah's lavish plaything, was reduced to begging in the street.

The public, however, was not terribly sympathetic. The arts, as always, were short of funds, and of all the many cultural institutions needing subsidies, the Harkness Ballet hardly seemed the most deserving. When the dancers themselves made a public plea for support in *The New York Times,* Clive Barnes declared the company unworthy. "The Harkness Ballet is not at present artistically viable," he wrote. "Does any independent, experienced voice in the dance world say it is? So far as the dancers are concerned, Mrs. Harkness has already wilfully disbanded a company of dancers far stronger than her present troupe."

The following year, a four-sentence article in *Variety* told the story: The Harkness Ballet has folded. As for the theater, Rebekah's grandest creation of all, her dance troupe had never even returned to it after its two-week run there in the spring of 1974. It was now available on a rental basis, and a handful of Broadway shows had brief engagements there, but more frequently it remained dark. Costly union contracts blithely signed by Rebekah ensured that even sellout performances rarely broke even. At best, it cost Rebekah more than $200,000 a year to maintain. Of Rebekah's dreams, only Harkness House remained.

"Because I'm loaded, they all look at me and say, 'Show me,'" she told a reporter. "It's a very hard thing to face the fact that almost all people wish you ill."

"She was disgusted with the whole scene," says Cappy. "She

really didn't want any part of ballet. She didn't want to be bothered. She'd had the best and fired everybody. Once she lost the ballet company, she said, 'I really want to go on to something else. I positively hate it.'"

In the fall of 1974, six months after the opening of the Harkness Theater, Rebekah anxiously prepared for a big weekend at Sneden's Landing with Lauersen. Cappy recalls: "She said, 'I need this dress, and I need that dress.'" "And when I asked why, all she said was, 'We're dressing.'"

On October 12, 1974, a minister arrived at the house. "There was every indication she was getting married," says Cappy. "But she didn't want to tell me and she didn't want to tell Joe. She was so ashamed of marrying him, and they did it so sneaky, but we knew that they were getting married."

One of the few people in whom Rebekah confided was her psychic, Frank Andrews, who argued against the relationship. According to him, Rebekah was desperate. "At around the same period, she even asked *me* to marry her," he says. "I tried to prevent her relationship with Lauersen. I said look, if you love him, then don't ask me my opinion. But she was incoherent. I couldn't even read for her anymore. She actually believed in these people. She lived in a world of fantasy. She had all this money she didn't know what to do with."

And so Rebekah took her fourth husband; she was now Rebekah Semple West Pierce Harkness Kean Lauersen. Ten days later, she met with her attorneys and rewrote her will. Among the provisions she added was one stipulating that if her new husband should survive her, he would receive the net income from "a sum of money equal to the value of one-third . . . of my net estate." For all her financial problems, she still had millions of dollars and real estate holdings in New York, Sneden's Landing, Nassau, and Gstaad.

Even those close to Rebekah did not realize the couple was married until the press reported it months later. "Terry and I didn't even find out until we read about it in *Time* magazine," says M'liss Crotty.

If Rebekah's method of informing her children was unusual, so was the marriage itself. Lauersen frequently worked late at New York Hospital. Rebekah had sold her place at the Westbury and bought an apartment in the River House, an exclusive East Side apartment building at which Lauersen often stayed when Rebekah went to Sneden's Landing. "She told me they had some kind of arrangement, and saw each other a couple of days a week," says Andrews.

More and more, Rebekah remained holed up in Sneden's Landing, refusing to confront the outside world. Like Norma Desmond, the aging beauty played by Gloria Swanson in the film *Sunset Boulevard,* she sometimes sat in the great hall of her thirty-room house perched over the Hudson and watched old movies she had rented. She rarely made it to the end without dozing off. There she sat in the forty-five-foot-long room with its thirty-foot-high ceilings, two grand pianos, sofas and chairs covered with yellow and gray silks and velvet. At times everyone was stranded there, with all three cars—the two Mercedes and Rebekah's Rolls—out of commission. By 1976, such chaos was the rule. Even when Rebekah didn't eat at home, the grocery bills topped two thousand dollars a month. The servants had huge meals. The windows and doors in the house were often left open, even when the rain poured in, ruining the rare Oriental rugs. The dog gnawed away at priceless objets d'art.

More than anything, Rebekah feared getting old. She told people she wanted to live forever, and she investigated cryogenics. The giddy, driven, highly disciplined energy Rebekah was known for had vanished, unless she was accompanied by her famous black doctor's bag. In the bathrooms, one occasionally stumbled across one of her hypodermics, used for her Talwin injections.

Some of Rebekah's friends blamed her husband. When Lauersen managed to make it out to Sneden's, he was frequently late. "If you were five minutes late, Rebekah would think you were dead," says Bobby Scevers, who was back on speaking terms with Rebekah. "Lauersen would tell her he was leaving the city and would be there in forty minutes, then not show up till four hours later. She was so nervous that by then, she would be into her sixth bottle of Bacardi."

According to M'liss Crotty, Rebekah was also taking more drugs than ever. "We got a sample of the pills she had. Whatever Sunny von Bülow was taking, Rebekah was taking more," she recalls.

Meanwhile, Sneden's Landing was rife with intrigue. For no apparent reason, anonymous obscenities were suddenly shouted over the household intercom in the middle of the night. Police found dynamite in the cliff on the property. Rebekah beefed up her security, but a prowler tried to break in by climbing the trellis. Joe Pantori was armed and instructed to sleep by the intercom. The place was surrounded by barbed wire. Helicopters patrolled the estate. "Once, someone actually climbed up the bluff and tried to get in her upstairs window and escaped by boat and they had helicopters chasing the boat and all," says Bobby.

One evening Rebekah invited M'liss to the theater with her. "Afterward, we all ended up at El Morocco, and Niels was all over the place, glad-handing all around the room, leaving Rebekah by herself. I could sense something was wrong," says M'liss.

The next day, Rebekah invited M'liss out for the weekend at Sneden's Landing. Lauersen did not make it for dinner, nor did he arrive later that night. M'liss noted that at least three new Scandinavian servants—a butler, a maid, and a gardener—had been hired. "I got the distinct impression Niels had moved them in to keep an eye on her," says M'liss. "I was aware that she was drinking, but I didn't know the full extent. Lauersen should have stopped her. She was drinking like mad. Some of the help were terrified of him. Rebekah was pretty ossified and not paying attention to what was going on. Outside of Cappy and Joe, she was isolated from anyone who might notice anything wrong. How the hell could they have confronted it? They would have been sacked immediately."

M'liss spent the night at Sneden's in the downstairs guest room, while Rebekah retired to her suite upstairs. At 6:30 A.M., M'liss was awakened by the sound of the dog squealing at the top of the balcony near Rebekah's room. "Get down here," M'liss called to it.

The dog refused, even though he generally obeyed commands.

"I climbed the stairs to drag him away, but he made a beeline to Rebekah's room," M'liss continues. "Then he made a huge scene at her door, crying and scratching on her door, and I saw he was covered in blood. I pushed open the door. Rebekah was lying on the floor. There was blood everywhere—on the walls, beds, sofas, wastebaskets. I called her name four times, and finally she looked up at me. She was so groggy.

"There was so much blood in her hair. She must have fallen and hit her head on the marble coffee table. Some of it had started to dry, so it must have happened sometime earlier. The houseboy drove us to the hospital and I ended up in the emergency room with her, holding her hand as they stitched her up. They said she was lucky to be alive.

"The fall suddenly put things in perspective, and she squeezed my hands. She didn't cry. She was really a brick. Finally, she explained she had gotten up in the middle of the night without the lights on and fallen, and staggered back to sleep."

When they returned from the hospital, M'liss, fearing she might be overheard, went out again to call Terry from a pay phone. Terry told her to find out exactly what Rebekah was taking. "I got into her medicine cabinet and I wrote down all the prescriptions," M'liss says. "She was taking the whole gamut— Nembutal, Seconal, Tuinal, Valium, phenobarbital. She was injecting Talwin and drinking heavily, including Pernod and her Pink Drink, that Bacardi cocktail. And as things got worse and worse with Niels, she had begun drinking more and more. Terry said something has got to be done, she is going to kill herself. So it was decided that I was to have a chat with Rebekah."

M'liss packed her bags, expecting to be thrown out of Sneden's Landing as soon as she confronted her hostess. "I walked in and said to her, 'My bags are packed. I am leaving because I can't stand seeing what's been going on here. You are mixing lethal combinations of drugs and alcohol. You are courting death . . ." She hesitated. "If you feel I am out of order, I am ready to leave."

"No, please," Rebekah said, "Sit down. Have a drink."

"Rebekah! This is not the time for Dubonnet. I can't stand by and watch what you're doing to yourself. I looked in your medicine cabinet. You're playing with fire."

"God, it's so clear," Rebekah said. "It's so obvious, and I have just been denying it: I have to get out of this marriage." Using all the strength at her disposal, she became as single-minded as she ever had been. "I want a divorce now," she told M'liss. "Where can I do that?"

In order to avoid suspicion, Rebekah returned to New York to spend the night at the River House, acting as if everything were perfectly fine. She secretly informed Edith, then living in suburban Maryland, of her plans. She also told Cappy and Joe, who awoke early the next morning and told Lauersen that Edith was having a crisis and Rebekah had to visit her right away. Early the next morning, Rebekah lied to her husband about where she was going. Accompanied by Joe and M'liss, she got in her Rolls-Royce and sped off to the airport in search of a Haitian divorce.★

★Over a three-year period, Dr. Lauersen declined more than a dozen requests for an interview by the author.

In brief telephone conversations with the author, Lauersen asked how Rebekah was. When he was told she was dead, he said, "Oh? I never really knew the woman."

Lauersen was asked how that could be since he had married Rebekah.

"No, I wasn't married to her," he replied.

He was then reminded that his marriage to her had been widely reported by the press. In addition, legal documents, including Rebekah's will, cited him as her husband.

"That is a lie, sir, you know? It is all a fake, a lie. It's all misinformation. And I don't know any more about the case."

Later, Lauersen said there had been "a short marriage, and it was annulled right after the wedding. It was an agreement, really not a marriage, simply an agreement. The reason was to give her human support."

18

ANGEL

s Rebekah went through her days in a drug-and alcohol-induced haze, it became increasingly difficult for her to focus on her granddaughter. Angel survived in spite of the family, not because of it, thanks almost entirely to the dedication of her nanny. Rebekah had made a practice of walking with Miss Weeks when she took Angel out for a stroll in her pram in Central Park. Now Rebekah seemed embarrassed by her damaged granddaughter. The child's features were beautiful, but she could not live up to Rebekah's expectations. "Granny wanted a little ballerina, but of course Angel wasn't up to it," says Miss Weeks. "She tried to get Angel to stand, but she couldn't do it. Angel never stood once in her whole life."

As the child grew and her problems became increasingly evident, the distance between Rebekah and her granddaughter became more pronounced. "She didn't disown us, but she didn't have us with her," says Miss Weeks. She and Angel were to stay out of the way; that meant using special entrances at Rebekah's various homes. When reporters came to the house to interview Rebekah, "It was made plain but unspoken that we were not to be seen," says Miss Weeks. "When Rudolf Nureyev—that awful man—came to the house, I wasn't supposed to be seen."

Angel had already survived longer than most of her doctors had predicted. But just after her fifth birthday, in the spring of 1972, she lapsed into a coma. Miss Weeks kept vigil at the hospital, but after several days the child showed no sign of improvement. The prognosis was grim.

"At the end of the weekend I was told that Angel wasn't going to get better," says Miss Weeks. "I replied, 'In that case, let me have her in my arms. If she is going to die, I want to hold her.'

"She was in intensive care. She was naked as a pug. I remember how little she was. They wouldn't take the catheter out, because it would have hurt. I was the only one she could respond to. My touch was the only one she knew. So I said, 'Let me hold her in my arms. If she feels me, she may respond. I know where she needs to feel.'

"I undid all my clothes. I looked a fool, but I didn't care. I undid my overalls at the top. And they put her into my arms attached to all these things and I put her up here at my chest and pressed her head against me. I held her the way I always held her, thinking I was going to say good-bye to her. But then she gave one mighty yell and hugged me with one arm. She just came alive. She just gave a shriek and kicked her foot.

"Dr. New had tears in her eyes. She cared. She said, 'Oh Miss Weeks!'

"I said, "Give me a bottle of something to drink, and I sat down and I held her, and she sucked and sucked as though she had never had a drink in her life. And she came round."

Miss Weeks was dismayed at Rebekah's and Terry's lack of attentiveness during Angel's crisis. Terry, then in Santa Monica, checked in by phone, but that was all. "I can never forget that whenever Angel was ill, neither Granny nor Terry came near us. Granny said, 'I won't come, Miss Weeks. Just let me know when anything happens.'"

In the meantime, Terry had divorced Tony McBride. The trauma over Angel had not been the only problem with their marriage. They lived in Kauai forty miles from the nearest restaurant or café, and Terry had never liked being so completely cut off from urban life as much as Tony did. In addition, she complained to friends that he was going overboard with his complete immersion in his "health conscious, natural life-style," eating natural foods, practicing vegetarianism, and fasting. Terry said he even made their dogs fast, a charge Tony later sought to disprove. When some huge German shepherds attacked his baby colt, tearing the young animal to pieces, he had it put to death. "Then I got the colt and carved it up as dog food and stuck it in the fridge," he says. "The dogs sure weren't vegetarians then." Terry paid Tony to leave, and he moved to the Fiji Islands.

After her divorce, Terry began to spend more time in Los Angeles, where she began seeing a new boyfriend, Mario Roman. Though born in Italy, Roman had become a naturalized citizen by virtue of his service in the United States Air Force. A rabid anticommunist, he gained notoriety in the Los Angeles area as the leader of the Minutemen, a right-wing paramilitary outfit consisting of several dozen heavily armed men. He boasted that he owned a half-track tank and a 50-millimeter cannon. That was just part of his image, however. An inveterate partygoer, with his silver hair, a perpetual tan, and Hawaiian shirts, Roman cut a striking figure. "He was a real ladies' man," says his former attorney, Eric Kitchen. "I saw him at one of the most elegant, stuffiest places in town with two incredibly voluptuous blondes, each wearing see-through dresses and no underwear." In addition, Mario made the most of his exotic, but vague family history. He was known as the No-Account Count.

In the spring of 1972, about six weeks after Angel was out of her coma, Terry arrived in New York to visit her daughter—without notice. Miss Weeks had finished the morning ordeal of feeding the child. The day nurse who assisted her was not yet on duty. While Angel lay in her pen, Miss Weeks went into the kitchen of the tenth-floor apartment to clean up. She heard a sound in the nursery: Terry had entered without knocking.

"We've come for Angel," she said abruptly.

"Mario was behind Terry, very strong, very smartly dressed. Terry was pale, dazed, almost hypnotized," recalls Miss Weeks.

Terry held out a small, empty suitcase she had brought with her. "Will you put her things in it?" she asked.

Mario went to the playpen. He picked up Angel, clad only in her diapers and a flimsy T-shirt, and suddenly ran with the child out the front door to the elevator. Miss Weeks tried to follow him into the elevator, but the door shut in her face. She hurried to the intercom and called the doorman. "Don't let that man walk out of here with Angel," she told him. Then she ran to another elevator farther down the hall. Terry followed. The two looked at each other in silence as the elevator descended. Terry was in tears.

By the time the two women reached the ground floor, Mario, carrying Angel, had already entered a chauffeur-driven Cadillac limousine parked in front of the building. Terry got in and Mario gave her the child. Terry, according to Miss Weeks, was shattered. After she got in the car, she began sobbing, "Oh, Miss Weeks, I don't want it to be like this. I don't want it to be like this."

"I don't care what anyone says," Miss Weeks recalls. "Terry may have been in cahoots in the beginning, but she was totally under somebody's control. She couldn't have carried it out by herself. She was given the child in the car, but she was literally at a loss for what to do. She wanted to give her back to me, but they wouldn't let her open the car door."

Angel, meanwhile, was draped limply across Terry's knee, screaming.

"Hold her up to you," Miss Weeks shouted at Terry. "Hold Angel's head up." She was afraid the child would have a seizure.

As the driver prepared to pull out of the parking space, Miss Weeks berated him. "I'm just a chauffeur," he said. "I'm just doing what they tell me to do."

"All I could think of was how to stop the car," Miss Weeks says, "So I stood in front of the bonnet." Then she stopped passersby on their way to work. "Will you get round this car, please," she said to three or four of them. "They are taking our little girl away. They are trying to take the child," she shouted. "Don't let them take the child."

The police finally arrived, but said they could not interfere in a family matter. "She is the mother," said Miss Weeks, pointing to Terry. "But she doesn't know the babe. She is very sick and needs medication. At least let me give her her medication."

A doctor had accompanied Terry and Mario in the limousine, and Miss Weeks insisted on speaking with him. Finally, the doctor, Terry, and Miss Weeks went upstairs, and Miss Weeks described Angel's medical condition. Terry was quiet, shaken. "The doctor didn't want anything to do with it," says Miss Weeks. "He washed his hands and disappeared. Mario disappeared. Terry disappeared. I was left trying to soothe the child." Before he left, Mario spoke to Miss Weeks. "Wherever you live," he said, "I'll get you."

Miss Weeks tried to reach Rebekah. "But Granny couldn't be wakened," she recalls." She was locked in her place in Sneden's with all the electronic stuff. Nobody had the guts to wake her. Carmine, the chauffeur, and Joe wouldn't put me through even though by that time it was three in the afternoon. I said you've got to wake her. But nobody had the nerve. She had told them not to disturb her.

"Eventually they got her up, and she came like lightning. After they had gone I found a note, signed by Terry, saying she was very grateful for all I had done for Angel, but she was making different arrangements. Granny tore it right up."

It was not clear to anyone why Terry suddenly wanted Angel back, nor why she had proceeded as she did. But perhaps she had been under enormous stress with Angel's problems and with the breakup of her marriage. Miss Weeks ascribed Terry's actions to being under the influence of the charismatic Mario and one can only speculate as to his motives. Even Terry's best friends couldn't understand it. "I don't know what got into her head," says M'liss Crotty.

Rebekah was furious over the incident with Terry. Terry had never been attentive to Angel and was oblivious to how much care she needed. Still, she was Angel's mother. Rebekah decided it was time for Terry to take over.

The new arrangement meant that Angel would still be in Miss Weeks's hands. The only difference was that Terry was to help pay Miss Weeks a modest salary, plus Angel's expenses. Like each of her siblings, she had inherited millions from Bill Harkness.

Miss Weeks was understandably wary after Terry's escapade with Mario, an event she called "the snatch." But since she was now well into her sixties, she had little choice but to accept the arrangement. She could not retire, as she had hoped, because Angel was completely dependent on her. As a compromise, she was allowed to move with Angel to Toronto, Canada, to be near her relatives. There, she began keeping an oral record of Angel's progress and her relationship with Terry and Rebekah. One night in 1974, she spoke into her cassette recorder:

In a matter of weeks, on March 7, Angel will be seven years old. I have had her in my care for six and one half years. During that time, I have experienced many things: great happiness and joy and extreme anxiety. She has needed great patience, which I thank God the ability for granting me to have. And I have enjoyed an experience that is something I will never forget. Whatever I felt I could do for her I have been able to try. I have never had anybody interfere with anything that I have wanted to do for her with the result that I have had complete confidence in myself, and the knowledge that I could help her with my own ideas. This has all come true, and now at the end of six years she has done many things we never thought she could do. She is almost seeing.

She has had good care. It has been made possible by her Granny, Mrs. Rebekah Harkness. For the first five years, we were with her and under her jurisdiction. We had every kind of moral and physical support—even spiritual, without her knowing it—that anybody could have. She gave me great confidence in myself because she trusted me so much. And with her at the back of me, I have been able to do all these things.

Now, in this dear little house in Toronto, Canada, I have been able to realize some of my most precious dreams. For two years or more, I have wanted to find somewhere Angel could go to be among someone like herself and have little children to play with and be taught more professionally than I can. . . . And she has just been accepted to go to the Ontario Crippled Children Centre. For five whole days she will go for two and one half hours and she will have swimming, music, speech therapy, and physiotherapy. And this is not going to cost us anything but the effort of getting there. I think this is just wonderful.

I will go with her for a while and stay in the background until she is more secure, and then I will stay behind. If anything happens while I'm gone, I'm certain she will be well cared for. . . . She is so long and skinny like a string bean, but well. Her feeding is still a tremendous problem. And I have asked them seriously not to touch it, for a week or two, until she gets settled. They think they can feed her, but they have another thing coming. In all the years I have had her it has been a very difficult thing. The least little thing that goes wrong with Angel, and she loses her power to suck, and that means an intravenous feeding. I don't think they will be able to do very much. But one never knows. Miracles can happen.

Despite the joy she took in Angel, Miss Weeks was disturbed that Terry had not observed the Christmas that had just passed:

I have taken quite a few photographs over the Christmas holidays to send to Terry. She never answers my letters in any way or calls to see how we are. And when I call her I can't get through or I don't get an answer. I only have to write to a box number. She didn't even send her little girl a Christmas gift or a Christmas card. Don't you think it's strange from a mother? I do.

Granny sent us a very handsome check. I used it to buy all my Christmas gifts. It came a little late, but it paid for all my gifts to my family and it made me very happy.

A day or so later, Miss Weeks made another entry in her diary:

It's rather strange. I haven't heard from Dr. New for quite a long time. She used to give me a call quite a number of times to see how we were. But I guess she is pretty busy.

It is now Saturday evening, a quarter past eight. I had a very happy day. Almost two hours in beautiful sunshine. The snow is beginning to clear. Angel has had an excellent day. After being out, of course, she drinks well. She is now tucked up in bed and sleeping.

I can't tell you how excited I am about next Monday, when we start our little school. I am going to order a car to take us for the first day, and after that I will try taxis. It would be rather wonderful if I had someone to drive for us and a car, but that we don't have. And I don't really and truly want it. I am seriously thinking of calling Mrs. McBride tomorrow and telling her of our progress. I did write it all to her, but she doesn't answer or acknowledge anything I send her. I might even call Gran, too.

A few months later, Miss Weeks reported that school had been a great success for Angel:

It is now April the 22nd, 1974. . . . We have had to give school a go-by once because Angel was low in fluid and could not spare the physical energy to do all that she is expected to do. She now has a bike of sorts, a four-wheeler with a funny contraption that makes her try to use her legs to propel herself, but she goes backwards, sideways, and never forwards! She is the funniest little thing. Now she is a little heavier and looking rather bonnie. Snow is all gone, the buds are beginning to show on the trees. Daffodils are shooting in the garden. We are going to have a little patio made at the end of the garden for Angel's swing, which I am determined she will have if I have to buy it myself. We are saving our little bit of money that various people sent her for her birthday. And then we will have garden chairs, and we are going to use the garden to its fullest extent, and we will have a little paddledy-pool for the hot weather. That way we will beat the heat.

As time passed, Terry's manner of paying Miss Weeks's salary and expenses for Angel had become a major source of concern:

I have to call Terry today and ask her for some money . . . I have asked her to send some money to the bank, from bank to bank, which I hope she will do. Failing that, I will have to call Mr. Bartwink to see what he can to. I just need the money. And that's that."

Miss Weeks's money problems with Terry had become chronic. When she first moved to Toronto with Angel, she incurred over seven thousand dollars in moving expenses, and it took many months for Terry to reimburse her. The monthly checks to cover her salary and Angel's expenses often arrived several weeks late. For her part, Terry complained to M'liss that Miss Weeks was too demanding and asked for too much money. As a result, she paid little attention to the woman's finances.

There was not much the nanny could do about it. Angel had become the most important part of her life; abandoning the child was the furthest thing from her mind. But it was also increasingly difficult for her—or for anyone, for that matter—to communicate with Rebekah; when Rebekah did think of Angel and telephoned, she was generally drunk or drugged. "I couldn't tell Granny because she was sick," says Miss Weeks. "She used to call me in the middle of the night and rattle on and on, rambling at three A.M. she was very erratic. I knew she was thinking of us and getting something off her chest. But she was not coherent. She used to ramble away and ask how I was, and then the line would go dead."

Disconsolate, Miss Weeks spoke into her diary:

"The last bit of this tape, I have been listening to it. I feel sorry I ever spoke it into the tape, but still I will leave it and see. . . . Very soon I'll have no savings left to help us out, so I think my next move will be to write a straightforward letter to Mrs. Harkness and see if perhaps she has not been told of my position. I am sure in my heart she wishes us to have at least enough to keep us going. She never begrudged us anything when she was taking care of us."

Ultimately, the climate in Canada proved too extreme for Angel. After two years, Angel and Miss Weeks had found the winters harsh and difficult, and the summers surprisingly hot, which did not help the child's susceptibility to dehydration. In early 1975 they moved to London and found a two-story house on Woodland Way. Miss Weeks had always wanted to return to England to be near her relatives, and a three-month visit there earlier had worked out far better than anyone had expected. The cold, damp climate enabled Angel to cope better with her diabetes insipidus, allowing her to put on weight. And since Miss Weeks had many friends and relatives there, the child was surrounded by more people who cared for her. In addition, Miss Weeks was able to obtain new nasal medication, unavailable in the United States, for diabetes insipidus. Angel thrived.

The attention Miss Weeks gave the child had resulted in a far richer life than anyone anticipated. Since Angel's only connection to the outside world was through sound, Miss Weeks did not tolerate silence. Angel was given noisemaking toys, which she played with when she was feeling well. The doors within the flat were always open, as were the windows when weather permitted. Angel laughed with delight when the nearby trains roared by. Miss Weeks played music constantly. She talked to the child nonstop and kept a tape of her voice handy when she tired of the one-sided conversation. When she was in the kitchen, she allowed Angel to roll around, banging pots and pans against the floor. In some ways, Angel even seemed capable of communication. "You often felt she understood what you said, but didn't know how to respond," says Miss Weeks. "I would take her left hand and say, 'Come along. Come along to Nan.' And I wouldn't move. And I would keep on talking. And she would wriggle over and come to me."

There were other signs of intelligence as well. "One of the most important things was putting in the nose drops, which had to be refrigerated between usages. They were essential to her. Once I gave her the drops and put them back on the table, and then went out of the room and closed the door. I had no sooner gone outside than she burst into tears, a thing we had never ever heard her do. I never saw tears like that before. I said, 'Whatever is the matter?' and put her face on mine, and she pushed me away. She knew I had not picked up that vial. Now how did she know that? Now as soon as I picked up that vial in my hands, she stopped crying and she put her face up and I kissed her. I said, 'You are a clever girl, Angel!' She knew they had to be in the icebox.

"Angel had a wonderful life. Nobody knows what a good life she had. Outsiders say she was brain-damaged. Yes, but a lot of brain-damaged children can have a lovely time. Angel didn't know what it was to bite or speak or tell you what she wanted, but she could push and shove, and my God, she was strong at times."

Miss Weeks knew quite well that Angel would never actually be able to walk on her own. Nevertheless—despite those who said it would be useless—she had special shoes made for her that compensated for the fact that her paralyzed leg was slightly shorter than her good leg. In her new shoes, Angel was able to walk when Miss Weeks and one of the nurses held her securely on both sides. She would swing her good leg forward, taking a step on her own. Then Miss Weeks would swing her paralyzed leg and Angel would make her way across the room. Angel had also learned how to move around the flat by twisting and rolling over.

Miss Weeks was delighted with Angel's progress but increasingly felt abandoned by Rebekah and Terry. In January 1976, she made an entry into her diary:

Christmas has come and gone and we are now settled down

once again in the old routine. Believe it or not, I have had not a phone call or single word from Mrs. Harkness, Angel's granny. She who always promised to be 'behind' me & help me with 'everything.' It is now over eight months since we spoke to each other on the phone. I called her to wish her a happy Xmas but was told she was sleeping and could not be disturbed. This was 10:30 A.M. in New York City. She did not return my call. Angel's mother did send us a card and a small gift of a candlestick, but never a cent to help for Xmas.

On March 7, 1977, Angel was ten years old. The child's birthday was always an occasion for Miss Weeks. Her sister Anne and she had both been born in March, so the three of them celebrated jointly. This year was a milestone for Angel: Dr. New had proclaimed that if Angel ever reached the age of ten, it would be a medical miracle.

The birthday party was a measure of Miss Weeks's pride in her achievement and was celebrated accordingly. Along with her sister, she invited one of her former charges, Angel's nurse, and Dr. Rex Barber, Angel's doctor in London. The six of them crowded around the kitchen table to eat the birthday cake. Angel was in particularly good form. She was able to sit up in her chair as the rest sang "Happy Birthday" to her. Then, as if to demonstrate the progress she had made, Miss Weeks posed a particularly difficult challenge.

"Give me your pretty hand," she asked her. "Give me your pretty hand."

Nanny and child had evolved a fairly elaborate, private means of communicating, includivng a variety of shrieks and squawks that Angel made to ask for food or to be taken downstairs and movements to acknowledge the presence of someone. But it was still unclear whether the child could understand plain English. More to the point, Miss Weeks, in referring to her "pretty hand," was talking about Angel's left hand, her paralyzed one. How could she possibly move it?

Angel smiled at her. Slowly, with her one good arm, she reached her right hand across her body, picked up her left hand, and placed it in Miss Weeks's grasp.

"Angel understood a great deal," Miss Weeks explains. "She understood me and those who were in immediate constant contact with her. But she had her good days and bad days. And on this day she was absolutely fantastic."

Her nanny was not, however. She had always had two assistants to help care for Angel. But her financial situation had deteriorated to the point where she had to let one go. "Suddenly things got more difficult," she says. "Those days were the hardest of my life."

Angel's relative strength and size, ironically, was part of the problem. For as Angel continued to grow and master more tasks, Miss Weeks, already afflicted with a bad back, just grew older; she would soon be seventy. With a bit of assistance from a specially constructed handrail on the stairway, Angel could actually get down the stairs alone. "You just call her name and she would plunk her bottom down to the next one. And step by step, she would get down." Sometimes on hearing her nanny's voice, she would twist her way to the stairs, then plunk down so rapidly that she would roll right into a collision with her.

When she was in a lively mood and in good strength, Angel, through her shrieks, demanded to go downstairs to play. Invariably, Miss Weeks complied. But by the time the child was ten years old—more than four feet tall and weighing eighty pounds—she was too heavy for Miss Weeks to carry back up. "She held the bannister with her left hand and she lifted the left leg," Miss Weeks says. "My arm would be under her other arm and I lifted her right leg. And that's how we would go up together. But going up was very hard on my back."

One night, Miss Weeks was too tired to help Angel up the stairs. The two of them, both on their hands and knees, had to crawl, Miss Weeks pushing Angel up one step at a time until they reached the top of the stairs, where they sprawled on the floor, exhausted, hugging each other, Miss Weeks laughing until the tears ran down her face.

Feeding the growing child had become so difficult that Miss Weeks did it in absolute privacy. "If anyone came in the room, Angel would stop eating. So I had to close all the doors. And I had to balance this huge child on my knee and press her head against my left breast. And as she grew bigger and bigger I don't know how I did it. She could never be taught to eat in her crib. That's the only way she would eat.

"Dr. Barber once came unexpectedly to check in on Angel and he caught me feeding and struggling and it shocked him. I don't think anyone knew the physical effort, how difficult it was to feed her. I am five feet four inches and Angel was about four feet, maybe eighty pounds, biggish, heavy. I had to watch that she didn't put on too much weight so we could still carry her."

In all the nine and a half years she had cared for Angel, a vacation had been out of the question. Dr. Barber suggested she take one now. She had not even had a weekend or a night off during that entire period. The only time she had been away from Angel for more than the three or four hours it took to go shopping and perform various errands was when she spent a night in Toronto while scouting for a house in Canada.

Miss Weeks and her sister Anne made reservations at the seaside resort of Worthing for the first weekend in May. Mrs. Lovell, a nurse who had been taught the fine art of feeding Angel, stayed at Woodland Way in her place.

"I made a point of speaking to Angel by phone morning, noon, and evening," says Miss Weeks. "Mrs. Lovell held the phone so that Angel could hear me, and she let me hear Angel kicking. And I left a tape of my voice so Angel could hear me throughout the day.

"When I went away I thought nothing of it. I didn't feel I had done anything wrong. But now I think of when Dr. Levine [from New York Hospital] first gave me charge of the child. He was a small, slim man, and he kept waving his finger—I still see that finger waving. Was he saying that if I left her for even a day, Angel would die? Dr. New was all for me when it came to taking care of Angel. She always said, 'If you take her from Miss Weeks, she'll die.' She said that many times! 'If you take her from Miss Weeks, she will die.'"

When she returned on Sunday, Miss Weeks was relieved to find that Angel was fine. "She had obviously been well cared for.

It showed. She ate me up, kissing me all over, clinging with one arm round my neck like a limpet."

Over the next week, however, Miss Weeks began to see slight irregularities in Angel's behavior. "She punished me for going away. She would hardly leave me. She would hang on to the back of my neck so tightly I couldn't take it, and I would have to put her in the pram, and we would go down to the park and feed the ducks and listen to the traffic.

"There was something you couldn't put your hand on. It wasn't uncommon for her to have low days. But this was different. She just didn't want to be out of sight, and she gradually fed less and less. She looked so lovely, you couldn't say she was ill. She was not ill. For some reason, she was insecure. She was not happy to leave me. When we came in from a walk, she would be floppier than usual."

One morning, about three weeks after her return from Worthing, Miss Weeks awoke at 5:45. She changed Angel's diapers, washed her, and gave her her morning feeding. Then she went about cleaning herself up. "When I came out of the bathroom, her crib was rattling. At first I thought she was sitting herself up by holding one side of the crib as she sometimes did. But the crib was shaking and rattling and I had never seen anything like it."

In the past Angel's bouts with epilepsy had been well contained through her regular dosage of Dilantin. The rare epileptic fits she had were of the variety known as status epilepticus, characterized by "silent fits," in which she simply went limp and lost consciousness. Never before had she had a violent seizure.

"She was shaking from head to toe and turning bluer and bluer," says Miss Weeks. Finally, Dr. Barber arrived, gave her an injection, and took her to The Hospital for Sick Children. She appeared to recover quickly once she got to the hospital. She stayed the night and returned to Woodland Way the next morning.

That day, she was still feeding poorly. When she sat in her pram, she slumped forward limply. Her pulse was slow, and she pushed her food away after only feeding for a short while. But, according to Miss Weeks, she had a "lovely color." The feeding was short of the fifty ounces Angel needed daily, but in the past she had gotten by sometimes with even less than twenty-five fluid ounces and come back with a hearty appetite the following day. Miss Weeks was not overly concerned. Nevertheless, as a precaution, she called Dr. Barber and put him on alert.

Miss Weeks's back had worsened as well. It was so painful she could no longer climb the stairs. "I had to crawl upstairs to bed the last three or four weeks on my hands and knees," she says. "I had to crawl upstairs; then I would stay there till it was time to go to bed, and I would go to bed without undressing."

The next day, feeding became particularly difficult. Miss Weeks had her helper bring Angel downstairs to play. "Ordinarily, she would pick her toys out of a little bowl one by one and give them to me," says Miss Weeks. "But as she sat down on the couch beside me, she just flopped against me and put her left arm up to get up on my knee. She put her head on my shoulder and didn't want to play."

Later that afternoon, Miss Weeks tried feeding Angel again. This time she drank a few ounces, for a total of about fourteen ounces for the day. Miss Weeks called Dr. Barber. In the many times Angel had been in such desperate straits before, Miss Weeks had resorted to nasal tube feedings, but this time there was an additional complication, Dr. Barber explained. As long as the fourteen ounces Angel had just eaten remained in her stomach undigested, a tube feeding would be impossible. Angel sat in her crib and closed her eyes. Miss Weeks sat nearby, doing a crossword puzzle as she watched over the child.

At five o'clock Miss Weeks wrote in her diary: "Angel is settled in for the night and is very limp and very sleepy. No cough, no fever. Dr. Barber—talked twice with him and he agreed that Angel is better left. Her mouth is very red and swollen. She has had a few ounces to drink but cannot have a nasal tube. She is not really unhappy and has played but was very limp at 4:30. Refused any food and started to gag so I left well enough alone. I am not happy about her."

She was sleeping soundly, however, and didn't seem to want to be roused. "I decided to leave the Almighty in charge until early in the morning and to be on the alert to feed her as soon as she moved," says Miss Weeks.

At eight o'clock Dr. Barber came to look in on her. She had no fever and was sleeping soundly.

Miss Weeks checked repeatedly on the child through the early evening. Her condition appeared to improve. At 9:30 she wrote in her diary: "Breathing nicely and quietly. Pulse much better."

At ten o'clock she called Dr. Barber and told him that Angel's pulse was a bit slower but that she was sleeping peacefully and was warm and had good color. Then she dozed off in the rocking chair by the crib. Every hour or so, she woke up and checked up on Angel. Around 3:30 A.M. she awoke again and looked into the crib. "I used to turn her over in her sleep. She loved that, just the change of positions. So I started to do that, and I put the sheet over her and I began to touch her, and she didn't feel as warm as she should."

Angel's breathing was rapid and short. Miss Weeks tried to rouse her, but she wouldn't wake. She was not just sleeping— she was comatose. Miss Weeks cold-sponged Angel's face and called Dr. Barber, who arrived within a few minutes.

He put a stethoscope to Angel's chest, then turned toward Miss Weeks. "She's just taking her last few breaths," he said.

"Then put her in my arms."

Miss Weeks sat in the rocking chair and Dr. Barber lifted the child so that her head could rest on the nanny's shoulder. "I could feel her so lovely and warm, and she just lay there with her face there, and I thought she might wake and come out of her coma."

Then Dr. Barber put the stethoscope to Angel's back. He listened and heard nothing. "Now we will put her back in the crib," he said. He laid her down and gave her a kiss. Then he turned to Miss Weeks's assistant. "You put the kettle on for a strong pot of tea." "It had to be one of you," he told Miss Weeks.

Miss Weeks wrote in her diary on May 26, "Angel fell asleep in my arms at 5 A.M. The sun rose, the birds sang and I felt a beautiful calm. Dr. Barber was so very good and helped me a great deal."

The doctor stayed with Miss Weeks as the sun came up. She called Terry in California, then called the Seaward Funeral to make arrangements. The men from the funeral home arrived a few hours later and put Angel's body in a canvas bag, which they dragged away, allowing it to bump on the steps and they approached the van.

"I heard her body thump against the steps," says Miss Weeks. "And I remember thinking, well, I guess she can't feel anything now that she's dead."

After speaking with Miss Weeks, Terry called Sneden's Landing. Rebekah had long since gone to sleep, but M'liss Crotty was still awake, having just returned from an evening out on the town. When Terry told her the news, M'liss made plans to meet Terry in New York the next day, where the two of them would fly on to London. Rebekah, still drinking heavily, was in no condition to travel.

Miss Weeks had arranged for the funeral at nearby St. John's Church, where she had often taken Angel in the past. "Sometimes I took her to church in the wheelchair and we would sit in the back for the singing. And as soon as 'Our Father' was said she went, 'Ahhh.' She knew. She never spoke, but she knew."

For months, workmen had been remodeling the apartment for Angel, making the garage into a downstairs room with a doctor's couch and basin so that she could come in on the ground floor and sleep there if she were ill. On the day of the funeral, they finally finished their work. They put down their brushes, took off their overalls, and came to the church for the service. Among the other people attending were Miss Weeks's relatives, the nurses who had assisted her in caring for Angel, and the drivers who had taken Angel to and from the hospital.

No one had brought flowers, so Miss Weeks took care of that as well, at her own expense, putting Terry's and Rebekah's name on them. Along with M'liss and Terry, she walked the short distance from the house on Woodland Way where Angel had lived to St. John's, with Terry holding her hand.

Miss Weeks accepted Angel's death with resignation. "I miss my wee lamb," she said, "But I am so happy she's in God's care." She wrote a poem in her diary expressing her sentiments. In part, it went:

> God needed one more
> Angel
> To sing for him that day,
> I am not sad, I'm only glad
> You are now in heaven.

Now that Angel was dead, Miss Weeks was worried the family would forget her. The nanny had reason to be concerned; she had not even been reimbursed for the flowers for Angel's funeral. According to Miss Weeks, after the funeral, the family refused to pay her the thousands of pounds it cost to renovate her apartment for Angel. The plight of Miss Weeks was especially hard to believe given Rebekah's reputation for extravagant generosity. But Rebekah had left instructions with the staff that Angel was not her responsibility. Any pleas to Rebekah for help from Miss Weeks were simply forwarded to Terry. Two years after Angel's death, when the checks did not come as promised, Miss Weeks wrote in her diary: "It is scarcely believable that anyone with so much money could be so niggardly as Terry is to those people who try so hard. . . . My shoulders are broad and they are caving in . . . I long to mind her mother's own words: 'Give her a chance, Miss Weeks, and she will either care for you or kill you off.' Not a bloody word from anyone. I hope they can sleep at night because I can. I owe not any man."

19

DESPERATE
MEN DO
DESPERATE
THINGS

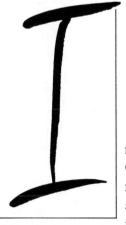

n the spring of 1978, Cappy Pantori went into Rebekah's room and found her mistress visibly upset.

"It's too terrible," Rebekah said. "I can't talk about it."

Cappy tried to be lighthearted. "You can't talk about it?" she said. "There's nothing that you can't talk about unless you murdered somebody!"

"Well, it's as bad as that."

Cappy thought Rebekah was joking. "Why?" she teased. "You murdered somebody?"

Rebekah was in no mood for humor. She paused, about to break into tears. She had to tell someone. "It's Allen," she said.

"Well, what is it? Is it really bad?"

"It's very, very bad," said Rebekah. "It's just terrible."

Allen and Rebekah had not had much contact for more than fifteen years. He had last visited her at Capricorn in Nassau in 1975. Then thirty-four, his feelings toward his mother were deeply ambivalent. He would do anything to please her, but he always ended up disappointing her. This time was no exception. He was certain Rebekah would be delighted by his association with Philip Mansfield. "My mother trusted people like that," he says. "The same type. Ordinarily I wouldn't have, but she was always saying how smart Jews were."

But when Allen told her about his investments with Mansfield and Triple B Security, Rebekah was appalled, certain that he was being swindled. He, on the other hand, had to confront for the first time the spectacle of Rebekah on drugs. "When you see your mother on narcotics, when she falls flat on her ass, it hurts," he says. He returned, angry and confused, to Florida.

After several years in Miami, Allen had moved with Mansfield and his wife, Mary, to Marathon, about one hundred miles south in the Florida Keys. In the old days, Marathon had been a haven for rumrunners and gangsters who used to hang out in nearby Blackwater Sound, as depicted in the movie *Key Largo*. In more recent times it had become a bedroom community for Key West. Allen patrolled the bar at the Hurricane Motor Lodge, a twenty-four-unit motel, complete with a marina, package store, bar, and office, which Mansfield had bought for $550,000.

In January 1975, Mary Mansfield was thumbing through *Time* magazine when she read about Rebekah's marriage to Niels Lauersen. She assumed Allen knew all about it. But when she brought it up, he was baffled. He began crying and pounding the walls furiously. "He would have broken the walls if Phil hadn't stopped him," she says. "I felt so sorry for him."

In Nassau, Rebekah had said nothing about it to Allen. "She never even mentioned the son of a bitch to me," he says. "Here my own mother was coming down on me and then this guy is giving her an outright con job."

Allen had had a quick temper even in childhood, and he sometimes appeared to lose control completely. One night Allen attacked a troublesome patron at the Hurricane. "Allen had that look in his eyes," Mary Mansfield says. "He couldn't stop. He wouldn't have stopped until he killed him. Not because he wanted to, but because he couldn't. He just couldn't."

The patron survived, and no one pressed charges. But Mary was petrified. "Allen's going to kill someone," she thought. "I don't want him in the motel anymore."

Increasingly, Allen's rage was directed at Philip Mansfield. "If he'd run the Hurricane the way we told him to run it, it would have been a success," Allen says. After he invested more than $2.6 million, he had certainly paid for the right to his assessment. And even Mary agreed with his opinion of her husband as a businessman. Mansfield was a King Midas in reverse: Everything he touched turned to dross. He had an unerring instinct for losing money. "I could see the handwriting on the wall," she says. "It was a nightmare just keeping the Hurricane afloat. Phil was a wild entrepreneur. But in some ways he was the dumbest person I ever met. He didn't know the first thing about business."

Mansfield spent a fortune fixing the motel up, and building sixteen additional units. Meanwhile, a Holiday Inn moved in nearby, providing unforeseen competition. The national gas shortage ruined the tourist seasons. Mansfield spent thousands on cash registers for a little tiki bar that took in a few paltry dollars a night.

If one business went bad, Mansfield bought another. When the Hurricane was losing money, he purchased the Tarpon motel nearby, thinking that might help the situation. It lost $300,000 the first year. He bought a farm and a kennel. He bought office buildings in Hialeah, but was unable to find commercial tenants. He bought a data-processing company, an insurance company, a clothing store. He offered one employee who was leaving the company a spectacularly high bonus if he returned.

Meanwhile, he lived the high life. He bought two airplanes, a Beechcraft Queenair and a DC-3. He bought houseboats, then left them to rot. He gave a Cadillac to one employee, and plowed hundreds of thousands of dollars into a lavish home for himself. He came to the office and tossed around a bag of money, claiming it had a million dollars in cash. He confided to a friend that his lieutenant's badge was a fraud. He thrived on intrigue, chaos, and other people's money—principally Allen's. And each time he ran low, he just went back to Allen for more.

Meanwhile, the Internal Revenue Service informed Allen he owed more than $200,000 in taxes on the money he had withdrawn from his trust—taxes he thought Mansfield had been paying. As it was, Allen had lost all his money except a $1 million spendthrift trust, of which he was allowed to touch only the income and none of the principal. Now, because of Mansfield, the IRS had attached the income on it. And one by one, each of Mansfield's businesses began to fold.

Finally, even Allen's patience was exhausted. Mansfield was no longer the "Old Master," as Allen had dubbed him when he worshiped the man. Now he called him "Hebo Manischewitz," and made him the subject of frequent anti-Semitic outbursts. Allen also referred to the IRS as the Israeli Relief Service and said it was run by "a bunch of conniving Hebes."

"I used to tell Phil, if he ever turns on you, I'm afraid," says Mary. "It was strange. I like Allen. I feel sorry for him. But I used to tell my husband he would make a good SS officer. Allen's emotions are strong. Everything is either black or white. He used to aggravate me no end. He would say, 'Do you know how to make people behave? If they don't do what they say, you shoot 'em.' I couldn't believe what I was hearing. Allen was a very dangerous man. He loved the thought of killing. Finally, when Allen was having problems with the IRS, Phil didn't know what to do with him. We had lost all the money. There was no business, no place to put him."

Mary says her husband invested Allen's money honestly but

stupidly, losing it on dozens of crazy schemes and lousy investments. "He didn't cheat Allen," she says. "He lost it in terrible
investments. If he had just taken Allen's money, he wouldn't
have ended up broke himself."

In either case, Allen was angry, humiliated, and out of millions
of dollars. "I was a fool to trust people without checking them
out," he says. "Anyone who would trust those assholes is a fool.
If someone did that to you, what would you do about it? You
fuck over certain people, you're gone. I started to play the same
way [Mansfield] played. You can keep the money. You just
bought it. And I told him he was going. I had a .38. He was
gonna get five shots right smack in the face. I'm not kidding.
Five shots. Bang! Bang! Bang! Bang! Bang!"

By 1976, Allen broke off completely with Mansfield and left
Marathon for a $225-a-month one-bedroom apartment at the
Kendall Arms, in a modest middle-class neighborhood in southwest Miami. He began taking a correspondence course in lock-
smithing and studied auto upholstering with an eye to fixing up
old cars.

At once trusting and angry, he was an enigma even to his closest friends. "He wouldn't hurt kids or old ladies or anybody that
needed help," says a friend. "He's a decent, honest guy. You
couldn't meet a better guy. You could take everything you got
and leave it here and come back in a hundred years. He'd guard it
like a damn Doberman pinscher. But don't fuck with Allen. If
you're gonna hurt him, you're in deep shit. Very deep. If he is
your enemy, he is a bad enemy. Allen has taken a lot of hits over
the years. Desperate men do desperate things."

The cream-colored two-story complex in which Allen lived is
home for secretaries, Air Force personnel, and working-class
people. It boasts a coat of arms with the initials K and A, for
Kendall Arms, an immodest affectation given its plain appearance. From the back parking lot, the building looks like an army
barracks. There is a simple courtyard with a magnolia tree. The
building was so poorly built, Allen said, that the downstairs
neighbors could hear him walking on the floor above. He had

come a long way from the worlds of Henry Flagler and William Hale Harkness.

On November 24, 1977, Allen planned to have dinner with his friend, Hialeah police captain Raleigh Jordan. He had become close with Jordan just after his falling-out with Mansfield; Jordan was horrified at what had happened to his young friend.

"Giving Mansfield $2.6 million is symbolic of Allen's honesty, truthfulness, candor, and innocence. That's the price you could put on his honesty," says Jordan. "It doesn't mean he was stupid. But he got caught by these tremendous emotional forces that beat him around."

Jordan had met Mansfield just once, and only briefly, but he didn't like him. "He looked like a big rat sitting behind a big desk, eating a big fucking piece of cheese. He looked like a possum with no hair—I swear to God he did. Little Mr. Kosher. Allen was taken by a bunch of slime, and they took everything he had."

Jordan had invited Allen over for Thanksgiving dinner but had unexpectedly drawn police duty that day and couldn't get off work. Instead, Allen stayed home alone. At about 9:00 P.M. he walked from his apartment through a parking lot to the Food Spot, a convenience store a hundred yards or so from his apartment. He planned to be gone for only a few minutes; he was just going to buy a few things and call Jordan to wish him a happy holiday from the nearby phone booth. (He did not have a phone in his apartment for fear it would be bugged.)

For protection he carried a fifty-two-dollar high-standard .22 magnum chrome-plated derringer. The small, two-shot pistol has an extremely heavy trigger pull—twenty-five pounds—so that it cannot go off accidentally. He had loaded it with forty-gram hollow-point bullets, specially designed to explode on impact. He kept it in his back pocket in a carrying case that looked exactly like a man's wallet. If someone tried to jump him, he was ready. "You want my wallet, you can have it," he says. "You earned it the hard way. It's all yours. Boom! Boom! You just bought it."

He got some chocolate milk and crackers, then stopped at the phone booth to the left of the store.

Nearby, a tall, wiry, nineteen-year-old named Patrick Bemben eyed Allen. Bemben had a reputation as a fighter, and had been linked by police to local residential burglaries. Earlier that evening, he had been playing checkers with his younger sister; then he and his fifteen-year-old brother Paul and a friend named Joey Tum had gone to the Food Spot to play pinball and hang out. They bought a six-pack of beer. Patrick drank four or five cans. He was slightly intoxicated.

Allen pointedly ignored the trio. He called Jordan at the Hialeah Police Department. Suddenly, Bemben got into the phone booth with Allen.

"He comes right in the booth with me," says Allen. "He goes: 'Whoooo!!' Breathes beer all over my face. I thought, 'Man, you want to talk? Hey, I'll give you the phone.' And then he goes like this: 'Blbb, blbb, blbb, blbb!!'"

"It sounded like a damn aborigine," says Jordan, who could hear him on the other end of the line. "It sounded like a chant, an African chant."

To Allen, Jordan said, "Who is that shouting? Is that a drunk nigger or something?"

"No," Allen replied. "It's not a nigger. The party is white."

Bemben, who was four inches taller than Allen, looked down at him. "Is that me you're talking about?"

"Yeah, it sure is," said Allen.

Bemben took the can of malt liquor he was drinking and deliberately poured the contents on Allen's leg.

Boy, I'm gonna start working his ass over, Allen thought. *He's going into the concrete.* Then he said to Jordan, "Don't worry about it. I can handle this." He hung up and started out the phone booth.

Bemben shouted, "Don't you ever call me a nigger."

At first Allen tried to calm him down. "I didn't call you a nigger," he said. "The party on the phone didn't mean anything. He didn't mean to offend anybody."

But when Bemben continued to object, Allen began to lose his temper. *Okay,* he thought. *I'm going to give this guy all the rope he needs to hang himself, he starts putting his hands on me, starts abusing me. Keep on, motherfucker. See what happens.*

Bemben continued screaming and shouting. By now, several people at the convenience store were watching.

"Listen, man, nobody called you anything," said Allen. "If you want, I'll be happy to introduce you to the guy I was talking to."

Bemben began to walk away, as if he were sick of the argument. Then, just as Allen let down his guard, Bemben struck him in the eye as hard as he could, using a beer can as a weapon. "Next thing I know—Wham!!" says Allen. "I got hit—I get this Colt .45 can in the eye. He hit me about four or five times in the face, good, hearty blows. This guy's no amateur. *Whew,* I thought, *where am I? We're back to school again. OK, fucker, if that's the way you want it, that's the way it's gonna be.* I went to work on his head. I got his head going like a Ping-Pong ball. I wasn't gonna stop. I was just gonna beat his head—because I've done it before. Up—down!! Up—down!! I don't stop. Then I saw my chance. I gave him an open slap. His head went back. Then my right fist came over. I hit him a beautiful shot."

Bemben tried to kick Allen in the groin and missed. Allen got up and kicked back. Bemben's brother shouted, "He kicked you in the balls. Let's get him." Then he joined in the fight, coming up to Allen from behind and kicking him.

Allen couldn't see out of his left eye because blood was streaming down his face where he had been hit with the beer can. Bemben, only six or seven feet away, started to retreat behind a van that was parked nearby. *He must be going to get something to blow me away,* Allen thought. He saw Bemben's arm reach under his shirt. "Blood coming' down my face, right?" Allen says. "So I see his arm come up. Not me, baby boy. School's out."

Bemben started to run away.

"Come back here, you goddamn hippie son of a bitch," Allen yelled. Then he reached into his right back pocket for his derringer. He drew and fired two shots. The first bullet entered the front of Bemben's chest and passed through it laterally from right to left. The second hit his right arm and went into his chest, eventually lodging behind his left shoulder blade.

Allen put the gun back in his pocket. He was hurt from the fight, but he was composed. He looked down over Bemben sprawled on the ground nearby, and watched his eyes fluttering.

"He just lay there," Allen says. He laughs as he remembers. "And then, I saw his eyes go like this—*ee-ee-ee-ee-ee. Oo-oo-oo-oo.* Bye-bye, baby, bye-bye. I was watching his eyes go *tt-tt-tt-tt-tt.*"

"I love it," says Jordan, reminiscing with Allen. "Little eyes are flashing. His eyes were pleading for help. And Allen thinks, 'There's no way we're gonna be able to save you. You're gonna die, motherfucker. You're going to hell. You're not going to court. I am. You're going to hell.'"

Allen went to the phone booth and called Raleigh. "I had to shoot somebody," he said calmly.

Jordan was startled. "Allen, put the gun down in the phone booth, in clear view, and shut up," he started to say. "Don't say anything to anybody."

But by now several patrol cars were approaching. Paul Bemben shouted at Allen, "You killed my brother."

Allen dropped the phone. He couldn't hear Jordan. He stood there mute, the gun in his back pocket as the cops approached.

At seven-thirty the next morning, Allen, anxious to tell the story of what he saw as a case of thoroughly justifiable self-defense, waived his rights and gave Officer Steven McElveen a detailed account of what happened. He was charged with homicide and carrying a concealed weapon.

To defend him, Allen hired Roy Black, an imposing lawyer from Miami who later gained fame representing drug smugglers as well as lawyers, doctors, businessmen, and cops. On the face of it, the case against Allen was not terribly strong. To convict someone of second-degree murder in Florida, the state must prove the defendant "acted with a depraved mind, regardless of human life." There were plenty of witnesses who could back up Allen's assertion that Bemben had provoked the fight. If a jury found that Allen had overreacted, the worst would be a conviction on the lesser charge of manslaughter. Black did not consider it an especially tough case. "Almost any normal, everyday guy would have been acquitted," he says.

In his zeal to cooperate, however, Allen had given a statement that was extremely damaging. For one thing, he described himself in terms a jury might not find particularly sympathetic. "I'm the kind of person, once attacked, I attack. I get like . . . a tiger," he said. . . . "I got hit in the face so fast and so many times . . . if I had gotten hold of him, I probably would have strangled him to death. . . . He like ran away. When I got him I could still see his frightened eyes. He knows he wasn't fighting with the average guy and he probably liked to get away or something."

All of which suggested that Allen was getting the better of Bemben—in which case a gun was completely unnecessary. Allen even described Bemben moving away from him toward the van: "I remember him moving. There was a van there . . . and I remember all the visions . . . the things that these people have done went through my head, almost like a computer tape. . . . Hippies. I've seen a lot of property destroyed by hippies, and he's just like one of them."

Ultimately, the issue was whether the shooting was justifiable. But before the trial had even begun, Allen himself had suggested he shot Bemben because he was just another hippie, who had provoked him initially but was frightened and fleeing when he was shot. His statement alone virtually ruined a plea of self-defense.

Black was reluctant to put Allen on the stand. "You don't do anything like that unless you're sure how it's going to turn out," he says. But there were not many alternatives. As the trial approached, Allen and Black had several sessions rehearsing his testimony, and Allen practiced diligently.

Once in court, it was a different matter, however. Allen could not resist telling everything. Among the more damaging tidbits he volunteered to the prosecutor was information about his collection of guns. He also told of his hatred of hippies, "people that are bad news. They vandalize property. They defecate on the beach. They usually hang out waiting to do something to somebody, to beat them up."

Black says, "Allen's testimony was incredibly self-destructive. When he got up on the stand to testify, it was as if he were committing suicide."

"That jury was terrified of him," says Jordan. "When he talks to you, you know how forceful he is? He scared the living shit out of them."

"When he got on the stand, he decided to take it all into his own hands," says Black. "If I had known that he was going to use it for a performance . . . we had gone over his testimony I don't know how many times. He became psychotic on the stand. The guy is a total nut."

The jury deliberated only a short time. They found Allen guilty of second-degree murder and of carrying a concealed weapon.

According to Black, Allen made things even worse while awaiting sentencing by calling the judge's chambers regularly. "He was pretty self-destructive," says Black. "He kept threatening the judge after the trial."

Allen, bitter over the way Black handled the case, denies that charge. "The only person who said that I threatened the judge was Roy Black. No one else. And he's an outright liar." He did exactly what Black told him to do, he says, and the strategy failed: "I gave them the truth in their phony little faggot-assed nigger courtroom down here, and they didn't appreciate it."

Raleigh Jordan concedes that Allen's demeanor and speech often seem threatening to people who don't know him. But on one issue he is certain. "You want my opinion?" he asks. "Allen should have walked."

Instead, Judge John Tanksley sentenced Allen to life imprisonment for second-degree murder, with an additional five-year sentence for carrying a concealed weapon. He was remanded to Raiford State Prison in northern Florida, while his lawyer pondered an appeal. Allen made it clear that he did not want to depend on his mother for legal help and had no intention of being more of a burden than he had become already.

"His family was not there for his support," says the prosecutor. "It seemed like he was an apparition to them."

20

THE
END OF
THE
TUNNEL

dith somehow had emerged as the sanest of the three children, even after years of being sent from one mental hospital to another, of being stashed away as if her existence were the deep dark family secret her mother couldn't deal with. In late adolescence she had been committed to the Institute of Living in Hartford, Connecticut. One summer, she was released briefly and visited a friend in Watch Hill. "She looked great," says the friend. "It was wonderful just talking to her. But she was self-conscious. She said, 'I'm embarrassed. I feel that because I'm a mental patient, it makes people feel ill at ease."

By 1969, she had left the Institute of Living for Chestnut Lodge in Rockville, Maryland. "Chestnut Lodge is a place where the very wealthy go, and they sometimes stay all their lives, if they have enough money," says one observer. "It is so easy to put someone there and forget them." Edith remained until Milton Kayle, one of Rebekah's lawyers, made it his project to bring her back.

A former special assistant in the White House under President Truman, Kayle had become an attorney to the dance company in 1969, succeeding Aaron Frosch. Rebekah eventually dismissed him, as she did so many of her lawyers. But Kayle stayed on to look after Edith, of whom he had become enormously fond. The feeling was mutual. Those close to him said he thought of their relationship as "sacred" and that he had become a father to her. He resolved that the days of being locked up in one mental hospital after another would end. He saw to it that she was released from Chestnut Lodge as an outpatient. She continued in psychotherapy, but with Kayle's assistance she bought a house on sixteen acres in Potomac, Maryland, and began to live a more normal life.

In 1970, when she was twenty-one, Edith met Kenneth McKinnon, a young attorney with the General Accounting Office in Washington, D.C. The son of a civil servant, and a graduate of the University of Maryland and Georgetown University Law Center, McKinnon was taken not just by Edith's physical loveliness, but by her charm, generosity, and her determination to shed her onerous family legacy. Edith dressed casually and lived modestly as if to conceal her wealth; many of McKinnon's law student friends lived better than she. She was somewhat shy, but she could be gregarious and brilliantly clever. She was well read, and her dry wit often went over the heads of others. "She was very straightforward," says a friend, "and she took great pleasure in cutting through to the heart of the matter in very graphic terms—all to my delight."

In April 1971, Ken and Edith were married at Rebekah's home in Sneden's Landing. They honeymooned in Nassau, then settled on Edith's Potomac estate. The huge, rambling stone house had more than a dozen rooms spread out on three levels, a swimming pool, sauna, stables, and large heated and air-conditioned kennels for Edith's five dogs.

Rebekah was delighted with Ken. At last someone in the family had taken up with a responsible human being. He had not even known Edith was wealthy when he fell in love with her. He later heard all the horror stories about Rebekah from Edith, and he sympathized with his wife. But it was more complicated than that; he also saw the side of Rebekah filled with generosity and wit and exuberance. She went through wild mood swings on occasion, but that, he thought, was a function of her alcohol and drug problems.

With her mother, Edith was polite but distant, visiting only when necessary. When she and Rebekah posed for *McCall's* magazine in 1966, the accompanying article asked, "Why does one seventeen-year-old move happily forward to meet the adult world while another, equally pretty and equally intelligent, is already sullen and disillusioned?" Edith was on display in a national magazine as the product of the ideal mother-daughter relationship, and no irony was intended. "She hated the duplicity," says a friend. "It made her sick."

At the grand opening of the Harkness Theater, Rebekah wanted the happy couple to accompany her in the family's box. Ken attended, but Edith begged off, claiming she wasn't feeling well. And when she visited the family's estate in Nassau, Edith tried to make sure Rebekah wasn't there.

In 1972, Edith gave birth to a daughter, Erin. "At first she thought she didn't want to have children because of what happened to her and her mother," says a friend. "But she got pregnant and thought about it. Obviously, she could have gotten an abortion. But she was very excited about having a baby. She thought it was wonderful to create a new life. It was a scary prospect for her, but she was excited and delighted when Erin was born."

Edith spent her days playing outdoors with the baby, reading, gardening, or caring for the dogs in the kennels. And in the summer, friends came by and hung out by the pool. She was happy enough that she finally gave up her psychiatrist.

But, three years into her marriage, Edith began spending increasing amounts of time inside the house alone. She withdrew from many of her friends. She became argumentative for no apparent reason. No one, not even her husband, understood what her problem was.

It was alcohol. "I didn't know what was going on," says one friend. "I didn't know she was drinking. There were a lot of arguments that didn't make sense. She wasn't herself. She was angry, irrational."

Edith hid the bottles and denied it. After several months, however, Ken realized she was drinking and got her to see a doctor. The problem was not new to her; she had just hidden it for years. It dated back to her childhood when she was given brandy Alexanders. And when she was a patient at Payne Whitney, she had had problems controlling her drinking when they served wine in the courtyard. Now it had gotten out of hand.

"The doctor told her he was aware that she was a very wealthy woman," says a friend. "But he said no amount of money could ever buy her health, and that if she didn't stop drinking, she would be dead in two weeks. Somehow he cut through, and it left a deep impression on her. And that was it. She stopped just like that. She didn't go to meetings. She didn't go for treatment. She just stopped. And she came out of her world that she was living in, and started to live again."

When she sobered up, she became herself again, and she continued to see a psychiatrist about it for a few months. But it was clear irreparable damage had been done to the marriage. After nearly a year of her sobriety, she and Ken separated and were later divorced. Edith told friends that although she loved her daughter, she felt she couldn't be a good enough mother to her, so she decided that Ken should have custody. "Edith didn't know what a good parent was like," says a friend. "She never really had one. She had grown up in institutions—not a real stable environment. There was something she saw in herself that she saw in her mother. I don't know what it was, but it scared the hell out of her. So she decided Ken would be a better parent. It was not that she didn't have the time or the responsibility or felt having a child would impinge on her life-style. It was the most unselfish act in the world. She loved Erin, but she was afraid she would do to Erin what Rebekah had done to her. And she didn't want Erin destroyed as she felt she had been."

Edith was also scared she might slip back into drinking. "She knew her limitations," says another friend. "That was a very courageous act. That was part of her tragedy. She had had emotional problems all her life. She was getting a divorce. She had to make that sacrifice."

After the separation, Edith traveled and renewed old acquaintances. Always believing the scars from the surgery after her suicide attempt were hideous, she finally underwent plastic surgery to cover them. At the same time, she had silicone implants inserted in her breasts and had a nose job. "It was out of character," says a friend. "I don't know why she did it. She was pretty. She didn't need [the operations]. The only explanation I can think of is she didn't like herself and was trying to change."

Then in late 1976, Edith met Eivind Harum, a tall, blond Norwegian who had danced with the Harkness Ballet in the sixties. For years he had been close to Rebekah—so close that Bobby Scevers saw him as a rival for her affections. Harum, however, denied having an affair with Rebekah. "I never slept with her," he says. "We liked each other and I was favored, but that was all."

Harum, at the age of thirty-three, had landed the role of Zach in the Broadway musical *A Chorus Line* in 1974. The play was finishing its London run and, around Christmas, Harum had some time off before the troupe began an American tour. He asked Rebekah if he could rest up in Nassau for a week. She was not there, but one unexpected guest was—Edith. "I had met her before and thought she was gorgeous then," he says. "But now she was twenty-eight years old and had totally blossomed. I fell in love with her."

Though he barely knew Edith, Harum was no stranger to her tortured relationship with her mother. "Rebekah commiserated with me about how badly she felt about Edith jumping out the window. She never got over that. That stayed in her gut. When we got drunk together, that always came out. It was one of the worst things in her life. That was her guilt."

When *A Chorus Line* played in Baltimore in February 1977, Edith spent almost every day with Harum. "As for her marriage, I never touched on those things," he says. "We were having a love affair for three weeks, full of touching, caressing, and loving. I thought there was plenty of time to get to know her later."

When the tour moved on to Detroit, Harum received a phone call from Edith. "This is not your fault," she said, "but I'm going to kill myself.'"

He called the sheriff in Potomac. When the police got to her place, she was lying down in her car in the garage with the exhaust going. She was hospitalized but was back home a week later. In the middle of March, Harum flew down to see her. "She was very sorry and very distant. We talked all about suicide because one of my pet things is meeting death and saying, 'Fuck you, I'm not going yet.' Dying is just as stupid as living. You're gonna die later anyway. We talked about how ridiculous the whole world is and how ridiculous death is. Her sense of humor was coming back.

"She didn't say why she did it, and I never asked. I told her I had tried to kill myself in 1973 and was unsuccessful. I hate those people who try to kill themselves and fail. I cut my wrist and took sleeping pills and vodka, but there I was, alive. Having lived through it, I realized it wasn't my time to go. This was her second time. I said, 'I thought you learned the first time. If you jumped out of the fifteenth story and lived, you're not supposed to go. You have to live the journey out.'

"But she didn't keep in touch. I told her to call me, but she didn't want to."

Even after her divorce from Ken, Edith remained close with his sister, Linda McKinnon, who lived in Florida, and took several trips to Nassau with her. "When I went through a bad time,

Edith was really there for me," says Linda. "She was very help-ful to others with their problems. When she talked about herself, she could be very detached. But when anyone else was talking about their feelings, she had a great deal of empathy. She couldn't have possibly been able to understand other people's pain unless she could understand—unless she could feel—some of her own. Sometimes I think the pain got too great."

Linda noticed Edith's strong attachment to the dogs at her kennels. "Their love didn't come with any strings attached," says Linda. "It was so pure. She was extremely affectionate to-wards them. She had been hurt so much by people. It was as if she was always waiting to be hurt. She was very vulnerable. She was like a lonely little girl who was looking for someone to fill the void. And I don't think she ever really knew what she was looking for. Her eyes were very expressive. And even when she was laughing there was a sadness there that never seemed to go away."

Edith began seeing a psychiatrist, who prescribed a wide range of psychopharmaceutical drugs. When she went to Nassau, her suitcase was so filled with prescription bottles that the customs inspectors were shocked. At times, she ate very little. "There were times when Edith was very active, hyper, very up," says Linda. "After one of these peaks, there was frequently an equally drastic downswing. She was like a manic-depressive. The mood swings were very extreme.

"I was extremely protective of her, and I knew that she couldn't drink. She had stopped drinking for over a year, and I went to Washington to see her for a week. When she ordered a drink at a restaurant, I was appalled. But it was obvious that it was a perfectly normal thing for her to do. I was very upset about it. The next day she asked me to go to the liquor store for her, and I said no. And she said, 'Well, I'll just call a cab.' I agreed to go to the liquor store and get it for her. But it made me physically ill.

"Someone who was working at her house used to bring her drinks into her room for her on a tray, and I was furious. When she wasn't drinking she had a zest for life. She always had many plans and dreams, and things that she wanted to do. But when she drank she was a totally different person. Her perspective was completely altered. She wasn't in touch with reality. Edith became extremely self-destructive."

When Linda was ready to return to Florida, Edith kissed her good-bye. "She wouldn't let go of me. She was hugging me so hard I thought she was going to break my ribs. She was sobbing. I think that we both knew we weren't going to see each other again. I wasn't helping her by trying to pick her up and keep her from hitting bottom. I knew I had to leave her. That was the most painful thing I've ever had to do."

Later, Linda discussed Edith's problems with a mutual friend. "I feel like I am part in a tunnel with Edith," she said. "We all know what the end of the tunnel is going to be. We just don't know how long the tunnel is."

Rebekah was at her best when she could relax at her
Bahamian retreat, Capricorn.

Terry, probably in 1966, not long before her marriage to Tony McBride

Rebekah with Angel, Terry's daughter. Initially, Rebekah gave the child enormous amounts of attention as if to make up for the way she neglected her own children.

Angel
was a perfectly
formed child and only
gradually did it become
possible to diagnose
her problems.

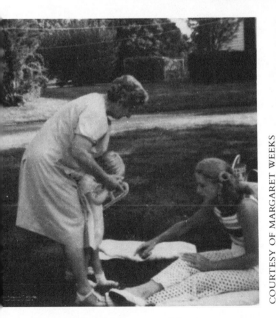

Miss Weeks helps Angel "walk" to
Granny.

Terry visited her daughter
occasionally, but more often found
Angel's problems so daunting she
stayed away.

MICHAEL AVEDON

When Edith was released from Payne Whitney for this 1966 sitting with Harkness House photographer Michael Avedon, Avedon was so thoroughly briefed about her mental problems that he expected a lunatic. However, he found Edith far more sane than her mother.

In July 1966, *McCall's* magazine highlighted Rebekah and Edith as if they had an ideal mother-daughter relationship. "Why does one seventeen-year-old [like Edith] move happily to meet the adult world while another, equally pretty and equally intelligent, is already sullen and disillusioned?" the magazine asked, apparently without irony. Edith hated the duplicity.

In April 1971, Edith married a young Washington attorney named Kenneth McKinnon.

JAY T. WINBURN

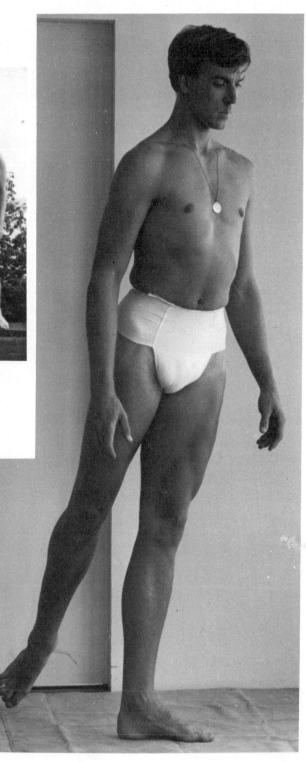

Bobby and Rebekah would often weekend at her estate in Sneden's Landing, New York, overlooking the Hudson River.

In the mid-sixties, Bobby posed in a dancer's belt so Rebekah could do a sculpture of him.

Throughout the sixties, Rebekah adhered to a strenuous
regimen and took class daily. Here she is, at
fifty-one, in Barcelona.

Rebekah with the company's assistant artistic director, Donald Saddler,
in Barcelona, 1966

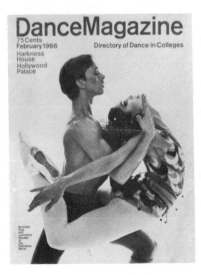

DanceMagazine
75 Cents
February 1966   Directory of Dance in Colleges
Harkness
House
Hollywood
Palace

In 1966, Harkness House had just opened and the Harkness Ballet was about to take the world by storm. Here are two of its stars, Lawrence Rhodes, who later became artistic director, much to Bobby Scevers's dismay, and Brunilda Ruiz, on the cover of *Dance Magazine*.

Rebekah in her suite at Harkness House. Above her is a portrait of William Hale Harkness.

DANCE MAGAZINE VISITS HARKNESS HOUSE

"Something permanent for the dance"

by Jack Anderson

Above: At 72nd St. off 5th Ave., the new home of the Harkness Ballet. Below: The mansion's old coach house is now the Harkness House Gallery, open to the public, without charge, Tuesdays through Saturdays from 10 a.m. to 5 p.m.

In the reception hall of the new Harkness House for Ballet Arts stands a golden chalice surmounted by jeweled butterflies which gently open their wings as the cup revolves on a turn-table. Near this "Chalice of Life" is an explanatory caption by its creator, Salvador Dali. It reads, in part: "Man exists amidst putrefaction . . . but by virtue of divine metamorphosis . . . he transforms into spiritual life."

A spirit of aspiration, of aesthetic metamorphosis, seems to dominate the intention of Harkness House. Its founder, Rebekah Harkness, declares: "I want to give splendor back to ballet. After all, ballet began in the French courts. And I think today our artists *deserve* such elegance, for they are our true aristocrats."

Dismayed at the tawdriness of most American dance studios, especially when they are compared with the Soviet ballet schools or the Paris Opera, Mrs. Harkness decided to provide a worthy setting

(over)

JACK MITCHELL

The former home of IBM founder Thomas J. Watson, Harkness House became a dance school modeled on the great imperial dance academy of St. Petersburg.

The studios at Harkness House were palatial compared to the dark, dingy rooms most dancers were accustomed to.

At the grand opening of Harkness House, Rebekah was draped with Salvador Dali's pet ocelot.

The Harkness Ballet won far more acclaim in Europe than in the United States.
Here, Rebekah and the dance company are showered with flowers in
Barcelona in 1966.

THE
ETERNAL
COCKTAIL
HOUR

n 1978, Rebekah was sixty-three, and the years had caught up with her. The testosterone had given her face a hard, stern, mannish cast. Rebekah had had to undergo painful hip surgery, and now walked tentatively. She put on weight. Her skin was slack.

At Sneden's Landing her presence was that of a haunted, stiff, ghostly figure ominously stalking about. "She was not precisely cold," says someone who enjoyed weekends at Rebekah's retreat, "but she was distant. Not entirely incoherent. But she was wooden, like a marionette, not very natural. It was as if she were wearing a mask. It was as if when she spoke, something would crack."

"Her appearance was bizarre," says another acquaintance. "She was perfectly put together the way very rich people sometimes are, but even more so, wearing a black mohair Chanel suit that was so impeccable it was glowing. She had jewelry and perfume and a great deal of makeup. Her hair was completely golden, in a youthful pageboy. But she walked like Frankenstein."

Hundreds of shots of Talwin had caused damage at the injection sites, restricting the movement of her knees. "She could only bend her knees about forty-five degrees," says Bobby. "The muscles of the thighs had tightened up like rocks. So she would fall over, and being loaded, she couldn't get up."

Nor were the problems just physical. Rebekah's attention span—never long to begin with—had grown shorter and shorter. She was brittle, almost incapable of caring about anything that took place outside her line of sight. As for her family, she was disappointed that Edith and Ken had gotten divorced. She loved Erin and kept in close touch with Ken, but she knew little about Edith's drinking problems. She kept up with Terry's life only through M'liss Crotty. And she knew very little about Allen; it was not until months after the killing of Patrick Bemben that she even heard what had happened. "She was very upset," says Cappy. "She said, 'They never told me. And now the trial is all over and I'd like to help him, but I don't know what to do.' Then she tried to get a lawyer, and they told her to leave well enough alone."

When she tried to find out exactly what happened, one friend told her the CIA had probably put Allen up to it. The story was a complete fabrication, of course, even though there may have been good intentions behind it. Allen spoke Russian, and there had been rumors of him being involved in gunrunning in Panama, so this exotic explanation was, in some ways, easier to swallow than the truth.

There were other things on Rebekah's mind. She had been advised her Haitian divorce from Lauersen was not valid, so she had had to get a New York divorce in 1976.

Through all this trauma, there was no man in Rebekah's life. However, when her marriage to Lauersen had started disintegrating, she had begun communicating again with Bobby Scevers. In 1975, Bobby, then living in Geneva, had written her when he heard about her hip surgery. "She called me in Geneva and said she was so glad to hear from me. She'd been very sick, and still didn't feel too well and was unhappy and lonely."

Bobby secretly visited her in New York, and Rebekah showed him their home at the River House, where Lauersen not only had separate rooms but a separate entrance as well. When Bobby moved to Texas, he kept in close contact with Rebekah by phone. She even rented an apartment in Dallas for him under her own name. There was always the possibility it might come in handy if she needed a different residency for her divorce.

When the divorce finally came through, Maria New urged her to see Bobby again. "At first Mrs. Harkness made jokes because of the way she had thrown him out," recalls Cappy. "But Maria would leave letters for her from Bobby. He used to say he loved her. And she used to say to me, 'I don't know what to do. It's over and done with, but Cappy, you know—'"

Still drinking heavily and addicted to Talwin, she entered Silver Hill Foundation in New Canaan, Connecticut, in July 1977, to try to shake her drug habit. That month she wrote to Bobby.

"Dearest Bobby-San," she began, using an appellation from the days when her Japanese masseuse had been part of her entourage.

> Believe it or not, I am here getting a rest & a few other things that are good for one I suppose. I will explain it all when I recover my sense of humor etc. . . .
>
> I hope you are well as it's a pain in the neck not to be. I miss you of course. . . . Don't forget I am still on this fifth rate planet.

> Love,
> Becky-Poo

In November, after returning from Silver Hill, she bought an apartment on the fourteenth floor of the Carlyle apartments adjacent to the Carlyle Hotel on East Seventy-second Street. Her new home had originally been two apartments. The entry led into a long hallway, painted with a mural of a garden scene. The huge living room served as a music room and library and was dominated by two grand pianos and a bar. There was a large kitchen, a small terrace, and a sun room, and throughout the apartment ornate molding and furniture that included Louis XIV reproductions, an elaborate Spanish bed, and a lacquer cabinet inlaid with ivory.

Meanwhile, Bobby was performing in *The Nutcracker Suite* in Beaumont, Texas, and Rebekah flew down to see him. "She was very, very quiet, very, very calm. I don't think she was taking anything or drinking anything at that time," he recalls. "She was just confused by all these little Texas hicks trying to think they were so high-class."

By now, Rebekah knew she needed Bobby again. But he was wary of a reconciliation—she had already thrown him out twice before, and he was living with Nikita Talin, his friend and mentor of many years.

Rebekah went so far as to investigate adopting Bobby. Not only would it help allay his fears about coming back, it would also ensure that he could take over Harkness House in the event of her death. Her lawyer, however, thought the idea was crazy and talked her out of it.

Finally, in early 1978 Bobby moved into the Carlyle with Rebekah—but he made it clear he wanted Nikita to join him. "Everybody hated Nikita, but Bobby wouldn't come without him," says Cappy. Nikita arrived in June 1979, and moved into his own bedroom at the Carlyle.

Even though Bobby was back, Rebekah's love life with him was over. "There was nothing personal at all," says Bobby. "I didn't want to. We talked about sex, but she said she understood. She said at her age she really didn't need it anymore. She told me, 'That's all right, I can love you just as much without that.'"

★   ★   ★

Bobby had been close to Nikita before he even met Rebekah. Indeed, it was Nikita who had shown him the world of dance and the arts. Without him, Bobby would never have gotten as far as Dallas, much less moved to New York and met Rebekah. In return, Bobby had been intensely loyal to Nikita, introducing him to Rebekah, who had been a patroness of Nikita's work in Dallas, and who used to fly him to her retreats in Nassau, New York, Rhode Island, and Sneden's Landing. When Rebekah had thrown Bobby out into the streets, bereft, on the verge of suicide, Nikita had always been there to catch him.

His arrival with Bobby meant there was a new inner circle around Rebekah, consisting of the two of them and their friends. That included Raymond Wilson, the pianist, and Joy O'Neill, the choreographer-dance teacher-psychic who read cards and told fortunes. "These were her parlor games," says Bobby. "She liked having these people around. It was hard, because everybody hated everybody else. But Rebekah didn't worry about that. They were there for her. Everybody else had to deal with it. It was like a royal court."

But as her health worsened, Rebekah began to lose her tolerance. "She'd invite everybody to dinner," says Cappy, "and everybody would be thrilled and have a wonderful time, and she'd say, 'Excuse me,' before coffee, and they'd be waiting and waiting, and she'd never come back down, and that would be the end of the night. She'd go upstairs and say, 'These goddamn people! They want to eat!' And she'd *asked* them there. If she didn't like the way the conversation was going, she'd just get up, never have coffee, just say, 'Excuse me,' and then send someone down and say, 'I'm sorry, Mrs. Harkness retired for the night. You go on with your coffee.' She did it constantly."

When the entourage went down to Nassau, they gathered each day at six-thirty for drinks, as they had for years. By now, though, many of them dreaded the Eternal Cocktail Hour, as they called the daily ritual.

"By evening she was a mess," says Wilson. "The maids fixed

her hair up, then she'd sit for dinner and try to find something to talk about that wasn't deep. Unfortunately, the weather doesn't change that much, so we had to find another topic. I'd try to get her to talk to about something she'd remember. Then she would frequently get mean, and Willard, the butler, would take me aside and say, 'Mr. Wilson, you must never talk about anything serious.'

"She was a strange beast. She got so drunk during dinner, she literally had her face down in the mashed potatoes, and Willard would try to get her face out as gracefully as possible. Then she would wake up about twenty minutes later and start screaming."

Rebekah's special drinks were always on hand, including the Pink Drink. "There was always something wrong with her stomach," says Wilson. "One night I had acid stomach and I went to get some Maalox. She bought it by the gross. I opened a bottle and it was rum. The poor woman was not supposed to be drinking, so she had stashed all the rum in the Maalox bottles!"

She carried so much medicine, she called herself Nurse Jane Fuzzy Wuzzy, a reference from the Uncle Wiggly books. She often fell down and hurt herself. She used to drop her handbag walking down the street. And at night, Bobby or Nikita or Raymond often had to carry her home when she passed out.

"I couldn't stand it," says Bobby. "I would be sitting in my room watching television and I would hear this big *whump!* *wham,* and she had fallen down in her room. She was drinking so much and still taking Talwin. How she didn't fall over and hit her head on the toilet or the bathtub, I don't know. And since she had this problem with her thighs, she couldn't get up off the floor. She was just so drunk, and I would pick her up and put her in bed. And she said, 'Oh, poor Bobby, you have to put up with this.'

"Alcoholics try to make amends to everybody they wronged when they were drinking," says Bobby. "By bringing us back, I always felt she was trying to reconstruct what she had when things were good. But she couldn't drink. She got so mean when she was drunk."

Celebrating her birthday at a Nassau night spot, Rebekah

asked the band to play one of her compositions, and when the musicians said they weren't familiar with it, she threatened to have them all fired. Those at Capricorn referred to it as "a rich man's Alcatraz," knowing full well they were the prisoners.

After returning from Silver Hill, Rebekah decided her estate at Sneden's Landing carried with it only bad memories of her marriage to Lauersen. She had the antiques and paintings in it auctioned off at Sotheby's, and sold the house for $1 million to Elaine Isley, wife of a member of the Isley Brothers singing group.

Her medical condition deteriorated. She was often in great physical pain from her hip, but she refused to take care of herself. "Rebekah wouldn't go through proper rehabilitation," says Bobby. "She would get bored. She had a real hard time sitting still."

In the spring of 1980, Bobby and she went down to Mexico for the Cervantes Festival. "Rebekah's music was being played, and I thought it would be good for her to get out and see people," he says. "She had been so reclusive since the company closed. So we went down to Mexico, and she started feeling real constipated. She was always complaining she didn't feel well."

In June, not long after they returned to New York, they went to Long Island to see a dance performance. On the way back, Rebekah said, "Bobby, I can't stand it. I've never had such gas pains in my life. I'm getting so bloated."

Maria New came over and took Rebekah to the hospital. At about 2:00 P.M., when Bobby arrived to see her, she was being wheeled out of her room on the way to surgery. "She was so distended, her stomach was like she was going to have seven children. You can't believe that someone can swell up like that," he recalls. "They said she probably had an intestinal blockage. It would be a real short operation, just an hour, so Nikita and I stayed in her room. And we stayed and we stayed. At around eight or nine o'clock that night, they brought her back."

After Rebekah came out of surgery, Maria told various friends and members of the household the grim news: Massive tumors were obstructing Rebekah's bowels; they had started in her uterus and spread to her intestines. There was some hope, but the chemotherapy that would be necessary to treat the growths could be devastating to Rebekah. Maria was not very optimistic.

"Don't tell anybody," she said. "She doesn't have long. It's cancer."

22

DARKNESS
HOUSE

ikita Talin was to take charge of Harkness House, but it had already been in serious decline for several years and it was not exactly clear what he and Bobby were taking over. An opportunity to study at the Harkness School of Ballet at Harkness House had been coveted by young dancers; even after Rebekah's many fiascoes, the school had continued to be a serious force in the New York dance world. One reason was that David Howard, a highly regarded dance teacher, was its director. He was so well thought of that even after the folding of Rebekah's last troupe, some of the best dancers in the world—among them Gelsey Kirkland, Natalia Makarova, and Peter Martins—took class with him. But he quit a few years before Bobby and Nikita arrived, and whatever glory remained at Harkness House quickly faded; it continued to exist only by virtue of the foundation Rebekah had created years before. She herself had completely lost interest. M'liss Crotty and Rebekah's administrators sought to maximize the building's return by renting it out to institutions and celebrities for private parties and receptions. Often, however, when the caterers left, there was not always someone there to clean up properly.

Those who knew Harkness House at the height of its glory were astonished by the decay. "The contrast was unbelievable," says a dance teacher whose tenure spanned both eras. "It had been a spotless, elegant town house, very open sexually, with gorgeous men and women hanging around in tights and leotards, the finest dancers, doormen, great paintings on the walls. Now there were no standards. The worst bunch of untalented people. Magnificent pianos were left untuned. The lights were literally dimmed—they used twenty-five-watt bulbs." People began to call it Darkness House.

By the time Bobby and Nikita took it over in 1979, it had become a travesty. "There was just nothing left of the school," says Bobby. "The draperies were ruined. The building smelled to high heaven. It looked like some horror movie place fallen apart."

Bobby and Nikita, of course, saw themselves as the saviors of Rebekah's defiled dream, armed with a mandate to restore it to its former glory. "We were like Christ driving the thieves from the temple," Bobby says. But exactly who the thieves were depended on one's point of view.

Nikita, for one, was hardly a popular choice to head Harkness House. Gruff, overweight, a cigarette constantly dangling from one side of his mouth, with his fleshy jowls and long stringy hair greased back, he was true Texas Gothic, a man whose persona seemed a product of another time and place. Born Howard Sperling in Chicago in 1920, he took a Russian name, as was the custom among many American dancers of his era. As a youth in the thirties, he danced with Ruth Page's Chicago Opera Ballet, the San Carlo Opera Ballet, and later the Ballet Russe de Monte Carlo, principally in character roles. When his career as a dancer ended, he moved to Dallas as a dance teacher in 1951.

In the fifties, Nikita married June Josey, a Dallas oil heiress, and gained a certain recognition giving dance lessons to the daughters of Dallas society. He was frequently written up in the Dallas papers, and his wife's family gave him an entrée to Dallas's establishment. "I was used to living with the Joseys, my dear," he says. "I'm not no little kid that somebody picked up."

In 1959, he went to El Paso to choreograph for a local dance company. There he met the nineteen-year-old Bobby Scevers, a sophomore at Texas Western University. They immediately hit it off, spending nights cruising the streets of Juarez across the border. Nikita had divorced his wife, and Bobby came to live with him in Dallas. "When I met Nikita, everything fell into place," says Bobby. "I knew this is it. He was like a god to me. He represented everything I wanted to achieve."

As he put on weight over the years, it became difficult to think of Nikita as a dancer. Instead, he affected an ursine demeanor full of bombast and swagger. He dressed extravagantly and became increasingly eccentric. "Others were terrified of him or hated him with all their hearts," Bobby says. "But I was never afraid of Nikita. He can be very brusque. And, as a teacher, he doesn't care if he hurts your feelings. He is difficult, temperamental, moody, demanding, sometimes so inconsiderate you can't believe it. He has an image of what he thinks a dancer is capable of and he won't accept anything else, and he will point out your sore spots and make fun of you, and it can be hard to take. But then he can turn right around and be so thoughtful, so wonderful, brilliant, and intuitive."

Others were not quite so generous about him. "Nikita was crude," says a former employee of his at Harkness House. "Bobby was very nice. But Nikita had a terrible temper. He would explode over the slightest thing. He was always afraid someone was going to take his place. If you ever left Nikita's name off anything, he would get paranoid. 'I am the director of the school,' he would say. 'Let it never be forgotten.' The stationery had to say 'Nikita Talin, Director.'"

"[Nikita and Bobby] exercised their power very arbitrarily," says Nancy Bielski, one of the more popular teachers at Harkness House. "They canceled class just to show you they had power. Bobby had very positive goals. He wanted to make it a good school. But I could never explain what Nikita was doing. Nikita would start screaming at me. There was always the feeling of conspiracy in the air, of one group plotting against another."

Bobby at least had paid his dues over seventeen years. But Nikita was new on the scene. "None of them wanted a man like me," he says. "I took all the power away from them. They'd had free rein. Then they had to answer to me."

Nevertheless, the disintegration of Harkness House continued unabated. One by one, the best of the remaining teachers left. Many classes were discontinued. Its physical condition worsened even further. Dancers complained that the floors were dangerously slippery, even unsanitary, from spillage after weekend parties. In the bathroom, the tubs were littered with cigarette butts and dirty linen. One employee who was emptying ashtrays was startled to find in one a rotten human tooth.

A student group called Noverre Society protested the canceling of classes, firing of good teachers, broken barres, and unsanitary conditions. Scores of teachers and students signed petitions criticizing Nikita's administration. Some of the protesters found their lockers mysteriously vandalized. Meanwhile, several members of the Harkness House board of directors pondered whether to take action against Bobby and Nikita. One director wrote another that it would be "difficult to prove moral grounds which, whether true or not, are judgmental at best and . . . can, if aired publicly, backfire and result in a possible lawsuit. It could end in a swearing match with nothing really accomplished." Instead, the letter pointed out that the foundation's fund-raising was possibly illegal, that its financial statements were "highly question-able," and that no financial audit had ever been done.

Bobby did not take kindly to the criticisms. "They were just a bunch of old women," he says. "Those old bags were nothing but trouble."

Even when Rebekah was in town, she was no longer in any condition to exercise any authority over Harkness House. Throughout the controversy, her name was rarely invoked. On her infrequent visits there, she wandered through the crumbling dance palace in a daze, usually accompanied by Nikita or Bobby. When she was out of town recuperating, Nikita and Bobby had free run of Harkness House and of her place at the Carlyle.

Attempts to get her involved were futile. "Rebekah was very sick," says one student. "She was oblivious to what was going on. Any letters we wrote to her were never received."

The prognosis for Harkness House was as grim as Rebekah's. "It was on its last legs," says one employee who worked with Nikita. "Harkness House had no bearing on what was happening in the dance world anymore. The dance world was not enriched by anything that was happening there."

It was not just Harkness House that was disintegrating. The huge entourage Rebekah had in the sixties was gone. So was her dance company, and many of the musicians, composers, choreographers, and administrators that went with it. There were no longer large staffs of servants at her remaining homes. Those who did remain engaged in open combat. As the various players jockeyed for position, Rebekah's relatives watched with dismay. "It was like *Rosemary's Baby,*" says Tarwater. "There was a center of evil that lasted longer than the individual people who came and went. It was very heavy. Diabolical. This was the House of Borgia."

Rebekah's wealth had once been reported as high as $450 million. Those close to her knew that was a gross exaggeration, but it was natural to assume she still had great sums of which to dispose in her will. "All these people thought they were inheriting money," says Nikita. "I came in and changed their whole world. Oh, they hated me."

No one was safe. M'liss Crotty had been on Rebekah's staff for several years, but her position was largely a function of having grown up as Terry's best friend in Watch Hill. She thought of herself as Rebekah's goddaughter.

"M'liss always had the information," says Cappy. "She was like *The New York Times*. She would keep Mrs. Harkness abreast of everything that Terry was doing." Such intimacy with Rebekah provoked jealousy from the house staff. "Rebekah helped M'liss buy a car and gave her other perks." says Cappy. "We were never compensated like M'liss. We were only employees."

Bobby and Nikita hated M'liss. "She had this whole group of real no-good worthless hangers-on that were her friends," says Bobby. "Every weekend we would go out to Sneden's Landing and M'liss would say, 'Oh well, wouldn't you like to have so-and-so and so-and-so?' And they would all come out to Sneden's Landing and just get loaded. Champagne would be going and steaks would be going. And Rebekah would have nothing to do with it. She was so out of it during this time. And they would all be standing around, laughing and drinking.

"M'liss was the last thing Rebekah needed, with these phony benefits for the Harkness Foundation that never made any money. They might raise fifty thousand dollars, but it would cost about fifty thousand dollars, and they would be lucky if they made one hundred dollars' profit. The phone bills were astronomical, and Rebekah thought all this was ruining her name. So Nikita stopped all the benefits, and M'liss's whole reason for being was threatened.

"Then M'liss started spreading rumors about Nikita. She was always trying to get rid of Nikita. Rebekah came to me, very nicely. She said, 'I don't believe what I just heard. I'm not going behind your back. I'm going to tell you straight out.'

"I hit the ceiling. It's just that same evil, vicious, malicious gossip. I said, 'That's it!! I'm not putting up with this. I am leaving. It's either her or me. I've had it. I'm going home.' It was a terrible scene. And Rebekah said, 'Don't leave, don't leave, no, no.' That's how M'liss got out of there. Superfast."

M'liss saw it differently, however. She claims the fund-raising events she planned were not nearly so bad as Bobby says and that her departure from Rebekah's entourage was neither sudden nor bitter. Moreover, when Sneden's Landing was empty, it seemed like a "mausoleum" to Rebekah. She had insisted M'liss fill it with houseguests.

M'liss was not the only adversary of Bobby and Nikita. Cappy and Joe Pantori had a feud with them that went back years. Their real antagonist was not so much Bobby as Nikita. "Nikita was very obnoxious," Cappy says. When Rebekah was selling her house in Watch Hill in 1973 and moving all her furniture to Sneden's, a statue by western artist Frederic Remington was missing. When Joe investigated, he decided it had been stolen by Nikita. Rebekah then sent her accountant, Ted Bartwink, and Joe down to Texas to find it.

"They appeared at Nikita's door, and his poor little old mother opens the door and they say, 'We're from Harkness,'" recalls Bobby. "They just stomped through the house like a couple of bullies. And of course there were no Remingtons. Nikita is not a thief. Because he can be so obnoxious, Nikita's really been the brunt of a lot of abuse that just isn't true."

"I was in a difficult position," says Nikita. "Every morning when she'd bring the tray, Cappy'd say terrible things about me. Cappy and Joe just wanted me out because Rebekah had faith in me."

Bobby detested the Pantoris. "If you could see how they were bleeding her," says Bobby. "Cappy would moan and groan about what a hard time they had. But they always had very good salaries."

As the battle wore on, Joe's position became increasingly tenuous. "They didn't want another man around," says Cappy. "They didn't get to her when Joe was around. We knew it was coming."

Finally, Cappy and Joe were dismissed. "[Rebekah] always

said to me, 'You're gonna be well taken care of.' So you feel bitter and hurt. Years ago, I had said, 'Joe, I don't want you to work for her. I want you to stay with the union, where you have a pension.' We never got overtime or anything for the late nights and weekends. And when you stay twice with a woman in the hospital and no one, not even her children, is there, and no one even cares and later someone gets to her and says, 'Forget about them. What do you owe them?'—it really hurts."

ENDGAME

 n June 25, 1981, Rebekah drew up a new will under the supervision of Barrett G. "Barry" Kreisberg, her latest attorney. Theoretically, she was still calling the shots, but she was impressionable and she could be easily swayed. Whenever new people—regardless of whether they merited suspicion or not—joined the fold in a potentially powerful position, the hackles went up on every member of her entourage.

Rebekah had first hired Kreisberg five years earlier, before her divorce from Niels Lauersen. She had become wary of the pricey Park Avenue attorneys she had hired and fired so often in the past. At the time, Joe Pantori had argued that since she owned a home in Sneden's Landing, a divorce nearby would be faster, less expensive, and likely to generate less notoriety. An acquaintance of Joe's recommended Kreisberg.

Kreisberg, a former minor league professional basketball player, had been a member of the town council of Greenburgh, New York. He had subsequently developed a general practice in nearby White Plains involving corporate, real estate, matrimonial, and estate work. "When he walked in, this big giant of a man, Mrs. Harkness was very impressed," says Cappy. "She was always impressed by someone who was big and tall."

Rebekah had not redone her will in some five years. That in itself was unusual. Previously, she had made significant changes as often as two or three times a year. So long as she changed her mind again and again, so long as she was in good health, it didn't really matter what her will said. But now she had cancer. Her entire fortune was on the line.

Following their dismissal, Cappy and Joe felt bitter about having recommended Kreisberg in the first place. "There's lawyers that'll come to you and say, 'Gee, if you could get me a job with Mrs. Harkness, I'll take care of you.' But he never went to bat for us. When she told him we were fired, he probably was so scared, he probably said, okay, take them out of the will. Never a good word in our defense.

"All the people stole from her—money and dresses," says Cappy. "But I was really very careful. Everything was aboveboard and on the up-and-up. You wonder. Sometimes people were better off stealing from her—everybody else came out smelling like a rose."

But Cappy's sentiments were irrelevant. Rebekah and Kreisberg executed the new document in her apartment at the Carlyle. One of the witnesses nervously made small talk. "I hope you never have to use it," he told Rebekah.

"Believe me," she replied, "so do I."

Rebekah was undergoing a rigorous course of chemotherapy, so toxic she often got violently ill. The only redeeming aspect of the treatment was that it made her not want to drink. But she became so susceptible to infection that rather than brave the New York winter holed up at the Carlyle, she went to Tucson, where her brother, Allen West, lived.

Called Frère to distinguish him from his father and his son, who were both also named Allen Tarwater West, he had been Rebekah's chaperon through the Bitch Pack days and had accompanied her on their notorious round-the-world voyage on the *Empress of Britain*. Both had been eager to leave behind the provincial midwestern sensibilities that had imprisoned them.

Frère had worked as a policeman in Washington, D.C., when he was nineteen, in an aircraft factory during the war, and periodically as a photographer and rancher. He had inherited enough from his father that he never really had to work for a living, but not much more. "He never entered the world of infinite choice, of yachts and estates in the Bahamas," says his son Tarwater. "It was very hard for an older brother to have a sister who is the bête noire of the ballet world, the gold-plated pariah of St. Louis. He was very sensitive to her tremendous monetary success relative to his own slight ability to exist without working.

"My father had the strongest sense of self-betrayal. It is not easy *not* having to work for a living. It is a curse—this tiny myopic existence vis-à-vis who gets what. *That* is the family heritage—their only sense of identity is what can be earned through inheritance rather than through personal achievement. They define themselves in terms of what they get, rather than what they produce. And it was not just our family. It is a universal flaw in that world of deb parties. In the outside world they melt like sugar candy."

After Betty, as Frère continued to call his sister, inherited her fortune from Harkness, the relationship became increasingly distant. "I always loved Betty," he says. "But I was out in Arizona raising cattle, and she went on tours with the dance company. She never included me. She didn't care about anything except her own little world. I didn't know where I fit in. I was just her brother."

Now that her life was coming to an end, Rebekah was ready to reconcile her differences with Frère. After all, they had a lot in common, sharing, among other frailties, "demon rum, mood-changing chemicals, and a profound need to justify an existence they had never earned," as Tarwater puts it.

Rebekah and her entourage arrived in Tucson in August 1980. "It was so miserably hot, and we stayed in her brother's house," says Bobby. "He had this miserable, pitiful little cottage house. It was awful. And he had these old alcoholic girlfriends who were so huge they could hardly get through the door."

Along with Bobby, Rebekah brought down Joy and Nikita. Bobby, with his characteristic tact and delicacy, describes Rebekah's relationship with her brother: "He was such an obnoxious old fart. He had a very funny sense of humor, but he was a professional playboy, and that's not very attractive when you're seventy-eight years old or whatever. He was really into porno movies and smoking pot. He would go out and get two or three hookers, bring them back to the house, and they'd all watch porno movies. She found that very unattractive.

"And he is the world's stingiest person. She thought he was a vulture sitting on a fence post. He'd ask what she was going to leave his kids when she died, and that made her mad. Everything about him irritated her—he smacked his teeth, he banged his fork on the plate, and made noises when he ate. He was hard of hearing and wouldn't get a hearing aid, and she hated that."

Even the most disparate members of Rebekah's entourage developed an aversion to Frère. "He was a real leech," says Cappy. "He never had a dime to tip when he came to visit. All he wanted was to get money for his family. He was just around for whatever he could get."

One night, Rebekah and Frère, accompanied by several members of her group, drove across the desert to Frère's favorite strip joint, where there they argued about her will. As the strippers strutted down the runway, she chided him over his taste for fleabag dives.

"All that schooling for this?" she said.

"Betty, there are many forms of schooling," he replied. "And there are many kinds of schools."

Then he started in on her will. "You're not thinking straight, Betty. Forget those people."

Frère insists Nikita's and Bobby's motives were mercenary. "They were just after the money," he says. "Frankly, I thought Nikita Talin had Betty hog-tied somewhere. Every time she would think of getting rid of him, she'd take him back. He was an operator."

Rebekah soon became disheartened with her rapprochement with her brother. She had bought a magnificent house near the University of Arizona and the hospital where she was treated, and each day Frère came over for dinner. "He just came over for his free meal," says Bobby.

Meanwhile, Rebekah hired a music teacher and studied composition as much as her chemotherapy would allow. "It was so awful to see her after those treatments," says Joy. "She came home, and she threw up until I thought her guts would come out. When she'd start to feel a bit better, we'd go next door to the Arizona Inn and swim and exercise until it was time to go back. She dreaded it. She said, 'Why do I bother?' She started giving up the fight."

Rebekah finally left Tucson for good in the fall of 1981 and returned to New York. But as winter approached, the climate again became too rough for someone undergoing chemotherapy. Just before Christmas, she went to Nassau. As her illness progressed, she lost some of the anger that had been such a driving force in her life. Terry visited her at Capricorn, and Rebekah showed her an almost maternal warmth she had rarely displayed before. "She was more sedate, more introspective," said one friend. "She had always been driven. But now she was calmer, more spiritual. For the first time, she almost became a normal mother."

"Rebekah loved the Bahamas," says Joy. "She loved her house there. It was quiet, peaceful. There wasn't all the ballet bullshit that we had here—all the conniving nonsense. She could create. She could go to her little studio and do her thing."

At times, Rebekah seemed far healthier than anyone could have hoped. "It was like the last burst of life," Joy says. "All the cells pushing together for that last burst. Suddenly she looked twenty years younger. Every morning we'd go and walk on the beach. Nobody else was there. When she found a sand dollar, it was like finding gold. Suddenly I saw her as a little girl who never grew up.

"But sometimes Rebekah just sat there, despondent, playing solitaire, knowing the end was coming. Whenever she had problems she would go to the studio. She just sat there in a chair, looking out at the sea. She was trying to deal with death."

Being in Nassau was good for her spirits, but it was not long before she took a sudden turn for the worse. "We went for these walks along the beach," says Bobby. "All her energy was gone. She'd walk just three or four feet and be so out of breath she couldn't finish."

"I got a phone call from the butler," says Maria New, who had begun to monitor Rebekah's health. "She was white as a sheet. She needed a transfusion." Nassau was too far from the kind of medical facilities Rebekah needed. On New Year's Day 1982 she returned to New York.

Maria Iandolo New and her husband, Dr. Bertrand New, a psychiatrist, had been undergraduates at Cornell University when they married, and both later attended medical school at the University of Pennsylvania. In 1954 they took internships at Bellevue Hospital, but Maria left after a year to work in pediatrics at New York Hospital.

Aggressive, high-powered, and ambitious, Maria, now fifty-three, had been appointed chairman of both the Department of Pediatrics and its division of endocrinology at New York Hospital, becoming the first woman to chair a department at that institution. It was a position that spoke to her adroit political and administrative skills as well as her talent as a medical scientist. Not that she was well liked; rather, she was known as "a survivor," someone who "played hardball." "She made enemies," says one colleague; "she didn't make friends." Nevertheless, Dr. New was widely published in the most prestigious medical journals and was nationally known for her research. *Harper's Bazaar* hailed her as "superdoctor," *The New York Times* as one of several "women ahead of their time" in raising a family while having a successful career, and *New York* magazine named her one of the one hundred top doctors in New York City.

Rebekah had been friends with Maria on and off since the birth of Angel fifteen years earlier. "We became friends from the point of view of true friendship," says Dr. New. "I was one of the few people in her life who had her own profession. I'm very busy. I had very little time to visit her. But I was there when she needed me."

Maria was not a cancer specialist, or even Rebekah's physician; but as a doctor, she could explain to Rebekah exactly how serious her illness was and could make certain Rebekah got the best medical care possible. "Maria was an 'in' to the hospital," says Bobby. "Any time Rebekah called Maria she had access to medical advice. And she had a horror of not being able to get to the right doctor or the right kind of care."

As Rebekah relied increasingly on Maria, various servants, relatives, and hangers-on went about their Byzantine machinations in hopes of being written into Rebekah's will; Maria became yet one more unforeseen obstacle. Her most bitter antagonist was Terry, who had loathed her since Angel was born in 1967, and thought she was after her mother's money. Many dismissed Terry's feelings as being tainted with displaced anger and guilt, and in her oblique way Maria expressed her own suspicions about Terry's motivations. "I always thought Terry trusted me as a physician," she says. "But I was wrong. Terry never said to me, 'I hate you because you saved my baby's life.' She never said that. That would have to be an interpretation made by others. But she did turn against me."

On the other hand, Terry was not the only one who suggested that Maria's motives might be less than altruistic. "Maria would jump," says Cappy Pantori. "Maria jumped through hoops. She would never hurt Mrs. Harkness, but she wanted to be in the picture because it was beneficial to her."

Even the starchy, proper Miss Weeks had found that when Maria came over to examine Angel, she was more attentive to Rebekah. "She would go upstairs and spend five or six minutes with Angel," says Miss Weeks. "Then she would say, 'You know, I really can't spare the time. Granny wants to see me at six.'"

More to the point, many were jealous because Maria had benefited financially from her relationship with Rebekah, including a loan—later repaid—to buy a country house in Sneden's Landing. Rebekah gave her furniture, and she gave $27,000 to Maria's children. Nor did it hurt Maria's standing at New York Hospital to be close friends with Rebekah, who had already given the hospital $2 million.

Maria, of course, gave considerably in return. "Who's to say what her motives were, or if her motives even mattered," says Bobby. "She was one of the few people Rebekah ever had over that I liked. She was wonderful to be around, so solicitous. She's an educated woman. She was very good to Rebekah. She performed services that Rebekah couldn't have gotten from any other doctor." As her illness progressed, Rebekah relied more on Maria than ever before. When she returned to New York, she arranged a special meeting with her attorney, Barry Kreisberg. On February 4, 1982, she dictated a one-paragraph codicil to her will leaving fifty thousand dollars to Maria.

In Nassau, Rebekah had spent much of her time with Joy O'Neill, the former dancer with the American Ballet Theatre. By now, all the misunderstandings, and Rebekah's suspicions about Joy having an affair with Bobby, had long since been cleared up, and Joy had become one of Rebekah's most trusted confidantes. They went for long walks on the beach in Nassau, and Joy was one of the first people to whom Rebekah turned while she was fighting with Frère in Tucson.

Some doubted the authenticity of Joy's psychic and card-reading powers, which were among her primary attractions for Rebekah. Maria New was one of them. "Of course, good old me, I told Joy what Maria said," Bobby recalls. "And I also told Rebekah. After that, Joy and Maria have never had anything nice to say to each other."

Joy was convinced that Maria was jealous. "She wasn't too happy that Rebekah and I were together all the time, having fun, traveling all over the world," says Joy.

Even Bobby, who was friends with both the warring women, thought there might be some truth in Joy's assessment. "Joy was a threat to Maria," he says, "another women close to Rebekah who might get in and get something."

Whenever Joy was present, one topic of discussion was the case of Claus von Bülow, then under indictment for the December 1980 attempted murder of his wife, Sunny, the daughter of utilities magnate George Crawford. Von Bülow was the *trompe l'oeil* lord of New York and Newport society, a man of "fatal charm," as social chronicler Dominick Dunne put it, who inspired feelings ranging from "detestation to zealotry." Specifically, von Bülow had been charged with injecting his millionairess wife with an overdose of insulin that left her in a coma from which she has never recovered. The charges did more than rock Rhode Island's Gold Coast. This was the most notorious society trial of the decade.

Joy's involvement in the trial came via a job she had had as an exercise instructor at the Manya Kahn Body Rhythm Exercise Studio, a chic Manhattan health club. It was there that she had met Sunny von Bülow; Sunny had chosen her, she said, as her favorite exercise instructor, working out with her five times a week for five years. The two had become like "sisters," as Joy put it, exchanging intimate personal confidences. As recounted in William Wright's book, *The Von Bülow Affair,* Sunny had even offered to set Joy up in a business. When Joy's mother died, Sunny invited her to spend the summer at Clarendon Court, her estate in Newport.

During one tête-à-tête about dieting, Sunny reportedly told Joy the secret behind her own slim figure. "What you need," she

said, "is a shot of insulin." She went on to explain that by injecting it, you could eat what you want, "sweets and everything."

Since the outcome of the trial was likely to be predicated on
medical evidence, such information could be crucial to von
Bülow's defense—and what better defense than a witness who
had knowledge that Sunny injected herself with insulin?

Initially, Rebekah was thrilled with the excitement of the trial,
and offered to go to Providence with Joy; Rebekah had known
Sunny's mother, Annie Laurie Crawford Aitken. As the trial
took its course in Providence, it made headlines day after day.
When the lawyers called, Joy took the phone in Rebekah's bedroom at the Carlyle. Rebekah listened intently, overhearing their
conversation.

"By the way," she said to Joy. "Ask where Sunny got the
insulin."

But ultimately, Rebekah was so disturbed by the chaos surrounding the trial that she decided she didn't want Joy to testify.
That left Joy in a bind: Everyone else was positioning themselves
to get into Rebekah's will. If she antagonized Rebekah now, she
might jeopardize her own standing. "I thought, Well, I'm not
here for that. I don't care about not getting anything. Because I
went on the stand for von Bülow—I knew I was gonna lose it. It
didn't matter to me. And so I went."

The prosecution was aware that Joy could be the most damaging witness to their case, and they set about trying to destroy her
credibility. It was not a difficult task. When she took the stand
on March 2, she quickly unraveled. Often, after answering a
question, she paused, then added an irrelevant, damaging
postscript. She admitted taking tranquilizers before coming to
court. Then, unprompted, she said, "Dancers are very hyper
people. Someone is always trying to shoot you down before you
even get onstage." On the witness stand she attacked her former
employer, Manya Kahn, an eighty-year-old woman in ill health.
Worse, she appeared to enjoy it. When questioned about her reluctance to come forward earlier to testify, she said, "I felt like a
criminal. I'm not used to that. You people frighten me."

In the meantime, Rhode Island state police detective John Reise and other members of the prosecution spent a weekend in the Mini-Yellow Storage Company in Yonkers, going through log-books and records of the Manya Kahn Body Rhythm Exercise Studio. From May 16, 1977, when Joy started working at the studio, until the end of the year, the logs showed that Joy had instructed Sunny von Bülow a total of five times—not five times a week as she had claimed. In 1978 and 1979 Sunny visited the studio 210 times—and had not been taught at all by Joy O'Neill.

When the prosecution put their rebuttal witnesses on the stand, Joy was eviscerated. Nancy Raether, another exercise instructor at Manya Kahn's, testified about her friendship with Sunny von Bülow, whom she had instructed some 255 times in 1979 and 1980. Then she was asked about Joy's reputation for telling the truth. She did not seem to want to answer the question, but finally she did.

"I'm afraid it wasn't very good," she said.

As the trial continued into March 1982, such revelations were splashed across the pages of the daily papers. "I never knew I was gonna be a key witness," Joy says. "If I'd known what was going to happen, I never would have said a damn thing. I was devastated." This was a particularly difficult period for her, Joy said, since she was losing the two women who were closest to her: Her "sister," Sunny, was now in a coma, and Rebekah, "the mother I never really had," was dying of cancer. Still, nobody believed her. Even her best friends found it hard to defend her. "Joy just went overboard," says Bobby. "I don't honestly think she was lying, but she couldn't back up her statements."

More to the point, since Joy was actually living with her at the Carlyle, Rebekah was disturbed about her testimony. "We've got to get her out of this house," Rebekah said.

When Joy returned to New York from Providence, she found Nikita had been clipping newspaper articles about the trial and had put them on top of the piano. She was furious. Rebekah had read the clips and confronted Joy: "I think you have a problem with lying," she said. "I think you really need help. And I think you've lied to me before."

"I looked her right straight in the eye," says Joy. "I knew she

meant sleeping with Bobby, and I said, 'Let me tell you something, Rebekah Harkness. You're wrong. You believe all the garbage you want. But I never lied to you. And I'm one of the *few*
people who never has.'

"Then Nikita, in his cute, flamboyant little way, turns around
and says, 'Oh, I have something for you to read.' Like, 'Joy, it
doesn't really matter. I've just slain you, I've just killed you.'
Nikita got me right out of the will. He got himself in. He
planned me right out of there. The whole ballet world knows
that. It was terrible to do to her, because she was already close
enough to death without showing her these horrible things in the
paper. She never would have read any of them."

Joy packed her things. "See what happens when you tell the
truth," she said.

BEDSIDE
MANNERS

n late March 1982,
Rebekah decided to
move to Palm Beach,
which had the ad-
vantage of having a
warm climate and easy access to New York for medical reasons. In
addition to her entourage, she had several contemporaries who
were regular visitors at the house she rented on Via Vizcaya.
Rebekah had never lived there before but was automatically welcome at virtually any party in town.

Of course, her health imposed serious limitations on how much socializing she could do. On April 17 she celebrated her sixty-seventh birthday with a party at her house for about one hundred people. But she rarely left home. "She would have lunches, but not much more," says a friend, Anne Cutler. "She could not entertain. She was not well."

It was difficult for many of Rebekah's friends to get through to her, and they resented it. "She was kept completely from her friends," says Cutler. "The moment I got there I called, and I wasn't allowed to speak to her. It was sad. She was so drugged. Bobby and Nikita were up for the main chance, and there were other people who would have liked to have seen her."

Meanwhile, Rebekah had decided to buy a house in Palm Beach, and Bobby and Nikita and she began to look over the real estate market. She discussed the possibility of Connie Woodward, a friend, writing her memoirs. Finally, she was joined by Terry, who rented a house nearby. "It was her attempt to make friends with Terry," says Maria New. "Terry was always her dearest child, the one she felt most comfortable with."

Of Rebekah's three children, Terry in many ways was the most difficult to figure out. "Terry is as cool as they come," says someone who has known her for years. "She never confides in anyone. She does not show her cards. With Allen and Edith, you knew exactly what they were thinking. They couldn't hide it for a moment. But with Terry you have to be extremely careful. She has an ingenuous way of communicating something so you think she meant something else when she really meant exactly what she said. She is much, much cleverer in a giggly, frothy way than you can possibly know."

Bobby had trouble tolerating her, but even he could be amused. "Everything about Terry irritated me," he says. "She was so rich and so stingy. We never had a cross word, but she was just a twit. Impossible as she is, she seems so scatterbrained it's hard to stay mad at Terry very long. But in a way I think she is a shrewd little cookie."

Shrewd or not, Terry, now thirty-eight, had had a propensity for getting involved with eccentric men. Her latest beau, Wolf-

gang von Falkenburg, known as Wolfie, was a tall German with an imposing Teutonic bearing, to whom Rebekah had taken an intense and immediate dislike. Brusque and abrasive, he infuriated Rebekah's friends and associates in Palm Beach. He was outspoken about his right-wing political views. But his past was a mystery. He was the subject of dozens of rumors that never checked out.

Rebekah was incensed that Wolfie referred to Terry as his wife, since they had not married. "He is *not* my son-in-law," Rebekah told Anne Cutler. More to the point, she intended to keep it that way and asked Kreisberg to investigate him.

"She never liked Wolfie," says Bobby. "Never, ever, ever, ever. If Rebekah could have found a way to get him away from Terry, she would have. When Terry and Wolfie had a fight in Palm Beach, Rebekah was really delighted."

In Nassau, just a few months earlier, Bobby had almost exploded at Wolfie. "Rebekah's tumor was starting to grow," he says. "Gas couldn't pass out in its normal way, so she would belch, terrible belches." One night when she wasn't feeling well, she went to bed early. Bobby joined Terry and Wolfie for drinks after dinner in the living room, when suddenly Terry burped. "Why Terry, you sound exactly like your mother," Wolfie said. Then they started making fun of Rebekah's belching.

Bobby was infuriated. "If I had been more secure," he says, "I would have made a big scene about it. But I just got up and left the room."

Not that Terry wasn't concerned about her mother's health. She was so disturbed about the ravages of chemotherapy that she persuaded Rebekah to discontinue the treatment. Then she hired a woman—described contemptuously by Maria New as a "vegetative therapist"—who fed Rebekah ground carrots. "They were looking for some kind of a health spa for miracle cures," says Bobby. "Terry was very anti-doctor. Especially doctors from New York Hospital."

Initially, Rebekah went along with it. "Maybe I don't need all this chemotherapy," she said. "Maybe I just need good food and the proper vitamins and minerals." But once the new therapist took over, Rebekah found the enemas painful and called a friend in New York asking for help. "I have nurses down here who are killing me," she said.

By late April, she had weakened considerably. Her search for a house had not gone well and, partly in desperation, she settled on an $800,000 home on Ocean Boulevard. The house was at a very good address, but was relatively modest and needed renovation. "Palm Beach was so expensive," says Bobby. "Rebekah didn't feel she could keep up some huge place. She didn't have the energy to look at any more houses. She couldn't even walk upstairs. This wasn't Versailles, but it was certainly nice."

Terry and Wolfie were against buying it. "Wolfie was screaming and yelling: 'What a terrible house. It's falling down.'" says Bobby. "He wanted her to buy some enormous Spanish mansion that was gorgeous and cost millions and millions of dollars." Others thought the biggest problem with the transaction was its timing: After all, Rebekah was dying of cancer. "It was a perfectly good buy," says one of her friends. "Eight hundred thousand dollars is not overpriced for Palm Beach. That wasn't the problem. But it only makes sense to buy if you have a long time."

On April 23 Maria New arrived in Palm Beach. "Rebekah kept asking me to come down, but I never could take a weekend off," she says. "Finally, I did."

The next morning at six Augusta Wallace, Willard's wife, knocked at Maria's door. "Madam is very sick," she said.

Rebekah was in bed, looking dreadful. "She had a very swollen belly," says Maria. "She had had a colostomy. It didn't take much medical knowledge to see she had an obstruction. I told her, 'We've got to get you to a hospital.'"

"Let me rest a while," Rebekah said. "I'll think about it."

Later that morning at about eleven o'clock, Rebekah signed the papers to buy the house. At the last moment, Terry and Wolfie tried to talk her out of it. "They tried to put the kibosh on it," says the real estate agent who sold it. "Wolfie tried very hard. But everything had been signed, sealed, and delivered when he got in the act."

Meanwhile, Rebekah's friends were unaware of her rapidly declining health. "I was meant to be having lunch with her that day," says Anne Cutler, who saw her just a few days earlier. "I thought she was in remission. She looked a lot better. Remission can be deceptive, but she was on an upper."

At the same time, Maria New confronted Terry about Rebekah's medication. "I'd like to talk to you," she said. "Would you put aside your hostility toward me? Your mother is very sick right now. She has an intestinal obstruction. She is going to die from the obstruction if we don't do something."

Terry admitted that Rebekah was no longer taking the medication. Then the woman Terry had hired went into Rebekah's room and closed the door. A few minutes later, Rebekah shrieked in pain. Maria went in. The nurse was trying to clear her obstruction by pushing water into the colostomy. Maria was horrified.

"I cannot be part of this," she told Rebekah. "If you will not go to a hospital, if you will not come to New York, I'm leaving. I cannot stand by and see this. It is too painful."

Maria went for a walk. When she returned, Rebekah called her into her room. She said she wanted to go to New York; and that her attorney, Barry Kreisberg, should charter an ambulance plane. Maria immediately called Rebekah's oncologist, Dr. Morton Coleman, who arranged for a bed in New York Hospital.

Terry had been having lunch with Kreisberg. By the time she returned, Rebekah's bags were packed. Terry was horrified that immediately after finally buying the house, Rebekah was being whisked away. "She only lived in that house for two hours," says Terry, "but they got a healthy commission for selling it."

Anne Cutler agreed. "I think she was coerced into buying it by the real estate business. They knew she was dying. They wanted the commission."

Rebekah had more important questions to deal with than real estate. She left Palm Beach on a chartered plane and a few hours later was admitted to New York Hospital under the care of Dr. Coleman. She was bloated and in great discomfort, with an enormously distended belly.

Rebekah responded quickly once she was back on her medication. She was greatly relieved to be in the hospital. Bobby maintained a bedside vigil, having obtained an "egg crate," as they call the rubber mattresses that are used to prevent bedsores, so he could sprawl out on the floor. He spent hours leafing through magazines with Rebekah. "We were still planning to go back to the house in Palm Beach, so she loved going through *Architectural Digest* to get ideas to decorate the house," he says.

Nikita Talin also spent a great deal of time at the hospital. In addition, Rebekah had brought Augusta and Willard, her servants, up from her estate in Nassau, as well as several other companions. The doctors and nurses tripped over them as they made their way through the tiny hospital room.

"I was criticized for being there all the time, but it was what Rebekah wanted," says Bobby. "She had a horror of being alone. As long as she was awake you couldn't leave her."

"She wanted a crowd around her," says one of the many health professionals who helped care for Rebekah. "The more people around her, the happier she was. They were all being nice to her, and she wanted to be nice to them in return and wanted to take care of everybody. You can tell when vultures are hanging overhead. Everyone wanted a piece of the pie. I questioned their motives, but there was no doubt she wanted them."

The entourage had been at war for more than two years, and their machinations were an open secret among even casual acquaintances of Rebekah's. The most recent casualties in the line of duty had been Cappy and Joe Pantori, Joy O'Neill, M'liss Crotty, and Frère, among others, all of whom were on the outs with Rebekah. Maria, Bobby, and Nikita were still in the ascendancy. In addition, Yuki Irwin, who had worked with Rebekah and the dance company in the mid-sixties, was brought back to give massages to Rebekah as her pain increased.

Rebekah's children, as usual, were most conspicuous by their absence. None of them were at her bedside. Allen was in jail in Florida. Terry and Wolfie had stayed in Palm Beach, with plans to come to New York later. Edith had visited once in March, but was still reluctant to come back and was not clear exactly how serious Rebekah's condition was.

Steadily, Rebekah got worse. Her kidneys were failing, and chemotherapy was discontinued because it was too toxic. "It was starting to look bad," Bobby says. "And then things got worse and worse and worse."

Rebekah still tried to deny how close she was to death. Even when she wasn't taking the chemotherapy, she was on morphine, Valium, and Seconal. Remarkably, she was alert and in reasonably good humor. But her condition continued to deteriorate, her kidneys continued to fail. Her faded hair was falling out, her skin was flaccid. Once she had had such a firm musculature, but now she was emaciated and weak, and the angular bones protruded where muscle tissue had been.

On May 18, according to Bobby, the doctors gave her the bad news. They asked Nikita and Bobby to leave the room, but Rebekah insisted that they stay.

"They told her the treatment just wasn't working," recalls Bobby, "and there was only one other kind of medication to try. Even it might not work, and it would make her susceptible to pneumonia."

If she didn't try the medication, Rebekah was told she had only ten days to live.

"Ten days!" she cried, sitting bolt upright. "I thought I had at least a year."

The next day, Rebekah had a discussion with Maria New about adding a codicil to her will. According to Dr. New, Rebekah had called and asked her to come to her bedside immediately in room 1409. The request was unusuual; Rebekah had always respected the importance of Maria's work. What follows is Dr. New's account of what happened next.

"I don't like to interrupt," Rebekah said, "but I've had some very disturbing news. Please come to me."

Maria ran upstairs. Rebekah told her that a doctor had said she should start putting her affairs in order.

"What does that mean?" Rebekah asked. "Does that mean I'm about to die?"

Maria had no answer, but said she would call Dr. Coleman, the attending physician.

Rebekah would not let it go at that. "In the meantime," she said, "because there is this risk, I want to dictate a codicil to my will."

Maria says she told her to call her lawyer. Rebekah got on the phone, but Barry Kreisberg was on vacation in Norway.

"I don't have to have a lawyer," Rebekah said. "I can dictate a codicil. What you need is a notary public."

Maria got her administrative assistant to take dictation and a notary public to witness the signing of the document. At some point, Maria left the room, and returned. Then, a three-page document was drawn up. It was entitled "Notes to lawyer (Mr. B. Kreisberg)." Just beneath Rebekah's signature was a statement, "This is to certify I have witnessed the signature of Mrs. Harkness on this 3 page codicile (*sic*) to her will dictated on 5/19/82 in Room 1409." Maria signed it as a witness. Then Rebekah asked her to give it to her accountant, Ted Bartwink.

Among other things, the document specified:

- that Yuki Irwin should get fifty thousand dollars.
- that the Palm Beach house would be sold, with the proceeds to be split by Nikita and Bobby.
- that Maria New would get an ermine coat, a sable coat, a string of pearls, earrings, and a pin.

The largest provision of all concerned the sale of Harkness House, whose value on the real estate market was $7 million. The text specified that half of the money should go to ballet, to be managed by Bobby Scevers and Nikita Talin; the other half was to go "to research in medicine to be managed by Maria New."

That meant the largest single beneficiary from Rebekah's estate—due to receive $3.5 million, as much as Rebekah was giving to dance—would be Maria New's medical research. Exactly how that would be administered remained open to interpretation.

Apparently, surprised by the shock waves caused by this incident, Maria insists that she never even read the document. "Whatever infighting there was, was never for my selfish motives," she says. "We had a very satisfying, deep relationship. I helped her as if she were my sister." Dr. New's assistant, Vita Amendolagine, who took the dictation for the document in question, says it was perfectly normal for Dr. New to be there. "She would often go up to see Mrs. Harkness and check on her," she says. "Rebekah would call anytime she felt something was wrong. But Dr. New wasn't manipulating her."

Nonetheless, when Ted Bartwink, Rebekah's accountant, read the three-page document, he was so alarmed he called Kreisberg in Norway and got him to return to New York immediately. Kreisberg had drafted Rebekah's last will a year earlier, as well as a February codicil giving fifty thousand dollars to Dr. New. But the May 19 document raised more serious questions about Rebekah's intentions and the people around her than had any single event at that time.

Kreisberg says, "In my opinion, it was not a valid document." Dr. New herself agrees: "It was an abortion."

First of all, there was the question of Maria New's signing the codicil as a witness—even though she later crossed out her signature. "It is improper for a beneficiary to sign it," says Kreisberg. "Chances are, the bequest wouldn't hold up in court." Moreover, the document was written on Dr. New's department stationary and dictated to her administrative assistant of nearly twenty years. And even if it had been legal, it was against the policy of New York Hospital to allow its employees to sign codicils or wills as witnesses. In addition, a last will and testament, or a codicil, must have an attestation clause declaring the exact intent of the document. This had none.

But it was the content of the "notes" that raised the most disturbing question of all. The biggest single stipulation of it—selling Harkness House and giving away the proceeds—was impossible. Rebekah didn't even own Harkness House; the Rebekah Harkness Foundation did.

"Rebekah couldn't leave Harkness House to anyone," says Kreisberg. "She didn't own it. I'm sure she knew that."

Rebekah, of course, had controlled her trusts and foundations for years. And it was possible, Kreisberg suggests, that these were just legal technicalities to her—that as far as she was concerned, they were all hers to do with as she pleased.

But others—including the family, medical personnel, people employed by Rebekah, and even friends of Maria's—had questions about what had really happened. They knew Rebekah had always been eager to please her friends, that she had lavished gifts upon them all her life. One person who spent a great deal of time with her during this period explains her suspicions. "Suppose I had said, 'I've been with you all this time, Rebekah. Wouldn't it be nice if I had something to remember you by?' Rebekah would have said, 'That's so nice. Why didn't I think of that?' "She was trying to please everybody. She was very emotional. She knew she was going to die and she wanted to make them all happy."

Two days later, on Friday afternoon, May 21, 1982, Dr. New, Bobby, and Kreisberg gathered in Rebekah's hospital room. She had been moved to a new, larger room, number 1404. Kreisberg and Rebekah had gone over the three-page document and had had a new codicil typed up. This time, they would try to do it right.

There was just one problem: getting someone to witness Rebekah's signature. As they had learned in their previous attempt, New York Hospital policy forbids its nurses to serve in that capacity.

At 4:00 P.M. Annette Gilbeaute, a private nurse not employed by the hospital, arrived to begin her shift with Rebekah. Kreisberg asked her to witness the will. She refused. If the matter came to court, none of the medical personnel wanted to testify. Kreisberg explained that since she was not a hospital employee, it would be fine if she signed the document as a witness.

"I know that I can," she said, "but I don't want to."

Meanwhile, Rebekah, ill as she was, was still concerned about her appearance. Due to the chemotherapy, her hair had become scraggly and she had called over to Kenneth's to have some wigs sent over.

While Kreisberg was still looking for a witness, the man from Kenneth's arrived on the scene. "You can be the witness," Kreisberg said as he grabbed the frightened hairdresser. Maria, however, was rounding up others for the task.

Rebekah put on a blond wig. "You look just like Marilyn Monroe," Bobby said.

Rebekah preened. "And what's wrong with that!" she said.

"It was complete chaos," recalls Bobby, "that one last outrageous bit of flair Rebekah had before she died."

"It was so wonderful—everybody running around signing wills and trying on different wigs."

Even Dr. New tried on a wig. Finally, two of her assistants came down to witness the signing of the last codicil to the will of Rebekah Harkness.

RECONCILIATION

dith, now thirty-three, was still profoundly ambivalent about seeing her mother. Edith had visited in March, just before Rebekah went to Palm Beach, but even then she had not been fully aware of the severity of Rebekah's illness.

Edith had not been having an easy time of it. She was seeing a psychiatrist, Dr. John Henderson, regularly—so regularly that her closest friends felt she was much too dependent on him and the drugs he prescribed. A year or so earlier, her weight had soared to nearly two hundred pounds. Now, even though she was on a severe diet, she pleaded embarrassment about seeing her mother until she lost more weight.

In fact, Edith's weight was now down to 125 or 130 pounds, so this was not the real problem. "Edith deeply resented Rebekah for neglecting her all her life," says a friend, "so she made up all sorts of excuses."

"Finally it became apparent she had nothing in common with her mother," says Kenneth Grundborg, Edith's boyfriend at the time. "She had no use for her. She didn't want to visit her."

Nevertheless, her friends persisted. Grundborg's sister, Jean Hope, lobbied as well. "We tried to force her closer to her mother," she says. "We sort of shamed her into it."

Grundborg had coaxed Edith into taking the train up to New York earlier, in March. But the result was a painful encounter during which Grundborg saw Edith's dilemma firsthand. "It wasn't the warm meeting you might expect between a mother and a daughter," he says. "There were strong guilt feelings, a strong resentment that she hadn't gotten the love she deserved over the years."

After that visit with Rebekah, Edith spent most of the spring with Grundborg in California. She had met him just a few months earlier. An army engineer, Grundborg had been stationed in Los Angeles and then in Santa Barbara. But his work required frequent trips to Washington, during which he visited his sister, Jean, whom Edith had hired to groom and exercise her dogs.

It was during one such visit on a cold snowy night in January that Grundborg had first asked Edith to dinner. The roads were so bad that Edith was reluctant. "But we had a marvelous time," he says. "She was fun to be with, the easiest person to be with I have ever met. Very sharp. If she had psychological problems she really didn't show them. She hid them well."

Edith talked freely about her past, however. "This was the first date, and she told me an awful lot," he says. They stayed up until seven in the morning and Edith told him about her so-called Peter Pan episode, her relationship with Rebekah, and her stays in mental hospitals.

Her real problem, Grundborg felt, was Rebekah. "Her mother didn't give her a tumble," he says. "Edith never wanted for anything except love." Grundborg was eager to provide that love. He was transfixed by Edith's beauty, openness, and vulnerability. Though he was stationed on the West Coast, he made every effort to see her as much as possible. Edith remained close friends with his sister, Jean, and told people that their family was "so normal you could talk to them and they would do things for you without wanting anything in return." They were the average, down-to-earth, all-American family she had never had. Meanwhile, she spent as much time as possible with Grundy, as she affectionately called him. In March she spent two months in California. They talked about getting married.

Not that their relationship was free of problems. Much as he loved Edith, Grundborg had his own feelings to protect. Never married, at age forty-four he had fallen head over heels for her, but he was wary of her reluctance to settle down. "I didn't want to get hurt badly on this," he says. "I knew she had many boyfriends before me."

Grundborg was also concerned about Edith sitting home alone in California, not even knowing the neighbors, while he worked during the day. For her part, Edith was already jealous of the time he spent on his career. She had more than enough money for both of them, and she asked him to give up the service. He would have nothing of it. He enjoyed his work, which dealt with landing operations of NASA's space shuttle, and he had just been promoted to colonel. He was about to be transferred to Duncanville, Texas, a prospect that did not make Edith happy.

Logistical and geographic problems aside, Grundborg seemed far too innocent for a woman who had been through as much as Edith, who had escaped from the surreal world of her driven, addicted, unloving mother and her entourage, into one run by psychiatrists and psychopharmaceuticals. When he and Edith had visited Rebekah in New York, in March that year, Grundborg got his first astonishing glimpse of the opulence with which Edith had grown up.

Rebekah adored Grundborg. She reacted with such delight when he brought videocassettes for her new VCR; she told him she couldn't believe someone would do something for her without ulterior motives. The nurses who cared for Rebekah liked him as well; in the midst of the various sycophants competing for Rebekah's attention, Grundborg—clean-cut, upright, brave, honest, and true—stood out like Dudley Do-Right in Sodom and Gomorrah. Only he, the nurses seemed to think, could be Edith's savior.

Back in New York, what remained of Rebekah's life could be measured in days, yet her children were not by her bedside. According to some sources, she was so bitter at their absence that she had no intention of letting them know she was dying. But others say she had completely reassessed her relationship with them and was reluctant to call them because she felt she had been such a lousy mother. "She said she didn't deserve her children," says one friend. "She had done them enough harm already. She didn't want them to come because she didn't have the right to impose such a burden on them."

In either case, Maria New interceded. "It was I who insisted that she call her children to her bedside at the last minute," she says. "I begged her to do it."

When Edith heard the news, she did not want to go. She had been trying to come to terms with her own alcoholism and was taking Antabuse, a drug that induces nausea when combined with alcohol. She was more dependent on analysis than ever before. Now that she was involved with Grundborg, she did not want to leave him, especially to see Rebekah. But Grundborg could not conceive of anyone staying away from a dying mother and urged to her to go to Rebekah's side. "Your mother is not going to live forever," he told her. "She's dying." It seemed that in order to keep him, Edith had to go—even though the very act of going separated them.

When she arrived in New York near the end of May, nothing

had changed in the drama over which Edith had anguished all her life. It still featured a cast of extraordinary eccentrics, all of whom stood between her and her mother.

"I could see immediately why Edith had left it all behind," says Grundborg, reflecting on his March visit. "This wasn't the real world. This was fiction. Rebekah said she was lonely, but there were all these characters hanging around and Rebekah was complaining that they were all out to get her, that they were all out for her money."

Edith was once again the reluctant heiress subject to her mother's perverse fantasies and expectations. She was both the only one there who truly belonged and the most out of place. She was the child Rebekah had always loved and feared more than the others, and the only real Harkness.

And now Rebekah was down to her last few days of consciousness. Emaciated, incapable of eating, literally starving to death as her tumors sapped her strength, she was surrounded by vultures, parasites, and sycophants, preying over her fortune. For the first time in her life, she openly expressed her affection to Edith. As she dozed off under the balm of her medication, she murmured again and again, "My beautiful darling daughter." When she was conscious, she expressed regret that her children never found a cause, as she had. "My kids never knew what to do with their money," Rebekah said. But for the first time, she took responsibility for the pain she had caused them. She told Edith she was sorry for giving her only all the material things, and no love. Friends of the two who came and went during the illness saw that Rebekah finally realized her failure as a mother. "I could see the love," says one friend. "Rebekah never really cried, but there was a loving tear in her eye. She was grateful to see Edith every day. At the end she regretted all she had done and was warm and kind, and she was genuine about it. You could see it."

Edith responded warmly as well. Prepared to stay just a day or two, she had come with only one pair of blue jeans, which the housekeeper had to wash each night so they would be clean the next morning. Instead, she stayed on, rarely leaving her mother's side. She had always made light of her emotional problems, but now, as the battle for her mother's affections reached the end-game stage, she was truly moved. This was the conflict that she had always avoided, always thought could never be resolved.

That didn't mean that Edith had Rebekah all to herself. On the contrary, Rebekah's retinue was a potent reminder of the years Edith had been in the way of her mother's career.

Bobby, Edith knew, was somewhat different from most of them. "When she and Grundborg visited earlier that year, Edith left an elaborate food processor for me," says Bobby. "There was a note saying, 'Thank you for taking such good care of my mother.' I was floored."

But others were still battling for Rebekah's attention. Yuki Irwin who was back at Rebekah's side, and Maria New were at each other's throats. According to Bobby, a few days after Edith arrived, Yuki entered Rebekah's hospital room, where Edith and Bobby were keeping vigil. Maria, Yuki told him, had claimed he and Nikita were "horrible and money-grubbing" and were badgering Rebekah about her will.

"I didn't know how to react," says Bobby. "I was stunned. This was the first time I'd had any indication that Maria was like that."

Later that day, Maria came into the room. Bobby was curt and hostile. When he confronted her in private, she turned ashen and denied everything.

"How could anybody be so mean?" Maria said. Over the next hour and a half, she assured Bobby she had always thought he was good for Rebekah, and that Yuki had fabricated the whole thing.

Then Bobby went back and told Yuki about his conversation with Maria. "Well, Yuki turned even a higher shade of yellow. After that, they never spoke to each other again."

Nevertheless, the infighting between the two women continued to escalate. "Yuki started saying things about the will which alienated first Edith from me and then Terry," says Maria. "Finally, I was visiting Rebekah when Yuki was there and Rebekah was in a coma. Then Yuki said, 'Leave the room. The children don't want you near her.'"

Terry also arrived that week, but she did not spend as much time at her mother's bedside as Edith. Bobby was horrified by what he thought was her apparent lack of sensitivity. "I realize that how people act is not always how they really feel," he says. "But if you ever see anybody dying of cancer, it's the most ghastly thing you could ever imagine. I was going through the agonies of the damned. I still get so emotional I can hardly talk.

"Rebekah couldn't go to the bathroom, but she could still urinate. And because she couldn't get out of the bed, I would pick her up and put her down on one of these portable toilets. And Terry would just sit there—with no reaction. None. I mean, I just will never understand how you can look at that and not have some emotion.

"Rebekah really couldn't eat anything. But once they thought she could try watermelon because it is all liquid. But she was so drugged and so weak that when she'd try to chew it, she couldn't hold the juice in her mouth and it would all drool down the front. She was starving to death, so gaunt. And Terry was just sitting there in her blank way with a hibiscus in her hair."

Edith, however, defended her half sister. "We each have our own way of coping," she said. "My way is to be here. But Terry has a hard time."

Later that week, Maria arranged for Rebekah to call Allen at Raiford State Prison in Florida. Rebekah was reluctant. She had not spoken to Allen in years, but Maria insisted she call nevertheless. Terry dialed the number, and she and Maria wept as Rebekah talked to Allen.

"Allen, I'm sorry," she said. Her tone was even and unemotional as she explained that she felt bad for sending him off to boarding school and neglecting him as a child. "I want to apologize for making you the black sheep in the family."

"It doesn't matter," he said. "Things happen for the best. Maybe it's better this way, maybe I'm better off. My name's not

351

in the paper like yours. I never had to put up with all the things you did."

Even as her condition deteriorated, Rebekah, in her way, was as strong and willful as ever. More than once, a doctor assembled friends and family to say that he was administering such strong doses of narcotics that if they had anything to tell Rebekah, they should say it then and there because she would probably never wake.

"She had such a high tolerance to narcotics that this happened again and again," Bobby says, describing those last few weeks. "But each time she would wake up again. And the next day she would be reading the *National Enquirer* and doing barre. She was so strong she had a hard time dying."

After one such warning from the doctor, Bobby found himself alone in the hospital room. "I sat there and I realized there were no secrets between Rebekah and me. She knew what my actual preference was. She knew I was homosexual. She didn't care. She never cared because she just didn't consider that anything. I think very often women are delighted, because they think, well, it's an ego trip for them. The last years, though . . . there was nothing personal at all.

"But then I felt, here she is, she's dying. Maybe I better tell her I love her."

Rebekah was half asleep. "I love you, Rebekah," Bobby said.

She sat up in bed. "You do? I always thought you hated being with me because I was so old and horrible."

"That's not true. It's always been an honor to be with you."

At that moment, Edith walked in and found the two of them crying.

"Edith, I'm sorry you have to see this," Rebekah said. "But Bobby is the only person I've felt comfortable with since your father died. I can't explain it and I don't understand it, but . . ."

Silently, Edith handed Bobby a napkin to blow his nose and tiptoed out of the room.

That week, the doctor announced the first bit of good news in quite some time. The tumor had shrunk a tiny bit and it was possible to make a last-ditch effort to save Rebekah's life with massive doses of chemotherapy. She had been taking so many drugs that she had been fading in and out of consciousness, but now the dosage of narcotics could be reduced to the point where she was able to talk again and to understand when the doctors explained that it would be an elaborate and painful process. Maria argued for her to take more chemotherapy.

But Rebekah was agitated and uncomfortable and rejected the idea. "I really just want to go to sleep," she said. "Can't they just give me something to make me go to sleep?"

A day or so later, the doctor asked her again.

"What good is it if I do live? How many years do I have at my age?" Rebekah said. "You can't guarantee me any kind of life, and I don't want to live in a wheelchair. It's like living inside your disease all your life. Just let me go to sleep. Just let me go to sleep."

Maria insisted that everything possible be done to keep Rebekah alive. "Maria was so worried Rebekah was not going to live," says Bobby. "It was like, 'I am a person of medicine and a person of science, and it's my job to save lives.' Well, maybe she really felt that way. But it was very obvious that Rebekah didn't want to live any longer. She was miserable and sick, and she couldn't see any reason to try any more treatment. But Maria kept coming in to encourage her to take some other kind of treatment to stay alive.

"And no sooner would Rebekah get to sleep—and it was very hard for her because she was in such pain—than Maria would come in and ask, 'Rebekah, are you awake yet?' And she'd awake and just jump up out of her skin practically. And everybody was getting pissed off at Maria for that. Then Dr. Coleman would come in. They wouldn't leave the poor woman alone."

But by late May Rebekah had given up completely. "If I can't get well," she told a nurse, "I don't want chemotherapy. When you can't do anything, just put me to sleep."

The nurse injected her with a narcotic to ease the pain, and Rebekah dozed off. Hours later, however, she woke up, puzzled and irritated. "You mean I'm still here?" she said. "I told you to put me to sleep."

The nurse was perplexed. "I did put you to sleep," she said. "I gave you that injection."

"That's not what I meant," said Rebekah. "I meant forever."

At the beginning of June, Rebekah was released from the hospital and taken back to her apartment at the Carlyle. All chemotherapy was discontinued; the best that medicine could do for her was ease the pain through morphine injections every two hours. Even that was not enough. As they strapped her to the stretcher, she looked so lifeless that the ambulance driver had to take her blood pressure to make sure she was still alive. The ride in the ambulance was just a few blocks, but it was rough, and with each bump Rebekah groaned in agony.

"She was so vain," says Bobby. "So vain all her life. And she was a beautiful woman—and to see her reduced to that."

Edith stayed with her mother virtually twenty-four hours a day. She called Grundborg daily, but had difficulty reaching him. She was planning to move with him to Duncanville, Texas, after Rebekah died, but was unhappy about the prospect of being a military wife in a small town. Bobby, who had lived in nearby Dallas, told her he thought the town was awful. "We'd joke about how Duncanville wasn't ready for Edith and she'd end up burning the place down," says Bobby. "She must have driven Grundborg nuts. She would call him every five minutes, and if she didn't know where he was she would call him en route and have a hundred fifty people calling him."

When she couldn't get through to him, she'd say, "Grundy's on the run. Grundy's on the run." At times, she thought he was becoming romantically involved with an old girlfriend—even though he wasn't. At others, she said, "He's such a good guy, I don't deserve him." Friends in New York were surprised she was involved with someone in the army. She had not been pleased when her former husband, Ken McKinnon, had been in the reserves. "It did not seem to fit," says one friend. "Either that or she changed. Maybe she was looking for some sanity."

When Edith did reach Grundborg, she told him she missed him and wished he was there. "I wanted to be there," he says. "But I couldn't go on an indefinite leave. So I told her, if anything developed where she needed me I would come. But she never requested that, even up to the point where the death was imminent."

In the week or so since she had returned to the Carlyle, Rebekah became semicomatose and was starving to death. Only occasionally was she capable of conversation. "She was quite dignified," says a friend. "She knew she was going to die. She faced it like a real old-fashioned warrior meeting death on the battlefield."

Meanwhile Frère arrived at the Carlyle to see Rebekah even though she had left explicit instructions that he not be allowed in. He paced impatiently back and forth outside her bedroom suite. "She's my sister," he said. "And I don't care what she said, I know she's dying and I want to see her before it's too late."

His demands put Rebekah's servants in a difficult position. To her closest friends she had said Frère was just waiting for her to die to see how much of her fortune she would leave his children. But no one wanted to tell him that, and he refused to take no for an answer.

Rebekah was usually asleep, rarely becoming more than semiconscious. Since it was highly unlikely she would be aware of his presence, it was especially difficult to refuse his request. Finally, they relented.

He entered the room to see his dying sister. She breathed slowly. Her eyes were closed; finally they opened, and Rebekah looked at him. Then she uttered her very last words.

"Allen," she said. "You asshole."

On Thursday, June 17, Rebekah's death seemed near. Bobby and Nikita were in the kitchen. Edith was angry that they were cooking dinner and entertaining friends without consulting her.

As if the imminent loss of her mother's love—so briefly regained—were not enough, Edith was increasingly disturbed by the comings and goings of the entire entourage. She privately referred to them as "the vultures." "Nobody can deny that there was political positioning going on as Rebekah died," says George Thomas Wilson, an assistant of Nikita's. "Maria New or Yuki was coming in every day. Everybody wanted to make sure they were on their best terms with Rebekah at the end. But it was not malicious. It was just inevitable. Everybody realized she did not have long. For weeks, everyone asked, 'Did she die today?' Everyday seemed like suspended animation."

Even one of the nurses thought the dinner plans were fairly innocent. "Bobby really did care about Rebekah," says one. "He and his friends just made up their minds they were going to go on living. This had been going on for weeks and no one knew how much longer they would have to wait. But Edith took it as a sign of disrespect. If you even have two or three people over, that's a dinner party, and Edith thought that was inappropriate."

Edith saw her mother's apartment filled with characters she didn't even know. It was one thing for Bobby to be there. However, there was also Nikita, and Nikita had George Thomas Wilson, who had moved into the apartment, taking a twin bed in his room.

"I didn't mind being an emotional whipping boy for Nikita," says Wilson, who was assigned the task of writing an obituary for Rebekah. "There was a great deal of emotional strain on everybody. I was there to absorb as much as possible of that. That was my function, to take abuse, from Nikita and Bobby."

But Edith did not want complete strangers in her mother's home at this most intimate moment. Yet they were coming and going as if they owned the place. She could not tolerate Nikita, and she despised Maria New. She said she was so disturbed by the episodes in which the codicils were drawn up, that if her mother hadn't still been alive, she would have raised hell.

And there was always Wolfie and Frère, not to mention the others who had been cast out but tried to remain in contact. Everyone waited breathlessly to find out who would get what. Edith could not believe they were so insensitive.

Around dusk, Ted Bartwink, the Harkness House accountant, and Barry Kreisberg, Rebekah's lawyer, arrived. In addition to Edith, Bobby and Nikita, George Thomas Wilson, Augusta and Willard Wallace, and a nurse were there.

At about seven-thirty Willard went into Rebekah's room. As

he began to clean up, Rebekah took her last gasp and stopped breathing. At 7:32 P.M. Rebekah Harkness was dead.

Augusta fixed a round of stiff drinks. Terry was called and arrived as quickly as possible. The nurse phoned Dr. Coleman. In the kitchen, the soup that had been simmering was just about ready.

Edith had never been more alone. "If only Grundy had been there," says one observer. "She felt terrible being there without him. She almost felt he didn't care, that he abandoned her, even though she knew his military commitments prohibited him from being there."

Still, Edith was seething. Only the servants and nurses had any business being there, she said. But she kept her temper in the presence of the guests.

George Thomas Wilson, still unaware that Rebekah was dead, asked Edith how she was holding up under the strain. "I guess I'm okay." She paused, and added, "Considering that my mother just died."

At the grand opening of the Harkness Theater in 1974, Rebekah, wearing a
Harkness-blue dress, stood in front of the mural by Enrique Senis Oliver that critics
called the "ugliest mural ever painted."

As Angel grew, it became increasingly difficult for
the aging Miss Weeks to lift the child. "It has to be
one of you," said the child's doctor.

Miss Weeks, at Angel's grave in Southgate
Cemetery in London

CRAIG UNGER

Allen Pierce in 1987. Allen's conviction was reduced to manslaughter and after being released from jail he opened a layout and design shop in Miami.

CRAIG UNGER

The Miami convenience store where Allen shot and killed nineteen-year-old Patrick Bemben in 1977

In 1973, Rebekah performed a Flamenco with dancer
Roberto Lorca at a charity benefit. "She was a tragic
figure, stiff and pained," said one spectator.
"It was so painful I was crying."

Dr. Niels Lauersen,
Rebekah's fourth husband.
"I wasn't married to her,"
Lauersen said recently. "I never
really knew the woman."

By the early seventies, the
testosterone Rebekah injected had
given her face and her musculature
a more masculine cast. In addition,
she was drinking heavily and
addicted to injections of Talwin.

When critic Clive Barnes
eviscerated both the dance
company and the theater in
The New York Times, Rebekah
had Senis paint Barnes dancing
aboard a sinking *Titanic,* and
hung the painting in the
theater lobby.

Rebekah, as seen by Enrique Senis
Oliver, who painted the mural around
the proscenium arch.

At the opening of the Harkness Theater, Rebekah wore her Dali tiara
and was accompanied by Frère.

Frère attempted to reconcile with Rebekah at the end of her life, but she thought
he just wanted his children written into her will. When he visited her—against her
instructions—on her deathbed, she uttered her very last words. "Allen,"
she said. "You asshole."

Frère in Arizona: Rebekah was
appalled by her brother's taste for
porno movies and strip joints.

MAURICE SEYMOUR

Choreographer Joy O'Neill regarded Rebekah as her "mother," but was written out of Rebekah's will when she testified for the defense in the murder trial of Claus von Bülow.

BLIOKH

Rebekah, not long before her death, with Dr. Maria New. If the handwritten codicil she signed had been legal, Dr. New would have received about $3.5 million for medical research.

BLIOKH

Nikita Talin, here with Rebekah, was not a popular choice to
head Harkness House.

A haggard Bobby Scevers after his 1978 return to New York, with
Rebekah at Harkness House

By the early eighties, drugs and alcohol and various medical problems
had taken their toll on Rebekah.

Just a few months before her death, Rebekah returned to the Bahamas where she
was visited by actor Burgess Meredith. According to Joy O'Neill, "There
was this one last burst of life."

"The Chalice of Life," the Dali-designed golden urn, was not big enough to hold all
of Rebekah's ashes and, after her death, was sold to a Japanese art gallery.

LAST
WILL AND
TESTAMENT

ow that it had finally
taken place, Rebe-
kah's death seemed
anticlimactic. After
the doctor pro-
nounced her dead, she was put in a green body bag, which was
taken away two hours later.

Edith called Grundborg in California. She was distraught. She
wanted him to come, but could not bring herself to ask him.

"I can't impose on you," she said. "And you can't help my mother live any longer."

On Friday afternoon, June 18, the day after Rebekah's death, Kreisberg went to the Carlyle to read Rebekah's will. Rebekah had changed it many times over the years, often relying on it as a court of last resort for her many tangled relationships. Such changes were not that unusual among people of her means, but she went further than most. Often she had written in servants, friends, or relatives for bequests as high as $100,000, only to revoke them later. She had made such changes in her will at least fifteen times.

Kreisberg called Terry, Edith, Bobby, and Nikita to the living room. He began to read from the fifteen-page document Rebekah and he had drawn up on June 25, 1981, a year earlier. In addition, he had the final two codicils Rebekah had written. The bequests were vintage Rebekah—whimsical, capricious, eccentric, confused, sometimes loving, more often unthinking and self-centered. They reflected the utmost seriousness and defensiveness with which she took herself as a composer. They rewarded some of those who were at her side at the end. But they also indicated her distrust of the deathbed politicking. Typically, they neglected many of the deserving people around her who had loyally served her for years, but who happened to be out of sight and out of mind at the end.

To Bobby Scevers, among other bequests, Rebekah left, apparently as a joke, her dog Bingo, who had died years before. "That's not meant to be Bingo; she meant Beulah," says Bobby. "She knew how I hated that demented dog. Whenever I would call its name, Beulah would just squat and pee. That's all that dog was good for."

The will made other stipulations that were equally peculiar, but more serious. It directed that Rebekah be cremated and her ashes deposited in the jeweled golden Chalice of Life by Dali, to be put on display at the ballet school in Harkness House. Most of Rebekah's extensive collection of jewelry, much of it designed by Dali, was to go to the United States government for use by the

First Lady and to be put on display at the Smithsonian Institution when not in use.

Edith was to receive the portrait Dali had painted of her.

Valuable pieces of jewelry, furniture, and furs were apportioned to Rebekah's various friends and relatives.

A $650,000 trust was created, to be shared by seven relatives, including her son, Allen Pierce, Frère, Tarwater, and other nieces and nephews.

Stipulation was made that her estate would pay for Rebekah's remaining compositions to be orchestrated by her music teacher, composer Lee Hoiby.

Yuki Irwin was to receive $50,000.

Maria New was also to receive $50,000, plus Rebekah's sable coat and her cultured pearl necklace and earrings.

Instead of leaving half the proceeds of Harkness House to Bobby and Nikita for ballet, Rebekah left each of them $250,000. In addition, Bobby was to receive $1,500 a month for life.

Willard and Augusta Wallace, Rebekah's loyal Bahamian servants, were left $600 a month for life—a small sum, considering they would not only lose employment with her, but would have to find a new home as well.

The biggest beneficiary of all was Rebekah's dance foundation, which would receive a few million dollars once her estate was liquidated. How much was left depended largely on the market value of Rebekah's homes in Gstaad, Palm Beach, and New York.

It was specified that "The document of May 19, 1982 entitled 'Notes to Lawyer (Mr. B Kreisberg)' . . . shall be of no force and effect." That document's stipulation that Harkness House be sold and half the proceeds—about $3.5 million—be given to Maria New for medical research was not mentioned at all. Instead, Rebekah requested that "either the Harkness Ballet Foundation, Inc. or William Hale Harkness Foundation set up a fund of $250,000 for medical research at New York Hospital," to be administered by Maria New. Not only did Dr. New not get the $3.5 million or so she would have gotten from the handwritten codicil, the

$250,000 was a request, not a provision, and as such whether or not it would be granted was up to those who were to take over the foundation after Rebekah's death. (The request was later turned down by the foundation.)

Another last change involved Joy O'Neill. She had been due to inherit some of Rebekah's furs, but was written out after the fuss over her role in the von Bülow trial. M'liss Crotty, who had once been in the will, was not mentioned at all. And nothing was left to many of her employees—servants, nurses, nannies—who had served her for years. Miss Weeks was entirely forgotten.

As for her children, Rebekah, with a few minor exceptions, left items whose value was primarily sentimental. In the document, she explained, "I feel that the provisions I have made for my children during my lifetime as well as the provisions of the late William Hale Harkness, made for them by his Will, are generous and ample."

Finally, as provided by a divorce settlement—not the will—Niels Lauersen, Rebekah's last husband, received $165,000 after her death.

Kreisberg explained to Rebekah's two daughters that if they agreed not to challenge the terms of the will, they should sign a waiver of consent. "Otherwise," he said, "you will be given a citation, to appear in court, to be served by a sheriff."

Edith was unsure of what to do. Like her siblings, she had been provided for by her father. She had never lived extravagantly, and the millions left her from her father's estate in 1954 had grown substantially over the years. All she wanted was the Dali portrait and her father's library. The former was taken care of in Rebekah's will, and presumably arrangements could be made for the latter. Still, she was always at a loss when confronted by lawyers and legal documents. She decided to wait until she could speak with her own attorney.

Terry, however, was angry, certain she would never sign any such document. Kreisberg, she thought, was just some cut-rate lawyer from a small town who had been recommended to Rebekah by her chauffeur. Rebekah had a history of alcoholism. The will was peculiar enough that it was entirely possible she had been drinking again. One item in it was mentioned twice, and Rebekah didn't even get her own dog's name right. In addition, during the last painful weeks, she had been taking powerful narcotics to ease her suffering. Had she been heavily medicated when she wrote those codicils? And who initiated the codicils in the first place, Rebekah or the people who benefited from them? As for the prospect of being served by a sheriff, even though it was normal procedure, Terry took it as a threat by Kreisberg.

At two-thirty, after the reading of the will, Edith called Bobby and Nikita together in the Carlyle. "Edith was furious," says Bobby. The reason for her anger had nothing to do with the will, however. She was appalled that Bobby and Nikita had kept Harkness House open rather than close it for a day in Rebekah's honor.

"It was a command performance," says Bobby. "I deliberately came late. Nikita and I didn't close the school the day after Rebekah died because we didn't think she would have wanted us to. But Edith made such a scene that we had to close it for a day, on the following Monday.

"At the same time, we were also told Kreisberg was in charge. He was doing everything he could to keep Edith happy. Then he posted a list of the people who were allowed to come into the apartment. Wolfie was on the list. I raised hell about that, and he was taken off the list."

Rebekah's funeral was held three days after her death. Bobby was angry that Terry and Edith insisted on a religious ceremony. Her own children didn't even know their mother, he thought. They were just spoiled society girls paying homage to the genteel rituals of a social order their mother scorned.

At the funeral, Terry and Wolfie saw Alex Donner, a friend of Rebekah's. As a pianist, Donner and his orchestra had developed a large society following, thanks in part to Rebekah's patronage. As a lawyer, he worked with Roy Cohn, whose notoriety spanned three decades, ranging from his role as a red-baiting counsel for Senator Joe McCarthy in the fifties to dozens of controversies as a power broker in New York society.

"They did not discuss the specific irregularities of her will,"

Donner says. "But there was a general discussion about [contesting the will]. I said Roy was one of the best, if not *the* best, for handling that kind of thing. He could tell them what could be done."

After the services, Wolfie approached Bobby. "Well, Bobby," he said, "are you happy now?"

Bobby was puzzled. "Why should I be happy?" he asked.

"Well, you were named in Rebekah's will."

"No," Bobby said. "As a matter of fact, I'm not happy. I'd much rather have Rebekah alive."

Wolfie also approached Maria New. Word was already beginning to spread that Terry and Wolfie might contest the will.

"Don't take it wrong, Maria," he said. "We are not out after you. We just want justice. We are not against you. We really admire you."

Maria was nonplussed. "I only know what Mr. Kreisberg told me," says Maria, "that Rebekah thought Wolfie was self-aggrandizing, and trying to take advantage of Terry."

Maria went up to Edith after it was over and told her how sorry she was and how much she would miss Rebekah.

Edith was polite and said, "Thank you." Then she jabbed Yuki, who was standing next to her, in the ribs with her elbow.

"It was a very unhappy gesture," says Maria. "As if to say, 'Look what she is saying,' that she hated to talk to me. I was very close to Edith and we were all very fine. But then Yuki decided to tell them about the codicil that had been dictated. They thought I had some nefarious purpose, which I did not. It was the wrong time for Edith to lose a friend like me. I was very close to Rebekah, and it was I who brought Edith to her bedside. I feel very badly about what Yuki did. It was a very destructive maneuver. I don't know why she did it, if she thought, 'Well, Rebekah is dying and now I will have Edith, another friend in the family.' I felt it was not only a betrayal, but a selfish thing to do. When a family is being hurt by a death, you don't try to send a friend of theirs away."

Following the funeral at a reception for friends of Rebekah's held at the Carlyle, Kreisberg again asked Edith to sign the waiver of consent, but Edith put him off. According to Terry, Kreisberg said he felt faint and went to lie down on Rebekah's bed. Edith brought him some tea and sandwiches. By the time he left the room, she had signed the papers.

Terry was dismayed. "Edith was just like my mother that way," she says. "She could be talked into signing anything without really knowing what the document said."

In the meantime, Edith had gotten together with Eivind Harum, the dancer she had gone out with five years earlier, who was still on Broadway, in *A Chorus Line*. With Grundborg absent, she was grateful to have someone to console her. She could never ask Grundborg to come to her side. "She felt if he loved her, why didn't he help relieve her of the burden," says a friend. "She wanted him not to offer to come, but to do it. She figured if he really cared he would come. He never did, and she was deeply hurt about it."

Now that Harum was there, at night, they lay on Rebekah's bed and talked. Harum stayed overnight, but the two did not make love.

"Edith was totally distraught, chain-smoking Marlboros," says Harum. "Her lawyer was trying to get her to sign various papers, and she was concerned about who was going to run Harkness House now that Rebekah was dead. I told her that Scevers and Nikita were the rotten apples. I couldn't take it with those two. She wanted to kick out Bobby and Nikita and the whole bunch."

Harum, meanwhile, invited her to join him and five friends on a sailboat trip around Bimini. "It'll be great therapy. You'll get away from this whole mess," he told her.

From the music room at the other end of the long hall, Bobby saw Harum coming and going. He did not say hello.

When Harum was gone, Edith called Grundborg. "She was very upset about her mother's death," he recalls. "She told me these people had suggested she go on a trip to Bimini. I said that sounds wonderful. Then she said an old friend of hers was going along on the trip.

"In our relationship, I could not be one of many. I had told her, it's either me or it's not me. She wholeheartedly agreed. I didn't want anyone else. All I wanted was her. That's the rule forever. When that rule is broken, that's the end. So when she told me this other guy was going, I said, 'Fine. You know the rules. I don't mind him going. But you know the rules.'"

A day or two later, Bobby came back to the Carlyle and found Edith alone in the kitchen, making a white wine spritzer.

"Oh, this is for Augusta," she said. "Augusta has a terrible headache."

"Suddenly, she got all defensive," Bobby says. "I wondered why was she explaining this to me. I didn't care what she did. A couple of other nights I came home late and her clothes were strewn all over, a shoe at the door and a handbag, with all the change thrown on the counter, as though she had started stripping on her way to bed.

"I never had any unpleasant words with Edith. Ever. But you could just feel the tension. It was awful. You could feel the hate and the anger. I can pick up those things. She talked about all her problems in the hospital. She was pretty friendly in a funny way. But I didn't care. We knew what she was up to, because we could see the way her clothes were thrown all over the apartment when we came home. She was obviously loaded."

Meanwhile, Terry was outraged about the will and had decided to fight it. Edith's feelings were less clear. But, according to Terry, Edith still objected to the various codicils, despite having signed the waiver of consent.

"I told her not to worry," says Terry. "That we could still fight this thing together."

To discuss a course of action, the two lunched on Madison Avenue with Edith's lawyer, Milton Kayle. Afterward, Terry told Edith she thought he seemed like a nice man. "I'm not so sure," Edith said.

"I thought you liked him."

"I've found out some things about him." She was vague, but she said that when she obtained more information, she would let Terry know the details. Two days later, she again raised the subject of Mr. Kayle: Soon after Rebekah's death, she said, he had presented her with some papers to sign. Now that she had read them, she was worried.

"You know what I found out?" she told Terry. "I found out that I can't fire him, that I made him trustee for life." Edith told the same story to several other friends, all of whom sympathized with her. None seemed to realize that trusteeships can easily be revoked.

On June 24, a memorial service was held for Rebekah at Harkness House. Even at this solemn occasion, there was hostility between the various factions. "I have no sympathy for anything having to do with any of the kids," Bobby says. "I never wanted to have anything to do with them. Their mother was doing so much for the world. All the money she just gave away! You can say what you want—her repertory was rotten, the company had problems. But dozens of people she helped have become important in the dance world.

"Rebekah was brokenhearted that the company folded, that Harkness House was so dilapidated, and that her children wouldn't help her with what she loved to do. That's why she said over and over and over she wasn't leaving her family anything.

"The kids were asked to furnish flowers, and they complained about how much the flowers cost. There had been some silk artificial flowers at the apartment and they wondered if [they] could use those. When you think how much money Terry and Edith are worth, how cheap can you be?"

Maria New wondered if she was welcome, but she came anyway. "Because of the hostility, she was afraid there would be a scene," Bobby says. "Nobody liked anybody."

At five-thirty, about a hundred people gathered in Studio B at Harkness House to remember Rebekah. During the heyday of the ballet, many had carped about Bobby's position. But even the most bitter of them seemed to feel that he had well earned whatever Rebekah left him. One attendee remembered "how gorgeous Bobby was circa 1964," and later described him to a friend as looking "drawn, gaunt, sunken-cheeked. The bloom is not only off the rose. He looks vampirized."

Nikita introduced five speakers to eulogize Rebekah: Donald Saddler, the former assistant artistic director of the company who had gone on to win several Tony awards as a Broadway choreographer; Helgi Tomasson, who had become a principal dancer at the New York City Ballet; Walter Terry, the dance critic; Gerry Arpino, choreographer for the Joffrey; and Carmen De Lavallade, dancer and wife of Geoffrey Holder.

Many of the major figures in the arts with whom Rebekah worked—Robert Joffrey, Jerome Robbins, Gian Carlo Menotti, among them—didn't even come. To those who knew Rebekah during her heyday it seemed like the organizers of the service had been desperate for eulogizers; Carmen De Lavallade barely knew Rebekah at all, and was there only by virtue of her husband, who worked with her briefly and couldn't make it to the service. Gerald Arpino adored Rebekah, but inviting him even so many years after the Joffrey debacle, as one observer put it, was like having "the Virgin Mary weeping at Pontius Pilate's grave."

In his eulogy, Saddler told a story of the Harkness at its peak, when Rebekah left her fabulous jewels with Leon Fokine for a few minutes and asked him to keep them in his lap.

"Boss, I've been between a million legs," he said. "But this is the first time I've had a million between mine."

One Harkness House regular later described the memorial service in a letter to another:

> . . . Pass into lobby, where a small crowd has gathered. This is the shocker; there they all are. Well, not all, but a lot. . . . The usual New York "you look fabulous" and what are you doing now's are exchanged. . . . Some are gracefully, almost elegantly preserved. . . . Terry is fat, turned out in a pink cotton-candy dress that would be appropriate at a Newport afternoon lawn party (which is probably what she thinks it is) and bears a resemblance to her mother that has everyone commenting. It is truly frightening: the toss of the head when she laughs, the voice, inflection, every mannerism. It is *all* there: fat Rebekah circa 1950.
>
> And to make the horror complete, there is a new painting on the wall. It is Rebekah in practice clothes (lavender), back

to the barre. And she is watching *YOU*. Talk about Dorian Gray. . . . There she is, a wrinkled sheep in chiffon; its one of the best portraits I've ever seen. It is *her*. Not a hideous mocking commentary with a gangrenous green claw-foot sweeping through the cosmos of Art and Beauty and Culture and Money . . . No, it is Rebekah, and she is watching you.

. . . The Chalice . . . which everyone wants to see, is not there. It has been taken out for cleaning, oiling, and possibly a valve job and brake relining . . . lovely as the gilded object itself may be . . . it has certain failings, and one is that it has not been adequately designed . . . to hold the charred and barbecued remains of a human body . . .

The master of ceremonies in this comedy hour is . . . your favorite and mine, Nikita Talin. He steps to the podium, an aging capon looking like a Bible salesman down on his luck. . . .

. . . Of course, if I am curious to know how much she had . . . just imagine how curious poor bereaved Terry (and Wolfgang) and Edith will be. I rather hope she left it to Bobby; he was with her, more or less, or at least in her life for 17 years. At 42 he will have time enough to spend it . . . He earned it. You can't say as much for Wolfie, you know. He's only recently come on the scene. It was amusing watching him walk in late to the service, after Helgi was finishing up, looking around at the coffered ceiling and gold paint. One could almost hear him exclaiming "Boy oh Boy," while humming "This Nearly was Mine". . . .

"Bobby tells me he is well aware that a big legal fight will be underway . . . Obvious The Family will contest because you can be damned sure she didn't leave either of them a cent. And if the girls have *their* way, Bobby and Nikita will be on the next bus back to Aransas Pass without a shoe box filled with fried chicken, thank you very much. He tells me that Terry and Edith have already installed themselves in the Carlyle and that several large and valuable objects have already disappeared. . . . Allen Pierce, I understand, is in some Florida jail and is happier than a pig in shit . . .

What will be her legacy? Aha, a good question! The only rational answer is for Bobby to marry Terry. He will then have another Rebekah (or a frighteningly accurate replica), and the money will stay in the family, and they can *both* fuck Wolfie (and one could do worse).

The next day, June 25, Terry went to Frank E. Campbell Funeral Chapel on Madison Avenue and Eight-first Street at midday. She had been selected to bring Rebekah's ashes to Harkness House to be put in the Dali chalice. Edith, Bobby, Nikita, Ted Bartwink, and Joy O'Neill, among others were there. After the ashes had been put in the urn, Joy went upstairs alone and began crying about having lost Rebekah. George Thomas Wilson came up, bearing a large Harkness House envelope, which he handed to Joy.

"I thought you might like to have this," he said.

"What is that?" Joy asked.

"It's Rebekah," he said. Then he left the room, leaving the envelope behind. "There were extra ashes on the table," says Joy, "and they scooped them into an envelope and said, 'Bring them up to Joy.' Nikita has her tooth. He loves that. That's right up his alley. God, that's sick!"

For Edith, the grotesquerie of these events was freighted with the baggage she had carried all her life. One friend at the memorial service had watched her carefully: "Here was Edith, passed over like she was nothing, watching all those dancers getting more attention than she. I saw all those people who Rebekah loved when she ignored Edith and I thought, 'Poor Edith, that poor girl must want to slit her throat.'"

27

HARKNESS
BLUE

hen Edith was finally alone in her mother's apartment, she went through Rebekah's drawers and medicine cabinets. There were over forty vials of drugs. Rebekah had hoarded medicine all her life. There was codeine, Seconal, Percodan, Dalmane, Librium, Nembutal, and many, many others. Edith's psychiatrist, Dr. John Henderson, had prescribed various drugs over the years and she was still taking them. But it could not hurt to have more.

A few days later, Edith flew to Miami. Then she, Harum, and five others took off from Dinner Key in Cocoanut Grove, Florida, for Bimini in two chartered forty-one-foot Morgan sailboats. Edith was slim, but not so emaciated as to attract concern. But it gradually became clear to her companions that she was suffering from anorexia nervosa, an eating disorder characterized by self-imposed starvation. She had lost eighty pounds in the last few months—she had been up to 200—and was continuing the severe regimen that had helped get her weight down so dramatically. In Bimini she ordered only salads, and barely touched even those. During the last three days of the trip, she ate absolutely nothing. Instead, she took vitamin pills, as well as chlorophyll, calcium, and potassium supplements. Harum was disturbed by her lack of eating. "The anorexia was obvious. I said, 'You got to eat something.' She was just taking pills."

Otherwise, Edith seemed in remarkably good spirits, especially in light of Rebekah's recent death. "In some ways, she was better than she'd ever been," said Harum. "For the first time, she said how much she loved her mother, that they had something of a reconciliation. Edith was determined to get Harkness House back in shape." She had been on the board of directors of Harkness House for years, but she had never taken an active role before. Now she was going to carry on her mother's dream.

Edith gave the impression of being happy, but it is difficult to know exactly what her state of mind was. In fact, she later told one close friend that during the trip she had great difficulty sleeping and was not feeling well. Such discrepancies between fact and appearance were not unusual for Edith. She had been extraordinarily successful at concealing her pain for her entire life. Indeed, she had jumped out of windows, taken overdoses, locked herself in carbon monoxide-filled garages, tried suicide again and again, spent years in mental hospitals, yet everyone who knew her— even those who loved her—described her as a woman who appeared remarkably normal.

Also on board was Harum's longtime friend, a choreographer

and former dancer named James Edwin Frazier who works under the professional name of Eddie James. A tall, handsome forty-year-old with the straight, regular features of a soap opera star, Frazier had been married to and divorced from actress-dancer Juliet Prowse in the early seventies. Harum describes Frazier as "sort of an Errol Flynn type," with dashing good looks and a streak of adventure in him. He had attended Texas Christian University in Fort Worth when Bobby Scevers was there, and he had trained at Harkness House in the sixties, during which time he briefly met Edith. He had ended up dancing and doing choreography in Las Vegas. A reformed alcoholic, he had been sober for nine months when Harum introduced him to Edith. "I thought it was natural," says Harum. "They could help each other."

After three or four days in Bimini, Edith and Frazier left the rest of the crew and chartered a plane to Nassau, staying at Capricorn. They returned to New York for a few days, then went to Edith's place in Potomac, Maryland.

Kenneth Grundborg had heard nothing from Edith for more than two weeks after Rebekah's death. "I got a call from Milton Kayle, saying at first he hadn't heard from her for a while," he recalls. "But finally he did. And he proceeded to tell me who was on the trip and what it was about. He went into quite some detail as to what was happening and who was staying with whom, and I was saying, 'How can Edith do that? Why is she doing that?'

"Then he made a comment I'll never forget. He said, 'I would have thought by now you would have known Edith. She's like that.'"

The next night Edith called Grundborg. He talked to her about the trip: "I didn't want to get hurt. When I talked to her about it, I said, 'You knew the rules. Why did you break them?' I was hoping she would say she didn't."

But she said nothing of the sort.

Back in Potomac, Jimmy Frazier had moved in with Edith. He had fallen in love with her, though it was not clear that she loved him in return. She had not gotten over Grundborg; she still thought of him frequently and hoped that the relationship could be revived. She told a friend that Jimmy couldn't hold a candle to Grundborg.

In the six weeks since her mother's death, Edith had lost another ten pounds, and was now below 110. Frazier, concerned with Edith's anorexia, prided himself on his cooking, and for at least part of the period they lived together Edith began eating again. However, she was no longer taking Antabuse. Whenever no one was looking, she took a few drinks of vodka. Frazier was with her every day and every night but he said he didn't notice it.

Now, as she drank, Edith worried about Milton Kayle being trustee. He had gotten her out of mental hospitals, so he could have her locked up again, she reasoned. And if he found out she was drinking, that's exactly what he would do. He was misusing funds, she said. She wanted to fire him, she confided in Frazier, among others, but she was afraid of him.

In fact, Edith's fears were the paranoid delusions of an alcoholic. "There was nobody who could have been more sincere and straightforward for Edith than Milton Kayle," says Ted Bartwink. "He met with her consistently and saw that her needs were attended to."

There was no evidence at all that Kayle misused funds. And Edith could easily have hired another attorney had she so desired. Anyone who had seen Edith's alcoholism firsthand felt that Kayle had only done the best he could to cope with her drinking, and that in doing so he became the target of her rage. "Edith had a drinking problem," says someone close to Edith. "She loved Kayle. He was like a father to her. But when she was drinking she would get angry and irrational and make things up. He had nothing to gain by having her locked up and everything to lose—a client and a close friend. All those things she said about him—I think that was the alcohol talking."

"When she was drinking her perspective completely altered," says another friend. "She was not in touch with reality. She would take things and blow them way out of proportion. She wasn't rational. She would become paranoid, very suspicious. She was a completely different person."

Still, at least four friends and relatives of Edith's—Jimmy Frazier, Jean Hope, Kenneth Grundborg, and Terry McBride— heard her complaints about Kayle and believed her. For the most part, they were not familiar with her problems with alcohol. There was so much chaos around Rebekah, so many charlatans and vultures, that it was easy to believe another horror story. And Edith could be very convincing. "We're masters of disguise," she had told Jean Hope. "When I drink I can fool anyone."

In early August, Eivind Harum called from Seattle and spoke to Jimmy and Edith in Maryland. *A Chorus Line* was on tour again. In September, the troupe would be performing in Las Vegas and he invited them to join him. "She sounded great," he says, "and we were all excited about getting together again."

On Thursday, August 19, Kenneth Grundborg came to Washington and visited Edith. Even though he had moved to Duncanville, Texas, and their romance had apparently ended, they remained close friends. "She had some type of bronchial condition," he recalls, "but she was not in bad shape. She was thin, but she always kept her weight down. As for her state of mind, she was perfectly coherent, perfectly normal."

Before Grundborg left, Edith raised the possibility of reviving their relationship and visiting him in Texas.

"Let's go out and talk about it," he said.

Edith, however, said she couldn't go because Frazier was in the house. Then she added that she had to run an errand.

"Then I'll take you to the store," Grundborg said.

But Edith begged off. "Looking back on it, she was funny," Grundborg recalls. "She kept saying she had to go to the store and I kept saying I would take her. She was not Edith. She was a different person. She kept saying no, no, no, I've got to go by myself."

Later, when he thought about it, Grundborg decided Edith

looked like she had been drinking. It was possible that she was going out to buy liquor and did not want anyone to see her.

At about the same time, Edith called Terry in Santa Monica. She said Jimmy and she were planning to go to Las Vegas to meet Harum, and added she was thinking of visiting Terry in California on the same trip. The two sisters had not been particularly close, but Terry was pleased to hear from Edith and fixed up her guest room in anticipation of her arrival.

Edith was so excited about the trip to Vegas that she spent eleven thousand dollars on clothes, buying almost an entirely new wardrobe, including three formal gowns. She rarely wore anything more formal than blue jeans, and it was not like her to spend so much money on clothes. Moreover, one of the dresses was in a pale blue velvet with a jeweled inset. Edith was not one to partake of her mother's indulgences, but it sounded very much like the color Rebekah had always chosen—Harkness blue.

Edith also phoned a woman in New York who had become a close friend. Her friend was aware of her depression over Rebekah's death and of the end of her relationship with Grundborg. But Edith seemed surprisingly upbeat and full of warmth, except for her respiratory problem, which she referred to as "walking pneumonia." She was ecstatic that she was down to a size four, and she talked about her relationship with men in some depth. She discussed a man named Carl, with whom she had lived several years before. "She went into a long detailed description of that relationship," Edith's friend says. "He sounded very sick—schizophrenic. I told her he must have placed an enormous emotional burden on her. I added that I couldn't have had the patience to stay with him all those years. I think she was instrumental in getting him back to Sheppard Pratt. [Sheppard & Enoch Pratt Hospital, a mental hospital near Washington, D.C.] She didn't think he was suicidal, but delusional. He said the Mafia was after him. Edith went into an elaborate analysis of his illness, which was too complex for me to comprehend. . . . But she said she had described it to her analyst, who was really impressed with her understanding.

"We discussed the fact that suicidal people give off 'cues'—

subtle pleas for help in advance—and she readily agreed. She asked me about working for a suicide hot line—what were the qualifications."

Then she told her friend, "I love you." She said it over and over again.

"Although I did and still do love her, it is not my nature to say it," says the friend. "People have said it to me in the past, like a common cliché, and it makes me wince. But Edith said it with absolute conviction. I said, 'Thank you Edith. You don't know what that means to me.'"

Edith switched the subject to her mother. "She felt that she could never hope to gain her mother's love. With her mother's death, the possibility would elude her forever," says her friend. Edith brought up the time just after her father's death when she went into the room where Rebekah was playing the piano, and her mother snapped, "What do you want?"

"Edith only wanted a little pat," says her friend. "But she could never ask for it."

By Friday, August 20, Edith's respiratory condition had worsened. Around noon, she called her mother's apartment at the Carlyle, hoping to speak to Willard and Augusta. They weren't in, and Bobby Scevers answered the phone.

Despite her anger at Bobby's entertaining his friends at the time of Rebekah's death, Edith was warm and sympathetic. "She said she was very concerned about me since her mother died and asked if I needed someone to talk to," Bobby says. "She was very good to me. It was a good conversation . . . but there would be periods when she would just fade away. She was very sick and extremely depressed and blue, and she invited me to come to Washington to see her."

Bobby told jokes and Edith laughed easily, but her laughter dissolved into a deep hacking cough. He suggested she go to a hospital for her cough, but she said her doctor was out of town. She was apparently referring not to her internist, but to John Henderson, the Baltimore psychiatrist who had been analyzing her for five years. The forty-two-year-old Henderson was a staff psychiatrist at Sheppard Pratt Hospital in Towson, Maryland, where Edith had been treated for alcoholism, and he had gained some notoriety in Washington and Baltimore as a forensic psychiatrist testifying in several murder, rape, and hostage cases that received widespread media attention.

"Edith talked about Henderson quite a bit," says Grundborg. "He ran her life. If she had a problem, if anything came up, she would say, 'I have to call him up and talk it over with him.'"

"She was so dependent on Henderson," says Jean Hope. "We took a trip together one Labor Day, and when the van broke down her first reaction was to call Henderson. She could hardly go to the bathroom without checking with him first. He made her feel so dependent on him."

On Saturday, August 21, Jimmy Frazier left Potomac to visit his theatrical agent in New York. That morning, he says, Edith seemed in fine spirits. Her respiratory condition did not appear to be a problem. Floyd Boring, the caretaker who lived on Edith's estate, drove him to the airport to catch an early afternoon shuttle. Before he left, Edith kissed him good-bye.

"Honey," she said, "hurry back."

Sometime that day, as she cleaned up the house, Edith's maid, Louise, found some empty liquor bottles in the house and called Mr. Kayle in New York.

That afternoon, Boring, the caretaker, went over to see Edith, who asked him if he had a gun for her. He told one of Edith's friends, "It seemed more for her protection and for something in the future."

"She was apparently quite drunk, and she called him a few choice words," says Jean Hope. "He knew that when she did that not to take her seriously, so he wasn't really hurt. Then he checked with Mr. Kayle. Mr. Kayle said, 'Wait outside. Henderson is going to meet you there at night.'"

At about 6:00 P.M. Edith called Jean Hope. They had discussed going to a dog show in Annapolis, Maryland, the following day. Jean offered to come over and make dinner, but Edith begged off. She talked as if someone was in the room with her; she had confided in Jean about her bouts with alcoholism, and Jean thought perhaps Edith was drinking again.

By the time the conversation was over, however, Edith sounded much more coherent. "She definitely agreed to go with me to the dog show the next day," says Jean. "I was glad of that because she had become so dependent on her psychiatrist. When she traveled with me to shows, she realized she was independent. By the end of our talk, she seemed fine."

Later, Edith took a few swigs from a bottle of Smirnoff's vodka, then telephoned Kayle. She was on a binge. Alarmed, Kayle tracked down Dr. Henderson, who was out of town. They decided Edith had to go back to Sheppard Pratt to dry out, and arranged for Henderson to fly to Potomac that night. Kayle told Boring to stay with her until they arrived.

Edith, however, was furious. She told the caretaker to leave her alone. She did not want someone to baby-sit for her.

At about ten o'clock Boring returned to the house. The lights were on, but Edith's car was no longer in the driveway. She had driven her Mercedes off into the woods, in an apparent attempt to make it appear that she had left. But she had returned; Boring quietly entered the house and saw her lying on her bed watching television. He left without attracting her notice and went outside to wait until the doctors arrived.

At about eleven o'clock Edith called Jimmy in New York. She knew they were coming to get her. She did not want to be locked up again.

"Please get back here as soon as you can," she said.

According to Frazier, she did not explain why. "It wasn't like Edith to explain things like that," he says. "That was one of her problems many of us have—she kept everything inside." He was at first unconvinced of the seriousness of the situation, but after Edith called him three times, he set out for Maryland by car.*

At about 1:00 A.M. Dr. Henderson arrived, accompanied by Dennis Michael Harrison, a colleague who had testified as a forensic psychologist in some of the same trials with Henderson.

---

*At least three people went to Edith's house that night: Boring; Dr. Henderson; and a psychologist, Dennis Harrison. All three have declined to discuss the events of that evening. But shortly afterward, Boring told his version of what happened that evening in separate conversations with Jimmy Frazier, Jean Hope, and Terry McBride. The events that follow were reconstructed from interviews with them, affidavits, and police reports.

Boring let them into the house. She was asleep. They woke Edith up and told her they intended to take her to Sheppard Pratt.

"No," Edith said. "I've spent too much of my life in mental hospitals." The doctors said they had the necessary papers to commit her, and if she didn't agree they would call the police and take her by force. As they talked, Edith went back and forth to her bedroom. She appeared to be increasingly drunk or drugged. Finally, she agreed to go with them, but said she first had to shower, change clothes, and pack. She excused herself and went into her room.

"Do you think we should let her in there alone?" Boring asked Henderson.

"She won't do anything," Henderson said. Then he proceeded to call the hospital to make arrangements for their arrival.

Edith locked the door to her bedroom and finished off what was left of the fifth of Smirnoff. Her blood alcohol level was .26 percent, an extremely high level of intoxication for an average person. For someone suffering from anorexia, it was dangerously high.

In addition to the alcohol, Edith had been taking Valium that day. The dosages were roughly at the normal therapeutic level, but doctors advise strongly against taking the drug in conjunction with alcohol. Worse, she also took Elavil, an antidepressant; since the drug was not one that Edith found in Rebekah's medicine cabinet, it is possible that it was prescribed by Dr. Henderson. According to the *Physician's Desk Reference,* a standard medical text on drugs, "Elavil . . . in patients who may use alcohol excessively . . . may increase the danger inherent in any suicide attempt or overdosage." Edith took roughly four times the normal therapeutic dosage of Elavil that day.

Edith went to the bathroom and turned on the shower so Henderson, Harrison, and Boring could hear the water running. Then she wrote a note to Jimmy that said, "It would take too long to explain."

The shower was still running, and Henderson, Harrison, and Boring were waiting impatiently. "As bad as she was that night," says someone who was close to Edith, "she wasn't really going to harm herself with a gun or anything else. She probably would have just gone to sleep. She was just loaded, watching TV, and making phone calls. And depressed, apparently. But she probably would have just stopped calling people and watching TV, and gone to sleep. She was put in the position where she was going to be dragged off, and she didn't want to go. And I think that's when she took the pills. I don't believe she meant to kill herself. I can see her pulling a power play, throwing a fit, saying, 'If these guys are going to take me, I'm going to make it miserable for them.' She had done this kind of thing before to get attention. She knew that there was a doctor there, and they probably would have done something to bring her back."

There were still more drugs in the bathroom. Edith sifted through the mood elevators, antidepressants, tranquilizers, and barbiturates she had brought from New York. Finally, she swallowed an enormous amount of barbiturates—most likely Nembutal, which she had probably gotten from Rebekah's medicine cabinet. She ingested fifteen to thirty times the normal dosage.

Strictly speaking, Edith had not taken a lethal dose of any one drug. But the combination, plus alcohol, was almost certain to be fatal.

About thirty minutes had passed since Edith had gone into the room. Dr. Henderson told police that he knocked on the door, but Boring told Terry that it was he who called to her. There was no answer. Boring tried to turn the knob, but it was locked. Thinking Edith might have left through the window, he went outside to check. He looked in through the window and saw Edith lying motionless on her bed. She was unconscious, a cigarette burning in her hand. Frantically, the doctors tried to revive her, but without success. Boring, meanwhile, called an ambulance. At about 3:00 A.M. members of Medic 1 and Ambulance No. 309 arrived from Baltimore's Suburban Hospital and tried to revive her.

At around 3:45 A.M. Frazier called to say he would be there in half an hour. Boring answered and told him Edith had taken an overdose. By the time he arrived a half hour later, Edith had been taken to the hospital. The house was empty. Boring had gone to sleep. Frazier called Suburban Hospital. At 4:37 A.M. Edith Hale Harkness was pronounced dead.

At about six-thirty the next morning, Edith's alarm went off. "She was not prone to do that unless she had something to do," says Jean Hope. "That shows she really was planning to help herself, that she really was planning to go with me to the dog show. I broke down when I heard that."

A service for Edith was held at Harkness House just two months after her mother's. There were not nearly as many people as at Rebekah's. The room was so empty you could hear the echoes. In light of the accusations of thievery that followed Rebekah's death, there was no reception at the Carlyle this time.

Many of the people there, of course, had attended Rebekah's funeral as well, so the sense of déjà vu was inescapable. Among those present were Milton Kayle, Terry, Wolfie, and some of the nurses who had grown fond of Edith while they were caring for Rebekah. Edith's ex-husband, Ken McKinnon, helped pick out the casket. Her hair had not been done the way she usually wore it, and he told them how to redo it. There was a quiet viewing of the open casket.

There had been warring factions present at Rebekah's funeral, but this time it was worse. Edith was young. It seemed her death could have been prevented. Everyone blamed each other for what had happened. There were dozens of unanswered questions. Why did the doctors have to take her away then, especially if she was asleep when they arrived? Given her history of attempted suicide and alcoholism, how and why was she taking Elavil? How could they let her go in her room alone? How long did they wait before breaking in? The medical examiner's report, newspaper accounts, and police reports were full of inaccuracies and inconsistencies. How could all this have happened while two doctors were present? Kenneth Grundborg, Jean Hope, Terry, and Wolfie were outraged. All thought the late arrival of the doctors drove Edith to take the pills. "She'd still be alive today if they hadn't come to take her away," says Jean Hope.

"There are a lot of unanswered questions," says Dr. Francis Mayle, the deputy medical examiner in Baltimore. He added that he tried to get answers from Dr. Henderson, but had met with a "stone wall."★

Jimmy Frazier, Edith's last lover, did not attend her funeral, but Kenneth Grundborg did. A close friend of Edith's who had been a confidante during her ups and downs with Grundborg went up to him after the services.

"You made Edith very happy," she said.

"Yes," he said. "But not happy enough." Then he began to cry.

Bobby, who did not attend the funeral, was not affected in quite the same way. "I'm glad Edith is gone," he says. "I think it is the best thing she could have done. I can't believe it took her this long to succeed."

★John Henderson, who, according to police records and other sources was Edith's psychiatrist, did not help explain what happened. When he was asked about the events surrounding her death, he said, "My official comment is that I know nothing about her. Never heard of her. Don't know the person's name. Bye-bye." Henderson's associate, Dennis Harrison, who accompanied him that night, was asked if he would answer a few questions about Edith's death. "No," he said, and hung up.

EPILOGUE
GUARDIAN OF
HONOR

he $27 million Rebe-
kah Harkness inher-
ited more than thirty
years ago might not
sound like an extra-
ordinary fortune these days. But, adjusted for inflation, it repre-
sents about $125 million in 1987 dollars. Yet at the time of
Rebekah's death, it was almost all gone. She had lost $38 million
(in 1987 dollars) on her dance companies and theater alone.

Capricorn, her beloved Caribbean retreat, was leased after her death to Spanish singer Julio Iglesias and then sold to someone else. Her chalets in Gstaad, the Palm Beach house, and her apartment at the Carlyle were also sold. Even Harkness House itself, Rebekah's splendid dance academy, which she had hoped would be her lasting legacy, was finally put on the market. Woody Allen expressed serious interest in it, but it was sold in 1987 to Leonidas, Inc., for $7 million, which, along with the proceeds from her other properties, went to her foundation. Finally, the Chalice of Life, the urn by Dali, was sold to the Mitsui Gallery in Tokyo for $600,000. Ted Bartwink and Barry Kreisberg personally took Rebekah's ashes to the Harkness family mausoleum in Woodlawn Cemetery, where both Bill and Edith Harkness are also buried. According to Bartwink, she had "no power to direct that her ashes be placed in the chalice because she did not own the chalice—the foundation did." He added, "She is now where she belongs."

What, then, was Rebekah's legacy? Many—especially those who benefited from her largess—say that her contributions will last for generations. A number of Harkness House alumni became important figures in dance. Helgi Tomasson became a star at the New York City Ballet and later artistic director of the San Francisco Ballet. Donald Saddler won several Tony awards for choreography on Broadway. Larry Rhodes became head of the dance department at New York University. David Howard remained one of the preeminent dance teachers in the country. And several others, Dennis Wayne and Finis Jhung among them, run their own small but successful dance companies.

Moreover, Rebekah's dance empire was not completely destroyed. Her two foundations, the Harkness Ballet Foundation and the William Hale Harkness Foundation, will continue to give to dance for many years to come. In 1987, their assets totaled $15 million, of which at least $750,000 will go annually to fund dance-related projects.

Rebekah's greatest contribution, some say, was in the way her dancers are trained. "I maintain," says one alumnus of the Harkness Ballet, "that for everything that went wrong, Mrs. Harkness gave more to dance than anyone since Diaghilev."

That is one way of looking at Rebekah's legacy. She was a generous woman—too generous perhaps—giving in the service of a deeply flawed vision, but it would be lamentable not to honor her love of, and dedication to, art.

At the same time, one cannot overlook the distrust, hurt, and anger that she left behind. With family and friends—as in dance—she had brought together a group of people who saw in her the answer to their dreams. Now she was gone and they were still fighting each other. In July 1982, just a few weeks after Rebekah's death, Terry Pierce McBride and Wolfgang von Falkenburg met with Roy Cohn and other members of Cohn's firm, Saxe, Bacon and Bolan, beginning a three-year attempt to have Rebekah's will declared invalid. Allen Pierce, then still in Raiford State Prison in Florida, joined Terry by giving her his power of attorney. Rebekah's children contended she was so heavily sedated when she signed the codicils that she didn't know what she was doing. "I think it's clear that my mother would have signed anything put in front of her," says Terry.

As court battles go, this one was a disappointment. No proof was offered that Rebekah was as drugged as they claimed. At no time were Rebekah's medical records submitted before the court or were her doctors or nurses questioned. Moreover, since neither Terry nor Allen sought a monetary settlement, it was unclear why they had taken the matter to court in the first place.

"I think that Terry got it in her bonnet that somehow Maria New was trying to influence Rebekah to do things against her will," says Bobby, who was angry that Terry was holding up distribution of his share of the will. "But Rebekah only did things she wanted to do. Terry has a vendetta against Maria involving that child [Angel]."

In 1986 the Surrogate Court House finally ruled against Terry and Allen and ordered that Rebekah's estate be distributed as outlined in her will and her last two codicils.

When the battle was over, its participants dispersed. Bobby Scevers and Nikita Talin were forced to leave Harkness House shortly after Rebekah's death. "It's the last thing Rebekah would have wanted," Bobby says, adding that she had wanted him and

Nikita to run Harkness House. In 1987, Bobby and Nikita began to receive their shares of Rebekah's estate, which, with interest, amounted to more than $300,000 each. Today, Nikita lives in Dallas and has real estate interests in nearby McKinney. Bobby lives in Dallas as well, and in 1987 was made visiting professor in dance at Southern Methodist University. He thinks about Rebekah a lot. "Whenever something good happens to me or I have some minor success, the first person I want to run and tell is Rebekah," he says. "But now there is no Rebekah. That's awfully sad. But I keep telling myself, 'You know, Robert, you are not the only person in the world to lose someone you loved.' "

Maria New is still head of pediatrics and endocrinology at New York Hospital, where Rebekah's third husband, Ben Kean, also works. Rebekah's fourth husband, Niels Lauersen, was linked with actress Liv Ullmann in a stormy relationship that surfaced in the gossip columns when she reportedly made statements—later retracted—that "she doesn't like him . . . thinks he is using her." He now has a gynecology practice in New York. After Rebekah's death, he received $165,000 as part of the condition of her divorce settlement.

Miss Weeks, Angel's nanny, lives modestly in a small one-bedroom, church-subsidized apartment in north London. She says she has never been entirely reimbursed by Terry for the many thousands of pounds she spent on Angel. In March 1987 she celebrated her seventy-ninth birthday. Her last wish was to be buried with Angel, but for that she needs the permission of the child's natural mother, and Terry has not responded to her. Moreover, the burial would cost more than she can afford. As a result, she has decided to be cremated and have her ashes scattered over Angel's grave.

Rebekah's brother, Allen Tarwater West II—Frère—died in 1986 of brain cancer. His son, Tarwater, lives in Spain, where he is a painter.

Edith's daughter, Erin, is fifteen years old at this writing and lives with her father, Kenneth McKinnon, on the East Coast.

Terry and Wolfie spend their time in Palm Beach, Florida, and

Hawaii. Like her mother, Terry rises early. In the mornings, she works on her music, recording serene lullabies that she writes and sings for her own Honeybee label. In addition, she works on her tropical paintings, which also show Dali's strong surrealist influence.

When I visited Terry and Wolfie in 1983, they lived in Santa Monica, which had just been hit by extraordinary spring rains. The sand was a dank brown and clumps of mud littered the Pacific Coast Highway. A local car wash put out handbills for a "Disaster Area" special, cleaning two cars for the price of one. "I've tried to explain to my friends exactly what happened to my family," Terry said. "They listen very politely. But I know they think I'm making it all up."

That leaves Allen Pierce, who, at this writing, lives comfortably but modestly in Miami, not far from the site where he killed Patrick Bemben in 1977. A heavyset, powerfully built man, his handsome regular features are somewhat obscured by his excess weight. His blond hair has turned steely gray, and his hairline has begun to recede. He has an easy smile, and he extends his hand to strangers with a grip whose force belies his friendliness and trust and suggests the anger beneath the surface. His nemesis, Philip Mansfield, died of a heart attack in 1979, and Allen frequently visits his burial site at the Star of David Cemetery in Miami, with a certain grim satisfaction. "He was going down," Allen says. "One way or the other he was going to die."

Allen's murder sentence was reduced to manslaughter on appeal, and he was released from Raiford State Prison in 1985 after serving eight years. Those years in prison—the Rock, he calls it—were the happiest of his life, he maintains. He says this repeatedly, and it is a measure of his family's tragedy that he really means it: Raiford was the best home he ever had. He had been in boarding schools since he was six. "It reminded me of my boarding schools, except that I had more freedom at the Rock," he explains. "You could go to school, the tag plant, the furniture factory. You could study welding. You could make your own choice.

"Many inmates didn't want to leave because they knew they couldn't eat as well on the outside. Damn good meals. God, they had so many. The best chocolate cake I ever had! The biggest chicken I ever ate, cooked in a Hawaiian sauce! And barbecued ribs!" If you wanted to drink, Allen says, there was a jailhouse drink called buck, made of yeast, fruit juice, and sugar, "so strong it could blow your head off."

Allen spends his days—and late nights—working in a small, unprepossessing layout and design shop he started in a shopping center in southwest Miami. His life is not what it once was—he drives a Ford Mustang, not a Bentley—but he is comfortable. He still has some money left from a so-called spendthrift trust, which stipulated he could use only the interest and not touch the capital. He has spent hundreds of thousands of dollars buying equipment for his new business. He is hoping to have better luck than he did during his days with Mansfield.

At times, it seems he has learned his lesson. "Anybody who trusts people like I did is a fool," he says. "It's as simple as that." He is more cautious when people ask him for things, but friends worry that he is still easy prey, that he is so impressionable and trusting that others will always take advantage of him.

Whether the past will repeat itself is anybody's guess. His friends say his future depends in part on the company he keeps. His temper is still explosive. Several months after getting out of Raiford, he was jailed for harassing and intimidating IRS employees, but charges were dropped and he was released a few days later.

Regardless of what happens, for all the anger and violence in Allen, one can easily make the case that he is a victim. Like his sisters, he must bear his mother's legacy. Yet he holds no grudge against her. "He absolutely adores his mother," says a friend. "He honors her. She made a lot of mistakes, but he speaks highly of her. His mother was a precious thing in his life."

Allen can be quite poignant on the subject. In a letter, he describes her as "one of the most eccentric personalities of this century, who, even though well meaning, still failed to see the world in which she lived from reality . . . Living in this world of fantasy cost her not only the fortune that she inherited . . . but also her life."

He has an extraordinary generosity of spirit. His intentions, however, have never been his problem. Rather, it is the combination of his limitless sense of honor, his anger, and his lack of control. "He does get carried away," says a friend. "The things that have happened . . . I just wish that somebody, somehow, somewhere could take that bitterness out of him. Hate and remorsefulness like that can destroy anybody. Allen is not a bad guy. He really isn't. But I pity the person who crosses him."

Allen remembers events from his childhood so vividly, so powerfully, in such extraordinary detail, that he appears to relive them as he talks. His moods change radically. One moment he is childlike, vulnerable, guileless, and innocent. The next, he erupts in a rage so uncontrollable and frightening that one cannot forget this is a man who has killed before. Yet it's hard not to sympathize with him. As he talks, the sadness and the anger and the pain visibly rise to the surface. Tears fill his eyes. He is the guardian of honor for a family whose honor has been defiled again and again and again.

Today Allen is still angry. He is angry at anyone who may have dishonored or hurt his family. That includes many people.

For one, it means Niels Lauersen. "I never even met him," says Allen. "What's more, I never really wanted to." But if he does meet him, he says, "I am going to pull the trigger on his ass."

Allen is also concerned about his sister Terry and her relationship with Wolfie.

But it is Edith and her fate that most deeply disturbs him. "My mother asked me to do certain things for her before she died," he says. "She told me to take care of Edith and Terry, to make sure certain things were done, and I'm going to do them. Whether I do them legally or illegally makes no difference at all. I will do them."

He has never met Edith's psychiatrist, John Henderson. "If I do, I'll say: 'You fucked over my sister. And I don't appreciate it one iota.'

"I'm not gonna put up with any shit like that. My sister was a tragedy. She never hurt anybody, couldn't hurt anybody if she wanted to. He's gonna find himself right in jail and skid row. All beat up.

"Edith is dead, but Erin is alive. I haven't even met Erin yet. But she's my niece. I will take care of my niece."

If anything else happens to anyone in his family, Allen says, he will have his revenge. He claims he is not alone: "There are people at the Rock, and I'm talking about guys that'll blow you away for less than a smile. When I say less than a smile, try it sometime. Less than a smile. They're all there because they did blow people away for less than a smile. And that's what time it is.

"If I have any more trouble with any of these people, you're going to be publishing a mortuary column. It's going to be: So-and-so died, and so-and-so died. That's what you're going to be publishing next, if they don't watch it. When you fuck with my family you're fucking with dynamite. I'm not playing games. Understand?"

ACKNOWLEDGMENTS

In May 1983, Richard Babcock, my editor at *New York* magazine, pulled a clipping of a "Suzy" column in the New York *Daily News* and pointed out an item about a fight over the will of Rebekah Harkness. He suggested I look into it. At the time, I had not even heard of Rebekah Harkness, though I was familiar with the Harkness family and its philanthropy at Harvard, Yale, and in medicine.

I went down to the Surrogates Court in Manhattan, where Rebekah's wills were on file. Over the next six weeks, I interviewed, both in person and on the phone, several dozen of Rebekah's friends, relatives, and colleagues. I spoke to Bobby Scevers, then in Hamburg, by phone. I had a telephone interview with Allen Pierce, then still in jail. And I flew to Los Angeles, where I spent a week interviewing Terry McBride. Her help was invaluable in preparing an article entitled "The Heiress," which appeared in the June 27, 1983, issue of *New York* magazine and was the genesis of this book.

The following year, I signed a contract with William Morrow and Company. I left *New York* magazine and began working on the book full time for the next three and one half years.

In its way, the life of Rebekah Harkness was exceedingly well-documented. The information in this book comes from many sources, including thousands of newspaper clippings, magazines, books, tape recordings, and court records. But much of the official record is wrong. Rebekah Harkness was not the richest woman in the world. She never had $400 million. Even the most banal newspaper stories of Terry's wedding to Tony McBride. — as in the announcement in *The New York Times*—were sometimes in error or were entirely fabricated.

This trail of exaggerations and falsehoods is not mere happenstance. The story of Rebekah Harkness is a Rashomon-like affair. Dozens of people made her the center of their lives, and each of them saw her in a different light. Each had his own "truth," one that frequently did not mesh with anyone else's version of what happened.

During the time I worked on this book, I interviewed an additional three hundred or so friends, relatives, and associates of Rebekah and her family. I spoke to some of them only briefly on the phone. Others I interviewed on many occasions, for hours and hours with a tape recorder. There were about four hundred hours of taped interviews, the transcripts of which ran to roughly 2 million words. When there were contradictions among the central characters, I would return to them again and again in an attempt to clarify what happened. For all that, I am certain I have not resolved all the discrepancies in their various versions of events. But I have done my best, and I hope I have done justice to those who were so generous in giving me their time and their trust. I am especially grateful to Bobby Scevers, Allen Pierce, and Margaret Weeks, whom I went back to again and again. Each time they patiently went over the most intimate details of their lives with me.

Among the many other people I interviewed, I would like to express my thanks to the following:

Salvatore Aiello, Malcolm Aldrich, Carlos Alemany, Jane Wells Alt, Angie Algieri, Wayne Alpern, Vita Amendolagine, Frank Andrews, Christopher Aponte, Lee Ault, John Archbold, Arnold Arnstein, Michael Avedon, Kathleen Bannon, Bud Barber, Clive Barnes, Theodore Bartwink, Michael Bettsak, Bert Bindschadler, Nancy Bielski, Roy E. Black, William Bonbright, Giselle Brady, Rita Brandt, Randy Brooks, Oliver Brooks, Howard Burdick, Michael Butler, Edith Camp, Margot Camp, Sophronia Camp, Kurt Cannon, Bertrand Castelli, John Caulk, J.B. "Jeannot" Cerrone, Charles Claggett, Bob Connell, Francisco "Toti" Cornejo, M'liss Crotty, Anne Cutler, The Salvador Dali Foundation in St. Petersburg, Florida, Alexandra Danilova, Mary Ellen Davis, Alex Donner, Pauline Dora, James Edwin Frazier (aka Eddie James), Wolfgang von Falkenburg, Robert David Lion Gardiner, Helen Gettemuller, Joseph Giordano, Peter Gravina, Spencer Gray, Helen Greenford, Kenneth Grundborg, Jack Harpman, Eivind Harum, Pamela Heller, John Heminway Sr., John Heminway Jr., Stuart Hodes, Richard Holden, Stanley Hollingsworth, Joel Honig, Jessie Holdredge, Jean Hope, Marian Horosko, Lee Hoiby, Edward F. Hutton IV, David Howard, William Illyes, Robert Jacobson, Finis Jhung, Raleigh Jordan, Eric Kitchen, Margarita Korell, Robert Larkin, George Lauder, Tanaquil LeClerq, Ruth Lief, Courtland Loomis, Roy Kahn, Louisa Kreisberg, Barrett G. Kreisberg, Georgie Lewis, Dorothy Livingston, Brian Macdonald, Mimi Manning, Mary Mansfield, Francoise Martinet, Anthony McBride, Anne Terry Pierce McBride, Jorge Mester, Norma Rogers Minnis, Anne Harkness Mooney, Reynolds Morse, Tony Movshon, Alexander Neave,

Pascale Olave-Uriarte, Dr. Neida Ogden, Joy O'Neill, Vicente Nebrada, Dr. Maria New, Hilary Newton, Cappy Pantori, Elizabeth Peabody, Allen West Pierce, Dr. John C. Pierrakos, Molly Pierrepont, Miquette Potter, Camilo Quelquejeu, Charitas Quelquejeu, Mary Rafferty, Jane Remer, Lawrence Rhodes, Betty Rosenstock, Mary Pettus Rowlands, Donald Saddler, Bobby Scevers, Xenia Schidlovsky, Carol West Scullin, Arthur Shepley Jr., Mr. and Mrs. Aaron Shikler, Mrs. Bradford Shinkle Jr., Jack Shinkle, Mark Shulgasser, Martha Simmons, Patricia Sinnott, Stephen Sohn, Anne "Breezy" Stevenson, Anthony Strilko, Mrs. Jane Suydam, Martha Love Symington, Nikita Talin, Bob Thomas, Sally Tiers, Margie Trevor, Charles Utter, Robert Vickery, Joe Wade, Dennis Wayne, Margaret Weeks, Rudy Wendt, Fred Werle, Allen Tarwater West II, Allen Tarwater West III, George Wheeler Sr., Jed Wheeler, Heyden White, Robert White, Allen Whittemore, Wade Williams, George Thomas Wilson, John Wilson, Raymond Wilson, and Melissa Wohltman.

I am no less grateful to the dozens and dozens of people to whom I talked on a not-for-attribution basis. Many asked me not to use their names because they feared for their jobs, privacy, friendships, or even their lives. I cannot name them, of course, but I am particularly grateful for their trust.

Several of my friends read all or parts of the manuscript and commented on it during its progress. Alan Weitz read the book in its early stages, and I am especially grateful to him for his supportive comments. I would also like to thank Marcelle Clements, Tom Moore, Felicia Rosshandler, and my mother, Barbara Unger, for their critiques, and Christina De Liagre for her encouragement and support.

Research for this book required trips to London, Chicago, Dallas, St. Louis, Miami, Palm Beach, Watch Hill, and Los Angeles. I am especially obliged to Natalie Koch of Beekman Travel for making travel arrangements.

For their hospitality during my various trips, I am grateful to Kerry Gruson, my brother, Jimmy Unger, and his wife, Marie-Claude Castonguay, and Mr. and Mrs. George Wheeler Sr.

I am indebted to the late Luis Sanjurjo, my literary agent at the inception of this project, for helping get this project off the ground. I am also grateful to Rob Scheidlinger, and my current agent, Amanda Urban, both of ICM, to my lawyer, David Hollander, and my editor, Douglas Stumpf, at Morrow.

I went through several thousand newspaper clippings about Rebekah, many of them in scrapbooks generously loaned to me by Barry Kreisberg of the Harkness Ballet Foundation. I was also provided with help by the staff of the New York Public Library's Performing Arts Research Center at Lincoln Center. The clipping files in its dance collection on Rebekah and several other major characters in the book were invaluable.

I also obtained research on Rebekah's family from the Culbertson Mansion State Memorial in New Albany, Indiana, where her family papers are kept. I am grateful for the assistance of William Krueger, an employee there. Likewise, Emmett D. Chisum of the American Heritage Center in Laramie, Wyoming, was helpful in providing me with original research on the Harkness family in Ohio in the nineteenth century, as was my sister, Chris Unger Majefski. Bill Ganahl of the St. Louis *Post-Dispatch* generously provided me with clippings on the West family. Mary Ellen Davis was an able and enthusiastic guide through St. Louis during my visit there.

My thanks also to Anne Watson for her help as a research assistant. For fact-checking assistance, I would like to thank Joel Honig, Della Rowland, and Raissa Silverman. For help with photos I am grateful to Allen Tarwater West III, William Bonbright, Joy O'Neill, Bobby Scevers, and Nikita Talin.

BIBLIOGRAPHY

The personal scrapbooks of Rebekah Harkness, her clipping scrapbooks at Harkness House, and the clipping files of newspapers and libraries in New York, Dallas, St. Louis, and Miami provided me with thousands of articles on Rebekah Harkness, her family, and her ballet. I list below those that are cited in my book:

PERIODICALS, MAGAZINES, AND NEWSPAPERS

(Page numbers are omitted because most articles were found in private scrapbooks and in the clipping files of newspaper morgues and libraries, where they were stored without their page numbers.)

The Bergen Sunday Record, August 20, 1978.

The Bombay Free Press Bulletin, February 18, 1962.

The Chicago Tribune, March 27, 1968.

The Dallas Times Herald, March 10, 1969.

Dance magazine, May 1955; May 1958; August 1960; March 1961; January 1963; December 1963; February 1966; June 1974.

Dance News, undated clippings.

Gray, Christopher, "All the Best Places," March 1983, *House and Garden.*

The Hong Kong Standard, September 17, 1954.

Jowitt, Deborah. "Poor Little Rich Girl." *The Village Voice,* November 20, 1969.

McCall's magazine, July 1966.

The Miami Herald, February 9, 1964.

The Miami News, February 28, 1984.

The New York Daily Mirror, January 30, 1955.

The New York Daily News, February 10, 1961; November 30, 1973; April 3, 1974; June 30, 1982.

The New York Herald-Tribune, November 18, 1962; May 19, 1963; October 19, 1963; October 1, 1965; undated clippings.

The New York Morning Telegraph, December 31, 1964.

The New York Post, December 6, 1961; February 14, 1962; January 12, 1969; February 15, 1975.

The New York Times, July 1, 1958; February 5, 1961; February 10, 1961; July 3, 1963; November 12, 1963; March 22, 1964; August 22, 1964; February 23, 1965; November 21, 1965; July 19, 1966; November 9, 1970; July 18, 1971; April 28, 1971; April 9, 1972; December 4, 1972; April 15, 1974; October 10,

1974; November 14, 1974; January 3, 1975; June 26, 1977; June 19, 1982; February 8, 1985; February 20, 1986.

The New York Tribune, June 2, 1974.

The New York World-Telegram, November 12, 1957.

Palm Beach Life, December 1963.

Rensin, David. "The Legend Lives." *California Magazine,* August 1983.

Rich, Alan. "Return to Sunnybrook Farm." *New York* magazine, April 29, 1974.

The St. Louis Globe-Democrat, September 2, 1952; December 8, 1926; March 11, 1928.

The St. Louis Post-Dispatch, June 11, 1939; January 6, 1946, "Mrs. D. W. Pierce, Active in Society, Sues for Divorce"; January 19, 1962; May 23, 1955, "Former St. Louisan Becomes Composer"; November 11, 1963; many clippings with date illegible.

Saturday Review/World, June 1, 1974.

The San Francisco Examiner, November 30, 1965.

Seaside Topics (Watch Hill, Rhode Island), August 29, 1954.

The Seattle Post-Intelligencer, January 30, 1964.

Show magazine, February 20, 1970.

Siegel, Marcia B. "The Harkness Ballet in Decline." *The Los Angeles Times,* June 29, 1970.

Swenson, G. R. "Is Dali Disgusting?" *Art News,* December 1965.

The Teheran Journal, January 7, 1963.

The Toronto Globe and Mail, April 18, 1974.

The Times of India, January 29, 1963.

Time magazine, September 28, 1962; April 2, 1965; April 22, 1974; January 20, 1975.

Town and Country, August 1970.

Variety, September 3, 1975.

Vogue magazine, October 1962.

The Wall Street Journal, November 11, 1969.

The Westerly Sun, September 1, 1954.

Women's Wear Daily, April 11, 1974.

DOCUMENTS, CORRESPONDENCE, AND RECORDINGS

"Banknotes" Publication of the Franklin National Bank, which later made its home in the Semple mansion.

"Biography of a Ballet." Press release by Isadora Bennett for the Robert Joffrey Ballet, undated, ca. 1964.

Boulanger, Nadia. Letter to Fred Werle, June 15, 1955.

Brooks, Randy (spokesperson for the student body of Harkness House). Letter to members of the board of directors for the Foundation Fund of Harkness School of Ballet Arts, July 16, 1981; letter to Zuma Renaud, board member of Harkness House, August 24, 1981.

Dreams of Glory ("Sonhos de Gloria"). Program notes, December 6, 1962.

"Empress of Britain, 42,500 Tons Five Day Atlantic Crossing"; *"Empress of Britain* World Cruise." Canadian Pacific brochures.

Hodes, Stuart. "Hail Harkness." Unpublished manuscript.

"Harkness Tour 1965." Harkness Ballet promotional brochure.

Harkness, Rebekah. Wills and codicils; letter to the editor of *The New York Times,* March 31, 1964, marked "not for publication"; letter to Bobby Scevers, July 14, 1977; death certificate of; personal scrapbooks of; taped interview by Terry Winters, November 2, 1965, 25 minutes, MGZT 7-83, courtesy New York Public Library, Lincoln Center Branch for the Performing Arts.

Honig, Joel. "Rebekah Harkness: Orchestral Works." Compilation of compositions by Rebekah Harkness.

"How to Win . . . Health—Beauty—Fame—Popularity." Ned Wayburn Institute of Dancing promotional brochure.

"The Pathwork." Brochure published by Center for the Living Force, Inc., Phoenicia Pathwork Center, Phoenicia, New York.

Pierce, Allen W. Letters to the author.

Renaud, Zuma. Letter to Dr. Samuel Meyer, board member of Harkness House, September 20, 1981.

"Safari." Program notes, Carnegie Hall, May 26, 1955.

Wayburn, Ned. Letter to Allen T. West, November 16, 1934, from personal scrapbooks of Rebekah Harkness.

"Save Our Company." Leaflet by members of the Harkness School of Ballet.

"A Special Place," pamphlet published by The Max McGraw Wildlife Foundation, Dundee, Illinois.

U.S. Department of State press release No. 504, October 2, 1963.

Weeks, Margaret. Personal written and oral diaries.

West, Allen T. Letter to Mrs. Anna Vance Culbertson Semple Rand, mother of Rebekah Semple, courtesy of Culbertson Mansion State Memorial, New Albany, Indiana.

BOOKS

Barrie, J. M. *Peter Pan*. New York: Charles Scribner's and Sons, 1911.

Birmingham, Stephen. *The Right People*. Boston: Little Brown and Company, 1958.

Blackwell, Earl, ed. *The Celebrity Register*. New York: Simon and Schuster, 1973.

Bruch, Hilde, M.D. *The Golden Cage—The Enigma of Anorexia Nervosa*. New York: Vintage Books, 1979.

Chandler, David Leon. *Henry Flagler—The Astonishing Life and Times of the Visionary Robber Baron Who Founded Florida*. New York: Macmillan, 1986.

Collier, Peter, and Horowitz, David. *The Rockefellers, An American Dynasty*. New York: Signet Books, 1976.

Dunne, Dominick. *Fatal Charms*. New York: Crown Publishers, 1987.

Elias, Norbert. *The Court Society*. New York: Pantheon Books, 1983.

Elson, Robert T. *Time Inc*. New York: Atheneum, 1968.

Fontaine, Joan. *No Bed of Roses*. New York: William Morrow and Company, 1978.

Gathorne-Hardy, Jonathan. *The Rise and Fall of the British Nanny*. London: Hardy, Hodder and Stoughton, 1972.

Goulder, Grace. *John D. Rockefeller, the Cleveland Years*. Cleveland: The Western Reserve Historical Society, 1972.

Harkness, William Hale. *Temples and Topees*. Private printing. New York: Derrydale Press, 1936.

——. *Ho Hum, the Fisherman*. Private printing. New York: 1939.

Kirschten, Ernest. *Catfish and Crystal*. New York: New York, 1960.

Koegler, Horst. *The Concise Oxford Dictionary of Ballet*. London: Oxford University Press, 1977.

Obst, Linda Rosen, ed. *The Sixties*. New York: A Random House/Rolling Stone Press Book, 1977.

The Physicians Desk Reference, 39th ed. Oradell, N.J.: The Medical Economics Company, 1985.

Primm, James Neal. *Lion of the Valley*. Boulder, Colorado: Pruett Publishing Company, 1981.

Swanberg, W. A. *Luce and His Empire*. New York: Dell Publishing, 1972.

Vaillant, George E. *The Natural History of Alcoholism—Causes, Patterns, and Paths to Recovery*. Cambridge, Mass.: Harvard University Press, 1983.

Wright, William, *The Von Bulow Affair*. New York: Delacorte Press, 1983.

COURT TRANSCRIPTS

Mario Roman v. Anne Terry McBride (California). Case No. 120574, Superior Court of the State of California in the county of Santa Barbara, filed, July 16, 1982.

State of Florida v. Allen W. Pierce. No. 77-33298.

Probate proceedings, will of Rebekah Harkness. File No. 2979-82, New York County Surrogates Court.

INDEX

415

INDEX

INDEX